M000076407

THE
DIVIDED
NATION

PRAISE FOR *THE DIVIDED NATION*

"Thought provoking… an action-filled, intense read!"
— Laura A. Grace, a book blogger at
unicornquester.com.

"It's the kind of story that I like - brotherhood, action, trying to do the right thing despite the consequences."
— Claire Banschbach, author of *Oath of the Outcast*.

"Wow. I'm still trying to absorb all that…This book is horrifying. The thing is, it tackles some very real issues that can't be brushed aside."
— S.G. Willoughby, author of *He's Making Diamonds*.

"Wow. *Wow,* y'all. Now, that was a ride."
— Kaitlyn Krispense, author of *Beloved*.

"The Divided Nation by Angela R. Watts is an important novel that shows the darkness of our times and the potential greater darkness of the future. This novel digs into the darkest parts of our world and still manages to highlight the good that lies under layers of grime… Recommend for anyone looking for a tough read that will challenge them as a person, rip of blinders and preconceived notions, and force them to see the world for what it is and what it could be."
— Kellyn Roth, author of *The Chronicles of Alice and Ivy*

"Angela Watts did an amazing job showing that even under the ugliest, dirtiest layers of rock and grime and dust, you can still find a gemstone that, when polished and cut and brought into light, can reflect a dazzling array of beauty."

— Merie Shen

"This book sucked-no, DRAGGED me in and had me slack-jawed and wide-eyed by page 34. It dragged me in so much, I lost sleep because of it."

— H. S. Kylian

Also by the author:

Emmanuel, an *Infidel Books* short story

Seek, Whispers of Heaven #1

The Thief, the Damsel, and the Dragon

Homeward

To the infidels. May our lives be proof

of greater Love.

Sara:
Thanks for being an
amazing friend!

Angela R. Watts

AUTHOR'S NOTE

This novel is for you. The broken, infidel, outcast, wanderer, fearful. The bold, ready, willing, scarred, strong.

This novel is for everyone with ears who will hear.

I will say now, I am not saying this dystopian is the future I see for our current world. I am a storyteller, not a nonfiction writer. I told this story because God gave it to me, and I could not run away from it. This series of books is about a dystopian world full of war. War is without bounds. Thus, stories of war cannot be contained easily, nor do I think they should.

By Christian fiction standards, this novel is not squeaky clean. By secular fiction standards, it is not deep water.

I did my best to keep the writing tasteful and without gory details, but it reflects realism: there is evil in the world as well as good. For the good to shine bright, we must go through the dark, and this series does just that.

So, reader. This one's for you, wherever you are in this world, wherever you're going—may you be an infidel who stands out against the world.

CAST OF CHARACTERS

GEORGE JOHNSTON

United Nations politician, businessman, and ganglord of his own large army that controls large portions of the UN across the globe.

WEST JOHNSTON

25-year-old gangster son of George Johnston, the Johnston heir.

KALEB SAVAGE

Ganglord and close ally of George Johnston. Father of Nate Savage and uncle of Jack Savage.

JACK SAVAGE

26-year-old gangster son of Hunter Savage.

NATE SAVAGE

18-year-old gangster son of Kaleb. Best friends with Simon.

JORDAN BUCKS

Ganglord and close ally of George Johnston's. Father of Simon Bucks.

SIMON BUCKS

19-year-old gangster son of Jordan Bucks.

GIDEON HOCHBERG

24-year-old close ally of George Johnston. Best friends with Alex Thompson.

ALEX THOMPSON

23-year-old gangster in George's gang. Comrade of Gideon Hochberg.

SPENCER ANDERSON

24-year-old gangster in George's group. Friends with West and Jack. Older brother of Randy Anderson.

ED and TY BROOKS

Brothers in George's gang.

BURL FISHER and KAY FISHER

Parents of the Fisher family and leaders of Springtown, Kentucky.

RENE' FISHER

17-year-old daughter of the Fisher parents. Friends with Simon.

LEE FISHER

15-year-old son of the Fisher parents.

BRIAN JONES

Secret Union soldier. Husband and father. Birth son of Kay fisher.

TERRI BREWER and **HOWIE BREWER** daughter and son-in-law of the Fisher parents, and their five kids, Dax, Jaycee, Paisley, Lily, and Aiden.

THE

DIVIDED

NATION

THE INFIDEL BOOKS – BOOK 1

ANGELA R. WATTS

ONE

MAY 1ST, 2027

"THE SECOND CIVIL WAR RAGING in this nation is the only reason you are still in business, Mohamad." George Johnston, mafia ganglord with more unrestrained power than most government officials, smiled across the table at his fellow United Nations ally. "I would not be so fast to condemn the Union as monsters when you send your own soldiers like pigs to slaughter, too."

The money transaction issue the allies faced did not affect George personally. Unlike the other United Nations officials, his fortune was secret, safe, and far from another soul's knowledge. It saved him many headaches, and he enjoyed watching the others scramble for control when he always maintained it himself. It had been three years since the 2024 presidential election and the dividing of the United States—government Union and rebel Confederates remained at war. Maintaining control came natural to George among the chaos.

"It isn't about the ten billion vanishing." Russian President Vladimir clasped his large hands atop of the meeting table where various other nation and sect leaders sat gathered. "It is about maintaining an image. If any of our civilians find we lost even a smidge of control…"

"*You* are not a leader of a torn nation, Johnston." US democratic President Kade spoke sourly, trying to put the other leaders at ease like he often did. "You strike fear into people— you're the boogey man waiting to kill them when they try to handle things themselves instead of counting on me. But you don't have to worry about maintaining respect. My country might be divided, again, but I am still the leader of the Union."

"And this money from Europe will maintain your respect? Did having money save President Lincoln's life as leader of the Union?" George chuckled, raising one eyebrow. "It is dangerous to be caught and have the money removed, but it is not the end of the world, friends."

"Oh?" President Kade laughed coldly. "You think we can make this headache go away by the snap of our fingers?"

"If we are caught—" Mohamad began, face flushing, but George cut the little leech off:

"It is unlikely that anyone will succeed in assassinating any of you. I agree, the transaction failure is unfortunate, but you have your best men on it. The money will be returned. So long as you stay to the plans, no one will see this as a weakness, if they find out." George waved his hand in dismissal. It wasn't his problem that the leaders lost focus on the bigger picture like children chasing a dozen balls at once. If they became greedy for material possessions, they'd become weak links, and George didn't allow weak links. His focus was on the legacy, the future, building the world into something his son could rule.

A pity he must play fair with the United Nation, but such was the life of an underling businessman, politician, and ganglord. He would rise to his complete power in time.

"Let us speak of other matters," the president of Mexico said, never one to waste time over trivial things. "I have many loads of cargo that have been unable to pass the border, Señor Kade. The Confederates put up a fight in Texas." His dark eyes cut to President Kade. The cargo loads could be anything from drugs, ammunition, or sex workers smuggled in or out of the US.

President Kade smoothed his hair. "I will have soldiers there to escort your loads at the designated time. Do not worry. You will be protected." Kade made far too much money on the Mexicans' affairs to risk interference.

"And," Mohamad interjected, glaring at George's cheery smirk. "You will leave my cities within these borders alone, Johnston. Let it be said here and now… come near my peoples again and I will—"

"It was a mere misunderstanding of my men, Mohamad. It will not happen again. Your Muslim sanctuaries are safe in the US. I handled the delicate matter and sent supplies as apology." George smiled wider, finding Mohamad amusing and not at all threatening. Respect for other leaders was crucial and came easy to George, but a few wide smiles and suave talking never broke trust.

Mohamad frowned and crossed his arms against his chest. "Understood." He probably didn't dare start another fight in front of the others.

The Russian piped in again. "Do the rebel scum show any signs of joining you in the UN, President Kade?" His obvious distaste for President Kade's lack of control over his nation showed in his cool eyes.

"The Confederates will not join us," President Kade said calmly, his pale blue eyes growing narrow. "There are too many things they disagree with. I have tried to bring peace, but they will die before they submit." President Kade met every face at the table. "If that is everything," it had been over three hours of talking, planning, and bickering, "then let's get out of here."

Eager to leave and return to their rightful abodes, the world leaders left the great mansion and, with their bodyguards, departed from the lush estate in record time.

George stayed on the mansion balcony, lit a cigar, and watched the leaders leave the premise. How amusing to see so many feared, powerful men and women scurry off like rats before his eyes. Power, greed, and lust were their motives, and no true ruler went far with such shallow requirements. They were textbook puppets and George could surpass and control them each, given time and appropriate planning. No one knew his true intentions and hadn't learned them for many decades. No one ever would until they were six feet under.

"Don't you have to get home? Or have some job to do?" President Kade appeared behind him. George handed a cigar to smiling President Kade.

"I train my men to handle themselves. Unlike a nation, they don't need a leader to breathe for them." George puffed some smoke, lips twisting into a smirk. The only pressing matter awaiting him at HQ was sending an Indian spy to his death, and executions were more satisfactory when there was waiting involved.

President Kade leaned on the balcony with a weary sigh. "That's one thing about this damn civil war."

"Hm?" George chuckled.

"No time to relax and have fun."

"You have far too much fun." George shook his head.

"Not as much as I would like." President Kade laughed softly as if at some joke. "Of course it is all worth it, but I do wish…" He looked to the setting sun that darkened the sky with dark blue and purple blotches, his expression one of a haunted man who'd lost much.

George had no pity, sympathy, or loyalty to the president, but since the president trusted him, he would act accordingly. "You miss your children."

President Kade straightened. "I think I'd best return home. The wives will be waiting, if you know my meaning."

"Of course. Until next time, my friend." George gave a respectful gesture and watched the president walk into the mansion again, still puffing his cigar. At least the President was above voicing his cumbersome emotions.

George left the building and went to his car outside. His bodyguards, Bashir and Winston, waited like hounds. Even though he was not a nation leader, as a mafia lord, he took simple precautions of protection. He did the dirty work the United Nation members gave him and while most didn't dare try harming him, it was a crazy world. Someone might try to take him out.

Winston drove them onto the narrow, winding road and Bashir kept watchful eye.

George made a phone call. "The meeting went well, my friend. The cargo loads will be guarded again. The Confederate militia in Virginia that you asked about is unarmed at the moment. The attack can continue there, if you'd like to dictate it." George smiled, knowing the answer he would receive from his closest, most trusted ally, Guns.

Guns often worked against Confederate militias, usually paid by George who was given information from the government and gave it to Guns. The Union didn't care how or who took care of the rebels, as long as the numbers of soldiers and amount of supplies decreased. Guns did his wicked job well, and George loved seeing the Union thrive, thus benefiting the UN, therefore making him quite the powerful man. Unlike many in the UN, he wielded his power wisely.

"Of course I would. The Confeds need to be knocked down to size. This might delay their D.C. expedition…" A pause, then Guns asked in a cool voice, "Did you find any information on the soldier?"

"I did. Brian Jones is valuable to the Union Army, you must remember, so I cannot recommend harming him directly."

"His wife or children are protected in government housing, George. I need to reach his extended family."

"His family in the South? The Fishers are easy to reach." George tapped his cigar and leaned back, closing his eyes. He needed a good night's rest. And whiskey.

"Step-father, mother, two little sisters, younger brother, nieces, nephews, grandfather, grandmother—I believe one of the sisters might do the trick."

"One's married, Guns."

"The one who isn't?" Guns asked easily.

"A teenager, I think. You could take her," George said shortly. He disliked meddling in Guns' personal affairs more than needed, and one constant personal affair haunted George's daily life, courtesy of Guns. But George trusted him, and they both understood the other's goal, continuing the cycle of comradeship and mutual power. "Now, I've got another call to make."

"Thank you. I will have Jed handle the situation."

"Well, if you plan on giving the honors to him, I can arrange for the kidnapping." George smiled at the thought. Jed was a scumbag who liked any jobs involving cruelty.

"If you wish," Guns said flatly. "I do not have to remind you of *our* arrangement?"

"No harm will come to that little town, my friend," George laughed. *Or your boy.*

"The men leave tomorrow?"

"Yes. Your cut of the supplies will be delivered, as always," George answered before hanging up. He dialed his wife and spoke for a short while, and when Cindy hung up, he was left alone with his thoughts.

The rather uneventful meeting had grown trust between George and the world leaders. His sympathy and harshness gave him a winning card among the leaders. It didn't hurt to remind them all of who they called when they needed a dirty job handled.

The leaders of the UN, the presidents, the government officials—they were slaves with nooses around their necks. They followed orders from higher beings, spoke as gods while being brainwashed fools, and thought themselves free. They were slaves to the cause of a united government. Their decisions often backfired: declaring martial law in 2024 hadn't fixed Kade's problems, it had caused a whole Confederate nation to rear its ugly head against the Union stomping over their rights.

The wars were ancient. George knew they didn't fight against flesh and blood. The supernatural interventions between many of the current battles were no small thing. Many of the leaders were spiritual: President Kade was a Mormon, Mohamad believed in Allah, the Mexican president was a Hindu, and so forth. He saw the leaders do unimaginable things to contact their higher beings.

George Johnston didn't need to do such stupid things. He didn't need advice from spirits. He didn't need to sacrifice things to fallen angels. He was a god himself.

George Johnston was a free man. He thrived off of the battles and quarrels of the Union and the Confederation, the gangsters fighting the mobs, and the foreign governments meddling in the US officials' affairs. The utter chaos delighted him—to some extent. Other times, it enraged him, seeing so many intelligent adults act like terrified children because the shadows might hold their demise.

George had bodyguards and escape plans and countless followers—if someone tried to put a bullet in his head, they'd die before they could finish the plot. Unlike the leaders, he did not fear the dark. He ruled it.

When the day came, after George was the dictator of the nations and had more power than any living soul in the western hemisphere, he would leave his legacy to his son, West. West would make a great conqueror of the East. Of course, West was often too much like his Uncle Richard for George's tastes, but George had spent the last twenty-five years polishing West. West's traits of loyalty, heroism, compassion, and mercy were something to be continually grinded into oblivion.

Though West didn't always follow instructions— such as having mercy on civilians, allowing prisoners to escape, and not torturing as George instructed him to— West was near his breaking point. George knew him better than West knew himself.

West would become a god. A leader. A conquerer. A son George could not just love, but be proud of.

But it was George's duty to make West into his prodigy. His heir. His second-in-command. West had fought long and hard, but his time was coming.

TWO

MAY 17TH, 2027

WEST JOHNSTON COULDN'T WASTE THIRTY seconds sitting behind a dumpster while a radical Jihadist shot at him from the street. Three rounds a second would take thirty seconds before the shooter hiding behind the side of the old brick shop would need to reload his AR-15.

Holding his Beretta in one hand, West pulled his radio to his ear with his other, snapping into it: "Jack, northside, now!"

"Occupied!" Jack answered. In that moment, West managed to hear distant gunfire coming from the east, but it wasn't heavy.

Occupied? How could the eastside be crawling with enemies? That piece of Miami, Florida was in crumbled ruins, and the caravan of Jihadists weren't exactly swarming the rubble, or at least, no one had known there were so many of them.

By the sound of the nonstop rounds, the shooter on West's tail wasn't a professional. He was scared.

West wasn't in Miami to assassinate enemies. He was on a retrieval job for twenty crates of ammo and supplies to create bombs. More technical, he was a block away from the actual building where the retrieval was going down. If he could get away with not shooting some trigger-happy teenager he'd scared out of hiding, he would take his chance and run for it.

Slowly creeping up from his hiding spot, sweat dripping from his temples and soaking his shoulder-length brown hair, the sun beating down on his broad back, West shouted, "Drop your weapon and I don't shoot!"

More firing. West knew the shooter heard the warning—he wasn't more than fifteen feet away now, maybe ten. *If I don't move, I'll be Swiss cheese soon.*

West eased up further and fired, hitting the shooter in the right shoulder. The wiry teen fell to the sidewalk and screamed. A headshot would've eliminated that cry of warning, but he didn't need to take such precautions now. The enemies knew George's men were in town already.

West ran down the sidewalk like a chicken begging to get its head chopped off. He didn't have much cover, so he just ran as fast as his long legs could carry him, darting inside an abandoned building when some sniper started shooting at his head. Pieces of brick grazed his skin as the bullets hit.

West ran through the building, the back half of the structure completely demolished, but he kept going over the rubble and stayed low.

"Jack, I'm coming to you." He spoke into the radio hastily. "Where's Hochberg and Thompson?"

"They're still at the trading post. They haven't come out and Clint's going in. I'm following him." Clint was a young man who worked odd-and-end jobs, usually with whoever needed him, but Jack and Gideon often acquired his help: he had the useful ability to blend in with the areas occupied by Middle Eastern, with his dark hair, eyes, and olive skin.

"Wait for me." West wove through the crumbled sidewalks and debris. He wasn't exactly athletic in his build—broadshouldered, strong and solid—so running wasn't his favorite pastime, but he was good at it.

Clint came over the radio then. "Guys, Alex and Gideon aren't coming out and everyone's almost evacuated. I'm heading in. I'm not waiting." His loyalty was almost childish. He never feared when someone was in danger, he simply acted. The trait gained him respect from West, but right now, the situation was too dire to laugh at Clint's youthful enthusiasm.

The transaction was a trap. Gideon and Alex are stuck inside the warehouse. Probably dead. But West didn't leave men behind. No matter how many times George tortured him for the moral decision.

He finally approached the trading post that stood strong beside a few other buildings, but was matchless in its size and the countless goods it contained. Gangsters, farmers, and traders gathered at the location to sell, buy, and trade whatever they needed or wanted. From food and animals to guns and slaves, the post in Miami was one of many popular hotspots.

A group of masked, black-clad men loading into a car out front made him duck back behind some rubble. They shouted in Arabic, waving machine guns, obviously trying to get away. Women and children screamed and fled into the streets. Men shot at the vehicle in vain, starting to run, though most packed up whatever they could.

Voices cried out in fear. "Bomb!" could be distinguished in various languages, only a few that West could make out.

The men were packing up shop because the trading post was rigged. And Gideon and Alex were in there.

"West!" Jack shouted, running through the crowd of maniac people. "There's a bomb! Clint went in!"

West ran for the post, darting inside and jumping over a few food supply crates that littered the ground. He narrowly avoided running into a cage of squawking chickens. "Gideon? Alex?" He shouted their names again and again but received no answer.

Jack ran to the backroom office where the leaders overwatched affairs, his long, lanky body easily avoiding any boxes that might get in his way. "They're not here! No one is!"

West kept going through the room that was bursting with supplies. Everyone had left in a hurry. Who knows what was still here? "Jack, I hear something!" he shouted, trying to get over a large crate that blocked his path to the stairs and a few other doors.

He heard Gideon calling for him. He looked to the top of stairs. Alex and Gideon had a small group of women—and was that a baby?—with them, both men trying to help the women downstairs, Clint taking in the rear.

The first explosion detonated. A violent surge of air and debris shot through the room and West lost all thought and being, losing consciousness as his body flew backward and heat singed his skin.

His last thought was if Jack had been close to the bomb when it went off.

ALEX TORE HIS BINDS OFF quickly, wriggling like a worm, then sat up and sliced his small, sharp pocket knife through Gideon's ropes, too. He remained focused intently on his work. "Do you think they'll use the bombs we paid for?"

"Probably. Those things aren't strong but if they're all they have to work with, we'd better move." Gideon jumped up and tried the door of the upstairs closet. Locked. Alex shoved a lock pick into his hand. If they had their radio or ear pieces, they could get a hold of Jack for help, but the Jihadists had only missed taking Alex's little surprises in his boot.

Gideon unlocked the door and stepped out. They'd been locked up for less than three minutes, but they'd been gone for at least ten, and three minutes of the Jihadists escaping was plenty of time for the people of the trade post to flee to safety.

So why did he hear a child screaming?

"Guys!" Clint called, voice strained. He was running toward a door across the hall. "Someone's in here, I hear them. I think some dude left behind his slaves."

The child's scream came again. Gideon and Alex rushed over. "Unlock it!" Gideon snapped.

"That's a bloody kid!" Alex hissed. He stopped in front of the door where the crying was louder, taking the lock pick and unlocking the door.

"The place is rigged," Clint panted. "Jack and West are coming—we gotta get outta here."

Alex shoved the door open. Five women, dressed in white dresses, sat chained to the wall. There was a young baby who continued to scream on one woman's lap.

Alex, Gideon, and Clint hastily undid the chains with

the lock picks Clint shared. They helped the women to the doors as fast as they could: there was no time to look the women in the eyes, or see their emptiness, but their will to live was evident, and right now, that was all that mattered.

"Downstairs," Gideon ordered. This was the part of his job George never knew about: mercy and compassion, sparing innocents. This was also the part of Gideon's job he knew would make his father proud. But his father had gone to heaven, and Gideon was on a hot road to hell.

Alex picked up one struggling woman. Gideon lifted the child into his arms, nudging and pulling the women onward. "*Run!*"

Clint helped the youngest woman, who couldn't have been older than thirteen, her legs were broken and bloodied. They reached the stairs, Gideon shouting once for West, but he knew help wasn't coming.

The fleeting thought of being blown to bits beside Alex and a baby wasn't something he was going to accept.

"Everyone, *down.*" Alex shoved the women downward into the corner and Gideon did the same in a matter of seconds, knowing it was too late.

And then the bomb went off downstairs. Another ripped apart the second floor down the hall where the women had been. Heat and pieces of demolition filled the room in a flash.

The last thing Gideon heard was a woman's scream and the baby's cry.

AS FAST AS THE BOMBS blew up, they ceased, and West had no idea how many had gone off, but it couldn't have been more than two or three.

Nothing made sense, but right now wasn't the time to sort out explanations. He stumbled to his feet, coughing. Smoke filled the room rapidly as various goods and the wooden beams set ablaze.

"Jack!" West tripped on rubble but kept going for the stairs. Jack coughed loudly.

"There's victims, Jack!" West reached the stairs but didn't see anyone at the top. "*Hochberg!*"

Movement at the top of the stairs. No screams, crying, or groans, and that wasn't a good sign. West dragged himself up the stairs, ears ringing violently, eyes beginning to burn. "We gotta move!"

"Al?" Gideon rolled over, hot blood rolling down his back from shrapnel wounds. "Take her." He pushed the child into West's arms.

Alex checked the women but his face was white as chalk. Two women weren't waking up, including the one in his arms, with blood all over their necks and backs. They'd been hit fatally by shrapnel.

Clint didn't move as the teenage girl pulled herself

weakly out from under his heavy body. Alex reached and grabbed Clint's arm, gasping. "C-Clint?"

Gideon saw the large piece of shrapnel sticking out from the side of Clint's neck. "Move." Was all he could manage. They couldn't save the living if they dragged the dead along, too.

The other three women staggered to their feet in total shock. Gideon and Alex left the dead and coaxed the survivors down the stairs quickly, Alex speaking Spanish to soothe one woman, who clung to his arm.

Jack reached them. "The front entry is destroyed. We can't get out that way. We gotta go to the back exit."

West pulled his shirt up to cover the child's face. The smoke was going to suffocate them before the flames ever touched their skin. "Back exit!" he shouted again.

It was their only shot.

Gideon and Alex guided the women through the smoke and scattered supplies toward the back of the room. Flames rose higher and darker, heat pounding down on them, the smoke growing black. The oxygen wasn't going to last. The women coughed violently, stumbling. The only thing giving them strength to keep moving was Gideon and Alex. And Alex was beginning to lose his cool—the man's absolute terror of fire clawing its way to the surface.

West kept the child close to his chest, trying to mask the girl's breathing with his shirt, and ran ahead of them.

The exit door was barricaded shut. The bombers must've done it before they left.

Jack looked around the room and grabbed an ax from a table of goods. In a matter of seconds, he'd broken the barricade and pushed the door open wide. West ran out with the baby and pulled the shirt off the girl's face when the fresh air hit them.

Gideon and Alex helped the women out into the alley. They all struggled for air as their lungs burned from smoke. But they couldn't stand there for long. Jack, Gideon, and Alex each picked one of the women up and kept going to the end of the alley, so when the trading post burst into utter flames, they wouldn't be killed.

Once they reached safety, there was that ethereal, split moment when time stopped. The women wept, covering their faces and crying out as the post burned like a piece of hell on earth. They wept for the two dead they'd left inside.

West sat and wept over the body of the little girl in his arms who'd died from smoke inhalation. He wondered if she was finally at peace. He wondered if it was a merciful God who took the children from the living, that maybe God wasn't so much of a monster as the world made him to be, that maybe West hadn't failed this little girl. The little girl hadn't deserved what this life had given her, but it was over now.

Then reality hit, as it always did, and he looked around to see Gideon and Alex bleeding from various wounds and women who needed oxygen masks. Jack's left arm was cut badly, too, but he kept a woman from moving around too much and hurting herself further.

West rested the body on the ground, covered her with his shirt, and headed to the truck parked down the street where they kept important medical supplies. His long legs carried him fast, but he didn't feel a single thing.

How many more bodies could he hold or leave behind? How many more times could he fail? They were all grown men and seasoned fighters, but how many more times could they face such things together?

ALEX COLLAPSED A SMALL DISTANCE from the others, panting, body heaving. Gideon stared at the destruction briefly before going to his best friend and kneeling down. "Alex. You're hurt. We have to get to the truck."

Alex covered his face as blood dripped from his blond hair, half of it shaven and covered in ash. His shoulders shook forcefully with sobs. Gideon grabbed his shoulder, cautious of his wounds. He didn't say anything. Words didn't comfort a man who'd held someone as they died. Words didn't help someone who'd been stuck in a burning building when that was their greatest fear. And words did not comfort a man who lost a comrade.

Gideon couldn't stand seeing Alex weep in fear, and he moved closer so Alex could hear him. "Breathe. Just breathe." It was hard to do when the smoke wrapped around your throat and lungs and threatened to end you. It was hard to breathe when you'd watched a person you loved breathe their last.

Gideon would never forget the screams, and he knew then that Alex wouldn't, either. There were so many screams they'd never forget. Gideon would take them to his grave.

West drove the truck over. Jack jumped in, grabbing oxygen masks, and Gideon helped pass them around. The women sat, using the masks with all the strength they had left.

"I called Vince," West said quietly. "He'll be here soon." Vince Zilinski was a trusted doctor who, while working for George, often helped whoever asked him.

Jack watched the trading post rise up into raging flames. "Did you call Ed and Ty?" The Brooks brothers were close friends of theirs and always came through during dire hours.

West just nodded.

Gideon began to clean up Alex's wounds despite his own. He barely felt West start to tend to him, too, as he worked on Gideon's injured back.

Alex didn't move besides shaking and running his

fingers through his hair repeatedly. He couldn't calm down. Gideon wouldn't be able to help him relax until they were out of sight of the fire. And the bodies.

Gideon had known Alex since he was seventeen, Alex had been sixteen, back before the nation divided. Even then, Alex could hold his own; he could fight battles and get out of terrible situations, nimble as a fox. But the bodies always got to him.

THREE

MAY 19TH, 2027

NATE SAVAGE ENJOYED FIGHT DOMES for the very reason that his father, George's right hand man, hated them. Kaleb's reputation as a powerful ganglord was put to shame by his son fighting at shacks for extra cash. But tonight, Nate didn't care about rules. He wanted some fun. Nothing he did made Kaleb proud, so he might as well deserve the punishments he received.

One night of fighting and earning cash wouldn't hurt anyone. For months, Nate had helped Simon do the right things: secretly carrying supplies to a town in hodunk Kentucky wasn't enjoyable. If they got caught by anyone, he and Simon would be punished, but that hadn't stopped them.

After all his hard work, Nate deserved one night for some fun. *Who knows? Maybe I can even prove Kaleb wrong and earn respect among the traders and owners here at the dome.*

Nate made his way into the Shabby Shack that burst with people of all kinds—rich men, poor men, slaves, owners. Most here to enjoy themselves and make money. The slaves and fighters had no choice but to fight.

Nate wasn't fond of domes, but he craved getting into the ring again, and unlike many fighters, he could choose to go home once he was finished.

The crowds gathered around the large square ring in the center of the first floor. Men jeered and waved cash. All eyes watched the brawl between two larger men, both fighting dirty on the ring floor, but no one stopped them.

Nate wove through the people, scowling at the strong smells of cigarette smoke, pot, and other drugs he didn't care for. He reached the back room where the slave cells were lined up.

"Hey, Big Daddy!" He called. As a freelance fighter, he'd have to go through the big guns in order to fight. Big Daddy owned the Shack.

"You ain't s'posed to be here, boy!" Big Daddy stepped away from a cell where a young teen was arguing with him. The teenager fell silent upon seeing Nate.

Big Daddy quarreled against Nate's offer, insisting Kaleb deserved more respect, but Nate suave-talked him. Nate was a good fighter, but he was just as good at talking.

"A'right, one fight." Big Daddy held up a large, rough hand in anger. "But that's it."

"Thanks for your business." Nate smiled slightly and scampered off. He watched a few fights from afar, ignoring the glares and glances he received. *Let the freaks all watch me like I'm an animal. I'll prove them right.*

He didn't enjoy watching the fights. One young man caught his attention, and he seemed to have real skills until he foolishly wore himself out. As he was finally pounded into the ground like a ragdoll, Nate grimaced. The slave's owner ended the fight but left the building in a furious huff. Nate didn't look away as a medic came to check the fighter; the young man was dead from head trauma.

"You're not supposed to be here, Nate." A large, burly man stepped beside him, shaking Nate's attention from the scene.

"Haven't seen you in a while, Reese." *Not long enough.* Nate cocked his head, watching two more fighters enter the ring before them. "How's it been?"

"Same old, same old." Reese glanced at the two fighters who danced around like weary boxers. "You fighting tonight?"

"Yeah." Nate almost asked Reese more questions, like what he was doing at the Shack—Reese was one of the best fighters any dome had ever seen. His martial art and street fighting skills weren't matched easily, and since his owner knew what he had, Reese rarely came to small domes. Nate knew this because Kaleb considered Reese a valuable man and kept up with his whereabouts, which was why Reese knew Nate and how he wasn't supposed to be at a dome.

"Good luck," Reese said.

"I don't need it."

"You do if you keep comin' around these places."

"Save your breath," Nate scoffed. There were plenty of domes in the beaten down parts of civilization and the surviving urban cities. So much of the United States had been destroyed, but in some parts, people continued to live sub-normally—if they followed all of the rules, gave their means of defense to the government, and jocked themselves full of medical enhancers. If Nate had to choose between one of those cities or a fight dome, he'd pick the dome any day of the week.

Reese headed to the ring as his name was called over the loudspeakers. He fought a skinny slave who darted around Reese like a lightning bolt. No amount of speed could withstand Reese's blows. The fight ended with Reese's victory. Reese made sure a doctor got the battered slave out of the ring.

Nate pulled off his shirt and laid it aside after his name was called. He stepped into the ring. The cheers and voices of the crowd filled his ears like a symphony from hell.

Nate watched his opponent enter the ring. He could tell a lot about how a fight was going to go if he paid attention to how the enemy approached: they could be confident, arrogant, shy, or stiff.

This guy strutted into the ring, called out to a few gamblers in the crowd, his grin big and crooked. Obviously, he planned on taking Kaleb Savage's precious son down in one fight.

Once the announcer started the fight, Nate sprang, not giving the man a second to start his game of cat and mouse. Nate faked him out—his front hand went to strike the man's temple. The man tried to block, but Nate popped him in the throat and grunted when the bugger got a good fist into Nate's gut.

The man threw punches, but Nate moved out of the way and threw a strong kick to the man's groin. A dirty move but not illegal. Nate didn't care about playing fair, and he wasn't letting his own athletic build go to waste because this fighter liked tossing his bulky weight around.

The man practically fell into the kick and staggered away. Nate needed him down for the count. He kicked him again and threw some head blows, taking some strikes to his own ribs, but the man wasn't able to move his legs much.

The crowd grew louder. Angrier.

Nate attacked the man full force, each blow having a specific job: throat, solar-plexus, and a good finishing kick to his kneecap. The man got a good strike into Nate's thigh as Nate took out his knee.

Nate chuckled as the man toppled, stepping back and taking a deep breath. The countdown started and ended.

Nate couldn't chalk it up to his best fight—he was pretty sure the bandage on the man's back was slowing his fighting abilities—but he'd won. That was something.

Stepping out of the ring and pulling his shirt on, he gathered his cash from the men who'd placed bets and smirked at those who'd lost. He didn't look back to see if the guy made it off the floor—he knew he hadn't hurt him beyond repair.

Reese followed Nate toward the door, away from the rowdy crowds. "You shouldn't waste your time, kid. You don't have to come here. Most of us don't have a choice." Reese wasn't phased by Nate's coldness. "Why do you do it? You don't need the cash."

Nate rolled his eyes, the smell of alcohol too strong for his liking, and the cigarette smoke made his head hurt. The bruises forming on his body ached. And he couldn't quite get the image of the skinny man with broken ribs getting dragged off the floor as Reese walked away.

"I like fighting." Nate didn't have to explain himself to Reese, however, and he was too sober to think about the slaves anymore. He opened the door and savored the fresh night air that hit his face.

"See ya, Nate." Reese didn't press further though the weariness in his voice made Nate wonder just how far Reese had fallen into his own oblivion. How could a man in a dome not be fallen, anyway? *Reese is everything I don't want to be: alone, broken, and doomed to die.*

But I'm none of those things. I've got Simon. I'm strong. I'll defeat anything and anyone who tries to stop me. If I can prove this to Kaleb, I'll be invincible, but Kaleb is unpredictable. I've never made him happy but I will, somehow. I have to. Like Uncle Hunter used to say, "A person fights hardest for the things they think possible."

NATE DROVE FIVE HOURS BACK home which was miles away from

Kaleb's HQ—Paradise—avoiding roads that might lead to any small blips of civilization, like the Islamic caravans, roadside robbers, or militia men looking for some fast fixes. Nate knew the roads better than most and so his drive was uneventful, which didn't always happen, but tonight, he had a lucky break and only saw wilderness and properties where houses used to stand before being burnt down.

He missed the old days, when America had been free

and strong. When the Army was for the United States and not split into another Union and Confederate bickering disaster. He missed when the Constitution had been law, but now it was adulterated with Sharia Law, martial law, and countless other things the nation had voted for.

When Nate had been small, he'd loved watching movies about apocalyptic worlds. Where the government was bad and ruling. Where the people fought back. Chosen people.

But that's not what the end was like. The end was slow burning—it'd been coming for decades. The election in 2024 was simply the straw that broke the camel's back—the nation snapped under the new laws and it chose chaos. One side chose personal freedom, self defense, and the protection of the innocent. The other side chose government control, foreign defense, and jaded moralities.

There are no chosen people. No heroes. No good. The government wasn't one wicked man—it was a lot of humans.

And every human could be wicked.

Like me, I guess. I don't even have a side—we gangs aren't Union or Confederates. We're like flies, swarming, jumping on any disgusting source we can. Technically, Kaleb was against the Confederates, but Nate didn't quite agree with that alliance. Nate snacked on some beef jerky to stay awake and switched his thoughts, since thinking about the disasters did nothing to change the world.

Jordan, Simon's dad, was slightly better than Kaleb. He showed more mercy and compassion—after all, he had underground railroads throughout the US and Canada. Nate knew Kaleb was aware of the big secret, but Kaleb never ratted Jordan out. He just ignored the smuggling of innocent lives out of danger.

Nate and Simon didn't live on base and hadn't visited in a while. Their small shack that was secure and smelt like mildew lay hidden in a small spot far from base and away from their fathers.

Nate parked outside his place, stumbling out tiredly, going inside, locking the door. He made it to the fridge and grabbed a beer.

"You freaking idiot." Simon's sharp voice came from behind him. "We have a supply drop tomorrow," his voice lowered to a hiss. "And you're out fighting!"

"*One* fight." Nate downed half the beer in one giant gulp. "I just wanted some fun, so ease off." Simon never eased off—not when it came to Nate doing stupid things. Nate did a lot of stupid things. He'd have thought Simon would grow accustomed, in the lifetime they'd known each other.

Simon cursed. "You're just being selfish! You could've gotten *seriously* hurt."

"Oh, c'mon, Simon." Nate scowled at him, finishing

the beer and popping the lid off another. *He's been hearing Rene' talk about God too much. He's getting annoying. Well, he's always been annoying, and naggy…* "I've worked just as hard as you to help Springtown for months! One freakin' night didn't kill anyone." His blood boiled with anger. Who did Simon think he was? Nate didn't get a single thing from helping Springtown. Simon had met a girl there and talked to her and would probably get some bliss at some point— but Nate received no reward.

Simon clenched his fists and leaned against the small countertop. "Shut up."

"I get home and you start nagging me."

"No, you're just touchy after you visit a dome." Simon shot back. "You aren't near as cold-hearted as you think, and you take it out on me."

Nate rolled his eyes, wiping beer from his mouth. "You're not a shrink."

"I'm not stupid," Simon said calmly. "I'm not apologizing for worrying about you. I'm grateful for your help, but these kinda careless nights are gonna get you killed." Simon got his kind heart from his dad. Nate got his coldness from Kaleb. He'd never do enough good deeds to change the truth. For Simon's sake, he helped Springtown, but it didn't change his heart.

"You say thanks too much." Nate scoffed. *Brothers suck when they're right.*

"We leave tomorrow," Simon sighed. "Just try to

sleep and not get drunk."

Nate lifted his beer slightly. "Love ya, big bro."

"Shut up, Princess Peach." Simon headed to his room.

Simon Bucks was one of the two people that Nate trusted with his life. Being Simon's brother by choice meant more than Nate's blood relation to his older cousin, Jack. Simon said Nate was simply bitter, and that was true, but he saw no reason to not be that way. He didn't need, trust, or like Jack, and it hadn't killed him yet: *yet* being the key word. Jack was a liable asset—good at his job and George trusted him—but Nate paved his own path quite well himself. Despite what Simon said, Nate didn't need Jack. Ever.

The other man that Nate trusted and needed was AJ McCall, the old vet who'd gotten Nate and Simon helping him support Springtown. He'd dragged them into the deal and Simon took over.

Nate finished his beer and grabbed a shower, letting the hot water run over his bruised torso, groaning as he moved his arms and neck. Fighting hurt but he liked the pain. He asked for it, asked for the blows, and he had control over his opponent, too. He didn't get that control with Kaleb. How many times had Kaleb beat him, locked him up, threatened him, all part of training?

Nate pulled his pants on, heading to his bedroom and crashing onto his worn, squeaky bed. He wished he could get his mind together and stop letting himself wander to the dark depths of his mind where he hid everything. He wished he didn't make Simon mad so often. He wished he didn't have to fight to make Kaleb love him.

He could wish a thousand things, but wishes meant nothing.

Absolutely nothing.

He closed his eyes, pulling his blanket a bit tighter. Uncle Hunter used to make him pray every night, back when the world was hellish but hadn't broken out yet, back when Nate could ride his bike and play games and be a kid and not a soldier.

The world kept changing. So did Nate. And Hunter was dead, killed by George's very test that would have sealed his alliance and made him an invincible friend of the Johnston legacy. Because of that turn of events, Nate hadn't prayed in a long time.

I'm probably just thinking of praying now because of all the God stuff Simon hears Rene' talk about. Satisfied it didn't matter to him if God heard him and therefore, he needn't pray, Nate fell asleep.

His mother walked away from his father and the baby in his arms— baby Nate himself.

From a distance, in the suffocating shadows, he watched as she walked away and Kaleb wept. His mother's figure vanishing in the shadows, Nate turned to Kaleb.

"This is your fault," Kaleb told the baby. "I didn't want you, but what choice do I have? I'd be a fool not to make you useful." He kissed the baby's head. "I'll make you stronger than me so you'll never face this pain, Nathan."

Nate jerked awake and groaned, head pounding. He always had strange nightmares but that one was simply unreasonable. His imagination, harnessed with far too much truth, had no right to hurt him so. *Kinda ironic, huh? One reason this stupid nation divided was over abortion. I'm one of the buggers who should've been killed off in the womb. What a disservice.*

FOUR

MAY 19TH, 2027

RENE' FISHER RODE HER MARE, Sugar, toward Springtown, her township in Kentucky with rolling hills and flat grasslands, dense trees near the borders, old and new buildings throughout the land. The town was lonely and battered from three years of surviving on nothing, of fighting tiny mobs and homeless who fought to enter and ransack whatever they could find, of scarcely sending any men to join the Confederates because their greatest cause to fight was to defend their very own border. They had no money and it was a miracle God provided supplies, but they'd made it, with very little help from outside sources. Until now.

Rene' wiped sweat from her brow, the summer sun merciless. Sugar moved eagerly past the mayor's house, but Rene' didn't let her go too fast in the heat. Mayor Knight didn't lead expeditions on the town's behalf, nor did he show much love or compassion. He cowardly stayed in his home and only appeared when he could say what someone else told him to say.

The leader of Springtown was a group of townsmen. The leader of that group was Mr. Fisher, Rene's father, a jack-of-alltrades, but he never quite expected God to put him in the position he was now. At least, that's what he told his family every night when they gathered for dinner.

Rene' dismounted, pushing her worrisome thoughts aside, tying her mare to the hitching post outside of the courthouse. Though Simon and Nate never came at a regular time or a set date—that was far too dangerous—they did contact her, or her father, before showing up at the border.

The two young men brought supplies, food, and medicine. Every little bit counted. The whole town needed them.

Rene' glanced up her fifteen-year-old brother, raising her eyebrows. She'd long gotten accustomed to him being much taller than her short height. "You OK?"

"Yeah." Lee pushed his dark hair back, sweat trickling down his neck. "Just tired."

They were all tired. Always. But she'd noticed some slight relief in the townsmen since Simon and Nate started bringing truckloads.

Rene' rubbed Lee's arm comfortingly. "I love you."

Even if you have grown far too fast than any boy should have to. He's practically a man now. It was always a strange thought to face.

"Love you too, midget," he smirked smugly.

They went into the courthouse where people gathered, mostly men and a few women waiting to help unload, all seeming almost happy. Springtown was constantly in a state of bickering beneath the teamwork—perhaps that was merely natural for a large body of people to be tense but survive. Still, could they seriously be this content?

Some people didn't like the thugs—they knew Nate and Simon were sons of powerful ganglords and raged about it, but the common-sense minded pushed on. "This is our only way," Mr. Fisher and countless others reminded the doubtful. In the end, the boys were allowed to enter the town after their truck was checked by an officer and they were kept under close observation.

Lee headed to help some men load up a truck of supplies for some elderlies needs.

Rene' watched him briefly before finding her dad. Usually, he dealt with the townspeople or handled jobs. Mr. Fisher had told his family, "I'd rather do a full day's labor than deal with another soul."

Rene' prayed her father got rest and wisdom. Her prayers didn't seem to work much anymore, but she kept praying.

Mr. Fisher was in Sean O'Malley's office. Sean was one of the adopted Fisher's now—a redheaded big brother Rene' never knew she'd needed. He was also good at defending the town and was so dedicated, if it weren't for the Fisher women, he would probably have starved himself to death by now.

"Hey, baby girl." Mr. Fisher smiled at her arrival, setting a small ammo box down on the table and loading his pistol.

"Hey, Daddy." Rene' hugged him. "Simon and Nate'll be here soon?"

He nodded. "You gonna help unload? How's Mom and Terri?"

"Mom's feeling OK. Terri's just napping with the kids." Terri, her older sister, had four kids with her husband, Howard, with the fifth due in a month or so. Rene' usually stayed at home, helped her family, and cared for the ranch animals, but she always made it to the courthouse when Simon came. During his visits, she found a sliver of relief. Of hope. Of happiness. Not only did Simon and Nate help her survive with her town, but Simon made her laugh. That meant something to her— it made her feel like she was capable of having a friend in the hellhole that was North America.

Mr. Fisher finished loading his pistol. "What's on your mind?"

She shrugged. The courthouse was so busy, and he was no doubt needed, so she didn't want to take up his time. "Just thinking."

"About?" He holstered the old gun on his hip.

"The supply drop."

"You mean Simon?"

She blinked, staring at her father in surprise. "What?"

Mr. Fisher's lips curved in a smirk. "Your friend?"

"Oh. Yeah, I guess." Rene' crossed her arms and glanced to the door. *Dad doesn't have to say* friend *like that.*

"He's not a bad man, despite what the town worries about." Mr. Fisher rested a hand on her shoulder gently. She already knew Mr. Fisher's thoughts—she did live with him and the Fisher family had no secrets—so she nodded.

"I've gotta help Mikey organize supplies. You wanna take that box to Ms. Fitz and be back before the truck?" Mr. Fisher headed to the door, Rene' following his footsteps.

"Yessir."

"Be safe." Two words that the family said far too often. Rene' smiled sadly and went to the storage room. She grabbed a small cardboard box and headed outside, walking steadily despite the humid heat.

Ms. Fitz lived nearby in the suburb behind the library. If Rene' hurried, she wouldn't miss the supply truck, but she also knew Ms. Fitz was lonely. Her visit wouldn't be short. Twenty minutes later, Rene' rushed back to the courthouse. Lee was waiting near the horses, smirking, offering her a bottled water.

"For a midget, you walk fast."

"Can it, beanpole." She gratefully downed the water. She disliked the terrible heat, but she supposed it was better than frigid winter with bare necessities. Simon and Nate had helped Springtown just in time last winter, and prayerfully this time, they'd manage survival again.

Lee laughed and leaned against his mare tied to the hitching post. "Here they come."

Every time Rene' saw the truck come into sight down the worn road, hope flickered in her chest, because each time offered a little bit more future. A little more hope. A little more trust.

Men stepped out of the courthouse, some eager, some tense as always. Mr. Fisher stepped close to his kids and watched as the truck parked near the doors. Simon and Nate stepped out quickly.

"Afternoon," Simon smiled at Mr. Fisher and glanced to the others. "We've got a bigger load this time."

Mr. Fisher came over with the others. Simon undid the lock again and everyone started carrying crates, boxes, and containers inside the courthouse.

Nate and Lee worked together in silence, hauling a

bigger box inside.

Simon turned to Rene'. "Hey." He offered her a small container. "How are you doing?"

"Good. You?" It wasn't like she could tell the honest, whole truth in the back of the truck. *I'm still scared and feel pathetic for not trusting God entirely? I'm tired? I hate myself for being tired because my family is even worse off?*

He chuckled and picked up his own crate. "I'm doing fantastic now that we're here."

They went inside and helped stack things neatly in the backroom. Rene's heart swelled with how full the rooms were becoming. Even when people used things constantly, it mattered it was restocked.

Rene' stayed to help the women organize things while the men finished carrying everything inside. Rene' followed them outside when they were finished.

Mr. Fisher, Sean, and a few others spoke with Simon and Nate: about the gangs, battles among the states or territories, and politics, no doubt. She kept up with the current disasters, and though she didn't feel like listening today, she went over beside Mr. Fisher and Lee.

"Nothing's going on too close, sir." Simon shook his head. "There were a few fights in Delaware, and a bigger takeover in

Ohio with a Union camp that no one knows who led–"

"What?" One man piped up curiously.

"The Union camp in Ohio was bombed." Simon shrugged. "No one knows much more than that."

"Anything from the Confeds?" Mr. Fisher asked slowly. Simon and Nate were their only ticket to the world news, and the right questions must be asked. As much as the majority in Springtown hated the war and prayed for the end of it, they also had the wisdom to know how much the war mattered.

"Two thousand were lost in Missouri last week when they were pushed back, but I've got word there are lots of big guns moving toward D.C. It's kinda secret and a long shot, but if they get D.C., after all these years, they're close." Nate's voice was heavy with anger.

A few men grinned proudly but Mr. Fisher remained somber. As if he knew such a blessing was as delicate as a flower sprouting on a highway.

Rene' chewed her lip. She held onto faith that God would protect her town. But reality was harsh. The Confederate armies and the Southern civilizations hanging on by the teeth could all be easily destroyed. The whole nation could be finished with a few nukes from a foreign nation who grew tired of the civil unrest that meddled with their own foreign affairs through the UN. But it hadn't happened yet. Rene' kept faith because if she didn't, fear would suck the life from her.

Simon met her gaze and offered a small smile, like he noticed her wandering thoughts and hoped to pull her back in. She quickly smiled.

The conversation continued, but she had trouble listening in on all of the pain and destruction. The Confederates weren't doing terrible, but the Union had the government funding that strengthened them in the long haul. It made her sick thinking of the fallen men who'd died protecting their freedom.

Springtown hadn't sacrificed men to the fight. The civilians protected their own town and succeeded thus far, but many young men yearned to join the battle that was sure to end soon. The nation might've divided three years ago, but with enough manpower and smarts, the Confeds would win and restore the nation, once and for all. Or so, Lee and Xander insisted. Rene' prayed they were right.

Eventually, the men dispersed and Mr. Fisher went to finish his duties so they could go home. Rene' followed Simon to the back of the truck. "Simon?"

"Yeah?" He pulled the truck door down and locked it.

"Thanks," she said quietly.

Simon's dark eyes met hers and they shined with a small smile. "For what?"

"The supplies." *And everything else.* But she didn't say those things.

"Oh. Right." He leaned against the truck. "No problem."

"And you, too, Nate." She smiled at him as he headed to the passenger side.

"You don't have to say thanks all the time." Nate didn't meet her gaze. Strange—he usually acted bold and arrogant. He had just a touch of quietness today. *He's probably hungover*—Rene' knew he drank more than Simon liked. Nate loaded up as she waved goodbye.

Simon groaned, running a hand through his dark hair. "Sorry. He's been rough…"

"I understand," Rene' said quietly. "Terri's been emotional lately. Family's hard."

"When's the baby gonna be here?"

"Aiden should be here in a month." Rene' grinned at using the new name for Terri and Howie's upcoming baby boy.

"You guys must be excited." Simon glanced to the courthouse where Mr. Fisher had disappeared.

"Yeah," Rene' sighed. "Kids are amazing… And the supplies you guys bring really gives us hope." Without supplies, children died. Simon had no idea the nights Rene' had comforted Terri about the surprise baby, praying with her that God would make a way for them all. God *had* made the way.

Simon shifted on his feet awkwardly, smiling. "I… uh… yeah… I mean, we're glad to help." He'd told her before it wasn't something he and Nate could do easily. They took jobs themselves, and while they avoided telling Rene' details, they told Mr. Fisher. All Rene' knew was they stole things, earned separate supplies, or ransacked empty places."And AJ and Mr. Fisher are the ones to thank for setting this deal up."

"Y'all get the supplies." Rene' tilted her head, long brown hair swinging in her ponytail.

"Fine." He smirked. "You're welcome."

Rene's smile faded and she looked down, gut twisting. "And… thanks for…" *For listening. For making me laugh before I go to bed with stupid jokes. For reminiscing about the 'old' days.* She got so lost in her thoughts she couldn't decide what to say.

"The talking? Because I wanted to thank you for actually talking to me. Even if you turn off your radio after ten o'clock."

"Hey, sometimes I use the little phone thingamajig you gave me!" She shrugged. "But the buttons are so small."

Simon grinned. "What?"

"What?"

"What'd you say—thingama-what?"

"Majig." Rene' crossed her arms. "Don't you know what that means?"

"Uh… sure." He rubbed the back of his head.

"Stop laughing at me. It's a real word!"

"OK," Simon cleared his throat and grew serious again, though his cheeks remained tinted red, his eyes shining.

"And yes, I was thanking you for talking to me, too." Rene' relaxed. It was easy to relax around Simon. "You don't have to." "Yeah, I do. You yell at me when I don't." Simon scoffed.

"I do not," she said indignantly. "You just wish I did."

Nate banged on the side of the van. "Si, we'd better head out!" he called from his open window.

Rene' offered Simon a small side-hug. "See ya, Si." She didn't have to force the happiness in her voice.

He saluted her, got into the truck, and drove toward the border.

Maybe there is some hope, her heart said as she watched them wind down the worn streets of old buildings. *God's gotten us all through things so far—He won't stop.*

FIVE

MAY 21ST, 2027

"EVERYTHING READY?" ALEX'S CALM VOICE came over the ear pieces that the whole team wore.

"All set, Al," Gideon replied, using binoculars to see across the city street of Little Rock, Arkansas, that stood like a sore spot against the barren state. Strong, glass buildings stood among the rubble of architecture that hadn't been gone for long. Such was the United States. Some cities were defeated and abandoned. In the western states, in the deserts and no man's land, not many wars between the two governments stirred. The Union and Confederates fought in the East, or a few bloody mob fights in the Californias and New Mexico. Gideon didn't have much use for either side of the battle, but each side fought for what they believed to be true.

"Phil?" Alex asked over the ear piece. Alex

Thompson, a top notch intelligence man, spy, and thief, worked solely with Gideon. He got along well with anyone else but only if Gideon was on the job, too. His past was a butchered one—he'd flunked enough jobs to have his confidence low as a field rat. "I could really use some sniper lessons, if you or Ed get the chance."

"Is the thugs' gun trade talk gettin' the best of ya, Aussie?" Philip Dunnham asked over the ear comms, chuckling. He and Ed Brooks were two of the best snipers George had.

"Shut up, Phil," Alex retorted.

Philip was a trusted ally—both of George and Gideon. He and Gideon shared a large secret from George himself: they'd been planning to smuggle Phil's little thirteen-year-old brother, Danny, away from George's vices for over a year. It hadn't happened yet, but it would soon.

"Almost there, gentlemen," Gideon interrupted calmly, making sure everyone was in position over his comm. Five men positioned around the building would shoot the situation back into control if Alex was blown, but so far, Antonio didn't see his new friend as a threat.

The con job had progressed for two months. Alex led it, portraying a capable businessman who joined the Catalysts in their expedition to money and power. The Catalysts weren't a large gang, but they were growing more controlling in the western states. After their group had tried to infiltrate one of George's Oklahoma camps, George ordered Gideon and Alex to "take care of it."

This con had been Alex's idea in approach to George's order. He'd reasoned that they couldn't wipe out the gang fast unless they were on the inside, where they could silently make it divide.

Within a few weeks, the con was in the works. Alex grew close to the leader, Antonio. Antonio liked "Beck" for his extreme talents in government intelligence and technology skills.

Gideon watched from his perch a few buildings away, up a few floors crouching near a window, as Alex stepped outside of the building, following Antonio and a group of other welldressed men. Antonio's bodyguards kept their eyes peeled but didn't see Gideon's guys in waiting.

Another group of men left the building, an even smaller gang who'd tried to strike a deal with Antonio. Thanks to Alex's hand in the matter, the deal had been vetoed, and it would ultimately lead to the Catalyst's demise. The small gang was a loose cannon—they would avenge the decision against them. A small group of men could cause great havoc.

While Gideon took care of things in the form of a bomb or a bullet, and was a spectacular spy, Gideon's go-to choices of dealing with matters weren't like Alex's.

Alex liked con jobs and spying, but never took a life unless it was self defense. Such a moral code brought him a lament countless times. Gideon couldn't let this time be one of those times. Hence, the group of men waiting ready.

Antonio spoke lightly with Alex as he walked, completely relaxed, without regard for the group heading the opposite direction.

That fool. You never turn your back to the enemy.

"Just keep moving, Alex," Gideon said into the comm. Everyone was in position and ready to blow heads off. Alex stayed a small distance away from the others, in case Philip had to snipe one of Antonio's men.

No one breathed another word. As soon as the Catalysts went half a block, the other men reached their trucks and grabbed their guns.

"Alex, down!" Gideon snapped into the comm.

The thugs opened fire at the Catalysts in seconds. Imprecise, but dangerous nonetheless. In return, Gideon's group shot them down.

Alex jumped down at Gideon's command, dragging Antonio down with him.

Gideon ran to the fire escape on his left and practically threw himself down the side of the building, landing softly, pulling his 9mm Parabellum from his holster.

Two men lay dead near the car. The other thugs had

sought cover from Gideon's snipers.

Antonio's men shot back pathetically at the unseen snipers surrounding them on all sides.

Gideon shot one of the gangsters hiding behind their car door. The body fell and blood soaked the road like even the dead refused to leave without a mark. From his current position near the corner of the building, Gideon didn't have much ability to shoot anyone, but he had clear sights on Antonio's men if he needed to shoot any of them.

The gunshots ceased. Eerie silence rang in Gideon's ears as the world fell silent for a second.

A scream of pain filled the air and a desperate yell, a plea. "Don't shoot!"

"Don't move!" Philip's voice came from down the street near the car of dead thugs, but obviously one wasn't dead.

Antonio snarled at his men, and they sprinted the final distance to their trucks and loaded up. Antonio snapped for Beck to get in with him first, obviously grateful Alex had saved his life. Gideon watched the trucks tear off down the road as he ran towards Philip. *For now, Alex's con is secure.*

What was Philip doing? They'd agreed no survivors except Antonio's men. Philip never took hostages, anyway. It wasn't his style.

Once the Catalyst's truck tore off down the street,

Gideon came out of hiding, too, speaking into his comm: "Alex, tell me if your end gets out of hand." He darted over to Philip. "What the hell?"

"It's Fred," Philip snapped, 9mm trained on the battered man leaning against the bullet-holed car. Bodies lay all round and the asphalt was dark with blood.

"Fred?" His eyes bored holes through the little man that writhed like a worm.

"Please, don't kill me," Fred blubbered, holding his tattooed hands up in surrender. "Please! I changed! I've changed from what you knew!"

"You raped kids. We failed to kill you once, we don't fail twice." Philip stepped closer. Three years and the incident was fresh in Gideon's mind. He knew it had never left Philip's consciousness, either.

Fred and two other men had betrayed Philip, taking the three children Philip rescued from a sex trafficking ring and selling the kids back. Philip hadn't known to stop them until it was too late.

"Tell us how many of you are trying to join the Catalysts and we'll make it fast." Philip's hands were steady on his sniper rifle.

Gideon came closer, but as he did, a small motion in the corner of his eye caught his attention. One of the bodies was moving. Before the man could reach for his gun, Gideon shot the dying man in the head.

He then smoothed his short jet black hair back with

one hand and eyed Fred again.

"I don't know!" Fred blurted hastily. "I don't know, we're not much of a gang. Just nobodies trying to get protection. The Catalysts were doing kinda well, we figured they might take some of us, some of us who are useful." He rambled on, licked his bloodied lips.

"How many?" Philip snarled, his chiseled features darkening with pure revulsion and rage.

"Over a hundred, we're from all over. We used to have more but a lotta guys died in the Wichita bombing. Look, we had no choice." Fred kept his hands up, sobbing fearfully. "Please, don't shoot me! We're not dangerous! We just want a break from the wars!"

Even with a hundred men, Fred was right—none of them were dangerous enough to threaten George.

Gideon shot Fred in the head before Philip could. "Let's go get Alex." Gideon motioned with his arm for the men in hiding to move out.

"THE JOB'S ALMOST FINISHED. THE Catalysts just have to kill themselves and divide what's left." Gideon sat the bowl of soup down onto the table in front of Alex. Alex didn't look up, pale-faced and tired as a horse. He'd been restless since he'd gotten home from Antonio's.

"I'm glad I don't have to go back. Beck was a jerk." Alex ate slowly, eyes downcast and mournful, though he mocked his con identity. He absently rubbed a small indent in the wooden table where Clint had dropped a heavy, unloaded gun only three weeks ago. Clint had been a handful—loud, messy, and constantly breaking something in the little cabin. Alex missed him, Gideon could tell. He didn't move on like Gideon did. Regardless of who was lost, Alex carried every name in his heart, and he didn't stop, no matter how heavy his heart grew.

Gideon was grateful Alex hadn't gotten hurt in the con while he'd been grieving. He hadn't made a mistake with Antonio the whole time—in fact, Antonio even thanked him for "saving their lives" before Alex left.

Gideon sat down at the table, eating hungrily. "You did good, Alex."

Alex gave a small shrug. "How's Danny doing? Kid's got it rough, not knowing he's about to be freed and reunited with his own brother."

"I imagine." Gideon smiled. "He's a good kid, he deserves this."

"He and Phil both." Alex ate some more.

"Yeah." Gideon briefly remembered Philip's anger with Fred earlier that day. "Danny does deserve freedom."

"We all do," Alex muttered. "You and I have each other, right? We've got a chance."

Gideon ignored the comment. Gideon and Alex had many things in common and many things that made them separate. Neither of them had family kin. Alex lost his family when he was five-years-old and entered the foster system, escaping when he was seventeen and joining gangs that'd take him. By the Second Civil War, he'd crawled his way to George Johnston—literally. Gideon had saved him from a ditch and gave him a position in George's group, which was an affiliate of the UN, so the group and every underling group remained Union. Alex deserved his place as one of the best thieves and hackers this side of the Second Civil War.

Alex leaned back in his seat and ran his hands through his hair after a long moment of silence. "We'll be free one day, too, Gid. God'll get us there." His voice was quiet, like if he voiced it too loud, the dream might shatter into the darkness and never be held again.

"Yes." Gideon didn't think God had much care for anything in the world. Losing his mother at age six and having his father go MIA when he was seventeen hadn't made him particularly ache for what was lost in the world—the destruction of his own family and his nation fueled him to make his dad proud. It pushed him forward to kill as many bad guys as he could, even if he'd become one himself.

Alex wouldn't become the enemy. But Gideon was a monster and one day, he'd do too many bad things in the name of good.

"You should get some sleep." Alex grunted in pain.

"We both should." Gideon finished his meal. "You grab a shower and I'll clean up."

"Thanks, mate." Alex got up and disappeared into the narrow hallway that led to two bedrooms and a bathroom. The cabin wasn't much, but it was safe and not in the middle of a base camp. Though they didn't need a roof to have a home— they'd survived on much less. They only needed each other. That was home. Wherever his brother was, Gideon would be there, and he'd do what it took to continue to be. Even if Alex wanted to go to West Virginia to retire and grow his own farm and have a little gathering of people to have home church with, Gideon didn't have much choice but to follow him into that jungle if that's what the years brought.

My gig has lasted almost eight years now. I doubt it ends soon. Eight years of following George, earning trust, being a master at his jobs, spying and killing like a machine. One day, George would see he was a spy and find out his role. One day, George would kill him.

Gideon washed the dishes in silence. *It hasn't happened yet.* In fact, it didn't look close to happening, but a man never got cocky. George entrusted Gideon with his own militia of men, but that didn't make Gideon invincible. Gideon treated his own group with respect but didn't go too far. He wasn't Kaleb or Jordan. If he practiced caution until he got his marking, then he'd have more weight in his role and more control over his group.

Gideon dried his hands on a towel. He thought of his secret alliance, Union officer Brian Jones. *At least I don't have to face these wars as a political figure. I don't enjoy the war like Brian does. I just take advantage of the chaos. As Dad used to say:* "A real warrior fights until his last breath, not when the world tells him he can stop."

SIX

MAY 24TH, 2027

BOLD DARK RED AND ORANGE stripes and blotches lit up the dawn sky, greeting the warmth of the rising sun over the basecamp. The heat of the sun promised another hot Kentucky day.

West preferred the heat to the cold—he'd spent too many nights freezing in basements when he was younger. Some punishments stuck in his consciousness, and he couldn't fight them because they became a part of him. A man could hide a scar but there was little hope fighting against his own psyche.

West put his 9mm Parabellum in his holster around his waist, looking around. His apartment room was barren: an Army cot, a small wooden dresser without a speck of dust, and dust-free old floors. It was West's own space in the basecamp but he hated it.

He preferred the hideout he and Jack had made

many miles away, but they hadn't been there in a while. Jack visited his girlfriend in South Carolina too many times to drop by. Meanwhile, West grew closer and closer to George—for the safety of his brothers. Thus George couldn't suspect him of foolish things.

West headed to the door and left the apartment complex. His phone buzzed and he answered it, looking about the quiet base. "Ready?"

"You really gotta remember to say good morning or something, bud." Jack sighed. "I'll meet you outside." Other men would head to mess hall and eat, but Jack and West avoided the mess because of the crowd.

"Gotcha." West hung up and moved to the front of the complex where a few cars were parked. Jack leaned against his expensive old Mustang, offering West a small paper bag full of breakfast.

"Good morning," Jack emphasized.

"Morning."

"Close enough, big guy."

West took the bag and got into the car, the sun beating against his white t-shirt.

"Hey," Jack frowned as he got in and cranked the car. "What's up?"

"Nothing." West opened the bag. They'd spent their whole lives fighting the whole world and George. West was failing and couldn't drag his brother down with him.

"Don't lie," Jack scoffed. "You've been acting weird

lately. Quiet."

"I'm always quiet." West ate some of his cold bacon. *My heart is a dark, frozen piece of coal and if I try to warm it up to comfort my brothers, I'll combust.* He'd never be able to control or stop that fire. It would destroy everyone close to him. So he let his heart grow harder. Colder. The cavern in his chest grew emptier, like his blood stopped flowing with life, replaced by nightmares, shame, rage, and hatred. Not hatred for George. Hatred for himself. *I'm a monster and I chose that. No excuses.*

Jack growled at West's silence. "We never keep secrets, remember?"

"Lotta jobs lately, just tired," West replied easily. That was a fair excuse. Jack and West were always busy with jobs and other meddling affairs. The things he saw often kept him awake at night, leaving him with no sleep, and Jack understood that.

Jack drove through the camp streets and shrugged slightly. "You can—"

"—talk to you. I've known you my whole life, I know the drill." West cracked a smile, finishing his breakfast quickly and managing to keep it all down. He took his coffee cup from the cupholder, taking a swig of the steaming liquid. "Thanks."

Jack rolled his eyes. "Did you hear about the mob fight in New York?"

"Yeah, why?" Mob and civilian uproars were pretty

popular and while he kept up with them, they became monotonous: people blew things up in protest against the government blowing things up.

"Just wondering." Jack sighed. "It got me thinking about Spencer, I guess."

Spencer Anderson, a close friend, was born in New York, along with his little brother Randy. They often complained about how their home-state was one of the first to join the Union, but every man had a certain fondness for where he came from.

West wondered how Randy was doing in Kaleb's group. Randy had been the first brother West fully trusted, back when they were young teens and just starting to have some fun in the gangs, back when they didn't have the weight of the world on their shoulders. Spencer and Jack were the older brothers—no nonsense, solemn, always trying to make sure George didn't catch them. While Jack's father was now deceased, he continually dealt with his uncle Kaleb's constant pressure.

West finished drinking his black coffee. The morning sun rose higher and reminded him of those mornings he'd spent as a little kid, hiding on the roof of the mansion he used to call home, hiding from the world and George. He remembered yearning for the sun to come and engulf him in warmth.

But the sun never saved him. Nor the stars, nor the

man on the moon, nor Uncle Richard, nor God Himself. Nothing had ever saved him from his father or the demons dragging him into depths.

Jack turned on an oldie CD and blasted the volume.

West, as usual, remained silent, lost in his mind like a shipwreck being tossed around at sea. He wondered what his mother was doing on such a beautiful morning, back home in the mansion, so far from where he and George roamed like lions preying the earth. Did she miss her grown son? Did she weep because of what he'd become?

I wanted to make her proud. Look at me now. A con, liar, thief, killer, monster. He'd become what George wanted over time. Slow. Steady. Like waves crashing mercilessly over a jagged stone, until the stone had no choice but to be reshaped or crumble.

Maybe I should've let myself crumble. Maybe I should've found a way to pull that trigger and rid the word of West Johnston, the demon-possessed businessman's son.

He couldn't do that to Jack. He'd never been strong enough to end his life. He wouldn't let George win.

WEST DIDN'T MIND BEING ALONE for the span of time, but he rarely got *left* alone. Too much went on in the base. Most of the time, if he wasn't on a job, Spencer wanted him to come over for beers, or Ed wanted to practice shooting, or a groupie needed some assistance. He didn't get left alone when Jack left base, as much as he wished he could have some free time, he was out of luck. *Life of a gangster's son.*

West locked himself into his apartment after Jack headed out of base to visit his secret girlfriend. Within the past year, Jack spent more and more time disappearing and going to South Carolina for Mels. No one else in the gang knew about her except West. Spencer might've gotten a slight hint, since he was around them quite a bit, but he kept his big mouth shut.

Jack never left longer than four days. Not long enough for George to suspect anything dangerous, though George couldn't hurt Jack or Nate. They were Kaleb's kin.

On the second day of Jack's absence, in the middle of the night when the room was heavy with darkness, West jerked awake. *Radio's beeping...* He answered groggily.

"Ty's having a nightmare and he needs you." Ed's pained, weak voice came through.

"Be right there." West scrambled out of bed, threw his clothes and shoes on, and ran outside. It took him three minutes of driving like a madman to reach Ed and Ty's small, run-down shack a few blocks away. The brothers lived alone when they weren't guarding Danny Dunnham at their place. The stark shack showed how the Brooks brothers rolled—give more for others and live off as little as they could.

West stumbled out of his truck and ran into the rugged house. He darted into Ty's bedroom as fast as his long legs could carry him.

"West!" Ty's weak voice screamed.

West pushed past the open bedroom door. "Ty?"

Ed sat on the floor, holding his brother close but unable to stop him as he wept in fear. Ty's episodes usually lasted ten minutes, sometimes longer. He rarely remembered them by morning.

West knelt down beside Ty. His chest ached at seeing Ty like this, but he couldn't stop the nightmares. Nightmares were tricky things. The state of teetering from reality and a reality far more real than the human mind could handle was not something easily wrestled against.

"I'm right here, Ty. I'm all right." He hoped Ty heard him, though Ty usually didn't hear him until he was coming out of the nightmare. Tonight was one of the rare times Ed called West out of desperation.

Ty sobbed harder, clutching West's arm and rocking back and forth. Back and forth.

"*I'msorryI'msorryI'msorry*. I didn't mean to let you get hurt." His words were incoherent and jumbled, but West made out enough of them.

Ed pulled Ty closer into his broad chest, rubbing his back, but it didn't calm Ty down. Ty's light brown hair grew dark with sweat.

"Ty, it's all right. I'm here. Ed's here. We're fine." West sat down beside him and just held his hand firmly. He didn't allow himself to think about what was going on Ty's head. Every time he did, it made it harder to stay calm, and it was his job to be the strong one, for both brothers. Being strong meant being numb to his own thoughts.

Ed prayed softly like he and Ty often did. West heard them muttering quick, full-hearted prayers before going into battle and heard them beg for mercy when the battles were over. They'd been Christians as long as West had known them. *Who knows, maybe the God they speak of exists—for them.*

After another five minutes of Ty weeping and shaking, he started to breathe easier. Ed rubbed his back. "Ty? It's all right. Just breathe."

Ty opened his bloodshot eyes, his shivering body giving out. Ed held him upright.

West grabbed the blanket from the bed and wrapped it around Ty. "Easy, Ty. It's over." He gently helped Ed get him into bed again.

Ty gripped their arms, gasping. He had that same fearful glint in his green eyes that he always did—the haunted memories of his nightmare just beginning to fade from his mind but lingering in his spirit. "Don't leave," he choked.

Ed smoothed Ty's damp hair. "Just sleep."

Ty passed out, thin body growing limp, and Ed kept running his hand over his little brother's head like he could soothe away the nightmares. The only sound in the room was Ty's steady breathing for a while, and when Ty remained asleep, Ed and West crept into the kitchen.

Ed sat down at the table heavily. "Thanks for coming, West." "Don't mention it."

"They're growing worse again," Ed murmured, running both hands through his dark hair unsteadily. "Since that job…" He stared down at his hands—the hands of a killer, a brother, a man who revered God but made choices that couldn't be blessed.

"It'll pass." West rubbed the back of his neck. The last job Ty had taken was a small retrieval, but he'd taken it with a few other gangsters, and once the job failed, they'd left Ty behind. Ty was captured and tortured for two days before Ed, West, and Jack found him.

Ty didn't speak of it. Three months later, he acted like it'd never happened: he smiled, laughed, and held no grudge against the thugs who'd left him for dead. But his nightmares showed how the torture had broken him.

"Yeah." Ed cleared his throat. "I don't know, West. I've been praying…"

"Damage to the mind is still damage. Ty's doing fine." West couldn't imagine what it was like in Ed's head. Surviving in the world was hard enough. But constantly facing God's judgment?

Of course, Ed often warned West that God judged all, but He loved all, too.

"You're right. I just keep praying for a miracle." Ed poured himself a cup of coffee, shoulders sagging. He rubbed the beginning of a beard around his jaw. "I mean, I've seen God do miracles. I just can't stand it not happening now. It isn't easy trusting God's plan is best when I can't make my little brother stop screaming."

What kind of wise God lets Ty, the kindest young man in this gang, be tortured by his own mind? "Sure."

Ed leaned against the small counter top and sipped his coffee. "How long have you known me?"

"Five years?"

"How many times have I proved to be a fool?"

"What?" West's eyebrows furrowed.

"Answer me."

"Never, I guess."

"Don't pacify me, West."

"I don't." West crossed his arms against his chest. "I never mock you or think you're stupid for believing in God. Ever," he said, anger flickering.

"That's not what I meant," Ed sighed wearily. "You don't have to lie and act like you believe everything. You can say, 'Ed, I don't think God gives a copper nickel about you.' You only started pacifying us this past year."

West slowly tilted his head. "So?"

"What's up with you? And don't write me off, because Jack's noticed, too."

"I didn't think anything was up with me. Just a lot going on." "Liar." Ed didn't shy away from kicking the bush. Hard. With a steel-toed boot.

West sucked in a slow breath, reminding himself that Ed would understand. "After all these years, I'm starting to believe the slightest image of a God you talk about, and I don't know what to do with it. After all these years, I've started accepting the fact I'll remember random Scripture verses when I'm getting tortured, and it doesn't even surprise me anymore. So, yeah, Ed. I'm at a loss here." West kept his tone even but it was difficult to do when he just wanted to stay silent. *And it terrifies me. It terrifies me that I'm growing weak enough to put faith in a God I cannot see who reminds me so much of the father who wants me to be his loyal little heir.*

Ed blinked. "So you're brushing me off recently because you actually…"

"Think it's all true? Just a tiny bit? Yeah." West gritted his teeth tightly. *I sound like a fool.*

Ed grasped West's arm. "I get it."

West licked his lips but didn't speak.

"West… Back when Ty and I were in the system, there was this orphanage we stayed at for a while," Ed began slowly. "One of the women who worked there would ask us every night—if someone was about to kill us if we didn't renounce Him, would we die for Jesus? If Jesus was right there holding our hand, would we choose death, or betray him? Ty and I always said we would die for Him. Not every kid did. Most kids hated the question, and I couldn't blame them. If God didn't even let us have a family, why die for Him?" Ed chuckled softly, eyes heavy.

West had never heard this story before. He didn't know what it had to do with Ed's years of constant faith. "OK..."

"My point is this…" Ed rubbed the back of his neck. "I know, if it came to it, I'm ready to die. When you accept Jesus, you accept that. When you choose God in this broken world, you choose persecution."

"Are you trying to scare me away now?" West asked dryly, smirking mirthlessly—Ed wasn't playing around and he'd not wasted his whole friendship just to ditch West at the last moment. But the way he spoke was unnerving.

"I'm telling you that none of us can make that decision for you, West. Not me, not Jack, not George. No one but you and God." Ed met his gaze, eyes no longer pained but burning with passion.

"I didn't say I was getting saved…" West muttered. "Just that I think there's something to God and His Word—that doesn't mean I'm changing. Doesn't mean

I entirely think God cares."

Ed studied him expectantly.

West bit his lip. "Thanks. I don't say it often, but thanks." He didn't have to say what he was grateful for: Ed always having his back and always knowing when to show up. And who knew? The prayers Ed constantly gave might be doing something. No matter what happened or what West chose, Ed wouldn't stop praying and that brotherhood dedication wasn't unnoticed by West.

"Thank *you*," Ed said, smiling and gesturing to the tiny living room that held one worn couch. "Sleep here tonight. Jack's outta town and he'll hang me upside down by my toes if I let you drive back."

"It's only three blocks."

"Just go to bed." Ed headed down the hall, going into Ty's room.

West went and sat on the ragged couch. He pulled the tattered throw over himself, closed his eyes, and tried to focus himself on something. Anything but the resounding screams he always heard at night.

As usual, he couldn't help but think of God.

He didn't need God's love or judgment—he got plenty of that from George. Though, Ed and Ty had lasted this long, hadn't they? *How? What kind of God lets this kind of war rage on the nation He's blessed?* Ed and Ty hadn't lost faith. They didn't have any family except each other. George's gang often ridiculed them, but they never lost hope or joy.

I don't need that kind of God. But maybe it isn't a bad idea to face the God my brothers trust. What did he have to lose? *The fate of the Second Civil War rests in my hands. I have everything to lose.*

SEVEN

MAY 26TH, 2027

"HOW LONG HAS IT BEEN?" Lee picked up a large box, arms strong and lean like the rest of his body. He smirked at Rene' playfully, his handsome features glistening with sweat from a long day's work in Springtown.

"Since November, so…" Rene' glanced at Simon, wiping sweat from her messy hair, wishing for a glass of water. They stood together in the back of the van, the rest of the men having unloaded everything except the box Lee had.

"Almost seven months." Simon's dark eyes widened. He whacked at a wasp that flew around his holed jeans. "It doesn't feel like we've been doing supply drops that long."

A lot of things changed during seven months, like all of the news reports and updates about the UN Simon and Nate told the town about during visits.

Rene' shuddered slightly and pushed the memories away. *Better focus on the good memories for a while.*

"Surprised your dads haven't found out yet." Lee chuckled, but Rene' detected the slight distaste in his teasing tone. Lee didn't fully trust Simon and Nate, mostly because of their fathers' roles in the war as "spineless cowards who fought for the biggest buyer which was the Union," and he constantly expected the too-good-to-be-true supply drops to fall through.

Simon flinched. "Guess your praying does something." He hopped out of the van.

"Appears so." Over the past seven months, though it felt like only three or four, Rene' had slowly watched Simon's interest grow about Jesus. He only ever asked a few questions and spent time processing what she, or Mr. Fisher, told him. Even the smallest bit of curiosity could change everything.

"Well, let's get moving, pansies." Lee hauled the crate off the van and sauntered into the courthouse.

"He's a good kid," Simon said quietly, helping Rene' down and shutting the van door.

"Yeah." Rene' grinned. "It's meant a lot to him and his friends to have you two helping. It gives 'em hope."

"Besides the few kids who'd beat us up in a New York second?" Simon winked.

"Sure. Besides the feisty boys."

"My money would be on them in that fight." Simon

followed her to the courthouse, keeping his stride small so he didn't outwalk her.

"Mine would be, too. Don't mess with teenage boys protecting their families." Rene' grinned cheekily, smoothing her t-shirt that hung loosely around her full curves.

Simon glanced down at her as they walked inside. "I wouldn't. We're fighting for the same thing."

"Oh, yeah?" Rene' smirked at him. What was that look in his eyes? A glint. Almost like he was happy. She liked seeing him happy, but it didn't happen much. Simon carried too many burdens on his shoulders. Rene' didn't do near as much as she wished she could to ease burdens: she couldn't save her family or her town, couldn't remove the stress from her parents, or take the fear from her nieces and nephew. She couldn't save the world. But with him by her side, her heart didn't comprehend the impossible.

Simon looked around and made sure no one was watching, then slowed beside the big stairwell. "Lee, his friends, Mr. Fisher,
Howard, we all share the same goal."

"Protecting Springtown?" Rene's chest tightened.

"Yeah. A wise man doesn't fight his allies, even if they disagree on some things."

"You're just scared AJ will tan your hide if you don't help." "No. I like this place." Simon glanced away.

"Huh?" Rene' fingered her cross necklace, cocking her head up at him.

"Springtown is a special place. Like a safe haven, ya know? Not many towns hold onto constitutional principles, or even survive. This one does. You guys fight off militias and nomads and you've won for *three years*. I don't want to lose you guys." Simon took in the busy townsmen before meeting Rene's gaze. "You give me something to have faith in. I haven't had that before."

Rene' slowly smiled, lump forming in her throat. "Y'all have given us hope, too, Si. We wouldn't've made it this far without you."

"Kinda makes me wonder if God does have a hand in this world." Simon rubbed the back of his neck, but before Rene' could speak, Lee called them from down the hall.

"Coming!" Rene' answered, patting Simon on the arm and offering a reassuring smile. She worried about him—he had so many questions and she didn't have all the answers. "C'mon, Si. You should drink some water and rest before y'all head back." She prayed nonstop for God to protect he and Nate. So far, God had.

"Will do." Simon chuckled. They went to the storage room and Lee tossed him a bottle of water.

Lee and his best friend, Xander, were carefully going through the new supplies with a few other men. Xander gave Simon a side-eyed glare before leading Lee to the next row of boxes.

Simon sighed softly but stuck close to Rene'. Rene' smiled up at him, popping open a crate.

"They don't like me."

"Nope."

"Anything I can do to help?" Simon downed his water in a few nervous gulps.

"Nah, I got it. I have to bring some more supplies around town today…" She didn't mind running supplies to the elderly or couples with little kids. But some families were unruly and caused problems among the town, so she left their supplies to the grown men.

"Guess I'll head out. Nate's probably dying to get back."

Simon rolled his eyes. "Little baby."

"We're praying for him. He'll come around."

"He's a good guy, he just doesn't want to be. I don't know how to get through to him. And I'm his best friend." Simon rubbed his temples, then grimaced like he regretted spilling his guts. "Sorry…"

"I'm grateful when you talk to me, ya know." Rene' shook her head. "But only God can soften his heart, not you, not me…"

"He doesn't want it." Simon muttered. "He says a soft heart in this world is a stupid move."

"God isn't done with him." Rene' believed that with all her worried heart, and sometimes, even the most fearful heart had enough faith to move mountains. Or so she prayed.

Simon paused a long moment. "Speaking of that, could you pray for Graham?" Graham was a skinny teen with a stutter who shadowed Nate and Simon. Rene' knew the gang bullied him often.

"Is he OK?" If Graham was in trouble, Rene' wanted to help. He sounded like the person she'd wrap in a blanket, give hot chocolate, and sit on the family couch for a while.

"Oh, no, he's fine. Just having a hard time lately—he keeps getting into trouble. Nate and I can't always keep up with him." Simon chewed his lip, worry dark in his eyes.

"I'll pray," Rene' said firmly. She trusted God to take care of them. But there were so many things, so many burdens, she yearned to take and demolish. But she wasn't God. She was a seventeen-year-old girl who had no control over anything but herself.

Surely, God would keep His promises, right? He wouldn't forget them, but it wasn't easy casting their burdens upon Him. Especially when the whole world sought their destruction.

RENE' SCRUBBED THE DIRTY DISHES, fighting to keep her tired

eyes open in the dimly lit kitchen. Lee and Mr. Fisher were finishing some chores outside and checking on the fast-growing foals. Terri, being too swollen to do much walking, had eaten enough to fill her and her unborn baby before heading home with the kids. Dax offered to stay and help clean, but Rene' assured him he could go play before their early bedtime.

"I'll help put up, dear." Mrs. Fisher stepped into the kitchen, her black curls pushed behind her ears and her reading glasses shoved up on her head. She always read from her Bible at night, sometimes reading aloud for everyone to hear, sometimes just pondering quietly.

"Oh, thanks." Rene' smiled briefly but her thoughts were too heavy to allow her much of a happy smile.

Mrs. Fisher dried a plate and set it aside on the counter. "You seem sad."

Rene' finished scrubbing another plate. "Huh?"

"You're very introspective, dear," Mrs. Fisher said gently. "Is something on your mind?" She always saw through Rene's greatest efforts to be OK, or when Rene' wasn't saying something. She always helped Rene' open up.

"Yeah…" Rene' stared at the dishwater like it would tell her how to let her thoughts come out in a smooth flow. She could write her heart out and make journal entries and stories vivid with life, but her tongue tripped her and her words faltered. "About Simon, I guess."

With everyone else, she didn't allow herself to speak of Simon more than him being an ally and friend.

Her mother knew better.

"Mmhmm." Mrs. Fisher waited.

"He said some things today that hit me." Rene' glanced at her mother expectantly. *Will she think I'm silly? Or overthinking? Or making something out of nothing?*

"Well?" Mrs. Fisher smiled.

"About having the same goal as Dad and Lee, protecting us." Rene' washed a cup. "But something about the way he said it struck me strange." If only she could describe the look in his eyes. *You could've been looking into his expression too much.* "Oh? What did he say?"

"Nothing really. Just… the way he said it… made me think."

"About what?" Mrs. Fisher prompted gently.

"About how much he actually *cares*. AJ isn't forcing him to be nice, ya know? No one is forcing him to care about us. And I know God's moving in him… It's just strange." Rene' finished cleaning a few more cups, chewing her lip.

"It sounds like you care about him, too." Mrs. Fisher dried the dishes slowly and carefully.

"I do. *Both* of them, I mean."

Mrs. Fisher shook her head. "Everyone in this family cares about those boys to some extent, but there are different types of caring, you know."

"Right. Some of the town hate them, and some only care about the supplies…" Rene' didn't like that fact but she couldn't change the mindset of a whole town.

"Then there's you and your father..." Mrs. Fisher glanced at Rene' with a smile.

"What?"

"You treat those boys like they're human. That shows more of God's love than any Gospel tract ever could." Mrs. Fisher stacked some plates tiredly.

"AJ's a Christian and he shares it with them, too. He's the one who planted the seed." Rene' helped her mom put away the dishes. "I guess we're just watering the seed, but it doesn't *feel* like that. I care about them, ya know?" She took a small breath.
"I don't know what to do."

"What do you mean?"

"It isn't *safe*." Rene' gritted her teeth, angry at how her heart quivered like a dam about to burst. "It isn't safe to trust them, not even a little bit." Logically, they were still gangmen. *They could betray the whole town— anything could happen. But I care about them, trust them, pray for them. What if things go wrong and I'm a total fool and we get hurt?*

"Rene', listen." Mrs. Fisher rested a hand on the side of Rene's face, her touch gentle yet firm, comforting yet strengthening. "You cannot carry the weight of the world on your shoulders." Her green eyes shined with

ANGELA R. WATTS

the kind of love that made Rene's heart ache. "You are our daughter, and your father and I couldn't be more proud of you. Springtown has survived this long because we work together, because God has shed mercy on us."

"I know," Rene' forced. *It just doesn't make faith easier. It doesn't make fear go away. I'm messing up—I should be fearless. But I'm not.*

"Trust that the Lord has a purpose for everything that's done. Don't be afraid of the 'what ifs'. Your father and half the town trust those boys, too, so don't think you've lost your mind." She chuckled and hugged Rene' close. Rene' sank against her mother's warm, comforting chest.

"God says be bold and not to be afraid, dear. *No one* learns those lessons overnight. Every day, we make choice after choice to obey Him. You're doing fine." She kissed Rene's cheek gently.

Rene' took a slow breath. *Fearless.* Fearless of the outcome of her life, her family's lives, and Simon and Nate's situation.

"Thanks, Mom."

"This war will end, Rene'. Have faith, baby."

She hugged her mother one more time, heart swelling with relief. And hope.

EIGHT

JUNE 27TH, 2027

"CRIKEY! YOU'RE COVERED IN BLOOD and smell like a dead wallaby. I'm not feeding you until you shower, Gid." Alex's Australian drawl thickened—as it always did when he was exhausted or annoyed—as he poured a bowl of vegetable soup. "I thought you said the job would be small and easy?"

"You know how it goes. And, I'm sorry, do you know what a dead wallaby smells like?" Gideon hadn't meant to get home at 12 AM, but plans changed often, and he rolled with the punches. Sometimes, overseeing another man's trade didn't go so well. At all. He had to pick up the pieces.

Alex ignored his question. "Are you hurt?" He tossed a rag over his shoulder, his white tank top, revealing his scar-covered arms and shoulders, splattered with soup. He usually covered his scars with clothing and gloves, but he didn't hide them around Gideon.

"Nah." None of the blood was Gideon's own.

"We'll talk after you shower." Alex sighed, turning back to the little gas oven he rarely used because of the flames, but he didn't always have a choice—face the tiny flames or starve. His stomach usually won.

Gideon went down the hall and closed the bathroom door behind him, stripping his bloody, sweaty clothes off. Dark bruises formed along his scarred, lean body, but no cuts and no broken bones.

He let the hot shower water roll down his back and slowly wash away the soreness in his muscles. He'd fought away men from George's trader—he hadn't killed them this time, but it didn't change the fact he'd hurt them. It'd been his job.

Twenty-four years old and he'd killed countless men. Bad men. Good men. He was a killer and there was no justice for every deed he'd done, but there didn't have to be. He wasn't a soldier, hadn't sworn any oaths, and hadn't trained on fair terms. He'd grown in a ruthless gang with rules far different than his father's rules.

His father would never have been proud of him for *all* he'd done. But he'd be proud that Gideon survived, as a monster, but a survivor, too. Gideon earned his nicknames, though he never stopped working to make Jeremy proud. His father would weep over the monster he was. Such was war.

"Gid?" Alex's voice called from the hallway, slapping Gideon from his tumultuous mind, followed by a sharp knock on the bathroom door. "You alive?" Gideon turned the shower off.

"Oh, good." Alex continued on as if the door wasn't muffling his loud voice. "Nate and Simon got back safe. I ran into them at the servo." Since Kaleb was George's subordinate, both gangs co-existed in various ways, such as sharing gas stations. The natural resources were only accessible to the Union and men in the government. Confederates and rebel scum couldn't maintain such luxuries.

"How'd that go?" Gideon dried off stiffly, tugging his underwear and pants on. He'd gotten hit hard enough to leave long-lasting bruises, and he was rather grumpy about it. It's what he got for trying to let the trader handle it for a minute instead of taking swift care of the situation himself.

"I reckon it went all right. Simon seems oddly happy. Nate's more angry than usual."

"Is that possible?" Gideon opened the door, smoothing his damp black hair back, tossing his t-shirt over his shoulder.

Alex chuckled. "Defo. Never underestimate a Savage man's anger."

"No one else knows about the surprise yet." Surprise

was code for Springtown. Gideon and Alex knew about the teenagers' endeavor but kept their mouths shut. Brian Jones was related to the Fisher family and part of Gideon's deal was making sure the town didn't get wiped off the map.

If Kaleb found out, he would put a firm end to the supply drops. Mercy was not a practice Kaleb condoned, especially not from Nate when he'd raised him to be his heir and the next leader for Kaleb's sect.

Gideon and Alex kept their eyes out for the teenagers. They silently ensured Nate and Simon didn't get their hides handed to them and kept up with loose ends or gossip. Despite the long months of the gig, no one in Kaleb or George's gangs knew about the little surprise.

Alex led Gideon to the kitchen. "Those boys are actually doing something good by themselves. Well, besides AJ's initial kick in the rear, but…"

"I know what you're trying to say. It's shocking to see Nate stick to so much of a good thing, right?" Gideon sat down heavily, groaning as he pulled the bowl of steaming soup closer.

"Yeah. I mean, he's probably doing it for Simon. Or out of spite because of Kaleb." Alex shrugged and grabbed two water bottles from the fridge. "But it isn't a small feat, gathering supplies successfully and transporting them."

"They're smart guys." Annoying and hormonal, like most teenagers were, but good at what they did. Of course, with their fathers both in cohorts with George, they had no choice but to be good. *Be the best or die.* That was Gideon's perspective.

"It's more than that and you know it," Alex scoffed.

"A miracle?" Gideon raised his eyebrows. "C'mon, Al." He sipped his soup, grateful for the warmth as the liquid filled his hollow belly.

Alex leaned back in his seat, gulping down water. "Maybe." He wiped his mouth, eyes twinkling but he didn't let himself smile. He had that annoying look, the kind when he thought he knew something Gideon didn't. It didn't happen often.

"What?" Gideon asked. Well, maybe the look did happen often, but Gideon usually knew more than Alex expected of him. That's how brothers worked.

"They're teenagers. Good at what they do, yeah, but you gotta admit, they've come this far, alone… Pretty impressive. Almost miraculously so." Alex raised his eyebrows, flashing a big grin like a kid on Christmas morning.

"Yeah." Gideon kept eating. He didn't believe in miracles like Alex did. God helped those who pulled their own weight and fought hard. Miracles were nothing to expect or believe in— Gideon's miracles consisted of sleeping without a nightmare.

ANGELA R. WATTS

Alex's faith was steady and centered in his very core. Gideon couldn't, nor did he wish to, break it, but he couldn't understand it.

Alex sighed but grinned.

"What?"

"Nothing." Alex finished his water. "I'm gonna hit the hay."

"Me, too." Gideon stood, washing his dishes carefully, weary of his aching ribs. Collapsing into bed sounded fantastic—but Alex wasn't leaving yet.

Gideon eyed him briefly. "You want to ask Nate and Simon to come on that job with us this weekend?" *No use trying to avoid the inevitable doom.*

"Yes." Alex didn't miss a beat.

"Fine." Gideon liked the boys fine, but taking a job with them was a different matter. Teenagers were eager for a fight and tunnel-brained. Gideon knew how it was.

"Good night," Alex said cheekily.

"You're a pain." Gideon cast him a glare.

"You're not a basket of roses, either." Alex disappeared down the hall with all the thief-like stealth he possessed.

Alone with his thoughts, a long groan escaped Gideon. He put the dishes away, turned all the lights off in the house, and went to his bedroom. He yearned for some peace and quiet. Or just quiet. Peace was a lie—something a monster like him couldn't obtain.

He pulled his shirt on and got into bed, the covers heavy against his bruised skin, but he found comfort in the familiar pain. If he stared at the ceiling long enough, he might fall asleep without any memories creeping into his mind.

Tonight isn't a night for miracles.

He dreamt of being alone in a room, chained up, bleeding out, but the only thing that he could hear was the screams of the women and child in the recent bombing.

More screams chorused those. Screams from Alex, West and Jack, Ed and Ty, Danny, Spencer—every soul he fought to protect, they cried out for help. He couldn't reach them. No matter how hard he tried. In the back of his mind, somewhere just far enough away where he couldn't find it, his father's voice echoed. *"Monster. Monster. Monster."*

"I NEED YOU GENTLEMEN TO kidnap Rene' Fisher." George set his cigar aside, a delighted smile tugging at his solemn features. He eyed Gideon, Alex, and Spencer before him like they were dogs being told what prey to kill.

Alex knew George enjoyed placing his favorite workers on jobs that benefited him. It was not always wise to have best men work together at all times—this made them an easy target for heavy losses—but it paid off to have a handful of the most skilled take on certain jobs.

Gideon sat casually and didn't respond, picking up the folder that George slid across the large wooden table that was meticulously neat, as most of George's belongings were.

Alex struggled to appear calm—maintaining a poker face was his job, though this conversation jarred him more than he liked. *What does George need Rene' for?*

"Kidnap?" Spencer managed, eyes wide. George rarely put him on such a job.

George crossed his arms across his chest. "A little jumpy today, Anderson?"

Alex peered over Gideon's shoulder, studying the the file: Rene' Fisher. Brian's teenage sister, with the gap in her teeth and freckles over her face. *Maybe I'm dreaming. Or having another lucid nightmare. Maybe I need to stop eating pickles before bed.*

"Kidnappings aren't my area of expertise, sir," Spencer said slowly.

"No, but they're Gideon and Alex's area of expertise, and you said you needed cash." George clasped his big hands together, satisfied his plan was best, his narrow eyes gleaming and his smile smug. He almost reminded Alex of a king cobra looming over his victim.

"Right, yessir." Spencer took the folder from Gideon, looked it over. Alex knew Spencer had no idea who Rene' was—after all, he didn't know about Brian's secret alliance with Gideon. His concern for her was rooted solely in his upstanding moral character that he didn't even see in himself.

"Any specific instructions?" Gideon leaned back in his chair. How he could look so matter-of-fact made Alex a bit jealous.

"She'll need to be at Jed's cabin in Arkansas, but there's no deadline." George tilted his head, strands of his oiled black hair falling over his forehead. "You gentlemen will have a few days
to recover after the infiltration of the caravan."

"Yessir." Gideon nodded.

"Don't harm her," George continued. "Springtown is a safe town and better left alone, for now. I'd rather not have to destroy them." He didn't explain why. That was strange. Why would he care about a town he could easily demolish for fun?

"Any ideas on how to grab her?" Alex asked half-heartedly. *No harm in asking, right?*

"I'm sure you'll come up with something." George picked up his cigar and lit it once more. "You are far from needing constant guidance."

Alex smiled and nodded but his stomach tightened. *Oh, this is bad. Very bad. Does Gideon understand how terrible this is?* They had to kidnap Rene' Fisher. Brian's *sister.* Brian, the big soldier boy who was growing into quite

ANGELA R. WATTS

the rising Union hero. Brian, the man who'd killed
countless and led even more into battles like some
samurai who could fly helicopters. And Rene', the one
girl Simon Bucks actually cared for. They were doomed
if they kidnapped the girl and doomed if they didn't.
Story of my life. Alex glanced at his brother.

"Of course," Gideon said firmly. "We can handle it."

"Good," George puffed smoke into the heavy
atmosphere.

Alex suppressed a cough, lost in panicked thought.
Jedediah was an old friend of George's and gave Alex
the heebie jeebies. *He could squash a watermelon with his bare
hands, and he's one of the worst womanizers I've ever seen.* Jed
made plenty of money from his sex trafficking circuit,
too.

Alex didn't dare ask why Jed wanted Rene'. He was
on a need to know basis, and that was something George
didn't need him to know. Maybe he could find the
answer later. He was the world's best hacker, after all.
Unfortunately, not every secret lies behind ones and zeroes.

Spencer spoke up after a moment. "Sounds good,
George." He stood and handed Gideon the file again.

Gideon and Alex stood, but Gideon met George's
gaze, eyes cold. "Payment?"

"The usual for this kind of job." George waved him
off with another huff of smoke. "Are we clear?"

"Yessir," they chorused.

Alex and Gideon had worked hard for years to gain this much trust from George. Occasionally, it made Alex's skin crawl, seeing just how messy the world was—thanks to men like George who had power and far too much lust for more, more, more. Alex wondered sometimes if his fighting was in vain but always went back to God's promises. Fighting the good fight was worth it, even if it meant death. As long as George would get his justice from the Lord, whenever that was, Alex could find strength to keep going.

He put on a smile with trust that God would have vengeance. "Jed branching out with his preferences?" he asked easily, though the question flipped his stomach.

George chuckled softly, shaking his head. "It isn't the job you think."

"No?" Alex often asked too many questions and it hadn't made George kill him. Yet. *Better keep up my annoying MO so no one gets suspicious.*

"No." George puffed on his cigar as he relaxed. "This job isn't about sex or money."

"Far away from Jed's preferences, then," Spencer muttered sarcastically.

George simply nodded.

"What motivation, then?" Alex asked.

Gideon closed the file. "Does it matter to us?" Gideon was playing the devil's advocate. Alex had seen the man get truly annoyed by his questions and it was a hilarious and terrifying experience all at once.

"Jedediah's simply doing as his orders bid him to. Revenge…" George eyed them. "It's a long story that doesn't concern you."

"She's a teenage girl—" Spencer started in disbelief.

George stopped him coolly. "She's merely a piece to use against the one who they have troubles with."

That explains a lot. And who is they? Alex nodded, eyebrows raising. "Sounds messy."

"As usual," Spencer scoffed. He wore his disgust as armor, because if he showed what he really felt whenever he felt it, he'd be a dead man.

George smiled fondly. "Many things appear as chaos, but calculated complexity is far from messy, my boys."

"Yessir." Gideon frowned, stepping to the office door. "We'll keep in touch."

They left the room and headed down the halls of the large, modern building. The place was quiet except for the light echoes of Spencer's careless footsteps. Leaving the lobby behind them, the three hurried outside into the warm sun.

"This *sucks*." Spencer glanced around the gravel parking lot where only a few cars were parked against the chain link fence out front. The premise was small but secure.

Alex followed Gideon closely and stayed clear of

Spencer's bubble space in case he got punchy.

"How are we supposed to do this?" Spencer pulled his car keys, huffing.

"Same as any other job." Gideon opened his car door and eyed them both. "We do what we have to do."

Alex frowned deeply, leaning on his car door and rubbing his shoulder. "And if she gets hurt?" She *would* get hurt. Jed was a cruel man and, unlike George, his target was often women and girls, and that never ended well. Alex fought the urge to throw up by biting his tongue.

"We won't let anything drastic happen." Gideon didn't seem concerned.

"Her dad is going to slit our throats. And Simon is gonna— " Spencer's clenched fists shook.

"Come by our place, three o'clock." Gideon got into the car and cranked the engine. He never let worries distract him from the solid fact that a job must be done. Consequences or issues that arose mattered little to him when he had a mission to overcome.

Alex waved at Spencer before getting in. "Gid…" He had to have faith. *Lord, help us find the wisest way to go about this. If we kidnap her, we're in trouble. If we don't, everyone is still in trouble because George will punish us and have her taken.*

Alex didn't want to see another girl get hurt. He was tired of seeing people hurt all the time. He couldn't stand hearing any more screams in his nightmares.

Gideon sped up onto the narrow street like he could outrace all of his problems. "We'll figure it out."

"Of course we will. We always do." A breath. "We can't let Rene' go to Jed. If this is a revenge plot against soldier boy Brian—"

"Of course it is." Gideon cut him off. "If we don't deliver, she'll be taken by someone else less merciful. We have control over the situation right now. We cannot lose that."

"How do we use it?" Alex rubbed his scarred hands together. "We take Rene' and find out who sent Jed to do this."

Alex scoffed. "She lives in *Springtown*. People will kill us before we reach the border. So how do we take her?"

"Then we find another way that won't cause bloodshed." Gideon kept his piercing eyes on the road but didn't slow down much.

"She's not allowed to leave. Ever."

"Then we find a way to make it work," Gideon said sharply.

"We should warn Brian. If someone wants revenge, they'll go after Brian's wife and kids," Alex muttered, unbothered by Gideon's coldness.

"No, they won't. If Jed had balls, he'd go for them now, but he's diverging. Whoever is sending Jed to do this isn't impatient... Taking Rene' as a torture tool isn't going to make a dent in Brian's armor—they have to know that." Gideon shook his head, running a hand through his dark hair, slowing as they rounded a corner in the narrow road.

"So…?"

"It's a slow game, but one Jed's going to play out," Gideon said. "He'll pick and prod at Brian just to show off. Brian's a secret Union soldier and there's not much that can get to him, but I doubt that whoever is behind this with Rene' will stop there. He could go after Brian's immediate family or the Fishers."

"Sick…" Alex finished the description of Jed under his breath. Gideon was right: if they didn't get to Rene', someone else would do their job after them, and that'd be worse for her. "How do we get Rene'?"

Gideon thought a moment. "Simon and Nate will kill us if they find out the truth, but we'll have to use their connection for this to work."

"Wait, what?"

Gideon cast him a glance before watching the road again and turning on the radio. It took him a minute before he reached Brian.

"Confirm identity," Brian said in an almost bored voice. "Knight."

"Grandmaster here. Roger that."

"I have news on the residents, Brian." Residents as in the Fisher family.

"Spill," Brian said.

Alex crossed his arms. What did Gideon mean their way in was through Simon and Nate? That was a terrible idea no matter how he shook a stick at it. He wasn't going to mess with a Savage or a Bucks. Especially not when a girl's life was at stake. *What choice do I have? We have to do messed up things that make me want to scream because no one else will. Worse things will happen if I don't do bad things. What kind of believer does that make me? God, forgive me.*

He steeled himself, set his jaw, and listened to Gideon explain the situation to Army boy. Once Gideon finished, Brian responded in a controlled, short manner:

"Jedediah and George will do as they wish. The unknown identity guiding this situation will not remain unknown for long—I will find out who it is. I will not conform to their scandal or retrieve Rene'. I understand that the harm that befalls her is not your doing. I won't allow this predicament interfere with our alliance, and I suggest you do the same."

Gideon paused a moment. Alex saw his eyes go dark.

"Understood, Jones."

"Is that all, Hochberg?"

"Roger that."

Brian ended the connection. Alex chewed his lip, feeling like that ended connection resembled something far worse was ending.

"A plan?" Alex looked at Gideon, determination

settling in his chest. As long as he was alive, he'd fight to protect the innocent, even if it meant playing dirty. He hadn't died in that explosion like Clint had. God wasn't finished with him yet.

NINE

JUNE 28TH, 2027

SIMON'S PHONE BUZZED ON THE floor near his cot where he'd left it after falling asleep texting Rene'. He hadn't seen her in twenty-four hours, and he already missed her. His father didn't know much of his feelings yet, but he'd have to explain some time, because Jordan's curiosity was finally piquing. Jordan usually minded his own business, a trait Simon appreciated, but he'd been acting a bit strange around Simon recently.

Groggy with sleep and pushing away his nightmarish thoughts, he grabbed his phone.

Buzz. Buzz.

His eyes adjusted to the bright screen. 2 AM. Graham's number. What on earth was the fifteen-year-old doing at this hour? Simon answered. "Graham? What's going on?"

"Help me." Two words. Two broken sobs. Simon

never heard such raw fear or pain in Graham's voice before.

Simon sat straight up on his cot. His blood ran cold like he'd fallen into a frozen lake. "Graham? What happened, kid? Where—"

"Please... p-please help... Si..." Graham choked out, voice raspy.

Simon shouted for Nate to get dressed. "Graham needs us!" He scrambled up, snatching on his pants and speaking into the phone again. "Graham, where are you? We're coming." "B-bedroom. Brock." Simon heard him throw up.

"Breathe, Graham, we'll be right there." Simon ran outside with Nate, both dressed lopsidedly.

Nate cranked the car, speeding onto the road. "What happened?" he snapped.

"Graham, can you tell us what happened? Why are you at Brock's?" Simon asked as calmly as he could. The fifteen-yearold really couldn't handle a dozen questions, but they needed to know what they were walking into.

Graham hung up.

"Why is he at Brock's?" Nate demanded once Simon put away his cellphone.

"I don't know!" Brock was just another hot-headed nobody thug. Graham always avoided the thugs, and Kaleb never put him on jobs with anyone because he couldn't handle stimulation or teamwork well. *So, what is he doing there now?* Graham didn't like Paradise any more than Simon did.

As Nate drove into Paradise, Simon texted Kaleb quickly. The base was practically a mini armory, but for most of the gangsters, it was the closest thing to home they'd ever had. Since Kaleb was George's second-in-command, he had lots of big toys.

Simon sucked in a breath. As much as he disliked the hubbub, most of the men kept in their lane. Nate and Simon had proved themselves countless times. Graham never had. *God only knows what they've done to him. He doesn't belong here and they all know it.*

Nate parked outside of Brock's apartment on the edge of the east side. A few other cars sat along the street. Simon spotted a few guys vomiting behind bushes in the yard. Screaming and hollering echoed from inside the rundown house. The thugs were all drunk and high, acting completely against Kaleb's codes, something they'd regret in the morning.

"He's having a party." Nate headed to the door, Simon on his heels. Once the door opened, the noise flooded their ears like a choir from hell.

Simon ran through the crowds of gangsters and nobodies, pushing whoever didn't move. No one dared stop him. He reached the hallway and searched desperately for Brock's room.

When a thug asked what they were doing there, Nate knocked him down, following after Simon.

Simon shoved the first bedroom door open, swearing when he saw it was occupied with a man and a woman that must've gotten smuggled in. He tried the next door. Simon froze in the doorway when he saw Graham.

Small, skinny Graham sat curled up in the corner near the bed, shaking. Naked. Bruised and bloodied like someone had beat him senseless. He didn't lift his head. He held his knees, trying to cover himself, weeping softly. A lamp lay shattered around him and the bedside table.

Simon stepped over, rage burning in this chest. "Graham, buddy, you're in broken glass. Don't move."

Nate stepped in, quickly taking the bedsheet off the floor and shoving it at Simon. Simon wrapped it around Graham's shaking body. Graham never made a sound, pale like a ghost, eyes dead. "I tried…" Graham choked. "I…"

"Shh, I know, buddy. We're gonna get you home." Simon put his arm around Graham and lifted him up gently. "I'm gonna carry you, OK?"

Nate went back out into the hallway and shouted at the top of his terrifying voice that reflected his father's: "Get out or I shoot!"

The party grew deathly silent.

Simon carried Graham to the doorway, glancing at the crowds.

Most stared at Nate in drunken anger or in a drugged up daze. One ran out the backdoor like a bullet. A few tried fighting him, and they didn't know what hit them. Nate throat-punched two and kicked the third in the groin hard enough to make the man blackout.

Brock came from the kitchen, eyes flashing, blond hair dark with sweat. "Beat it, Nate, this party isn't for daddy's boys." He took a swig of his beer.

Nate pulled his gun from his holster. More thugs ran because they knew Nate wouldn't hesitate, and if they tried to fight, Kaleb would send them to their grave. Some weaseled their way off through the back door like they weren't scared.

The dumbest three followed Brock toward Nate.

Simon snarled. He wouldn't stop Nate, but Graham sobbed against his shoulder. Simon covered his head. He didn't want anyone to see the kid in such a broken state but he couldn't leave Nate behind. Graham's grip on Simon's back grew weaker.

Brock smiled. Mocking. He put his beer onto the counter. "You come for Graham? Trying to play hero? You guys have been gone too much, Nate. C'mon, the kid *liked* it. The little Yankee wanted it!"

Nate shot down two thugs before Brock and the other jumped on him. He jammed his Glock against their heads. Kicked the man's knees to break them. When Nate was down, and Brock was trying to knife Nate in the gut with his switchblade to break free of Nate's grip, Nate had justice.

He punched Brock, over and over, in blind rage.

"Nate!" Simon shouted, He'd seen enough. Brock was dead and he needed to get Graham out of there. But at least Brock was dead.

Nate got up, hands bloody, dropping Brock's limp, bloody body to the living room floor.

Graham blacked out in Simon's grip. Simon figured that was best—he didn't need to see Brock's corpse.

They took Graham outside and Simon got in the back of the car with him, tending the boy's wounds with the first aid bag. It was tenacious work to do in small quarters, but Nate drove fast and careful.

Simon finished patching the wounds and gashes. He grabbed the blanket from under the backseat and wrapped it around Graham's frail body. Simon held him in absolute silence, save his shaky breathing, and stared outside. *When Graham wakes up, what am I supposed to do?* His stomach twisted like someone took a knife to it.

What do I say?

They'd failed Graham. They hadn't been there. Had there been warning or had this been one of Brock's crazy, impulsive ideas?

Graham was a kid. He didn't have anyone but Simon

and Nate and a sister who didn't live with him. They had failed him but he still needed them.

He'll think this was his fault. That he was too weak and that's why they chose him. He'll believe their manipulation, even after they're gone.

It wasn't true, those ugly lies that would swim around Graham's head like a tsunami. The truth they were in a world full of evil men who preyed on those who couldn't defend themselves. Even the strongest couldn't control everything. Even the bravest men could be broken.

Simon didn't know how to convince Graham the truth. It made him want to scream and yell and burn the whole world to the ground. He was sick of fighting one fight and turning around to see he'd lost another.

I can't give up. I've gotta be strong for Graham and care for him. I have to care for Rene', her family, her town. I have to tether Nate to reality. I have to keep Jordan and Kaleb pleased.

Simon's demons crawled about his mind like a thousand snakes wrapping around his heart. Constricting tighter. Tighter.

You're fault. This is your fault. Graham is broken because you weren't there. He won't trust you after this.

You break everything you touch. Do you really want to take this risk with Springtown? It will go up in flames. Because of you.
"Si?"

Nate's voice made Simon jerk out of his depth of

despair.

"What?"

"Every time I start thinking maybe God's there—"

"Don't pin this on God," Simon snapped, looking up at Nate in the rearview mirror. Graham stirred slightly in his arms. He could almost feel the boy's pain. He wished Nate hadn't done all the fighting. Simon wished he had killed some of those gangsters, too. All of them, even the ones who hadn't had a clue what Brock had done—he just wanted to kill them. If he killed enough, the pain in the world had to lessen, right?

"Graham believes in Him and what has it gotten him?" Nate whispered. "God's not gonna piece Graham back together—we are! We're gonna be the ones to wake him up and hold him after his nightmares, we'll be the ones guarding him, we'll—"

"Just shut up, Nate." Simon lowered his head against Graham's. "Just *shut up*."

"Answer me!"

"I don't have answers! Are you happy? Simon Bucks has no freaking idea about anything!" Simon almost shouted, but didn't want Graham to wake up, even though Graham didn't even flinch. God only knew what nightmares were raging behind the kid's eyelids. And Simon was powerless to stop it. Powerless to take away Graham's pain. Just like he was powerless to keep anyone else safe, or take care of Springtown, or make his father proud.

Nate grew quiet. Cold. *Well, let him go cold. I don't want to talk. All I want is Graham to be OK, but he isn't. He won't be. I don't know if he'll ever be OK. But God does.* And the fact both stung like fire and comforted like rain all at once.

I gotta be strong. Dad would be strong. Dad will know what to do. I'll call him tomorrow. I'll figure out how to do this right and be a good brother.

"YEAH, DAD. IT WAS BROCK." Nate paced the tiny living room of their apartment, hand running through his thick blond hair because he couldn't calm down and really needed to. He grimaced, pulling a hand down and staring at the blood beneath his fingernails. It made him hungry for more. *More. More.*

More death. More blood. More fighting. More pain. *Simon hates the pain. I'm nothing without it.*

"Brock's dead. I'll handle the rogues. What else do you want from me?" Kaleb asked, emotionless, and the muffled sound of papers on the line made Nate scowl. He wasn't even paying attention!

"Graham whispered for you in his sleep and I know how much you care about him," Nate snarled, tone breaking. *Why can't he show mercy? If not for me, what about Graham, who can name every battlefield and date of Kaleb's best fights and gang wars?*

Silence.

"I'll be there," Kaleb said.

Nate hung up and put his phone away after checking the time: 5 AM.

The cold, heartless father was coming to comfort an orphan boy he'd dragged into his gang. *He never showed such compassion for me.*

He stabbed me. Watched Simon drag me to a car like I was a dead body already. Two years ago, two whole years... He watched... He just watched... And he still held the knife in his hand like he forgot to let it go...

Nate shook himself and went into the living room. Graham lay in a pallet near the propane heater where Simon had made him comfortable.

"We need a doctor," Simon muttered.

"I called for one. He won't be here until seven." Nate stepped over and knelt beside Graham, checking his pulse. His breathing wasn't strong but his injuries weren't fatal. He'd probably need stitches in his arm where the glass shards had done damage, and from the bruising around his chest, probably needed his broken bones to be tended. But nothing lifethreatening.

Nate was grateful Kaleb would handle the group of rebels who'd been acting like scoundrels. Kaleb's men were ruthless gangsters who did what jobs that must be done, not demons who preyed on the weak. They'd broken the code, and Kaleb wouldn't stand for it.

Nate's brothers were not something he defended

lightly. He'd been nearly beaten to death more than once protecting Simon over the years, but Simon was his equal. Graham was a little shadow, never staying in one place long, lurking, trailing, too scared to show himself. *How can I protect a shadow who runs from war?*

It was my fault. I should've made sure Graham was safe before we left for the supply drop; I should've asked Kaleb to watch him. I was stupid assuming Graham would stay hidden. He's growing up and that leads to curiosity and independence.

"He's doing OK." Exhaustion covered Simon's face, bags under his eyes, but he met Nate's gaze calmly. "We'll just make sure his vitals stay strong until doc gets here."

Nate wasn't about to sit beside the kid as sentry when Simon would. Nate could patch himself up without problem, and he did Simon, too. He knew Simon could handle alcohol on a gash if he just let him yell through it.

But not Graham. He was a kid that Nate couldn't handle seeing in pain. Brock had taken that brotherhood bond, and he'd used Graham against Nate. Brock's jealousy toward Nate and Kaleb had caused this, most likely.

This is on me.

"Nate. Snap outta it." Simon drew his long legs up, holding his knees and watching Graham sleep peacefully.

"Huh?" Nate slowly sat down, taking up a water bottle from the floor, downing some.

"You look like you're plotting a murder," Simon muttered, eyes downcast. The last word fell from his tongue like a haunted memory.

"Kaleb's coming." His tone was matter-of-fact. Empty. Business-like. *Simon knows better.* Nate couldn't hide from him. If anyone in the world who knew Nate's soul better than he did, it was Simon.

"Kaleb caring about Graham doesn't mean—"

"—he doesn't care about me?" Nate cracked a bitter smirk.

"It doesn't change the fact you're his *kid.*"

"He didn't *choose* me, Si. He *chose* Randy, Robert and his wife, and Graham." Nate wanted to say that calmly, too, but his emotions threatened to break the dam he'd spent eighteen years building up in his heart. So, he stopped talking before his voice broke. *I'm a Savage. I don't lose control. A man without control is a fool who deserves demise.*

Simon watched Graham for a moment. "He still wants you. He wants you in the gang as his right-hand man."

"I haven't worked to earn that rank, and he knows it." Nate stared at the blood under his fingernails.

"He leaves it open for you. He wants you for it."

Kaleb's right-hand man, son, prodigy. Nate

wondered if he left the position open out of love or out of torment. *Maybe I won't earn it. Dad just might want me to drown in worthlessness forever.*

The front door opened abruptly. Kaleb stormed through the darkened house. Nate got to his feet, heading over.

"Where is he?" Kaleb demanded.

The first thing Nate noticed was that his father was sober—he couldn't trace a whiff of alcohol. Kaleb caught sight of Nate and followed him to the living room, his stern, stoic features dark with pure rage once he saw Graham curled up on the pallet. Nate looked away quickly.

"His vitals are OK, but he'll need the doc. He won't be here until seven, though," Simon said. Always the calm one when it came to dealing with their fathers. Often, he went as far as telling jokes. Those didn't always end well.

Kaleb squatted down beside Graham, reaching a calloused, scarred hand out and gently brushing the boy's shaggy curls from his forehead. The vein in Kaleb's neck quivered. "I'll need names of who was at the party." He didn't pull his eyes away from Graham.

"We can give those, but I don't think most of them even knew about this. A few did, but I handled them," Nate answered. Kaleb nodded. "We'll finish it."

We'll. Not an 'I'll' or a 'you'll.' Strange of him to say.

"Hey, easy, Graham." Simon soothed Graham once he started stirring. "You're at our place. You're safe."

Graham opened his eyes, blinking hard when he saw Kaleb.

"It's just me, G." Kaleb smoothed Graham's hair again.

Simon put a water bottle to Graham's busted lips and helped him drink. Once Graham finished, he closed his eyes again, but even from where he stood, Nate saw tears trickle down the boy's black and blue face.

"Rest, Graham," Kaleb said quietly. His tenderness reminded Nate of how he used to soothe Nate when he'd been five years old and got sick with pneumonia. Nate remembered that as the first and last time Kaleb had comforted him like a boy, not a baby.

"I-I'm s—" Graham fought to speak.

"Don't apologize, boy, you have nothing to be sorry for." Kaleb wiped a tear from Graham's bruised cheek. "You did just fine. You're safe now."

Graham fell asleep without another peep.

Kaleb stood, eyeing Simon and Nate coolly. "Brock's dead but the others need their lesson."

"We're in." Nate spoke for both of them.

TEN

JUNE 30TH, 2027

"THE BABY'S COMING!" LEE SHOUTED, stumbling inside the farmhouse like a mad man. "The baby's coming!"

Rene' looked up from cleaning the kitchen from the family dinner. "What?"

"The baby's coming. I'm going to get Doctor Graceson." Lee grabbed his saddle pack from the foyer wall hook. The full moon shed some light on the barnyard as Lee used his flashlight to run outside and to the barn. Rene' watched him through the window before darting to the hallway.

"Mom—"

Mrs. Fisher was already getting dressed again in her room. "Go over there and—"

"Yes, ma'am." Rene' already knew what to do. This was the first time Terri would give birth in a fallen nation, but that didn't change much about birth, and

Rene's job was watching the other four kids.

She shoved her boots on and ran outside, heading down the dirt road. Terri's little house didn't lay far from the Fisher farmhouse, and it only took Rene' a minute to reach it.

"The baby's coming!" Little Lily cried in delight when she saw her aunt come inside. Her blond curls bounced as she clapped her chubby hands. "The baby, the baby, the baby!"

Kids aged eleven, nine, six, and four weren't easy to keep calm when there was a tiny sibling on the way, but Rene' could manage. Dax and Jaycee, the oldest two, were calm enough to know they must keep Paisley and Lily distracted.

Rene' picked Lily up with a big smile. "Let's go play in a room, OK? So we stay outta the way."

Lily pouted but Dax reached and took her into his skinny arms. "I can, so you can go see mom, Aunt Rene'," he said seriously.

"Thanks, bud, I'll be right there." She patted his back, smiled at the girls, then disappeared into Terri's room.

Terri knelt on the floor near the bed, moaning softly. It didn't take a doctor to see she was going along rapidly. She usually took a while—at least half a day—to deliver. Rene' didn't think that was the case this time.

"Hey, sis," Rene' said gently, rubbing her shoulders.

"Where's Howie?"

"Getting supplies from the kitchen." Terri's cheeks flushed red. "It's happening a little sooner than usual. Did Lee go for the doctor?"

"Yep. Graceson won't be too long." Or so, Rene' prayed. Graceson was always at the hospital which wasn't a close distance from their farm. "You're doing great. Mom's coming over. Don't worry about the kids. Just focus on getting the tiny one here, OK?" Rene' kissed Terri's cheek. As much as she loved her sister, and loved babies, she didn't ever feel much need to be very close to her during childbirth. Their mother did that job well enough.

"Love you, sis."

"Love ya." Rene' headed to the kids' room, smiling at Mrs. Fisher just as she came through the front door.

"All right…" Rene' closed the bedroom door and faced the four children.

Dax pushed his dark hair from his forehead. "How's Mom?"

"She's doing fabulous and it shouldn't take long." Rene' picked up Lily, grunting.

"Baby coming now?" Lily frowned.

"Yep." Rene' sat down on the messy bed. Jaycee and Paisley grabbed some dolls from their toy bin, playing quietly, and Lily squirmed out of Rene's lap to have a part of the doll action.

"You're a good big brother, Dax." Rene' put her arm around Dax as he sat beside her.

"I'm worried," Dax said softly.

"What about?" Rene' rubbed his back. He always told Rene' his fears and dreams. They'd been close throughout the years, and when the US split, wars started, and doom became real, he withdrew from his parents, but not Rene'.

"*Five* kids." He never let his voice grow loud enough for any of his sisters to hear.

Rene' considered his words. "It's not too much. We'll be OK."

"That's a lot of food." Dax tugged at the leather bracelet—a homemade gift from Lee on Dax's last birthday—on his wrist like he did when he was nervous.

"We'll be just fine, Dax. Lots of people in Springtown have babies." Lots *might be an overestimate, since there isn't more than, what, five thousand citizens? Maybe seven?* She forgot numbers easily, but whatever it was, it wasn't like women went infertile just because supplies were hard to find. *Even if that might be easier.*

Dax sighed, unconvinced. He was just as stubborn as Lee. "I guess."

"Simon and Nate are doing pretty good at getting supplies. That's been going strong for a while now, right?" Rene' wished she could take away his concerns. He was just a child. When she'd been eleven, she'd been playing in the dirt without a care in the big, bad world. But Dax? He worried about what food his sisters would eat, he worried about his parent's health, and he had nightmares his town would get blown up by Union soldiers or Islamic caravans.

It wasn't the life Rene' wanted for him or any of her nieces. *God is in control. His purpose is better than my desires.*

"Yeah, I like Simon and Nate." A small smile curved on Dax's lips. "Not everyone else does, but I do. I have more hope we'll win this war when they come."

"Some of the town just see surface value and get scared." Rene' pecked his cheek. "But not us, right?"

He chuckled and hugged her. "Simon gave me those pencils for my birthday—did you tell him I liked to draw?"

"I might've… Or maybe he's a mind reader." Rene' teased.

"He's too goofy to be a mind reader." Dax watched his sister's play around on the bedroom floor, his shoulders slowly relaxing.

"Goofy?" Rene' asked in surprise. "He's a pretty serious dude."

"Not with you," Dax said matter-of-factly. "What do you mean?"

"He's goofy with you sometimes, when no one looks. He likes making you laugh." Dax eyed her solemnly. "I notice things when Dad brings me with him to the drops. I've seen Simon act like that a few times now."

"Aren't you the little spy." Rene' smoothed his silky hair.

"You're a watchful knight in shining armor."

Dax scoffed and got down to play with his siblings. They kept to themselves for about twenty minutes. Rene' didn't hear anything outside of the room—no screaming or yelling from Terri's room, nor did she hear the doctor enter the house.

After thirty minutes, Rene's gut twisted harder and harder. She focused weakly on the board game with the kids. *I should go check on Terri…*

By forty tiring minutes, the bedroom door creaked open. Mrs. Fisher looked in, expression serious but eyes shining, so Rene' knew nothing bad had happened.

"The baby is here," Mrs. Fisher smiled at them all.

The kids cheered and Lily danced around Paisley. Dax smiled but kept himself composed, watching his Granny closely, expecting more news.

"How's—"

"Terri and baby Aiden are doing great." Mrs. Fisher gave her grandchildren big, mother bear hugs before turning to Rene'. "Lee and the doctor haven't arrived yet. Your father will go looking for them soon."

"I can," Rene' offered.

"That will be fine. He's too tired to get on a horse

right now. Be careful and get your bag and gun—" Mrs. Fisher paused a moment at Rene's small grin. "Oh, hush and go."

"Won't be long!" Rene' saluted her nieces and nephew before heading out. *I'd better not go see Aiden just yet. He'll have plenty of adoring family members hovering around him soon enough, and Terri should rest for now.*

Rene' went home, donned her small backpack which held her .22, and went outside to grab Sugar from the field. She tacked her up fast and rode down the dirt road. The moon glistening overhead like a marble stone in a sheet of black, Rene' prayed. *Protect baby Aiden, Lord. The gift of life is never vanquished by circumstances. Despite the difficulties and dangers that lay ahead, bless him, and help us guide him.*

She let Sugar trot until they reached the asphalt road about a mile and a half from the farm. Sugar plodded on, accustomed to nighttime riding and trusting Rene' for guidance.

About halfway to town, Rene' spotted Lee riding up the hill, the head light wrapped around his head growing larger the closer he came.

"Lee?" Rene' called, grinning. Her own headlight probably blinded him, too, but she didn't care.

"Doc can't come!" Lee called breathlessly.

"The baby's here!" Rene' urged Sugar closer and both horses halted on the side of the road. Rene' watched Lee's eyes grow wide in the light of the flashlight beams.

"What?" he gasped.

"Aiden is healthy and Terri's just fine. No doctor needed tonight." Rene' moved Sugar closer, reaching out and patted Lee

on the back gently. "You did good,

bro!" Lee laughed out loud.

"You? Speechless?" Rene' shifted in her saddle. "The doc can drop by when he can. You must be beat."

"Not as much as Terri," Lee teased.

Rene' scoffed. "C'mon, Uncle Lee. Let's go home." Home, where her family was safe, happy, and had a future in God's Hands. Home, where the world didn't seem so big or so bad.

BABY AIDEN SCREAMED AND CRIED most of the time, the fussiest child that Terri and Howie had faced so far, but they did the best they could. Lee and Howie offered Aiden happiness, but he didn't like being away from Terri for long, and no one else stopped his crying.

Rene' adored the pink-faced, dark-haired fellow, but she couldn't comfort him and had other things to busy herself with. For the next two weeks, she did as many ranch chores as she could, kept both houses clean, and helped the children daily. Dax stuck by her side and even helped repair a small hole in the chicken coop. The girls grew grumpy by the second week and spent more time with an over-exhausted Terri.

Fourteen days was a long time for two families to be at their wits' ends. The problems didn't end with the stress of the children and work, either. Mayor Knight stirred strife with the townsmen. He declared their reckoning with Simon and Nate must end. "They are no longer welcome past borders." While many agreed, many more condemned Knight for his lack of leadership.

"Those two bring us valuable information and so far haven't mislead or lied to us about anything." Officer Sean had recited his words with the mayor to the Fisher's over dinner one night, as he often did after a hard day's work and needed a meal. "I think Knight is rethinking his boldness."

"It isn't like he's done a thing to help this town. You two have done far more than him," Mrs. Fisher fumed, glancing pointedly at her husband and Sean.

"Something's prompted him to try to play leader." Mr. Fisher's tanned face grew tight with anger.

"Well, no one's following." Sean ate hungrily before continuing. "Seems most everyone knows we'd all be goners without those boys. The risk is worth any doom that might come. We've defended ourselves before and can do it again, but we can't get supplies alone right now."

Rene' pushed homegrown zucchini around on her plate. *Lord, please, calm the town down. I can't stand the thought of anything happening to Simon and Nate, or people getting angry again, or…* Her imagination could run wild but it wouldn't help. *Just guide us in wisdom, Lord, and help us to focus on Your will. Fear will get us killed.*

Her prayer didn't help her feel any stronger. By the time dinner was over and they bid Sean goodbye, she cleaned the kitchen with Lee's help but still stressed.

When she got into bed that night, numbness engulfed her, a safe, cool shell that kept her eyes dry, her heart steady, and her thoughts mindless. Alone, in the darkness of her room, the shell around her quivering heart crashed down like old stone walls.

I'm scared, Lord. It's been almost a year now, but the town is angry. If Simon and Nate are shunned entirely, we'll all die, won't we? Don't the people see that?

She curled up tightly. Her eyes burned with tears and her throat tightened until she could hardly breathe.

Tired. Her spirit was broken. Like a thousand shattered pieces of the darkest night sky dumped on the lowest desert floor, far from the warmth of the sun, far from the comfort of the moon. Her prayers became monotonous to her own ears.

Her pleading heart bled until she was sure there was nothing else in her to give to the Lord.

I have to keep going. I'll give all these broken pieces to God and won't cry when the pieces cut my hands. I'll fight on because that's what a believer does. They fight in faith that no pain is endured in vain. They fight through anything and everything.

On nights like tonight, however, Rene' couldn't focus on God's promises. She just needed to weep. She needed to mourn for what was lost and for what had never been. Perhaps it was a sin to mourn for the past, but she couldn't help it. She couldn't help but yearn for how the world used to be. She missed security, a functioning society, and joy that wasn't so hard to come by. She missed when her family could visit the city or leave the county, when things were normal and safe, when people weren't divided over abortion laws, tax laws, importation laws, and foreign treaties, among countless other nightmares she could hardly list. *I miss my family being happy and not fearing for survival.*

Rene's silent sobs shook her body. She never made a sound when she wept at night. The darkness sucked the breath from her but it comforted, too. If she closed her eyes tight enough, she could imagine Jesus sat beside her and whispered His promises.

I miss the past, Lord.

I know the thoughts that I think towards you, thoughts of peace and not evil, to give you an expected end.

I'm scared. Condemn me or punish me, but I'm afraid of this world. I do my best to have faith in the mundane daily tasks, but

Satan is pulling me down. Hard. It's so difficult to find joy when everything is in ruins.

Cast your burdens upon me and I will sustain you.

Rene' gulped until her tears subsided. She rubbed her hot face and stared at the ceiling. Crying helped, but not much, and her thoughts tossed around.

The small, phone-like device Simon gifted her buzzed beside her bed. She grabbed it off her Bible and read the message Simon had sent: *"Are you awake?"*

"Yes." She texted back.

"It's late there."

"Just eleven." How long had she been lying awake and crying? *"How's Aiden and Terri?"*

"Doing good. It's really tense here, though: Aiden's super fussy and the kids are getting upset about it. Terri's snappish. Mom and Dad are worried about the mayor trying to cause trouble." Rene' paused just after she sent the message. He had asked a simple question. Not a mission report. He had his own problems—like Graham, whom Rene' prayed for daily.

He texted back immediately: *"Can you call me?"*

Rene' took a shaky breath and propped herself up on her elbow, clicking the call button. It only rang once.

"Hey," Simon said quietly.

"Hey, Si." Rene' rubbed her face. Deep breaths. In, out, in, out. She could talk to him without sobbing.

"Have you been crying?"

She didn't sound like she had been, had she? "Uh, kinda."

"Don't cry. Is Aiden OK? Is fussy normal?" Simon's concern weighed heavy in his voice.

"Yeah. Sometimes babies are just like that." Rene' curled up under her blanket.

"Oh. Sorry. You said everyone was struggling?"

"Everything's just pulling a toll on all of us. And I'm not holding up well as I'd like." Shame burned Rene's cheeks. *Just because I trust Simon doesn't mean I should blurt this kinda stuff.*

"It's the end of a nation. It's OK to struggle—we all do," Simon said.

"It's an untamed Civil War II out there, and I'm crying because my family is stressed—"

"You guys are surviving, your town is scared, and you guys have kids who are hard enough to raise in a *normal* nation." Simon interrupted once again, voice firm and calm. "You're too hard on yourself, Rene'."

Rene' clamped her eyes shut to hold back tears. "Because I'm scared, Simon. I try so hard to trust God with my everything, but I don't have enough faith. I am so scared I'll lose my family, or this town, or I won't be enough to keep everyone safe… I miss how the world used to be…" Her heart hammered in her chest like a bird repeatedly slamming itself against a glass window.

Trapped. *I'm trapped in a reality far worse than any nightmare imaginable. I want to wake up.*

"Listen to me," Simon whispered. "Everyone is afraid. If we're not afraid, we're not human. You said God created us to fear Him."

"Yeah," she managed weakly.

"We gotta fear *Him*." He sounded like it was the simplest thing ever. "We don't have to be afraid of anything that can happen to us… or anyone we love… We fear God and all other fear isn't gonna hold us down."

"What?" How did he know so much about fearing God? It wasn't a topic she addressed much.

"Your dad talked to me. Since Graham got hurt, I've been thinking nonstop about fear and fearing God." Simon drew in a breath like it pained him. "Fear means letting something take over your mind, like you worship it, so if you fear God, nothing else can take away that trust or worship… I think."

Rene' had heard her parents discuss that truth before. "If we put our faith, our fear in Him, it's harder to let anything else take our fear… It's easy to forget."

"I know."

Rene' could hear Simon's breathing on the phone. He didn't sound hurt. "Si?"

"Yeah?"

"You don't think I'm a fool for not having more

ANGELA R. WATTS

faith?" It wasn't like she should rest her thoughts on someone's opinions, but she couldn't stand if Simon saw her as a hypocrite who spoke of God's love but still feared doom. That's not who she fought to be. *But I fail enough to be a total hypocrite.*

"You blow me away by how much you believe, because you don't give up. Not even now. You hold on," Simon said firmly.

Rene' relaxed like a great weight shifted off her shoulders. "You… seriously?"

"You show me how it *could* be, Rene', what faith looks like, and I want that." Simon paused after he got those words out. "I know you think you don't do enough, but you do. You've done more for me than I can ever tell you."

"You're the one who listens to me." Rene' fought the lump in her throat. "You don't have to do *any* of this."

"You don't have to pray or listen to me rage at night because of what I failed at." He spoke of the second night after Graham was hurt, when she'd called and he'd asked many questions about God and evil. He'd been a mess.

"Guess we're even," Rene' whispered.

"I'll… I'll see you in two days, OK?"

Rene' closed her eyes. "See you, Simon."

"Try to get some rest," he said gently.

"You, too."

"Goodnight." He hung up.

She tried not to cry herself to sleep. Simon hadn't been lying, had he? He might be a Bucks gangster, but he'd never lied to any of them before, and had no reason to listen to her cry. Yet, he did. It meant more to Rene' than she thought it should. Tonight, she was too tired to wrestle with what she truly felt. She fell asleep knowing she'd found relief from the Lord and from Simon, and maybe, that wasn't so bad.

ELEVEN

JULY 21ST, 2027

WEST JOHNSTON WAS UTTERLY ALONE, drenched in sweat, mind pounding a thousand miles per second. His heart rattled against his ribs.

Thump. Thud. Thump. Thud.

Any second, his heart might erupt into a million little pieces. He'd choke on his own blood, and he'd just die. He'd be a corpse on the kitchenette floor for Jack to find in two days after he returned from the weekend with his Mels.

A corpse.

Dead.

Free. Released from this world.

Thump. Thud. Thump. Thud.

West crawled from the foyer floor to the fridge. His flesh burned like he was on fire. If he could just cool down…

His vision hadn't really returned, but he pretended it had, and he opened the fridge. He hit a beer bottle with his hand. It fell, smashing onto the floor, the sound ringing in his ears like rockets going off. West grabbed a water bottle and downed half of it in one gulp, then poured the rest of the cold liquid onto his sweaty face. Of course, it didn't help. He'd been drugged and tortured by his own father. A splash of cold water was like slapping a bandaid on an amputated leg.

He needed sleep. That was a good idea. He could handle himself just fine if he got out of the beer and broken glass pieces. He tried dragging himself upright but failed. He yelled in agony as his body kept throbbing. Thump. Thud.

One part of him screamed in fear.

I'mgonnadieI'mgonnadieI'mgonnadie.

The other part, the experienced, trained soldier, whispered and took control. *It was a test. George is gone now. He took you here and left you alone because you aren't dying. You're safe. Breathe.*

He screamed again in pain, anger, and grief. Mostly pain, but anger kept him fueled so he at least could breathe.

He flashed in and out of consciousness. For hours, there was nothing on planet earth but him, his heart that wouldn't slow down, his body that fought the poison his father had given him. Nothing else. No Jack, no Ed, no Spencer, nothing except flashes of his father's face looming over him.

Oh, his father. And the voices.

Screams. His own screams that rang in his mind were always battle cries and never pleas. Some were his mother's screams, begging for West to be spared. He hated those most.

Sometimes, it was Ed's cries. *"Make it stop, West, oh, please... I can't take it."* Memories of Ed being chained, his back torn up from a whipping from some crazed gangster, all flooded West's mind.

Writhing on the floor, panting, West dragged his broken body across the floor. Inch by inch. Desperate for his bed. Or maybe he just needed to move because that meant he was fighting for something. Fighting to live and not just reach his bed.

Fighting to live. For his brothers. For the innocent lives he'd keep saving, no matter the cost. *For them. Not George.*

More cries pummeled his mind. He couldn't fight the memories that cut him into little pieces and threw him into a salty sea—those memories crushed him and withdrew every bit of spirit he had left. What was left of him? Nothing.

The memories came in waves, and West kept screaming against them.

Spencer, drenched in blood, sprawled out in West's backseat. "My fault. It's my fault Randy left," he sobbed, again and again.

Gideon, surrounded by bodies. Men he'd killed. And when he looked at West, for a split moment, West could've sworn the man was crying. Cold Eyes. Crying.

"God, make it stop. Make it stop!"

Why him? Why did he have to survive? Why did he have to be George Johnston's only son? *Why why why?*

"This is what you deserve for refusing to walk in my footsteps, my beautiful son." George kissed his head and walked away as West convulsed from the punishment. The poison. The choice, to be George's son and take his path, or be a coward and try escaping his own legacy.

"God… *please*… I'm…" Trying? Fighting? Begging? Broken? *Shut up, West. You have to take this or someone else will.*

George knew West wouldn't let the pain heap on anyone else's head if it was in his power to take it all himself. It made George proud and gave him hope that West would choose *his* path one day. *One day soon.*

West wondered what his brothers would think if they saw him right now. They would be enraged he hadn't called for help before he'd gone with George. But they wouldn't blame him for allowing this to be done to him. They knew he had no choice.

And for their sake, he hoped that if he were to ever die like Jack's father, Hunter, had, no one would find his body, either.

WEST SAT UP ON THE floor, dawn's light peeking through the windows, almost blinding him. He groaned. *Alive. I'm alive.*

West dragged himself to his feet shakily. Slow and steady... He went to the kitchen, but the floor was clean, like someone had scrubbed where the beer had spilled. No traces of glass that West could see.

A small bottle of painkillers sat on the kitchen counter. West picked them up like they might explode in his hands. He popped a few after smelling them a bit and making sure they were legit painkillers—they were the ones he carried in his own bag. *Strange.*

Ignoring the shiver running up his spine, he went and got a cold shower. He dressed in a clean—he was fairly certain they were clean—t-shirt and jeans.

He wondered who'd been in his house. He didn't have security cameras, and his big guard dog had been shot two months ago. He hadn't replaced the dog, and security cameras were useless to him because they always got shot or hacked.

Maybe Spencer dropped by, cleaned up, and left me on the floor—though I doubt he would've cleaned or left me. He checked his phone.

A missed message from Gideon about how they needed to meet up soon.

Three from Ed asking if he was all right.

Zero from Jack, since the states' time zones were different.

West headed outside, sucking in fresh air and getting into his car. He dialed Ed and looked around George's base, groggy and sore.

For many of the thugs, the base was a refuge, a haven of power and the sight of what the world could be for those who took what they deserved. West just saw it as a speck of hell he could never run from, because it had shaped him into the man he was. It was a part of him. A part he could never rid himself of. George had always made sure of that.

West would never escape.

"West!" Ed finally picked up the phone. "Where are you?"

"I'm fine," West sighed. Not a lie, since he wasn't dead.

"Ty headed out this morning to check on you. He should be there soon."

"Thanks," West muttered, trying to hide his pain. He kicked a small rock but his legs didn't like the motion. "I'll swing by later. Gotta meet up with Gideon first."

"OK," Ed sighed tiredly.

Ty picked West up and they went to the mess hall, but West didn't have much of an appetite. His mind was drifting to his meeting with Gideon. He couldn't help it.

Jobs kept him focused and pulled him along. Jobs with Gideon usually contained some sort of justice, even if it was the slightest smidge, because Gideon understood West's need for jobs that weren't useless or vain.

However, West couldn't always be picky, and Gideon didn't always recruit him for jobs. So this meeting nagged at West's gut throughout the day, but he was far from unaccustomed to his gut being a bother. He was a Johnston. If his gut wasn't nagging, he was dead.

TWELVE

JULY 28TH, 2027

AFTER HOURS OF PORING OVER the blueprints and information George had sent them, Nate and Simon faced one choice: take the job with Gideon and Alex for extra supplies. Gideon and Alex were good con artists, so if the con was almost over, why not help them finish? They'd get a huge chunk of supplies in return.

"It's simple enough and would keep us on schedule. If we don't do this, we're two weeks out because we'll have to find another source..." Nate crossed his arms.

Simon rubbed his stubbled chin, straightening from bending over the table. He didn't think anything was as easy as it appeared to be. "I don't think the town can go that long right now. It's too tense. They might think we're chickening out or scheming."

"So, we take this job."

Simon grit his teeth in annoyance. "A job with

Gideon and Alex isn't small. There's a thousand things they aren't telling us about this con. We're supposed to play clean up like it's no big deal?"

"Yes," Nate said. "That's exactly what we're gonna do, curiosity cat. We'll get the supplies and get them to town without stepping out of line. For Springtown, for Rene', we're gonna stay on a need-to-know basis."

Simon shook the empty coffee pot on the counter top, surprised he'd downed all of it during their brainstorming session. "I guess we don't have a choice."

Besides, if they impressed Gideon and Alex, what other jobs could they get with them? Simon knew they'd need to enter the big leagues soon, and a clean up job a practical start, since Gideon didn't trust them with anything bigger.

"We'd better get to bed early." Simon gathered the blueprints, tossing them in a metal bucket and setting them on fire with a lighter. He watched them burn and then disposed of the ashes.

By Friday, they'd be driving toward Springtown with a load of supplies that would give the civilians hope, and most importantly, keep the trust they'd fought so hard to gain.

ACCORDING TO ALEX, THEIR CON was over and the Catalysts had hightailed it to Brazil. "You guys are a little late to the party, but we're gonna clean out their old supply crates today." Alex led them away from the parked vehicles on the side of the dirt road. The area in Kansas was secluded and, in Nate's honest opinion, about the same as it had been five years ago. He'd never been fond of the West. Too hot and monotonous. The perfect place, however, for supply hiding spots.

"Who's been guarding it?" Simon adjusted his belt where his gun hung.

"Philip, Jin, and Braddock, among others." The blond Aussie approached the large shipping crates which were giant eyesores in the middle of a field near the dirt road. Various men stood about, waiting to fill up the vans and trucks they'd driven over.

"Nice job, Al," Simon said to Alex. "Must've been quite the con."

Alex smiled brightly. "C'mon. Let's get packing."

Gideon spoke with Philip at the mouth of one crate. His white t-shirt and pants were dusty like he'd been busy for hours. They glanced over at Nate and Simon, Philip giving one of his token glares, his brown hair ruffling a bit in the breeze, but saying nothing.

"Let's get this done!" Gideon called out sharply. The men finished opening the crates, and in an orderly fashion, the supplies were moved into the trucks and vans. Everyone worked hard, helping each other carry the heavier boxes and pallets. Gideon made sure Simon and Nate had their fair share.

When everyone finished, Nate couldn't wait to get out of there. Being out in the open like a zebra waiting to be lunch in the plains? He didn't like it. Wiping sweat from his brow, he glanced over when Gideon yelled for everyone to head out. They'd come for the shipping crates themselves later.

Simon got into the van after thanking Alex and cranked the engine.

Nate stepped over to Gideon while the others loaded up. "Thanks." He offered Gideon a hand. He noticed the thin scars running up Gideon's neck and along his wrists. He often wondered about Gideon's past, and his future, but Gideon never spoke about such things. Nate didn't mind it, but he didn't trust him, either.

Gideon shook it without hesitation but didn't smile or show any sign of satisfaction. "Quite a lot of supplies for two men."

Nate didn't look away from Gideon's gaze, something flickering in his chest. *He knows about Springtown...* "We'd be fools not to stock." He shrugged casually.

"You would be." Gideon glanced to the van. "Drive safe." He followed Alex to their truck like he'd been speaking to Nate about the weather and hadn't looked right past his disguise.

If it was one thing Nate hated more than a man who

peered into his soul, it was a man who did so like it meant nothing to him. Gideon Hochberg was a man Nate didn't want to lose as an ally. *Something is up with him. Why else did he let us come and get supplies without payment?*

Nate got into the van. "I got a bad feeling, Si," he muttered, buckling up.

Simon followed the other vehicles down the dirt road at a brisk speed. "Huh?"

"I think Gideon knows." Nate glared at Gideon's truck ahead of them.

"About Springtown?" Simon's eyebrows furrowed.

"He's Gideon freaking Hochberg, man. If he wanted to know, he could find out, and we should've realized!"

"He's not the worst person to know, OK? Our dads don't, George doesn't, I have a list of people who'd we'd be screwed if they knew—but Gideon's not on that list," Simon said calmly. "If we just keep our mouths shut, he probably won't care."

"He's too close to George. He won't allow this kind of thing." Nate rubbed the dog tags around his neck—they'd belonged to Hunter. Hunter had gifted them to Nate, not Jack, one night when he'd found little Nate crying in his bedroom because "Daddy hurt me again and I can't do anything to stop it." Nate didn't go a day without wearing them, like they were his armor.

Armor protected a man in combat. Armor couldn't protect a man from another man's mind or a scheme where brute force meant nothing. *A man can be strong, but if he can't keep a secret, he's a dead man.*

If they couldn't keep the secret, Springtown was doomed. It was possible the town might be destroyed anyway, of course, but Nate and Simon had a chance to protect the people. If anything happened, it became their fault, their duty, their job.

"We have to stay calm. Gideon's not as much of a monster as we think." Simon worried aloud as he drove. "If he was, West and Jack wouldn't do so many jobs with him. Right? I mean, no matter what he's done or how close he is to George, he's not a snitch…"

Nate drank some water from his canteen, eyeing the fields surrounding them for dangers. "We have no way of knowing if he'll turn us in, get anything from doing that, or if he'll blackmail us later."

"So we keep doing what we're doing." Simon shifted his hands on the steering wheel. "Besides, Alex is sincere, and he hates George."

Nate scoffed. "Oh, c'mon. He's a con artist. He could fake that." No one survived without both having a healthy fear of George Johnston and burying that fear at all times.

"I can read people, Nate." Simon acted like that was the final word he needed to defend his statement.

"You think they'll keep quiet out of the kindness of their little black hearts?"

"I think we gotta trust God to watch our backs, because we're powerless to know every outcome." Simon glanced at Nate briefly, the van bouncing over a hole in the chert, but he didn't slow down.

"You're taking all that seriously, huh?" Nate asked quietly.

"Isn't like I've got much to lose."

"Your life," Nate muttered. "Don't you remember anything? What about the Christians being executed in the Californias, Si? What about those Catholics slaughtered in Maine two months ago because of the Islam caravan? What about—"

"I know just as well as you do what believing in God can cost. But we could die at any given time, so is loving God really gonna make us bigger targets?"

Nate set his jaw at Simon's dark tone. He remembered Yemmy, the twelve-year-old boy they'd known at that age. The boy's father had been eager to join the gang and get rich. Yemmy befriended Simon and Nate fast. It'd only lasted six months. He had believed in God and constantly brought God up, though his dad didn't believe. His father had flunked a job and his car was bombed. And Yemmy'd been killed. A meaningless death before he'd ever gotten to become a man.

Loving a God who lets that happen to people who love Him? I'm not that open-hearted. I can hold my own.

Simon sighed. "Nate—"

"I'm not angry at you for believing, Si."

"I'm not saying I *do*."

"You want to." Nate shrugged. "What's the difference?"

"I want to *understand*," Simon said. "I want to learn about God. That doesn't mean I don't have doubts or fears."

Nate could sense Simon's struggle. *Graham. Simon's torn between trusting God with the one person he can't heal and being angry at Him for the damage caused.*

"But…" Simon steeled himself. Squared his broad shoulders like he was making a decision. "I'm not a child. I'm not a fool. I'm not a coward. I'll hold on."

"You think believing matters, after all this?" Nate hadn't addressed their argument after Graham's incident, but the hidden tension remained in his question.

"Yeah, Nate," Simon said without hesitating. "I do. I think God has a bigger role in this damned world than any person gives Him credit for. He's not just playing Judge."

Nate laughed softly, but if he dared speak, Simon would knock him out.

"I'm not gonna force feed the Gospel to you." Simon rolled his eyes. "Let's just focus on getting these supplies to

Springtown."

"That I can do, brother."

OF ALL THE PLACES SIMON traveled since 2024, his favorite place was Springtown, Kentucky. Between the fresh air, lack of demolished urban setting, and Rene', he decided it was a bunch of things piled together that made it heaven. It certainly beat Paradise.

Officer Mikey led them past the border and toward the courthouse where they parked and got out. Simon and Nate went around to the back of their van. Nate unlocked the door and shoved it open wide.

Officer Sean came down the courthouse steps, smiling at Simon, his red hair wild from the breeze. "Hey! AJ told us you were coming earlier than usual."

"Yessir." Simon shook his hand. He tried not to be obvious when he looked back to the courthouse, but he didn't see Rene' anywhere.

Sean tilted his head. "Rene's running a little late."

Simon stiffened and quickly led him to the van. "Got loads of stuff this time, even some baby supplies." He didn't need to voice his confusion as to why diapers and baby formulas had been in a gangster's storage supplies. The Catalysts hadn't been the heartwarming, humanistic type, but it didn't matter. *Even monsters have family.*

Sean looked the shipment over. "You two are miracle workers."

"Where's Mr. Fisher?" Nate asked, pulling a box from the truck.

"He's occupied right now and won't make this supply drop." Sean shrugged. "He wanted me to thank you both."

Men started unloading, and Simon kept to himself and carried the boxes he could. After the truck was emptied, he followed Nate outside of the courthouse. The warm sun bore down on the asphalt beneath him. He glanced down the road again but didn't see anyone on horseback.

"She'll come," Nate scoffed softly. "You little love-struck rat."

"The animal for that expression is *puppy*," Simon snapped. "And I'm not. She's my friend."

Nate rolled his eyes. "I know what I said." He drank some water that Sean gave him and Sean tried small talking with him. He was a master of kind words and comfort, like an Irish dog that Nate couldn't run from.

He's the total opposite of Nate. Who knows? Maybe Sean can be the one to soften Nate's heart. Simon chuckled to himself.

Just when Simon knew they'd have to head out soon, Rene' came up the road on Sugar. A smile tugged on Simon's lips, but it quickly diminished when he saw the state she was in. She dismounted near the hitching post and tied Sugar as Simon came closer. "Rene'?"

Her long hair was in a tangled ponytail and her face was ashen—she hadn't slept in days. Not properly, anyway. By the looks of her dirty clothes, she hadn't had much peace to sleep. "Hey, Si. Sorry I'm late."

"I wouldn't have let you lift anything the way you are now," Simon said, jaw tight. "Are you OK?"

"Yeah. No. No, I'm not." She paused, taking in her surroundings like they were the most important thing to see in the world.

"What's going on?" He frowned. "C'mon, let's sit on the steps."

She grimaced as if welcoming that idea like a slap to the face. "I don't wanna talk in front of everyone. Let's go behind the courthouse. I'll tell Sean we're talking." She squared her shoulders—he thought it was adorable when she did, because how much taller or stronger looking could a short person become?—and went to Sean and Nate.

He wasn't sure why his gut nagged so bad, but he followed her. She hadn't told him anything drastic since the last time they'd called that night when she'd broken down. She would've told him if something was wrong, right? *What if the baby is sick? Or Lee? Or Mrs. Fisher?*

"Sure." Sean eyed Simon after Rene' told them they'd be speaking out back. "Just don't be long, yeah?"

Simon led Rene' to the back of the courthouse where it was relatively quiet and private. "So—"

"Nothing's wrong." Rene' crossed her arms. Simon noticed the cuts on her arms, he assumed from barbed wire, since she'd told him about the fence work she did recently. She didn't take care of herself very well—at least one of those scratches needed a bandaid, but he didn't have one on him. He'd remedy that when they went back to the truck.

"That's a lie."

"I mean, nothing big." She sighed. "I saw the look on your face when I got here. I didn't know I was so scary lookin'." She offered a weak smile but Simon wasn't playing into her attempts to be invincible.

"Rene', you're upset, and I wanna help. Friends worry about each other." He didn't want to be creepy, and if he was even capable of it, clingy, but he did care about her. He didn't understand how or why, exactly, but he did, and it didn't hurt. His reasoning was that Rene' was in just as much danger without being regularly helped out by a gangster.

Rene' leaned against the brick building, shoulders sagging. "Right."

"Yeah." He cracked a smile. "So…?" He wished there was more he could do for her, but with the world as it was, it wasn't like he could just whisk the world back together. He couldn't heal the United States and thus, couldn't fix the heartaches Rene' faced, but he could be there with her throughout it all. That's what friends did.

After the moment of silence, Rene' met his gaze. "It's been better. Mentally, I guess. I've focused on God." She chuckled a bit bitterly. "Then life got harder. Aiden's colicky. Dax fell in the creek and bumped his head, so he hasn't been able to get out of bed since yesterday. Lee and his friends won't stop asking me about joining their group."

"Group?" Simon asked hesitantly.

"Lee and others, like Xander and Mo, claim they'll be the town's best defense in a year or two." Rene' took a slow breath, worry heavy on her face. "I really don't want them all to become cops or soldiers, Si... But what else can they do? Can you really stay a farmer, or a small town boy, in this kinda world?"

Simon thought a moment. "Maybe that's what the world needs right now. Maybe they don't have to change as much as you fear." *They're teenage boys who will defend their home. Nothing will get that duty out of their head.*

"I can't help them, Si, I can't take the role they'll take. I feel absolutely helpless, no matter what I do, and I'm... I'm struggling to not be afraid and trust God. I don't like it, but it's how it is..." She didn't meet Simon's eyes now. Was she ashamed? Simon didn't see anything to be ashamed of. She was stronger than most people he knew—at least she admitted fear and tried to conquer it. He couldn't even say the same for himself. He usually shoved his fears back until they went away. It didn't work.

"You've got nothing to be ashamed of, Rene'," he said gently but firmly. "You've helped more than you know, remember? You help with supplies, with your nieces and nephews, with the ranch, with keeping everyone's hopes up… I see it, you know."

Her eyebrows furrowed. "What?"

"You keep *everyone* having faith. You don't see that?"

"No." She was nothing if not blunt.

"You keep Mr. and Mrs. Fisher having faith. You mean the world to Sean, too, and the guy's got no family left. Lee and his friends would snap our necks if Nate or I ever hurt you." Simon shook his head firmly. "You mean more to this town than you realize. You all have a part to play."

Rene' paused, rubbing sweat from her temples. "Yeah…" She glanced up with a smile, like she didn't have to fight for joy anymore. "You're wiser than you think."

"Oh, I know." Simon tossed his hair. It got a laugh out of her, and he hid his satisfaction.

She nudged his arm. "Don't get cocky."

"I'm Simon Bucks. I'm always cocky."

"No, you're not."

"Am too! Try to stop me," he scoffed. Just as Rene' went to nudge him again—probably harder this time—Simon's radio beeped. "Ack, gotta take this, hold that beating, please." He lifted a hand.

Rene' crossed her arms with a sly smirk. Waiting like a cat to strike.

"Hello?" Simon spoke into the radio. "Can you hear me, over?"

"Simon, you're needed at the location in Tennessee. The plan's a bust. How soon can you make it?" His father's familiar voice, as worn and sharp as ever, crackled over the radio.

The heat drained from Simon's blood. "It'll take us about five hours, Dad." Probably longer.

"What?" Jordan demanded, then changed his mind just as quickly, like he didn't want to know where his son was. "It'll have to do. We've got about six hours until the men realize something's wrong."

Simon glanced at Rene' and headed to the front of the courthouse. "We're on our way." He shoved his radio back in its strap around his waist.

Rene' scrambled after him as fast as she could. "What's—"

"Sex trafficking in Tennessee. The job's been on the low for over a month, but it's going down tonight. There's a lotta kids there and if we don't move them soon, we'll lose this chance."

Simon waved at Nate, tossing him the keys. "You drive, let's go!" Nate got in and cranked the van without any question.

Simon opened the passenger door after waving at a police officer hastily. Sean must've left because Simon didn't see him, and he wasn't about to waste time explaining their hurried departure.

"I'm coming with you," Rene' said like it was the most natural thing in the world.

Simon almost didn't hear her. "No!"

"Are any women gonna be there?" she asked.

Jordan's women workers weren't able to make it to this job and Simon knew it, but he didn't like where Rene' was doing with this. "There might be—"

"You're lying." She grabbed the door.

"It's dangerous—" A million things came to his mind to argue her with but his tongue jumbled. "Rene', you can't—"

Rene' ducked under his arm and jumped into the van. She shouted at a young officer, who stared with wide eyes: "Tell my dad I'll radio!"

Simon paled, hearing Nate snarl at them both, hearing Rene' say that she knew what she was doing and that the kids needed her, but Simon slammed the door shut to block it out for a moment. "Rene', please. You could get hurt. Killed. The world isn't what—"

"The kids, Si. God needs me to do this." No fear or nervousness came through her words or expression. She sat calm and stiff as Nate sped down the street. She paid no heed to Nate's swearing.

"You shouldn't be coming." Simon clenched his fists, looking down at her. "The world is hell. You shouldn't have to see it!"

"I know kids, and I can help them, and another set of hands isn't gonna hurt. We'll come back." She met his gaze but didn't falter at his anger. How could she be so calm? Simon's stomach was in knots, and she looked like a little soldier ready to kill someone. *Her dad will kill me. Slowly. I'll deserve it for ever letting her come with us.*

She'd said God had told her to. Who was Simon to dump her out of the van? As much as he wanted to get her home right that instant with every fiber of his being, something stopped him.

Trust. His gut wouldn't stop nagging at him to trust, but trust who? God? Was he really willing to trust God with Rene' right now? Because she was in Simon's care if she passed the border.

Nate kept driving. He didn't stop or slow down.

"Rene', please, listen," Simon began slowly. "This is dangerous."

"I could get hurt or killed." She squeezed his arm. "God's gonna take care of me, and I don't care what happens. I've got nieces and nephews, Si. If I sit back and not help other little kids…" She shook her head, chin quivering briefly like the words pained her. "I wouldn't want anyone else to sit by if it were my kids."

"It's my job to keep you safe, and you've got a whole family. A whole family, a freaking town..." *But you let her in the van! It is already your fault! You messed up, Simon, and why? Because of God?*

"I can handle myself." She glanced down at the .22 on her waist. "Dad'll understand..." She grabbed his radio.

"Would you just trust me on this?" Simon demanded sharply, heart hammering. "This is *crazy*!"

"You let me in the van! You wouldn't have if you didn't think I was needed!" Rene' said firmly.

"Rene', we can handle it alone. You need to stay here, you're needed *here*."

"I'm needed where God tells me to go." She tried to find her father's connection on the radio waves. "And He told me to go, so no matter how crazy it is, I'm doing it."

Nate snarled again, speaking up. "Needed or not needed by those kids, you shouldn't come. You've never done this thing before."

Rene' reached her father on the radio, sucking in a breath.

"Dad?"

"Hey, honey—"

Rene' quietly and calmly explained the situation.

"What?" Mr. Fisher's voice rose. "What are you—"

"God told me to go." Her hands trembled. "The

kids are in danger and there's no other women helping so I have to help, Dad… I'll be back, I promise."

"When? Where?" Mr. Fisher pierced her with questions.

"Some place in Tennessee. I'll be back—"

"Tomorrow evening," Simon managed.

She repeated it to her father.

"Rene', you know how dangerous it is out there." Her father paused. "I told you when you were young that no matter where you ever were, I'd always find you." Mr. Fisher's voice was thick with emotion.

"I know, Daddy, and I'm coming home after I do what God told me to do."

"God *really* told you to do this?"

Simon wondered if Mr. Fisher didn't believe that. If he didn't, Simon wouldn't, either, and he'd gladly take Rene' home.

"Yessir, I'm sure of it," Rene' said, lowering her head like the pain in her father's voice cracked her.

She never wanted to hurt him. Simon gulped.

"You're leaving now?" Mr. Fisher choked.

Something in Simon snapped. He'd never heard Mr. Fisher—strong, tough, smart Mr. Fisher—sound so broken. But Simon didn't move or make a sound or order Nate to turn the vehicle around.

"Yes, Daddy, I am. But I'll be back. I just have to do this… the kids… please, if you don't want me to—"

Rene' couldn't finish, wiping tears from her flushed cheeks.

"We trust you, Rene'. If God told you to do this… He'll take care of you… But you come back. Hear me? Radio me. I'll come." He paused a long moment, composing himself, no
doubt. "Let me speak to Simon, baby."

Rene' chewed her lip, handing Simon the radio.

Pushing all thoughts or emotions aside, Simon answered. "I'll protect her, sir, or I can bring her back right now."

"Protect her. And tell me everything that's going on." He left no room for argument or lies.

Simon watched the Springtown welcome sign grow smaller and smaller behind them as the van bumped along. He wished he'd taken Rene' home. "Yessir." He didn't look at the others as he began to explain the situation to Mr. Fisher.

"Have her home by tomorrow evening or I come to get her.
Rene', use your head. You'll be fine."

Simon's father had never spoken to him like that. He'd never heard such gentle but firm, loving but threatening, commands before in his life. Mr. Fisher held his daughter dear to his heart, but he was letting her go. Why? He'd never even let Rene' out of town since the war started.

He can't protect her from everything… But we can do our best to. Simon sucked in a breath. "Yessir."

"I'll radio," Rene' whispered. "I love you, Dad. It'll be OK." His voice was choked but Mr. Fisher said, "I know, baby girl. We'll be praying."

THIRTEEN

JULY 28TH, 2027

THE WHOLE SIX-HOUR DRIVE MADE Rene' unusually quiet. The world wasn't the same—spots of humanity had been totaled, like they'd never been there. The remains of ashes and broken buildings sent shivers down her spine. She knew Nate and Simon picked the safest, most quiet route, but destruction was unavoidable. She thought of how the nation used to be, before the nation divided, when people lived in peace.

Now, the gangs fought for whomever, the Union pushed for central government, and the Confederates bled for freedom. If she'd doubted the realism before, she couldn't after seeing the ruins of what used to be along the worn road.

She kept calm by praying and trying not to think about anything too much. It didn't work very well. The destruction along the road bore down on her heart, like she could feel the pain each acre held deep within her spirit.

She couldn't fix any of what was done. But she could go help some kids. *That'll make this all worth it.*

The location was a small house in a suburban area—or what used to be, anyway. It all lay abandoned now, it seemed to Rene, and creepy. She didn't ask questions about the location or the situation. She didn't really want to know more than necessary.

Peering out the window, she saw another truck parked outside beside a large black van. A large flashlight sat on the hood of the truck, piercing the darkness like a welcoming beacon. Simon said that the truck belonged to Jack and West.

Nate parked out front and stormed over to his cousin. "What happened?"

Jack crossed his arms over his chest. Was it the way the flashlight beam hit him or was his arms covered in blood? "The men are dead. We got here early and they were moving out, so we ended it. Like Jordan asked."

"Where are the kids?" Simon got out, handed Rene' a little black backpack, and went over. Rene' stayed on his heels, trying not to stare at Jack.

Jack's eyes narrowed upon seeing Rene'. "The kids are inside. A few need medical attention—Vince is doing the best he can, but they aren't being easy about this." He gestured to Rene'.
"You said you can help?"

"Yes," Rene' said. "Can I go in?"

"Be careful." Jack jerked his thumb toward the little house.

"Is West inside?" Nate asked tautly.

"Nah, he's burying bodies. I'm gonna go help, if you guys wanna guard." Jack didn't seem bothered by what he'd said and he didn't look at Rene'.

His words rang in her ears a bit, but she ignored them and headed to the house. *Lord, help these kids. Guide me because I have no idea what I'm doing, but You do. You brought me here. Use me.*

She stepped inside and the smell of liquor and mold filled her nostrils. She quickly breathed through her mouth instead to avoid the stench so she didn't get sick. Simon followed her into the living room. There weren't many signs showing the place had been lived in except the blood stains on the hallway carpet.

She heard soft sobs coming from behind one of the hallway doors. She went closer, peeking in. There was no way to prepare herself for whatever she'd find.

Five little girls sat in the small, bare room, all wearing dirty dresses. A few were blonde and the rest Indian. They stared at Rene' in utter surprise but didn't speak. None of them looked in drastic need of medical attention, besides bruises around their necks, faces, and bare arms. Rene's heart might as well have stopped beating at the sight of them. *But where's the sobbing coming from?*

"Vince is in the next room." Simon's voice came from behind her. "You might want to come."

Rene' smiled at the girls weakly. "We're going to help," she said. "I'll be right back." Simon stayed at the door to guard the little girls.

Deep breaths. In through the mouth. Out through the nose. She had a job to do and emotions would only stop her from doing it. She went to the other bedroom.

Vince, the southern doctor Simon had told her about, knelt on the floor beside a pregnant teenage girl. The girl was hysterical, gripping the pallet and snapping at Vince in Spanish.

Vince tried speaking to her, but she didn't seem to hear him, and he evidently didn't know Spanish. A few other older girls sat off to the side, silent and somber, watching with dull eyes.

Rene' stepped closer, noticing the dark blood stains on the teenage girl's dress. The girl sobbed and braced herself against the wall.

"She's in labor and won't let me help." Vince didn't look up, not even phased by Rene's unusual presence. "There's a little girl in the other room who needs my attention." He stood.

"But—" She'd only seen two rooms of victims.

"There's three rooms." Vince grabbed his black bag from beside the girl. "Two girls are in bad shape, left for dead. Nate! You come with me." He disappeared into the hallway and Nate followed grimly.

Rene' knelt down beside the teenage girl. She didn't

know Spanish very well at all. "Can you speak English?"
She asked gently. *Goodness, she's terrified… Lord, help her!*

The girl panted, nodded.

"What's your name?" Rene' dropped the black bag
from her shoulder and opened it. This was why God had
brought her. She couldn't mess up.

"Onya." The girl rubbed her swollen belly.

"I'm Rene'. I'm gonna help you, OK?" Rene'
grabbed out some rags and a bottle of water, helping
Onya drink. "Here, for you guys," she gave out two
more bottles of water. The girls took them fast.

Onya writhed in pain. "Have you done it before?"
Her accent was thick with pain and fear. Rene' couldn't
imagine how she felt in that moment.

"Yes," Rene' said. It wasn't a total lie. She'd helped
Terri deliver babies before. *Kinda.* "Just take deep
breaths. Breathe— that's it, in through the mouth, out
through the nose."

Onya shook but obeyed. She had a strong will, at
least. "It's happening fast…"

"That's good." Rene' tried to comfort the girl. A
midwife would check on the baby, but Rene' feared if
she tried something, she'd do more harm than good.
She'd have to trust God with this and do what she knew
how to do. "Are you ready to push?"

Onya cried out in pain, nodding without another
word. Rene' hated how skinny the young woman was,

with a tooth-pick thin body besides her bulging belly.

"You can do it," Rene' said. "I'm gonna help. Just push and keep breathing." She glanced at the other girls. "Can one of you hold her hand?"

A tall Asian girl scooted over and took Onya's hand, whispering gently to her. After fifteen minutes of pushing, Onya was only growing weaker, and the baby wasn't coming.

Rene' tried to stay calm and focused. She didn't like this one bit. "Keep pushing, Onya... You gotta relax, sweetie."

After another five minutes, the baby came. Rene' caught the tiny newborn and quickly rubbed its back.

"Breathe, sweetheart," she said firmly. The baby began screaming, not as loud as Rene's nieces or nephews screamed when they were born, but it was a cry and that counted.

Onya sank back with a sob. The Asian girl held her and smoothed her sweaty, short black hair from her face.

Rene' took the towel from the bag and dried the baby off as gently as she could, like the baby might break if she breathed too hard. The baby cried and kept breathing. Rene' laughed weakly. "It's a little girl, Onya."

Onya sucked in a breath and whispered something in Spanish, outstretching her thin arms. Rene' gently placed the baby against Onya's chest but hadn't cut the umbilical cord— she didn't know how and it seemed to delicate a thing to wing. "Hold her gentle—I'll go get the doctor."

"Don't leave!" Onya gasped, chocolate eyes wide with fear.

"I've gotta get the cord cut," Rene' said gently. "I'll be right back." She glanced to the other girl before going into the hall.

How could so much happen and her insides feel like a foggy night sky? *I should be terrified, but feel nothing at all, like a dandelion seed wafting through oblivion, but somehow, knowing exactly where I'll fall.* She bumped into Simon blindly.

"Is it over?" Simon asked quietly. There was blood on his arms, like Rene's, but he had no signs of joy in his eyes. Only a haunted pain, the kind of pain of a life lost instead of gained.

"Simon, what happened?"

"One of the girls didn't make it." Simon didn't blink. "Did yours?"

"Y-yeah, the baby's fine. I need Vince." Rene' could hardly breathe. *Dead? A girl died?*

"I'll get him. You should go to the little girls. They're crying," Simon managed, expression empty. He headed down the hall. Rene' wanted to comfort him—but how? She couldn't right now.

She went back to Onya. She took another towel

from the bag and rubbed the blood from her arms as best she could, not looking up. "I have to go to the little girls, they're upset. I'll be back. The men are safe, they're good, OK?"

Onya held her covered baby to her chest, whispering weak confirmation.

Rene' went inside the other room. The little girls cried and one stood up, begging to know what was happening. Rene' had no time for overthinking or panicking over anything. She was strangely calm—like focusing on what had to be done overruled the pain. "We're getting you guys to safety."

"Why is Onya screaming?" one girl, her blond hair tangled, asked meekly.

"Onya had a baby, and they're both just fine." Rene' nodded. "Will you girls come with me? We'll take you to a safe place, away from anyone who wants to hurt you."

The one who'd asked what was going on threw her arms around Rene' and wept.

"I've got you." Rene' stood, fighting the shudder that crept up her spine, holding the little girl close. "Let's go," she told the others.

"We don't like those men." The blonde girl shook her head. The others nodded in agreement, some looking sheepish and others looking more terrified than ashamed.

"They're here to help, and I'll take care of you girls,"

Rene' promised. "They want to get you somewhere safe. They're helping me." She had no idea what she was supposed to say to persuade them.

The girls got to their feet slowly. One Indian girl whispered, "Will they hurt us?"

"No," Rene' said firmly. "No one's gonna hurt you again." She hid the fury from her gentle voice. She was glad Jack and West had killed those men, and she hoped they'd done it slowly. "We'll go with you." The girl nodded.

It wasn't like they could stay, but Rene' had earned some trust. *Thank God. Now, help me get them out.*

"Let's go outside to the truck." Rene' picked up another little girl and led them all outside into the night. West was waiting near the truck and opened the back quickly.

"Thanks," Rene' hoisted the two girls into the back carefully, arms shaking. She helped the others since they didn't let West touch them. West didn't tried helping them up, but he glanced at Rene' and warned her that they all needed to hurry now.

Rene' went inside. "Simon? Nate?"

Nate came out of the back room, expression dark. "Ready?"

The girls would panic if they saw him and Simon's bloodstained shirts and arms. "Don't let the girls see the blood," Rene' whispered.

Vince came into the hall, carrying a young girl in his arms, but the half pint didn't look conscious. He muttered under his breath and took her outside quickly.

"What—" Rene' began, but Simon came into the hall and led her to the other room.

"You get the baby, I'll help the others."

She went in but showed no fear. It was strange how the mind could function without feeling anything. "Onya, girls, we're going."

The girls got to their feet. Rene' gently helped Onya stand, relieved when Onya let her take the baby. Vince had cut the cord and wrapped the newborn up snuggly.

Once everyone got outside, Jack and West helped load them all in the back of the van where pallets of blankets waited. Rene' laid the baby in Onya's arms before passing out bottles of water. The little girls clung to her so she hadn't much choice but sit down with them.

Simon paused, meeting her gaze. "Here." He pushed his radio into her hand. "I'll be driving right behind you guys."

The back door shut securely and a little girl fell fast asleep against Rene's leg.

"Thank you," Onya whispered. Her exhaustion pained Rene'.

"We're going somewhere safe," Rene' said. Now that she couldn't keep moving, her heart threatened to pound out of her chest, and her stomach rolled. But she couldn't be sick now. *Thank You, Lord… Almost everyone made it out…* She thought briefly of the child Simon said they lost but couldn't let herself for long, because then she'd break. She couldn't break. Not now.

The girls didn't relax much, but the youngsters eventually drifted off to sleep, most of them curling up beside Rene' or the older girls. Onya held her baby and managed to feed the newborn a little after Rene' helped her figure it out.

After a few hours, Rene' kept the flashlight on but stared into the shadows of the van. She could hardly think of what had happened. What she'd done. She felt hot tears trickle down her cheeks, but she felt nothing else. *Where did all these girls come from, Lord? Not all of them are from America, or what's left of America, that's for sure. Where are their families? How long have they been used like this? How long can they face the war ahead of them?*

FOURTEEN

JULY 29TH, 2027

WEST WATCHED THE ROAD BEFORE them and kept the van at a steady speed. They were only slightly behind schedule. The girls were alive and they'd pull through, and though losing one girl was a harsh blow, it hadn't been as bad as such jobs often were. Even Jordan would have to admit it had gone smoothly, and the man pushed for perfection, especially when it came to young children being involved.

Despite the fair outcome, West couldn't find satisfaction. Perhaps his struggle was due to the fact he was driving them into a trap.

It's for Rene's own good. If Gideon doesn't kidnap her for Jed, someone else will, and she'll be as good as dead. This way, Gideon can protect her. This way… she'll be OK… she can go home… His spirit wouldn't agree with his logic.

"West?" Jack asked quietly. He never stopped

looking around the roads—staying alert for ambushes, thugs, or homeless thieves was vital. He was good at keeping his eyes peeled.

"Hm."

"We have to do it."

"I know."

A pause. "Not every right thing feels right."

West set his jaw tightly as if to bite back a thousand memories that were tinted with that truth. "I know." *I know we have to do this. I know Rene' is innocent. I know it will be terrible for her. I know Gideon will protect her the best he can.* But knowing, as he'd learned over the years, did little to soothe the human heart. His heart hardly mattered. What mattered was protecting the others and right now, that meant giving Rene' to the devil himself.

After five hours of driving, they reached the Borsch Haven. Jordan Bucks kept all of his underground railroad stops secret, secure, and small—but this one was one of the tiniest. A few cabins tucked away in a pine forest, with a stream out back, wasn't a bad place to hide or protect.

Jordan waited outside the main cabin. He ran over once the vehicles parked. Though he'd received word over radio of how the mission had gone, it didn't appear to have relieved his worry. He ran to the back of the van. Jack went to him, unlocked the door, and kept his distance again for the sake of the girls.

West shoved the van keys into his pocket as he stepped over but didn't get in the line of sight of the girls. He watched Nate and Simon come over with Vince, then glanced to the sky, where bold yellows and oranges morphed across the light blue sky. They'd made it in time, even if the trip had been hard.

Jordan spoke to the girls gently and helped Rene' unload them. Simon helped the best he could and tried to talk to the little ones soothingly, strongly resembling his father in that moment. They took the girls into the main cabin.

West glanced at Jack and Nate beside him. Miracle of miracles, the cousins didn't jump at each other's throats. Nate turned away to radio someone—probably Rene's parents, but West didn't dare pry. He wondered what Mr. and Mrs. Fisher were like. If Nate respected them, they'd have to be saints or something.

Jack and West cleaned out the van. Nate came over after a few minutes but never looked at either of them. After five minutes of them taking their time, the job was done and they had nothing else to do unless they risked going inside, which wasn't their place.

Besides, we just need Rene' to come outside. As long as no one was watching and she was vulnerable, Gideon could take her. Gideon wasn't far from the Haven at the moment but hidden from Jordan's guards. The sooner it was over, the sooner Rene' could go home, after the hell session was over.

West grabbed a water bottle from the cab and drank. *Focus.* He had a job. Disliking it meant nothing. He'd done plenty of those before. That's what the war was all about. *But handing a teenage girl to Jed?*

Half an hour later, Simon and Rene' came outside like dead folks walking. Jack brought them both a water. "How are they?" he asked.

"They're all gonna pull through," Simon said, shoulders sagged, expression hollow. Rene' stuck beside him as if she were freezing and he was the only thing that warmed her. Her trust in Simon might make things messier, but just a few seconds of her being alone would be sufficient.

"The baby?" Jack asked Rene' slowly. Jack didn't often single out victims on any job. A man got too attached that way.

"She's a bit tiny and needs lots of nutrients, but she and Onya will be fine," Rene' said after finishing her water. Her hands shook and her legs buckled slightly but she tried hiding it.

Simon firmly gripped her arm. "Let's go."

West stepped toward the cabins. "Jordan wanted us to do one repair to the second cabin before we left. Simon, Nate, do you mind helping? It'll only take a minute."

"You two can do it." Nate scowled.

"Dad did ask me, but…" Simon frowned. "I really need to get Rene' home."

"Fine." West headed to the cabin, hearing Rene' speak softly: "It's just a minute, Simon. I'll radio Dad. You go."

Nate and Simon came over to the second cabin, behind it, so the trucks were all out of sight and a considerable distance away. West picked up a hammer from the tool box waiting beside some old boards. "We gotta replace this plywood. Just gonna take a second."

"This isn't a cabin, it's a shack," Nate mumbled, staring at the gaping hole in the wall. They set to work quickly, but West knew it was too late. Once the job was finished, they headed back to the vehicles with zeal in their weary steps, but Simon froze in his tracks.

Jack lay sprawled out near the van, blood running from his temple, Glock in his hand though there'd been no gunshot.

Rene' was gone like dust in the warm summer breeze. No sign of her anywhere.

Simon darted over, panic in his eyes. "Rene'?" he called, over and over.

Nate picked up the radio lying in the cab seat. "She was *just* here!"

West dropped beside Jack and lifted him up, trying to wake him. *Oh, really, Gideon, you make a good scene.* The blow hadn't been much more than a knock-out blow, but there was a sleeping dart in Jack's neck.

"What happened?" Simon snarled. "Where's Rene'?"

"They drugged Jack. They must've drugged Rene', too, so we didn't hear anything." West shoved Jack into his truck, situating him quickly so he didn't flop about like a fish.

Simon ran for the woods but Nate grabbed his arm. "They're gone. They've got an escape route and you getting lost in the forest ain't gonna help."

Simon shook him off, knocking Nate off balance. "We have to find her! Who would take her and not *anyone* else? She's a nobody!"

West'd never seen the young man quite so furious and desperate before. "We'll find her," he said quickly. "You put that tracking chip in her shoe on the way here, remember?"

Simon ran to the van and dug around in a duffel bag. Retrieving the tracker, he turned it on, waited. After a long moment, he called: "She's moving west!"

"Let's go," West slammed the door shut on Jack's limp body. *Lord, if You're real, forgive me.*

FIFTEEN

JULY 29TH, 2027

RENE'S SKIN BURNED LIKE SHE was a bug under a microscope death ray. Her pounding head didn't allow her to open her eyes for a while, but when she did, all she saw was a dark room with one large light to her left. Where was the heat coming from? Sweat poured from her temples and she vaguely noticed she was mostly naked. But all she cared about was making the pain in her blood stop. She jerked but straps around her wrists, ankles, and torso bit into her skin.

Calm. Stay calm. Even if she couldn't see straight or think right.

"The poison will keep you disabled for a while." A man's voice, rough and hard like gravel. Rene' turned her head painfully to see a man near the door. His dark brown hair was overdue for a trim, and his smile was tight. "Hello, dear."

Rene' shivered. Her heart pounded like a thousand horses ran around in her chest. "Wh—"

"Don't bother asking stupid questions. I'm not telling you where you are or who I am." He stepped to a small metal table.

Rene's vision blurred in and out, making it difficult to take in details.

"Why?" She didn't put much thought into that one little word, it just came out.

The man chuckled. "That's a question I *can* answer." He picked up a small knife from the tray that stood nearby and ran a finger over the blade lightly. "Brian Jones did some bad things, and I'm out to settle the score. Petty sounding, huh? It's not my battle, but Brian's a good Union soldier and my boss doesn't like hotheads much. He thinks the war won't be won by Union warriors, and Brian's gone too far... But enough of that, you won't remember any of this..."

Rene' shivered on the metal table. *What is he talking about?* She tried hard to understand what was happening but couldn't focus.

It might be another nightmare...

He came over and cupped her chin. "You are prettier than the files show you to be."

"Brian?" Rene' repeated weakly. She couldn't get her mouth to work! *The poison...* Where was Simon and the others? What had happened? Who'd taken her? Who was this man?

And why does Brian have anything to do with this? He hates my family. He left us!

"Yes. There's nothing else you need to know, dear, and I promise, I won't rape you. Spencer out there," he gestured to the door, "agreed for no payment if he had you all to himself, and I'm nothing if not a businessman, yeah?" His eyes shining with dark mirth. "Hold still and this will go much better."

"N-no—" Rene' struggled as hard as she could to no avail. She could hardly breathe.

"Don't fight. It's a terrible trait to have in a woman." Jed traced a small cut on Rene's thigh.

Rene' cried out. "Go to hell!" Tears ran down her face and she begged God for mercy, but her mind was like a hamster in a wheel, spinning out of control. Her chest contracted tighter. Tighter. Tighter.

"Oh, hush, child." Jed cut another line and Rene' tried to break free but could barely move.

"Brian won't... won't care..." Rene' fought the sobs tearing from her throat. How pathetic was she? Weeping like a baby when she should be bold like a lion in the face of danger. Maybe it was the poison messing with her.

"You cannot convince me to release you, and there's nothing you know that I don't." His voice grew distant. Fuzzy.

Another cut. She felt it like it was a gash over her heart.

"Brian won't save you, and that is exactly my point."

Darkness and burning agony engulfed her. Nightmares plagued her like claws penetrating her spirit and ripping her apart from the inside out. *Trapped on the table, watching Brian and Kelsey stand by with grim expressions, but they did nothing when she cried out for them. They laughed when she begged God to save her. The pain didn't stop and Rene' couldn't face it. She couldn't even hold onto reality. Couldn't wake up.*

Lord, help me!

Have faith.

I can't do this, it hurts! Everything hurts!

Be bold.

I need... Dad. Simon. Lee. Sean. Anyone. Just make Brian and Kelsey stop. Make them stop watching.

The nightmares shifted constantly. *She was standing in the horse pasture, but the horses fled in a panic. Screams filled her ears, the screams of her family, and she fled to the treelines across the fields. Fire fell from the sky. She couldn't understand the flames, but the fear in her heart was something she understood. Her town was losing, the war had arrived at their front door, and she was helpless. As always.*

SIXTEEN

JULY 29TH, 2027

TIME HARDLY EXISTED, YET IT meant everything. Simon radioed Mr. Fisher immediately, telling him they were tracking Rene', while Nate called for the Vets. The Vets were AJ's band of merry men who looked for fights where they were required. Now was one of those fights where they were desperately needed.

Simon cut off contact with Mr. Fisher to give his full attention to tracking the chip. However, fifteen minutes later, the signal died. Simon swore.

"What happened?" Nate demanded, driving steadily onward. "Lost the signal. Someone must've found it and killed it. Who would've known to look for the tiny little thing? It can't be a sloppy kidnapping, Nate, this is serious. But how? Why?" Nate didn't speak.

"I can't call Mr. Fisher back and say we lost the signal. He'll lose his mind. We have to find her." Simon rattled on, heart hammering as he tried to get the chip to send off waves again but of course, it was hopeless. So he tried to think. Using the phone on Rene' was a pointless shot, but he dialed the number.

It didn't even ring.

"Si, it's clear we have no contact," Nate said calmly. "And we've got no eyes in the sky."

"West might have a helicam in their truck." Simon radioed them.

"Sorry, Simon, I don't." Jack answered the radio and spoke quietly. "We're already an hour behind, and in these woods and roads, they could be anywhere."

"What do we do then?" Nate snarled, grabbing the radio. "You two are the professionals. Are you just going to doomsay?" His rage radiated from his whole body and Simon knew better than to interfere. Obviously, Nate would fight for Rene', too, and when it came to dealing with Jack, he could handle it.

"We have to work together." Jack stayed cool. "We already have guys coming to help search. They owe favors."

"Guys on the ground isn't gonna do anything!"

Simon interjected. "We have no way of getting a location! We need to set someone up on the main roads—maybe where the highways are for the caravans?" He paused. "But only a pro would've found the chip, and pros won't be traveling in the open or in a group." It was an educated guess, anyway.

"Ah…" Jack said slowly. "That info narrows it down. We'll try to make some possible routes…" He hesitated briefly and in that moment, Simon could sense every doubt or fiber of common sense running through Jack's head, but he refused to doubt for a moment. They'd find Rene', even if it was absolutely impossible and every odd stood against them.

If he couldn't do this, what kind of gangster was he? What kind of friend? *Lord, guide us and keep her safe. If You care about her, prove it, please.*

"All right. I'll call Alex." Simon hung up, dialing Alex's number by memory. Alex was amazing at tracking, hacking— anything involving this kind of thing. Simon needed his help now more than ever. As soon as Alex answered, Simon calmly told him what was going on—or, he tried to be calm; he didn't know if he was.

"We have no idea who took her?" Alex asked quietly.

At least he doesn't sound hopeless. "No. I mean, it seems professional, but they didn't take anyone else valuable or dangerous." If anyone was in danger of being taken, it would've been him or Nate. Anyone but Rene', who was just a nobody from a tiny speck on the map with no history that wrapped her up in the demise of the nation.

"Right…" Alex agreed. "I'll see if I have any towers

near your location, if they ping images in real time, I can find them. At least see what kind of vehicle it is." Alex had access to many towers all over the US—usually, they loomed over heavily trafficked areas, but Alex installed a few in more desolate areas— like around Jordan's underground locations. He was the kinda dude who kept his all-seeing eyes out on the people who needed extra help.

"Thank you. Can I help?"

"You guys just keep driving. There's no other road out of Busch except the one you're on—it goes West for—"

"Eighteen miles and then it splits." Simon tried to hide his panic.

"We'll find her, Simon. The tower is at the split," Alex assured him, always the one to give hope and guidance.

"If they're pros and saw the tower, they might be equipped to go off road," Simon argued.

"We can't know yet."

Simon didn't want to hear that. *I gotta have faith we'll find her. I'll do whatever it takes. I promised I'd bring her home. I just need a lead to follow and I can't do that alone.*

I can't lose her, Lord, she means too much… Help me get her home… show me what to do. Show us how to find her. Praying felt strange somehow. Instead of weakening his spirit, or feeling like a fool, his heart grew stronger with determination like he'd yelled a battlecry.

SEVENTEEN

JULY 30TH, 2027

RENE' WOKE UP WITH A violent jerk. *It was so real... I could feel it all... Hear my parents cry... see the... No.* She couldn't think about it. It was just a nightmare. Her family was alive. *They have to be.*

Wretching weakly, unable to move because of her binds, she clamped her eyes shut. She didn't want to be unconscious anymore. Whatever reality held, whatever the man wanted her for, it couldn't be worse than what she saw when she closed her eyes. It couldn't be worse than the poison boiling her blood.

"Easy, kid, easy." Another voice, far more gentle than the other man's voice. "I'm Spencer. Simon told you about me, right?" He whispered but he sounded close.

Rene' grimaced when a rag wiped over her mouth. *Spencer... Spencer Anderson... that bigmouth Yankee...*

What's he… doing here? Able to think only slightly clearer, she couldn't get her tongue to cooperate as well and only managed opening her eyes.

"You can't talk just yet but that's OK. The poison's pretty bad, but you listen, yeah?" Spencer offered a weak smile, his expression tight.

Hadn't the man said something about Spencer… about… the payment? He's here to rape me? Rene's heart pounded hard but she couldn't move. Defenseless. Powerless. *Think. He isn't hurting you yet, he's talking, so stop being afraid!*

"No one can see us or hear us right now, so listen close, Rene'. You're gonna get out of here. You just have to hold on. I'm gonna patch you up, so just hold still, yeah?" As he spoke, he opened a first aid kit, but he didn't stop talking in a low, comforting voice. It made Rene's head swim to focus on his words, and she couldn't watch him for long before the light from the left blinded her so she shut her eyes tight again.

"D-dad…?" she choked.

"Not Dad," Spencer said gently. "But someone else will come." He didn't give a name. Rene' prayed it was Simon.

"Brian…" Rene' licked her lips. Her throat was dry like a desert and every swallow burned.

"Oh, sorry, here." Spencer held her head up slightly, holding a water bottle to her lips. She drank gratefully and tried not to flinch at his touch. "It's OK… They only wanted to ruffle Brian's feathers, but you'll be just fine. Hey, you're a Confed, right? I'm a Yankee, but I like the Confed side. That's our little secret," he spoke gently.

Simon said he was a friend. A friend. So stop crying... be strong... She opened her eyes again and gave her body one last look. Seeing the blood trickle from her legs and stomach wounds made her sick. She groaned involuntarily, a sob choking her again. *Be strong... It's over... isn't it?* The torture had to be over. She couldn't take anymore. She wanted *home*. But what would her family say when they saw her like this? What would they do? *How bad am I...* She glanced down weakly, head swirling.

"Nonono, don't look," Spencer whispered. "Don't look, kid. It makes it worse. Trust me."

Rene' shivered and closed her eyes. *Breathe.* In and out. In, out. In, out. *Like Dad taught you to do when you practice self defense.*

"You're just fine," Spencer continued. She clung to the sound of his voice merely to keep herself tethered to reality, and she couldn't hold on alone. Alone, the pain stole her entire existence until she was nothing left but a storming cloud of redness and blackness, a scream in the dark, a pile of dust in the desert. Alone, she was dead. A goner.

But as long as she could hear the Voice in her spirit

telling her exhausted heart to continue beating, she'd survive. As long as she heard Spencer talk like she would be all right, and see her family again, she could survive.

And then silence. Brief silence that almost brought Rene' to tears. "K-keep talking, please," she rasped.

Spencer had finished the wound on her stomach and started on the cuts along her thighs, but strangely, the pain grew numb.

"The painkillers in your water should be kicking in by now," Spencer said softly. "I only have a short time left."

"Why?" Rene' whispered. "That man…" She could hardly talk but questions pounded around in her mind.

"He's Jed. Your brother Brian has bad blood with someone he works for. They knows Brian won't reply to the video footage of you, but it's kinda a warning. He won't kill you, he just wanted to show Brian what he could do, and he'll go after Brian's wife and kids later, if Brian doesn't stop playing hero…" Spencer spoke hastily but somberly. "Not that… you need to know that. It doesn't matter yet. You did just fine, kid."

She'd never had anyone call her kid before. For some reason, it offered a strange sense of comfort, too. It made her feel less like a failure, bleeding out behind her bonds. It made her feel more like a survivor. Somehow.

She took a slow, pained breath. Of all the questions

she had—*who took me? Where am I? Is my family OK?*—she couldn't force them. "Brian… he's been gone a long time." She could barely hear her own voice. "He left. We didn't even know if he was alive… He'd never come for me." A sob died on her lips. Tears ran down her cheeks, but she hardly felt them.

"Shhh, kid. You don't have to talk about it. Don't think about it, either, just focus on something else. You don't need to go into any more shock than you already are. Think about your family. About Simon." Spencer's voice brought her back to reality again. The pain in her body numbed. She couldn't move a single part of her body, but it was better than agony.

"Talk…" she asked softly.

"I can definitely do that, kid…" And so he did. Until his time was up, he told her little stories about Simon and Nate when they were younger, as fast and as brief as he could. Rene' listened about Simon and Nate learning to drive cars, about them pulling all-nighters together in haunted houses, about accidentally shooting themselves with BB guns.

Spencer finished cleaning Rene' up, grimacing. "I'm… really sorry, kid. I swear I didn't, uh, pay much attention…" He'd put his coat over her but had to patch her wounds up, regardless of trying to be modest.

"Thank you." It was all she could manage.

"I'll see you, kid."

Recalling Spencer's story of how Simon set a bar on fire helped the pain more than imagining Springtown, and the winding word roads, and the towering oak trees near the courthouse, and the suburbs of kind civilians, and the warm summer sun pounding on their backs as they readied summer crops. She tried to block out the yearning for home, every little detail that lay etched in her brain, and failed.

EIGHTEEN

JULY 30TH, 2027

THE JOB WAS ALMOST OVER. Gideon had done far worse, but this job hadn't come easy for him, and especially not to Alex. What pained Alex worse was the fact he'd lied to Simon about catching images of the thieves.

"Nothing," he'd said. "They must've had another route." Suffice to say, Simon and Nate had no idea Rene' was with Gideon and Alex, and the boys were still looking. Their goose chase wouldn't last long. Just long enough for Jed to finish his business.

Jed hadn't taken long, either—two hours tops before he left Rene's room. Gideon had video footage of Jed's torture session and sent it to Brian's contact number Jed gave him, along with Jed's note: *"Worse will be done to Alyssa and the children if you do not follow orders from the UN."* He referenced the UN's constant protection of men like Jed—the smugglers, traders, traffickers, con-men, liars, and gangsters who kept the nations running. A soldier sticking his nose where it didn't belong wasn't tolerable. Jed could take care of such nuisances himself without court martials if he was bid to. And he'd just been bid and pulled the job off flawlessly, with Gideon and Alex's help.

Whoever was paying Jed probably wouldn't stop until the Jones' family was dead. Gideon doubted Brian would react to the video of his baby sister tethered, bleeding, and screaming. Brian was too cold. Such a sight was his *job*. Blood kin undergoing that agony wouldn't push him to anger or revenge. It would make him angry that anyone dared tried to order him around, but not make him grieve for Rene'.

Gideon would know. He'd worked with Brian for too long.

Brian did not reply to the footage. Jed laughed when he heard but wasn't surprised. "A pity," he paused a moment. "Well, I'll bid Rene' goodbye and part ways."

Once he was downstairs in the basement, Gideon eyed Spencer coolly. "Did you call them?" he mouthed.

"They're on the way," Spencer mouthed so only Gideon could read his lips.

Gideon took a slow breath and texted Alex, who was waiting outside of the cabin in godforsaken nowhere. "Why care about her?" he asked Spencer quietly. "You aren't one to drop a deal out of the kindness of your

193

heart." Spencer was the opposite. He wasn't a coward, but his need and love for possessions and money got to his mind.

Spencer scowled, eyebrows furrowed as he crossed his large arms. "I'd say the same for you, Cold Eyes."

"We have our reasons." *My reasons are not solely saving a girl. There's logic to them, too, a necessity to it all. I must maintain alliance with Brian. He told me to allow this to happen, and to him, it'll look like I am. But I didn't just let this girl get tortured for nothing. She'll go home.*

"I have a whole group of brothers who would drag my sorry hide out of trouble. Bo, Nabeel, and I were really in trouble, even you and Alex. But this girl didn't have a chance if she was only counting on Brian," Spencer finally whispered. "It's not out of kindness or pity. I'm just sick of people being left behind, and she means too much to Simon."

"Good reasons, charm-boy." Gideon headed to the hall. He understood Spencer's reasoning. Rene' might have a father, a brother, and a family and town who would go through hell for her, but having your older brother not lift a finger to save you? Gideon understood what that was like. He'd taken his chance to give Rene' a shot at life, and she'd take it because of the ones who loved her, but what Brian had done would haunt her. Gideon knew what that was like, too.

"What are your reasons?" Spencer never dropped

anything, even when he should, and it's why no one liked him. Besides his brothers and the men he conned into liking him.

"Let's say they're the same." Gideon went to the basement, steps silent. "Jed? Would you like me to leave her here or drop her off somewhere?"

"Oh, no, do as you will with her. Brian won't care so I don't, either." Jed stepped back, putting away a small needle into his pocket.

Gideon frowned. *He poisoned her?* "Yessir."

Jed headed to the door, smiling wide like he'd just won the lottery. "Torture isn't quite as good as some guilty pleasures, but it was nice tonight, hm? I'll see you gentlemen." Jed left the cabin.

Gideon peeked out the window, but the man disappeared down the road fast. Gideon let Alex in through the back.

"If we leave, they'll be here and never know we—" Gideon started, but Alex cut him off.

"We're telling them what we did, Gideon. That's final." For a spy, he disliked keeping secrets from people he trusted.

"Fine." Gideon watched Spencer go down to the basement with a large blanket he'd snatched from a closet bin.

"Simon and Nate'll understand." Alex feigned hope.

"We're not getting near her father," Gideon

muttered without meeting Alex's eyes, glancing at his wristwatch. It was growing late. He just wanted to be done with it all—he hated hearing Rene's screams play in his head, and he hated knowing he'd hurt the others. But he'd done his job, what needed to be done, and it could have gone a lot worse.

At least Gideon had helped Danny. Philip had gotten his little brother, Danny, back from Ed and Ty— though it had been mutual, a scene had to be shown so George would believe the Brooks had fought hard—and would be heading west soon. Gideon hadn't said goodbye to the boy. He didn't like goodbyes. He hoped Phil kept to the plan and moved fast.

Perhaps that was why he had so much pain in his chest. Even jobs well done hurt him. It wasn't always easy being Cold Eyes. Sometimes it was, however, like when he'd woven a whole cover story about Islamic extremists supposedly killing Danny, so Phil could take Danny and George thought it was some other group seeking revenge.

He steeled himself and went to the basement with a bottle of water full of electrolytes that Alex handed him from their duffel bag. "Spencer?"

"She's OK." Spencer's voice traveled softly from the basement. Spencer had cut her bonds, wrapped her in the blanket, and started carrying her upstairs. Gideon got out of the way quickly, following him to the cabin, but there was no furniture to place her on.

Spencer sat beside the door and rested Rene' nearby so she leaned against him. She wasn't responding. Spencer took the bottle from Gideon and put it against her mouth, but she didn't get much down before falling back.

Spencer frowned darkly. "She's… not doing well, Gideon."

"I think Jed poisoned her again." Gideon glanced at wideeyed, shamefaced Alex. "He took the evidence— we'll have no way of knowing if this is George's batches or something of Jed's own design." If it was George's, he could easily retrieve an antidote. If it belonged to Jed, they very well might lose her— assuming Jed didn't see a difference in her living or dying. He hadn't made it clear to Gideon: he didn't talk to Gideon much at all, since he feared Gideon more than he'd ever show, which was why George had orchestrated the job.

Rene' fell asleep and a small grunt of panic came from Spencer. "You guys talked to Simon and Nate on the radio, right?"

Gideon nodded silently. Alex had made the call and explained things the best he could, as much as it had broken his spirit.

"They'd better get here soon… She needs a cure, Gideon. What if it's not George's stuff?"

He obviously didn't want to hear the answer that she

might die, so Gideon thought for a moment. "I can run a blood test. It'll catch the bigger lethal poisons, if they're George's, and we'll go from there."

Alex stepped beside him before he even finished speaking, shoving one of the test kits at him. "Let's run it."

Gideon quickly took some blood from Rene's arm and ran it through the tester, which wasn't big, but ahead of its time. Most government soldiers had no use for identifying poisons, but gangsters did, and it wasn't a piece of equipment easily sought. It ran the test in a timely manner.

"Well?" Alex asked, leaning over to look at the screen. He disliked other people working jobs he could do himself, and he could do practically anything on a machine, but he hadn't wanted to jab Rene' with the needle when Gideon would.

"It's one of George's poisons," Gideon sighed. "A strand of a common one, but it's not in great supply. I don't have the antidote in the truck. But I have one at the cabin…"

"That's over nine hours away! We can't get it in time." Alex's face grew white as a sheet.

"The poison isn't fast acting. I'll call West and see if he has any." Gideon stood and took his phone out, dialing West. Alex paced along the living room floor and peeking out the window a million times.

Gideon got a hold of West and updated him on the situation. "Do you have an antidote for that? I can make the drive to my place for my antidote if I have to, but that's over half a day of driving."

"Can Ed get it and bring it to AJ's?"

"You're taking her to AJ's and not Springtown?" Gideon frowned.

"It's closest and safest. AJ and Mr. Fisher already worked it out," West said tightly.

"I'll call Ed," Gideon said. "You don't have any?"

"George destroyed most of my antidotes recently." West didn't say more, voice taut as if he struggled to hide emotion. "Understood. Keep us updated." Gideon hung up and called Ed. Ed agreed he'd gather the antidote from Gideon's cabin and would be at AJ's as fast as possible. Gideon gave him the address, hung up, and rubbed his face.

"Ed'll get it?" Spencer asked.

"Yes."

"Remind me to buy him a beer."

"He doesn't drink." Gideon joined Alex at the window, nudging him to stop looking out so much.

"Well, then a puppy." Spencer looked down at Rene', taking a shaky breath. "You're gonna be OK, kid."

Gideon didn't bother telling Spencer that the girl couldn't hear him. Spencer knew, he just talked to her anyway and there was no harm in that. It probably helped Spencer calm down, too, since he was deathly afraid of poisons. Gideon couldn't blame him, but Gideon didn't tremble before things he feared: he'd stopped doing that when he was eight years old. Back in the early 2000s, when he'd gone to the doctor with his father and had cried over being given a needle jab.

"Needles only hurt for a second," his father, Jeremy, said. "Be a big boy. It'll help you feel better."

"Are you scared of needles?" Gideon asked his father, who seemed invincible, like Batman, while Gideon shook in his seat. He didn't like doctors—they hadn't saved Mom—and he didn't like his father seeing his fear, either. His fear needed to be hidden. Deep, far from his mind.

"Used to be," Jeremy replied.

"Now?"

"I'm scared of other kinds of pain now, son, but everyone's scared of something. What matters is how you face that fear. That is what makes a man. And you're growing into a man quickly." His father squeezed his shoulder, tone serious. Gideon wasn't scared any longer.

Gideon wished things were that simple now. He wished he had someone offering him a comforting hand on his shoulder while he made countless decisions that jabbed him in the heart like a thousand needles. Such was life. *Such was war.*

"Gideon?" Alex rested a hand on Gideon's left

shoulder firmly. "They'll be here soon." Despite his comforting words, his own nerves showed heavy in his eyes.

Gideon paused a long moment. Squared his shoulders. Met Alex's gaze. "Let's finish it."

NINETEEN

JULY 30TH, 2027

COLDNESS DUG INTO RENE'S BONES like canine teeth. Farther, farther, farther. She whimpered, not hearing anything but the ringing in her ears and mind, like a jackhammer humming in her skull. As much as she tried to open her eyes, she couldn't. Once again, the pain took her entire existence and ripped away every shred of being she possessed.

Why can't I open my eyes?

Despite her greatest efforts to wake up, she was powerless to defeat the demons tearing at her spirit.

Cold hands around her neck. Claws slicing her skin. Screams of laughter from shadowy creatures hovering above her. Needles pricked her skin, over and over. When she opened her eyes, she was in a little room without windows or light, and flames of fire flooded from the corners. It came closer. Closer. Closer. She heard screams. Her family. Where were they? They sounded so scared. And hurt.

*Strangely, a window appeared in the wall, and Rene'
struggled to see. Her family fled outside and flames followed them.
The raging fires swept over the farmhouse, the barn, and the
fields—Rene' watched it all turn to ash as her family ran on.*

She had to reach them. She had to get free and go to them.

*She jerked. Cried out. Fire lapped at the metal table she was
strapped to. Binded, she couldn't move. Trapped. Dead.*

Dead.

*"Help me!" She screamed. Again and again, she screamed,
and hoped someone would hear her. "God, help me!"*

"Whoa, whoa, whoa, easy!" A firm voice pierced the
nightmare like a knife slicing through a veil of thorns.
"Easy, kid, wake up."

Rene' gasped for air, cheeks stinging with hot tears.
It took a long moment for her eyes to adjust to the light.
She shivered against someone—who?

"Hey, it's just me, Spencer, remember? Simon'll be
here soon." Spencer frowned down at her like she'd
been screaming. Had she screamed?

Rene' tried moving, but her head lolled against
Spencer's arm. Her thoughts jumbled. *Simon? He's… he's
coming… and Daddy, too?*

"Here, drink some." Spencer's voice penetrated her
mind again. He held a bottle against her lips, and she
drank but choked on it. "Sorry…" Spencer wiped her
mouth quickly.

"What… what's wrong with me?" Finally, her tongue worked!

He paused. That pause scared her.

"It'll be fine, Rene'." Spencer pulled the blanket around her snuggly.

She shivered but kept her eyes open, fighting off sleep. She couldn't face the nightmares again. "I-it isn't. I feel… terrible."

"It'll be fine," he repeated. "I've got good news, kid. I got word that some of the Confeds made their way into Florida," he whispered. "Your team's been busy! That's great, right? My team, well, we gangsters just work for the highest bidder."

Rene' sucked in a breath. If she was home, the pain would all stop. She'd be safe. She'd be all right.

But she wasn't home. Agony coursed through her body. Her mind scattered in dark, jagged pieces. And she couldn't hear God's comforting voice.

She fell asleep, crying from pain and wishing someone would take her home, but Spencer's voice comforted her a little.

TWENTY

JULY 30TH, 2027

JED'S CABIN NESTED IN A speck of trees about two miles from the empty highway. Nothing too top-secret or threatening. Jed didn't care if nomads came along and rested there a while before continuing their journeys through the US, so the place was barren and ugly.

Nate parked near Alex's truck. Simon jumped out before the vehicle stopped completely and ran for the front door. *She has to be alive. She has to be.* He practically dove through the unlocked door, looking around and utterly ignoring Gideon and Alex. His eyes landed on Rene'—she lay on the floor beside Spencer, wrapped in a blanket.

Simon dropped onto the floor and cupped her face. "Rene'?" he whispered. "Rene', can you hear me?"

"She can't hear you," Spencer said quietly, not lifting his head as if a dog who expected a beating for something he'd done wrong.

"She's poisoned?" Simon stroked Rene's sweaty hair, rage rising inside of his chest like a lion clawing through a cage. "You guys said she was OK!"

"Ed is retrieving the antidote, he'll meet us at AJ's." Gideon kept his distance and eyed Nate wearily as he came in. Nate scowled at him and Alex, fists clenched which made Alex step back instinctively.

West and Jake came to the door but didn't come inside. "Gideon?" Jack asked. "Can we talk for a minute?"

Simon carefully lifted Rene' into his arms. Her ragged breathing sent shivers down his spine. *She's in so much pain. This isn't right. She shouldn't be hurt.* He carried her outside, keeping her head against his chest.

Nate followed him outside, keys in hand. "Let's go."

Simon placed Rene' in the front seat of the van where he could hold her.

"Is there anything I can do to help?" Spencer asked quietly.

He stood right behind Simon but Simon hadn't noticed.

"No," Nate snapped.

"Nathan, Spencer helped her." Simon cast him a calm look.

"This is also all of their fault!" Nate gestured at Gideon, who spoke quietly with Jack and West without noticing Nate's furious gaze.

"No, this is Jed's fault." Simon smoothed Rene's hair gently again, his voice tight with rage, but he wouldn't explode. He'd fix this quietly, so no one would ever expect it was him when Jedidiah showed up dead in his own bathroom with his brains blown out.

Nate got into the truck and cranked it without another word. The most important thing was getting Rene' home safe. Revenge and blame could wait.

Spencer stepped back. "Call me if you need me." Pain weighed like a mountain in his voice.

Simon got in and held Rene' as Nate started driving without so much as a glance behind them. Rene' moaned in her sleep and curled up against Simon's chest. He knew she couldn't hear him, but he comforted her. "We're going home, soon, Rene'. We're gonna go to AJ's first. We're getting you the antidote. It'll be just fine, Rene'... Your Dad will be there."

Rene's eyes fluttered open. "You came," she choked weakly.

Did that surprise her? "Of course I did. I promised you I'd take care of you."

Rene' closed her eyes again. "It hurts." Her body trembled and her voice broke, all her strength to fight slipping away. What had Jed done? What had he told her? Simon didn't know what Rene' had faced, but he knew he had failed her, and he couldn't let that happen ever again.

Simon would help her fight or at least carry her to the finish line. She was broken, in body and spirit, and it broke Simon, too, like someone set his heart on fire. He kissed her forehead. He'd be strong, for her, and get her home—she'd survived this far and he would protect her now.

"It'll be all right, Rene'. You just hold on. I'm gonna take care of you. Don't worry about a thing." He held her closer, praying her shivering would stop if he could warm her up, but that wasn't how poison worked. Until they got the antidote, there really wasn't a thing he could do to stop her pain and comforting her was most likely in vain. He did it anyway.

"The nightmares…" she mumbled. Though she said nothing more, Simon understood. The nightmares were worse than the pain. With a sound mind, a person could withstand physical agony. With a broken mind, there was no reason to fight.

"You just listen to my voice," Simon whispered, keeping her face close to his so his voice would frighten off the demons running around in her head. He wiped the tears from her hot cheeks.

And he prayed. He prayed like never before while he told her the same things she used to tell him—promises God had made to His children. He spoke them because, while he wasn't a Christian, the other pointless, comforting lies would hold no strength for Rene'. He had to give her spirit a reason to fight. What better way to do that than to call upon the Lord she loved?

AJ AND HIS BIKER GANG of Vets lived hours away from Springtown. They used to live on the Alabama state line, back when Nate first met them, but that'd changed after their homes were burned down. The gang of old men had nothing left to lose in life. That made them dangerous. They had fun scaring thugs, killing bad men, and saving innocents. Even George Johnston hadn't killed all of them.

Nate had run into AJ as a fifteen-year-old, speeding around in his brand new race car Kaleb stole for him. Nate tore that dirt road up for hours, fuming his anger through racing. He raced to survive, bask in freedom for a time, be alone.

That night, his freedom was jarred by a group of bikers camping near the road.

Like a total fool who had too much dark rage burning in his chest to think straight, Nate lit some bottle bombs and threw them at the bikers as he sped past. It was just for fun. Just to have some power over someone else, after hours of being the one learning his place in the hands of Kaleb.

To say the prank backfired was a cruel understatement.

All he remembered after that was taking a left turn

and hitting a ditch, crashing his car into a tree. When he woke up, he was in a foreign room with a strange, older man frowning down at him. His injuries were patched up and the old man, AJ, had smiled and said: "I need to teach you how to use that wrist of yours better, sonny. You didn't hit any of us."

Nate smirked when he recalled that time. It'd been rather terrifying, facing the man he'd tried harming, but AJ had grown into more of a father figure than Kaleb had ever been.

Nate brought his attention back to reality, parking the van outside of AJ's tiny house that stood strong, even if it was ancient. It was just like the last time Nate'd seen it. He helped Simon get Rene' out.

West and Jack parked nearby. They'd followed them after their conversation with Gideon and Alex was over. Nate hadn't radioed a single word for the whole drive. His anger toward them all burned hotter than he could control. It was best to focus on the matters at hand or else he'd regret his actions.

AJ stood on the front porch, guiding them inside. "Your old room, Nate. It's all ready for her." His button-up, short-sleeved shirt was wrinkled and his glasses perched on the bridge of his nose—a picture-perfect example of a man who could deduce far too much in the matter of seconds they'd been there.

Nate followed Simon into the room. Though the

bed lay waiting for Rene', and a bowl of water and rags sat on the table, the room hadn't changed much since the last time Nate had seen it. Bare and yet cozy at the same time. Just how Nate liked it— no emotional material possessions, but the room meant more to Nate than memorabilia ever could.

Simon tucked Rene' into the bed with a sheet. "Her fever's erratic."

"Keep her cool." AJ stood in the doorway. "Jack radioed me about what needs to be done. The fever won't become regular, and she'll get hot and cold, but it's best to keep her temperature low."

Simon dampened the rags and placed them on Rene's forehead and neck. "Yessir."

Nate turned on the little fan nearby. He wished there was more he could do. Something to focus on besides Rene's pain. Twiddling his thumbs in wait wasn't something he did.

He left the room and went outside. West and Jack stood on the porch, both sweating from the summer humidity. West spoke into his phone urgently like the world was tumbling down. Nate listened in without meeting Jack's concerned gaze.

"What do you mean the antidote is gone?" West asked. "It has to be there!"

"Unless George took it?" Jack suggested.

West's face paled a few shades. "Abort the job, Ed.

ANGELA R. WATTS

We'll have to go find George for the antidote." He hung up.

Every fiber in Nate's body tingled with rage. "We don't have the antidote?"

"George must've taken it from Gideon's place, same as mine. It can't be a coincidence at this point. George knew I'd help you guys, even if he never breathed a word about this mess to me directly." West didn't meet Nate's gaze, running a hand through his shoulder-length brown hair. "I don't understand why. She means nothing to me. Why test me?"

"Well, she means something to *us*!" Nate swore. "We need that antidote *now*. If you big boys can't do it, I'll do it myself." He could call Kaleb—there might be a chance he had the same kind of antidote. *I'll have to admit that Simon and I know Rene'. Everything would be ruined if Kaleb finds out... Assuming none of them already know... Wait.*

West opened his mouth but Nate lifted a hand. "If George has the slightest clue about you guys helping Rene', what if he knows about Si and me?" Nate's head swam like a flopping fish. "If George is testing you with Rene', he's gotta guess it means something to you, but it doesn't, so why?"

"I don't know," West answered honestly. "I didn't know a thing about you guys in Springtown. He'd have no reason to believe I did. If this is any kind of test, it would be for you and Simon—teaching you a lesson for helping and keeping secrets, but it can't be."

"Not that we can tell," Nate corrected sharply. "What if this isn't for you?" *What if George found out? What if he's gonna punish Simon and I? Or blow Springtown to smithereens, just because they tried to survive and we dared to help?*

"It has to be for me." West frowned. "Even if George knew about you guys, he'd have to assume I was in on it, too. He took *my* antidote for this poison, remember? This is my test."

"No!" Nate insisted, clenching his fists. "What do you two always do when we get into too much trouble, huh?"

A pause. Neither wanted to speak but Jack answered slowly, "Help you?" He might've doubted the answer, since Nate never considered their interference to be valuable help.

"Exactly." Nate nodded. "So if you guys always help us, George would've known you'd help us *now*, too."

"That's assuming he—" Jack started, but Nate stopped him once again, like a bull on the run.

"Yeah, it's *assuming* he knows, because he knows everything! Don't tell me he doesn't."

West stepped closer. "You think this is a test for *all* of us? If George has known, he could've just sent guys to Springtown to end it."

"He likes games," Nate hissed. "You know it better than anyone."

West's Adam's apple bobbed. "He doesn't always."

"Right now, he has four prodigies in his hands. Me, Jack, you, and Simon. We're the sons of some of the most powerful ganglords out there. Why destroy what we're doing when he can play with us? Show us we can't do it all without his guidance? Why not play with us?" Nate asked coldly.

"We don't have proof," Jack snapped. "Sure, it might be true, but he hasn't taken action yet on any of us."

"Let's focus on getting the antidote," West said calmly. "We'll go to him and get some answers."

Nate crossed his arms tightly, heart hammering. He wanted to kill someone—had he missed the obvious? Had George known all along? Had George created some grand scheme to destroy all of them? Or was this happenstance only, and George only found out recently that Rene' was connected to them? Nate had no way of knowing, and not knowing was enough to drive a man to violence. It didn't take much to drive Nate Savage to violence to begin with. *Whatever George is doing, whatever is going on, we can't lose this fight. I won't lose.*

TWENTY-ONE

JULY 31ST 2027

"IT'S A SHAME TO LOSE your own son to the world you created."

George grabbed another beer from his fridge in the warehouse bar. He preferred stronger alcohols, but since his son and his little band of merry men would arrive at the warehouse location he'd text them in, oh, two hours, he didn't want to be drunk.

Guns sighed and took a long sip of his bourbon. Unlike George, he wouldn't be there for the visit and didn't mind getting drunk. George knew the man thrived off it. No soul could say it was his downfall because he'd survived a long, long time. Guns thrived, too, in the military and out, as a gangster and as a politician. These facts were why George liked him so much since they were young.

Times changes and much of that change came from

George and Guns. Men like them couldn't be stopped.

"I know better than you that the world you create can bite back," Guns muttered haughtily.

George scoffed. "It's hardly a competition. Your son should've left the Navy and you know it. Not your fault he's gone."

"I'm in no mood to talk about such things tonight, George."

"Well, I am." George sat down on a bar stool. He couldn't lose his son. Deep in his soul, he knew that. Adopting Daniel Dunnham was a simple second plan, in case West died and George needed a new heir to his legacy. While he loved the skinny, angry boy with all his heart, Danny he wasn't West. He wasn't his own flesh and blood.

Now, Danny was gone. Kidnapped by some Islamic extremist who sent George evidence of the boy being slaughtered. George sent assassins after the killer, but it didn't change the fact that Danny had been taken from Ed and Ty Brooks, and that Gideon had been in charge of the boy's safety. It was a matter George disliked having to deal with—but he would. He would deal with the matters he created because they were small issues compared to others.

West was George's only son and he could not lose him to the world he'd created. *My son will lead this world.* George simply needed to keep pushing him forward on the correct path. West was everything to George—unlike Danny, who was an unfortunate loss, but George knew how to deal with mere losses.

Being a father was far harder than being a politician, businessmen, or ganglord. He could kill innocents without a second thought. The idea of West going to sleep at night with no trust for George, when all George did was for him, made his stomach twist. Every torture session was a step closer in their bond—father and son, teacher and student, legend and prodigy. It was not about fearing West into submission. It was about molding his mind into what it must be.

Guns leaned against the counter, eyeing his glass. The silence must've gone on long enough because he smirked. "For a chatty man, you've been awfully silent."

"Thinking, as always."

"Well, I have no reason to stay if you're just grinding gears."

"I can't wait to see his face…" George sipped his beer slowly, savoring the taste on his tongue.

"You torture that boy too much." Guns laughed jokingly. "You know that he'll be cautious. He knows a test when he sees one, as he should."

"This is a bit more than that. Simon and Nate'll learn their lesson, too. It's satisfactory, having so many ducks lined up. I gave Gideon, Alex, and Spencer a job, and the others rise to the occasion? How could I resist some fun?" George smirked. *It's a priceless chance.*

"You knew they'd kidnap Rene' through Nate and Simon?" Guns asked dryly.

"It was a mere hunch. I didn't base any plans on that option," George scoffed.

"So, you not only watched those two young men work for the town—"

"You're the one who said Springtown was off limits, my friend, and I'm a man of my word."

"—and you plan on scaring them, but you know it will end in a rebellion with bloodshed." Guns' cold eyes pierced through George. "I think you should explain, brother."

George hated that nickname. George had only one blood brother, Richard, although he'd worn out that terms years before; Richard, the elder, no longer recognized George as a brother. As far as George cared, he was a brother to no one.

"Oh? You wouldn't prefer to let me drink in silence?"

Guns didn't look away or respond. Well, George would give him answers, since it wouldn't hurt and Guns was the only man he truly trusted.

"Let's see." George thought for a long moment, just so he got that usual grunt of annoyance from Guns. "I know Nate and Simon will fight back, but Kaleb agrees that it is past time those boys learn their place. Once this is over, Kaleb will have Nate take his role as Kaleb's right-hand. The same for Jordan and Simon. Those boys have played rogues for long enough. This situation is a reminder of where they belong. They do not belong in a civilian town." George cut Guns a look. "You disagree?"

Guns shook his head. "I never said I wanted the town to survive—I said it was off limits. That's not such a ridiculous rule."

George chuckled. "I see. Anyway, it is a challenge for West, but a lesson for the boys, as well. They're not my sons, so I will not punish them. That is Jordan and Kaleb's job." He waved a hand and set his beer down with a sigh of contentment.

"West is your son, and he had nothing to do with the kidnapping or the supply freights. His attention is very keen on the war." Guns cocked his head. "Like I said, you're too hard on him." Another wicked gleam came to his eyes. As if he were one to speak about being too harsh to one's son.

George laughed heartily and patted him on the back. "Where would I be without our silly conversations, friend?"

"You would be dead without me." Guns lifted his glass and George held his bottle to the toast.

"You cocky cuss!" George laughed again.

"So, another test for your son…" Guns didn't waver from the topic. He never did waver or yield. That was the annoying thing about a military man, but George could usually overlook it, since it paid off many times.

"He must learn bad things happen without him causing them," George smiled. "Such as losing a brother he cares too deeply for."

"A murder?"

"Oh, you sound so hungry for one."

"You usually make them something to hunger for." Guns poured himself another glass of bourbon and downed it in one gulp.

"I do," George chuckled. "We have time left before they come for the antidote for the brat."

"I'm listening."

Once George finished telling Guns his plan, Guns stood up steadily. Guns mumbled, "You'll brand Gideon?"

"It is a bond he *deserves* by now, Guns. The loss of Danny is unfortunate, but his victories triumph it. I trust him, he belongs to me, and once word gets out he failed to keep Danny alive, they might lose respect... It is not the final test, but it's the first step to that kind of respect. He has an important role in this war, and I want him with me." George eyed him darkly. "Don't tell me you're concerned about it?"

Guns set his glass down, the muscles in his weathered, stern jaw tightening. "Make the cold-eyed brute scream." He left the warehouse after pulling up his stiff coat collar.

TWENTY-TWO

JULY 31ST, 2027

WEST LED THE BROOKS BROTHERS and Spencer toward the address George had sent. Jack didn't say much during the drive. West knew it was because of what had happened and what was yet to happen with George. Jack worried too much about everything. Perhaps that's what a leader did. In West's case, there was a fine line between overthinking and thinking the correct amount. If anyone could understand his father's motives, it was him, but if he let his imagination run rampant, that wasn't much help, either.

He turned his vehicle onto a small trail that curved for over fifteen miles into the North Carolina wilderness. They still had a chance of reaching AJ's in time.

The location was an old HQ ground that George had conquered from some little militia of civilians. The wooden cabins, rushing river, and dense forest all added up to a secure and maintainable spot for a man's brief survival. The warehouse was more of a large, plain building George built in addition to the cabins. He had scarier, more intimidating locations to meet up. West deduced that this wasn't nearly as terrifying as he'd expected—but he shoved the idea away. If George wanted his guard down, he'd strengthen it, instead.

He parked and got out, Jack following him. Spencer and the Brooks brothers had stayed at the end of the trail as backup— they'd insisted on having a part in this mission. Spencer's guilt over Rene' would be the death of him, but in this case, they could use his help. If it gave the man some relief after what he'd watched happen to Rene', so be it.

He took a breath, opening the front door and going inside. Without a moment's pause, he headed to the bar to the right corner of the room.

"Hello, son," George said softly, leaning upright from the counter top. He wasn't drunk—West could tell if he was drunk from a mile away—but the beer in his hands and empty bottles on the counter told West he wasn't afraid of relaxing a bit tonight. Since no goons stood in the open to guard George, that meant his bodyguards were hiding. West disliked guards even more when he couldn't see them.

"Father." George always liked it best when West

called him that, so he rarely did. "We came for the antidote."

George eyed Jack. "Must he always follow you around like a lost dog?"

Jack clenched his fists and smiled his biggest smile. "Lost dogs bite hard."

"I suppose it's best you brought him." George pulled a small vial from his coat. "*You* won't be returning to the girl."

West eyed the vial briefly. It looked like the right stuff.

"What?" Jack asked, somewhere on the verge of anger and exhaustion. "We just need the antidote, George, why do you have to string this out?"

"Why must you doubt me like your father did? Where did it get *him*?" George smiled almost innocently but there was no such thing as innocence with George Johnston. West used to lay awake at night wondering if his father had ever been innocent as a child. He could never imagine such a miracle.

Jack set his jaw tightly, the vein in his neck bulging. "I am not my father." Jack's bitterness hung heavy in his sharp tone.

"Here." George gave Jack the vial. Jack snatched it like a snake but stood close to West.

"Go, Jack," West said flatly. He'd already warned Jack if this was another grab-and-ditch, that Jack grabbed and ditched him without hesitation. It'd never been a technique Jack had ever done well—he rarely did it, even when it was what was best.

Jack eyed George darkly. "When will he be freed?"

George laughed as if at a grand joke with an old friend. "He's my son, not my slave, Jack. Freed is hardly the word to use after he passed a test."

"He's passed enough tests—"

"Jack," West said, without looking away from George.

Jack licked his lips and left the warehouse without looking back. West took a slow breath. *At least he didn't fight.*

"You know that Danny is dead?" George asked nonchalantly.

Unsure by the sudden turn in conversation, West nodded. "Yessir."

"Ed and Ty failed that job," George continued, staring at his beer bottle. "I'd truly hate for you to fail like that, West, which is why I push you so hard."

A yell came from outside. West's blood ran cold and the second he stepped toward the door to see who was yelling, George smiled up at him. "I wouldn't bother, son."

West ran outside, boots pounding on the wooden floor until he hit the door and jumped out into the evening daylight. "Jack!" "West?" Jack screamed again.

He never screamed. Never.

West darted around to the back of the warehouse building, but stopped cold. Ty lay near the river, a dart sticking from his exposed neck, blood splattered on the front of his coat. Ed was nowhere to be seen.

Jack tried desperately to wake Ty, kneeling in the mossy ground. "He's not responding."

"Where's Ed?"

"I don't know!"

George's voice came from the back door of the warehouse, bored and dry. "Take him away, Jack, and tell him he needn't bother recovering his brother's body."

West froze like someone shoved a cattle prod into his ribcage. He slowly forced himself to look at George, the whole world spinning in a sickening, tilted twirl. "You... killed him?" The words sounded distant, like someone else whispered them, or maybe he was just in a dream.

Jack lifted Ty's lean body into his arms. George met West's gaze, the thin smile on his face causing West's mind to crumble.

"Of course I did."

"Where is he?" West took a step closer.

"Gone, so the precious little Christian boy can't bury him to turn to dust. A nice touch, if I say so myself." George waved at Ty like dismissing a fly.

"He was one of your best men!" Jack shouted from behind West. West couldn't look at him—he could barely bring himself to hear him.

"Yes, he was, but what leader would I be to allow such a futile mistake pass unpunished such as Danny's demise?" George stepped back once, twice, but West lunged for him.

"Make a move and I kill Tyler." George lifted his voice sharply. "You have no idea who are in those woods."

West stopped. But his mind wouldn't stop racing, and his blood boiled with rage. He opened his mouth to speak.

"Why are you so surprised, West? I've killed good men before—men you've cared about." George kept his distance, not looking at Jack holding Ty in his arms as if he could protect him from anything.

West's lungs tightened. Breathe, he couldn't breathe. "You killed my *brother*."

"And I will do so again. You should know how to handle such a loss."

West slowly nodded. Like a switch went off in his mind, every emotion faded into blackness, locked in a crevice of his heart where he could not feel them. Not now. He would survive and protect. Not break. "You wanted me to stay. I will stay."

"Yes," George said. "Jack, do as I told you."

West didn't look back, but he could imagine the horror and sickness behind Jack's eyes clear enough. In times such as these, comrades fought on, even if brothers died. That didn't change what the living must do. He heard Jack leave, his footsteps heavy, his breathing ragged. West just stood there in front of his father until he heard the truck engine fire up and start down the road. Safe. Jack was safe. He'd get Ty away and he'd ensure the antidote was taken to Rene'.

West didn't allow himself thought of anything else.

"Let's take a walk, son." George stepped out of the building.

West followed him toward the path near the rushing river—the summer rains had flooded the creek and softened the mossy bank.

"I regret having to handle that situation as I did, West, but it is a good lesson for you."

"I have lost family before." West's voice barely registered in his own mind. He spoke like another man lay in him—a robot who did what had to be done when the other West couldn't.

"You are a man and must continue on without a moment's hesitation." George paused, eyeing the river a long moment as his eyes shifted between rage and melancholic sadness. "The time is coming close, West. The Confederates are hustling to take the capitals, the gangs are at an all time high, and you must take your place among the battles."

"I have." No pause, just emptiness, just what needed to be said.

"You have made your name as my *son*. You must be my *equal* to survive." George frowned and stepped closer on the riverbank. His calm aurora matched the thick, forbearing forest's atmosphere. "You must make me proud, West, and lead the men into victory. Once the Union and Confederates fall, this nation will be open for the powerful men who are not morally bound. Men like us who can build a new empire. A better one."

"I know."

"You are not ready," George's voice sharpened. "After all these years, why is that?"

"I am more ready than you think, Father." Control. West had self-control. Or, the robot in his head did.

"Prove it."

"This is another game, not the test. I want the test."

"You do not always *act* as if you do, my son." George looked back to the river almost pointedly—like he wanted West to look, also. He'd always feared the water since he was a boy. But now? What did he have to fear? What harm could be done to his body that he could not withstand? What terror could grip his mind that he could not control? Was he not the monster George created?

Nothing could change West now. It was for the best.

"You have created me, Father, and what I am, but I

have rebelled. I have made decisions against your orders. That time is finally over." West gave one glance to the woods, his entire being empty, like his father's.

"One death is all it took? After years of your rebellion?" George chuckled, voice like venomous honey.

Those words rang in West's head. *Strike him down.* Every fiber in his body begged. One swing, and his father would fall into the gushing river. West could imagine his head busting open against the rocks. He'd do anything to see his blood mingling in the water and drifting far, far away.

But West didn't move.

George sighed when West didn't respond. "Then you will return with me to the base. You will spend time on elite missions before I give you the test. I am sure you will pass it. You are not weak," he said, fondness heavy in his quiet voice. "You will make me proud."

"I will."

"I am curious, son, what changed your mind?" George stepped closer. "A man can wage war for years until he breaks, but a worn spirit and a snapped spirit are two different things.
Which are you?"

After all this time of molding West into an heir to be proud of, George still doubted his final agreement. West met his gaze, jaw tight. "Both, Father. I fought in vain. I choose now to fight for a cause that is not hopeless." He would fight for his family in a wiser way—as the monster George loved and as the monster who killed ruthlessly for his family. He wasn't a rosy-cheeked teen ready for a fight. He was a man, older than his years, who wanted control over what happened to him and his family.

George was his way to that path and he'd take it now. It was his duty, legacy, end.

George let the silence settle a long time before resting a firm hand on West's shoulder. "I believe you," he smiled. Oh, how he smiled. Like every demon that possessed him bared their sharp, gleaming teeth behind his eyes.

West didn't pull away and followed George to the vehicle out front. George hadn't always treated West without mercy. When he locked West in the basement after his childhood punishments, he would come down, hold his son, tell him how beautiful things would be once West became the god that George was rearing him to be. As a child, West hadn't cared much for the terrifying promises, but he'd craved being held by his father. He'd craved kindness from the very hands that had administered poisons for immunization hours later.

West left the river behind, but it's crashing echoed in his ears, over and over. Instead of fearing the depths, he wished to be engulfed by them, yearning for the water's dark comfort and everlasting promise. A promise of peace before death. What was more peaceful than death?

TWENTY-THREE

SIMON RAN HIS FINGERS THROUGH Rene's damp hair countless times, but nothing could free her from her agony or remove her pain. His constant prayers hardly did a thing. God didn't intervene or heal her like the Bible stories spoke of. Simon wondered if God could even hear Rene's screams. If He could hear them, how could He just listen and not stop them? God didn't wipe away the tears from Rene's feverish cheeks or hear her nightmarish cries, just like God hadn't held Graham when the boy woke up yelling from nightmares.

Despite his disbelief, Simon kept praying because there was nothing else he could do. He'd always been one to analyze a situation and take action in the wisest way possible. This time, he hadn't gone for the antidote, and he couldn't do a single thing to help Rene'. He could only hold her.

She was far from him, trapped inside another reality, a prisoner to her nightmares. He held her so she wouldn't jar her injuries. In the dimly lit room, he could remember the last time he'd sat on the bed—Nate'd been under the sheets then, pale as a ghost, his groans ringing in his ears. That night, two years ago, Simon'd been terrified—just like now. He'd rescued Nate from Kaleb's wrath but had almost been too late. A stab wound to the gut wasn't a small matter. AJ had saved Nate's life, but Simon's greatest fear of losing Nate had almost come true that night, and he wouldn't forget it.

The image of Kaleb standing on the front porch, watching Simon haul Nate's body to his car, covered in blood and holding that knife... It never left Simon's mind. It always made him wonder. Why did their fathers, Kaleb and Jordan, choose this life? They'd lost the women they loved to the world, to the darkness, and they'd just pushed in harder.

Hearing Rene' cry tonight... I'll never choose the darkness or the job or the greater good. I'll choose her.

And tonight, I choose God. I have to. I'm a worthless coward without You, Lord... I'm not as strong as my dad... He was so much stronger when Mom died, and he always said that's because he started believing in secret... But I can't think of losing Rene', not like dad lost Mom.

"H-help," Rene' murmured. He couldn't tell if she was dreaming or lucid.

"Shh," he whispered. "I've got you." He adjusted the damp rag about her neck. "Help's coming, Rene'. I promise. They're getting the antidote and your Dad'll be here." A part of Simon couldn't get the man here fast enough, for Rene's sake, and for his own, too. He didn't want to cause Rene' more harm. She'd probably find more comfort from her adoring father. *I'm just a gangster who breaks everything I touch—who am I to help her when it's my fault she's hurt?* His guilt, however, could wait. Just like Jed's death could wait, for now.

"C-cold…"

He pulled the sheet around her and rubbed her back. Her fever was wishy-washy and he should keep her cool, though the sheet wasn't thick enough to warm her any. "It's all right. Here, drink some water." He helped her down a few swallows from the water bottle, but she wasn't drinking enough. "C'mon, baby, drink some more. That's it, there ya go." He pulled the bottle back and set it aside on the table.

She closed her eyes again. Her silence scared Simon more than her cries.

"Keep fighting, Rene'. It's almost over." That wasn't the total truth—he didn't know when they'd return with the antidote—but lying to help those he loved was a natural skill. Old habits died slow deaths.

She licked her lips and fell asleep again. He didn't like the quiet, so he prayed aloud, stumbling over his words, even though he was usually an eloquent speaker, but he didn't care.

"Lord, have mercy on her. She didn't deserve any of this. This is on Brian and Jed and… and me. Not her. Please, take away this pain… You can do miracles, right? Why aren't You doing anything? I don't understand." Simon's throat tightened, but he refused to cry when praying to a powerful God.

"Because He's God." AJ's firm voice came from the doorway.

Simon jumped a bit but looked up, jaw tightening. "How long—"

"God is a God of miracles, Simon, but He doesn't cater to our wishes. He's not a genie." AJ crossed his arms against his chest. The old man's smile was not condescending or belittling— he gave a firm kind of love Simon didn't know how to respond to.

"This is hardly a wish," Simon whispered bitterly. "Rene' is a believer. He's not doing a single thing to help her."

"Are you blaming Him?"

Simon gritted his teeth, looking away while letting the question dig into his mind. "No. I'm not. I just don't understand how He's considered merciful during times like this."

"Would it help you to believe if you had all the answers, boy?" AJ asked quietly.

"I have faith in what I can see." Simon frowned. "I could love a God that helped the innocent or the good in heart, but God lets this happen. Just like I let bad things happen. He's not any more powerful than I am, is He?"

"You don't believe that and you know it. You're just furious right now. You think Christians don't get furious like this? Boy, my father died of cancer when I was fourteen—do you think I was trusting a benevolent God while standing in that hospital room?" AJ asked softly.

Simon blinked. His stomach knotted and his hands grew sweaty as he rubbed Rene's back. "No, sir... How could you?"

"Because I knew who breathed life into every single soul in existence," AJ said, stepping closer, footsteps heavy on the wooden floors. "I knew who rejoices when we rejoice, who weeps when we weep, who loves us more than we could possibly imagine. I knew that people die, Simon, and people go through absolute hell—but it does not make God less of a God. It makes us human, but it doesn't make God any less."

"Why?" Simon whispered. He peered down at Rene's ashen face. Stroked her cheek. "Why can't He just make the pain stop,
AJ?"

"He will," AJ whispered. "He will, boy."

"Not soon enough." *Look at her! God, can't you see this*

world? How much evil is done? How many people die every moment? Why can't You end it?

"Perhaps to our flesh, it isn't soon enough, but He cannot end the wickedness until every soul is created in flesh and blood and makes a choice to follow Him or not. It's bigger than our petty wars, Simon." AJ sighed and dampened another rag in the bowl, handing it over. Simon rested it on Rene's forehead.

"Yeah?" Simon mumbled. "Rene' says it is, but…" He was too tired for more talk like this. He just wanted to be alone.

AJ must've sensed his sudden mental departure, because he went back to the door, murmuring, "Your prayers are heard, Simon."

Once he was gone, Simon sank back and wept silently, his trembling hands brushing Rene's cheeks. *God, I hope they are, because I can't keep facing this world alone. Not alone. Not without the kind of heart Rene' has. I can't face it without her, either.*

RENE'S PULSE WEAKENED AND SIMON checked constantly, but he knew it wasn't much longer until her heart gave out. Nate never came back into the room. AJ helped keep up with Rene's vitals, but restlessness settled over the whole house like a thick fog. Mr. Fisher hadn't arrived, either.

An engine roared outside and AJ left the room, leaving the house as fast as he could. "Jack?" he shouted.

Simon heard loud, frantic voices from outside before the front door slammed shut and AJ appeared in the bedroom door. "They brought it." He held a vial in his weathered hands.

Simon watched him put it into a needle, inject it into Rene's bloodstream, and step back. The moment was brief but shook Simon—this was it. The last chance.

Slowly, after two hours, the antidote kicked in. Simon watched as Rene's fever weakened. He held her and everyone else left the room—except Spencer, who must've snuck in once AJ, Nate, and Jack left.

Simon eyed him coldly. "She's doing better. Her pulse is stronger now. How long have you been standing—"

"She's gonna be OK?" Spencer's brown eyes widened in grim relief.

"Yeah," Simon muttered.

Spencer's whole body deflated in a large sigh. He shoved his hands into his pocket and stepped for the door, jaw so tightly set Simon saw it quiver.

"Spencer? Where's West?" Simon asked quietly.

"He stayed with George…" Spencer whispered.

"What aren't you telling me?" Simon stiffened. Spencer might be one of the best con-men around, but he wasn't even trying to hide the pain in his face, or the tremor in his hands. Something was wrong—worse than usual.

"Ed is dead." The words tore from Spencer's throat in a whisper. Simon must've misheard so he just stared blankly, jaw agape.

Spencer clamped his eyes shut and lowered his head. "George had him killed—they knocked Ty out. He's... he's in the other room asleep... Ed... he's..." His voice broke and he said no more.

Simon pulled Rene' closer. As much as his mind begged him to disregard the news as a total lie, he couldn't. It was real. And it cut Simon's heart until he could scarcely breathe.

Spencer disappeared into the hall. The man who always had something to say couldn't open his mouth again. Simon clutched Rene' and tried to process the truth. He failed. *How? Why? What happened?*

And why didn't You stop it, Lord? Ed loved You—He was constantly talking about You and praying and worshipping with his blood-stained Bible. How could You let him die? How can You let this war rage on— how many soldiers and rebels will die for their causes when You could stop the bloodshed? Answer me!

TWENTY-FOUR

AUGUST 1ST, 2027

"I KNOW WE HAD THE hideout scoped out, Gideon, but I was behind schedule. I had a job from George and Danny hidden somewhere safe until I could get away, and we just got to the shelter. Some homeless guys found the spot and got angry at us. I'm shot but Danny's driving us—just not all the way to you." Philip's weak voice came over the secure radio. "Where do we go?"

Gideon's mind spun at the information. The shelter had been safe last time he checked, but if it wasn't safe now, that changed things for the worst. "How bad are you hurt?"

"Not too bad." Philip paused. "Just tell us where to go, Gideon."

"There are no other safe locations!" Gideon exploded, breathing growing ragged. He hadn't had any time to even process Ed's death after Jack's phone call—

and helping Philip was the last thing he'd expected, but he had to do it anyway. *Always be ready for the unexpected.*

Everything about the situation threatened to claw Gideon's heart to shreds. *Philip and Ed were so close—how am I supposed to break the news to him about Ed's death? I can't. Not now.*

"I'll send you an address," Gideon said calmly. Since Danny was a child, AJ would keep his mouth shut about the boy not being dead. Gideon didn't have any other place cleared for the night that didn't risk George's goons finding.

"Thanks, Gideon."

Gideon gave him a location and promised him he'd be there in time before hanging up. He never broke a promise. Sometimes, he wished his father hadn't taught him the extremity of a man's word. It'd be easier to break promises and not his own spirit, time and time again, but such was being a fighter.

THEY MET GIDEON TWO HOURS away from AJ's cabin. Danny pulled over on the side of the road, the car's headlights gleaming in the dark night, practically jumping out of the car. "Gid!" he cried. "Gid, he needs you!"

Gideon got out of his car, running over, Alex following right on his heels. Philip was unconscious in the front seat, the gunshot wound in his shoulder tended to by a sponge injector. The bleeding had stopped, but the sponges only worked for four hours.

"Let's get him fixed up. Alex, grab the kit and call Vince." Gideon couldn't exactly remove every sponge, since some could get buried and it took and X-ray to find them all, but Vince had the right equipment. The doctor always did have a soft spot for Philip. Hopefully, he wouldn't strangle Gideon for allowing this harm.

Alex scurried off to do as he was bid.

Danny stood behind Gideon, breathing hard, his straight black hair falling over his eyes. "Is he gonna be OK, Gid?"

"He'll be fine, Dan. He handled himself well—just needs some help." Gideon patted Philip on the face. "Philip? Wake up."

"I tried that," Danny said weakly. The boy always wore longsleeved clothing, but now he shook as if the August breeze chilled him. "He won't wake up. He just keeps mumbling about Ed. Why?"

Gideon hesitated at the question. *He can't possibly know about Ed...*

Alex brought the kit over. "Vince is nearby, he'll meet us at AJ's."

"All right," Gideon said. "Let's do the best we can and drive."

After patching up Philip so that he wouldn't lose more blood, they drove him to the road near AJ's property. Vince was waiting at the fork in the road, opening his van once he saw them approaching. The doctor had plenty of mobile medical supplies—X-rays, ventilators, and more.

Gideon carried Philip over to Vince's van and got him onto the stretcher in the back. "Need help?"

"You know the drill," Vince muttered, beginning his work with the focused intensity of a hawk. He gave Philip a dose of medicine to numb the pain. "Who did this?"

"I don't know."

"You said the cabin was safe for the boys." Vince rapidly and gingerly tended to the bullet wound. Gideon helped the best he could.

"It was. We changed the plan. AJ told me he could take them in until Philip healed. George won't find out."

"You had better pray he doesn't."

"I'm not a prayer," Gideon said flatly.

"Now's the time to start, boy."

TWENTY-FIVE

AUGUST 2ND, 2027

MR. FISHER WENT INTO THE bedroom like he'd run the whole way from his farm to AJ's cabin. Eyes wide with fear and rage, he didn't stop until Rene' was in his arms. Kissing her forehead, checking her pulse and breathing, he asked: "Did it work? Is she clear?"

Simon moved away a bit, explaining calmly how she was doing better. "The poison's gone, fever broke, she's just resting now." He couldn't meet Mr. Fisher's eyes. *Thank God he's here.*

"Thank God," Mr. Fisher breathed, pulling his daughter closer against his chest. The way he held her... Simon bit his lip, trying not to let his pain show. He had to be strong. He couldn't break now—not in front of Mr. Fisher. He wasn't a child.

Mr. Fisher whispered softly near Rene's cheek— praying. Tears ran down his weathered cheeks.

Simon lifted his head at the sight of tears and soft whispering. *He's… crying? Mr. Fisher is crying?* Simon froze, too scared to breathe. A part of him screamed *run*. The other part didn't dare leave Rene'. So he sat there like a statue, not staring as the father wept and rocked his daughter.

It wasn't right, just like Graham's pain hadn't been right, just like Yemmy's death hadn't been right, just like his mother dying hadn't been right, just like everything else in the blasted world wasn't right. Simon's chest tightened. It wasn't right for good people to hurt like this. *Now is hardly the time for a panic attack.*

"Thank you, Simon."

Simon barely heard the voice, or registered it, until he felt Mr. Fisher watching him. "W-what?"

Mr. Fisher rubbed Rene's back, eyes on Simon's like a lion— except Simon didn't feel like prey. "I said thank you, for saving my daughter and keeping your promise."

Simon's jaw dropped and his eyes widened, unable to breathe. "But I didn't—"

"You did." Mr. Fisher raised a hand. "AJ explained it all."

"Then you know I didn't stop it! I *failed her*, Fisher! I didn't protect her and she got hurt and it's my fault." Tears burned Simon's eyes but he pushed those far away, covering his agony with pure rage instead that turned his heart hard instead of broken.

"Stop right there, Simon," Mr. Fisher said sharply.

Simon fell utterly silent like his tongue'd been cut out. It was worse than getting beaten by his own father, getting told to shut up by Mr. Fisher.

"Jed is not a man easily matched." Mr. Fisher's voice dripped venom in that one name. "You did the best you could do to save her and you did. She is alive. You couldn't have stopped it."

"You don't believe that," Simon snapped. "You made me promise to protect her—not rescue her—and I broke it and that's inexcusable." He wanted Mr. Fisher's wrath, his pummeling fists, his vengeance. He didn't want the father's tears or forgiveness or pain. He was strong enough to take his own death but never Mr. Fisher's broken heart. A broken heart wasn't something Simon had trained for. All he saw in the gangs was the cruel lesson that a man shouldn't have a heart.

"I never say something I don't believe," Mr. Fisher said firmly, tone biting. He wasn't a man to argue over his word. "What happened is not your fault. What good would it do me to blame you, not Brian? Am I supposed to kill you? Beat you within an inch of your life, as if that will undo what happened to my daughter? As if that will change how she loves you?"

Simon stared at him. His face burned with shame and anger. *He doesn't blame me... He doesn't want to hurt me... Love? She loves me?*

"The only man I want to kill right now is Jed and whoever put him on the job. I want to take my adult son and ask him what the hell he was thinking when he decided to play hero but didn't lift a finger to save his sister." Mr. Fisher took a slow, pained breath as he gently pulled the sheet around Rene' tighter. "You got her out, Simon. I didn't."

It's my fault I failed the first step of protecting her. "M-Mr. Fisher?" Simon finally managed.

"Yes?" Mr. Fisher wiped a hand over his face, tears trickling into his graying beard.

"I… I'm sorry… I… She…" Simon looked away and blinked hard, fighting tears. *Don't be weak! You cannot be weak! Rene' deserves better!*

"I know, Simon… I know…" Mr. Fisher lowered his head, kissing Rene's forehead. "I'm sorry, too."

In that moment, when everything was so wrong, things weren't as wrong as they'd been merely hours before. Mr. Fisher, so different than Simon's own father, offered similar comfort and strength as Jordan did.

Simon sank back onto the bed, mind swimming at the things Mr. Fisher said. *I failed Rene', Fisher, and the whole family… But he said she… No, no point in thinking of that now. Rene' is broken. Hurt. I'll keep doing what it takes to provide and protect—but I'll keep my distance from now on. I can't let her be destroyed like everything else I loved. Not her.* His hand curled around Rene's, and when Mr. Fisher noticed, he simply kissed Rene's pale cheek.

Rene' never stirred or woke up, but she didn't scream, either, and Simon prayed she had at least one good dream.

"MY HOUSE HAS TURNED INTO a hospital and I don't think I have the tolerance to deal with your attitude tonight, Nathan," AJ said coolly, opening a kitchen cabinet and pulling out one of many rubbing alcohol bottles. He tossed it at Nate.

"What do you want me to say?" Nate unscrewed the lid of the bottle. His tone was as hollow as a politician's mind.

"Nothing." AJ turned away to gather water bottles from the fridge. He'd never played Nate's games or bought into his cold, angry attitudes—not that Nate cared. He had reasons to let hate fester inside him and didn't need a God, or AJ, preaching otherwise to him.

Nate went into the bedroom where Ty was resting. He hadn't woken up since Spencer and Jack brought him there. Whatever drugs that'd been shot into him were no small thing—his cries and pained breathing over the hours proved that. Nate dunked a rag in the rubbing alcohol, vigorously rubbing Ty's bare arms and back. Long, thick, ragged scars curved all around Ty's back and hips—some from knives and some from whips. Nate avoided the fresher scars.

Ty had the scars one didn't expect from a man who laughed and joked around louder than anyone else in the group. After all, how could a kind man with a genuine heart survive what his body had been through?

Nate shivered slightly. *Ed didn't survive. He finally lost.* How would Ty smile again?

How would any of them get the memory out of their mind?

We have to. We don't have a choice. Life moves on. Especially during war, and civil wars don't end fast.

Ty groaned softly in his sleep. Nate kept rubbing, harder and harder. "C'mon, Ty. You're gonna be fine." Nate muttered those words like they would be true if he believed in them enough, but that's not how it worked.

Nate didn't know how long he rubbed the alcohol over Ty's body, but a loud thud from the other room jerked him from his muddled thoughts. He eased upright, made sure Ty didn't wake, and left the room to investigate the sound. His old room where Simon, Rene', and Mr. Fisher rested remained silent.

Hadn't Danny gone to bed already in AJ's room with Philip? Nate snuck down the hall, easing the door open and looking inside the dimly lit master bedroom. Philip lay in the bed, exactly where Jack and Spencer had put him since gathering him from down the road earlier. Danny wasn't beside the bed on his pallet. Nate stiffened. "Danny?"

Silence. Where could the boy have gone? Nate stepped into the room—knowing Danny had the knowledge of killing a grown man in less than ten seconds—and whispered, "Danny?

It's me, Nate." *Not that he knows me.*

"Get out." The sharp voice came from behind the door.

"What was that sound?" Nate didn't step back, glancing down. Danny was like a terrifying little gremlin—though, that might've been George's influence and training.

"Nothing. Philip's fine," Danny said tightly. He stepped in front of Nate like a guard dog. Nate couldn't blame the boy for being overprotective. He'd just gotten his brother back after years and years of being a slave, a tool, a pet. Now, he'd found freedom.

"Was it you?" Nate frowned. Even in the dark, he could've sworn he saw blood trickling from Danny's temple. Had the boy jerked awake and hit the bedside table?

Danny got in Nate's space, snarling, "Get out."

Nate lifted his hands in mock surrender. "There's a rag and band-aid in that black bag under AJ's bed." AJ kept nothing else under there, no guns or weapons so carelessly hidden, just a first aid bag. Nate left the room and closed the door again. Well, he'd tried being nice. Simon would've been proud of his attempt.

He went back to his duty, rubbing Ty down with the alcohol and hoping Ty's fever broke. Ty never did handle drugs well. Nate himself was immune against most.

As he worked, he heard voices in the hallway—Spencer and Jack. Quiet, controlled tones that reeked of anger and tension. He got up, creeping to the door, brushing his blond hair back. Knowing his cousin and Spencer, they were drowning in guilt over Ed's demise and West's departure. *I'm not sure why. As much as it hurts, we knew it was coming. Not everyone makes it. West has warned us for years that he'd have to make this decision one day.*

"He won't come back, and you know it," Spencer whispered. "He's told us this'd happen. We just thought we were invincible and that he wouldn't have to submit."

"George will kill him," Jack mumbled, fuming as much as he tried to be quiet.

"No, he won't, you're just angry."

"Angry?"

"*Shh.*"

"Why would I be angry? I just lost two of my *brothers!*" Jack's voice cracked and silence rang in Nate's ears until Spencer spoke softly.

"West is strong, and he's prepared for this all his life. He'll be OK."

"No, he won't be OK, not without someone there,

Spencer. He can't be alone!"

"He's not alone, OK? Once he starts jobs, we can help…"

"It'll be different." Jack's tone hardened. "He'll protect us by staying away. He warned me and I thought… I thought I changed his mind…"

"We can't change the past. We gotta change the future," Spencer whispered. "Maybe the Confederates will win, and we can make our choices instead of taking orders all the time! Ed had faith, so maybe if we believe, things'll change."

"Why should we believe in a God who let Edward die?" Jack hissed.

"Why do so many of you blame God? Why not blame Satan? He's just as real and you know it. We've seen things and felt things that God wasn't orchestrating, Jack, we've seen demons—"

"Why *wouldn't* I blame God? He could stop all of this."

"You don't blame Him when things are going right, either, Jack! Ed went through hell, too, but he had more joy than anyone else. I want that. I'm sick of living like this, and since I can't escape it entirely, I might as well escape it inside. George can kill us, but he couldn't take away what Ed had. What better way to flip George off?" Spencer insisted, voice lowering but Nate managed to hear his zealous words anyway. They hit Nate square in the heart and ground his spirit into the dust.

They must've done the same to Jack because he shut up for five seconds. Then, a whisper, "I guess I see your point, bigmouth."

"Believing isn't gonna keep us alive, but we're dead men walking anyway." Spencer didn't sound too brave about that. He feared death more than West or Jack. Nate couldn't blame him for the fear, but he didn't understand it himself. *Maybe I do have something in common with Jack, after all. Our mutual indifference for death.*

"You're right," Jack said firmly. "I'll go watch over Ty for a while."

Nate practically leapt over to Ty's bed again, silent as a cougar, and dampening the rag again when Jack stepped in. Nate didn't turn around.

"You heard." Jack sighed.

"If you didn't want someone to hear, you should've gone outside to talk." Nate started rubbing Ty's back again.

"Nate?" Jack didn't step closer.

"Hm."

"Do you and Simon believe in God?"

"Simon's starting to," Nate said matter-of-factly. Ty shuddered at Nate's touch, but Nate just hoped he didn't wake up.

"You're not?"

"Why would I?"

"I know all the reasons why we *shouldn't* believe. I guess I'm hungry for the reasons why we should." Jack came and gently took Ty's hand in his own strong one. "I know it sounds juvenile. I mean, I'm Jack Savage, after all. Gangster, thief, killer… The last person who should care where I'm going after a bullet to the head." He chuckled mirthlessly.

Nate just kept rubbing. "I guess."

"Ed killed, too, and he still believed he'd go to heaven…" Jack's voice grew choppy so he took a breath and tried again.

"What if there is a chance that God loves us, Nate?"

"So what if He does?"

Jack thought a moment. "Nate, do you know a man who doesn't have faith?"

Nate laughed out loud, clearing his throat. "Are you serious?"

"Yes."

"George. Dad. You. Me. West—"

"We don't have faith in God, right?"

"Are you feeling ill, Jack?" Nate asked bitingly.

"We have faith in smaller things. Like faith that our guns won't jam up in a fight. Like faith that our brothers will stay awake when they're on watch. Just faith in our brothers and friends and inanimate objects."

Nate didn't acknowledge Jack's silly statement. He wasn't in the mood to talk of God or faith when they'd just lost a man— two men—to two different, terrible fates.

"Why don't we have faith in God?" Jack said slowly. "I've carried around this doubt for so long, Nate, pushing it away and blaming God, instead. Why do we have faith in men who have killed, betrayed, lied… We trust and love our brothers anyway, even when they hurt us or ruin things, but we can't do that with God?"

"Our brothers aren't *God*." Nate tilted his head. "I get you're trying to find answers, but I'm not the man to talk to. Try Simon, or AJ, or, hey, Mr. Fisher. Not me. OK? You won't want my answers." He reached and smoothed Ty's hair from his face, laying a cool damp rag on his head.

"I do want your answers, Nate. I know you hate me—"

"Don't assume anything about me."

Jack leaned over and grabbed Nate's shoulder. "You assume things about me. Like that I didn't care about Rene'."

Nate jerked away. "Don't you dare touch me."

"What did I fail to do for you, Nate? What did I do to make you hate me? You didn't even hate me before when Kaleb was drilling you to do so! It only started a couple years ago and I don't understand. You're my cousin. You're the only blood kin I have that I care about!" Jack whispered, jaw actually quivering like he might cry.

"I don't know what you're talking about. I'm helping Ty, so help or get out." Nate managed not to shout but his tone was just as cutting. *Why should I tell him what happened with Kaleb that night? Why should I admit I was weak? He wasn't there, Simon and AJ were. I don't need him. He's gotta figure that out sometime.*

Jack took a slow breath, pulling back and looking down at Ty. He squeezed Ty's hand. "I'll take care of Ty." A teardrop ran down his weathered, tan face, and he looked far older than his age.

Nate put the rag and bottle aside, leaving the room without looking back. He shut the back door behind him so it didn't make a sound, collapsing on the porch steps. He tried focusing on something that didn't rip his heart into shreds, something that didn't scare him to death, but there was nothing else.

Clouds swallowed the moon and stars above and a rather humid wind ruffled Nate's hair. He'd never liked Tennessee until he met AJ, though maybe the annoying weather grew on him when he'd started walking again after his stab wound. AJ had helped him out onto the porch every morning, and Nate sat outside for a while in the autumn sun, waiting for his body's recovery. But he hadn't been so impatient to leave as he'd acted. He'd liked the time with AJ and Simon back in that shack in no man's land. This place was similar to the other. The old cuss's taste didn't change much.

Nate didn't know what to think. Some people never changed, like his father and George. Some people changed, but he was too close to see every detail—like Simon. Nate didn't know how to handle Simon's curiosity about God, but he loved him too much to be as cruel to him as he'd been to Jack. *Jack deserved it. Simon doesn't. I can't lose Simon, so if he chooses faith, I'll have his back. That'll never change.*

Jack's the one who wasn't there for me when I needed him.

Vengeance and unforgiveness, Nate decided, did change a person. It wasn't a change he liked about himself. *Drowning.*

Trapped. I'm hopeless but I can't stop fighting the only way I know how. If I change, I'm nothing. As I am? I can go to Dad and do what he wills in order to protect everyone else. My time of playing rebel is running out, just like West's. Jack wouldn't understand but I do. I'm not gonna be a coward. I'm gonna face my fate and I'm gonna change it the best I can. I don't need to beg God to change it for me.

Nate stood up, determination firm in his mind, but when grabbed the doorknob, he heard something. Something soft and muffled. Frowning, Nate stepped away from the door, listening. Another muffled sob.

Where was it coming from? Nate headed around to the side of the house closest to the little shed. He kept one hand hovering over the Glock on his side.

Curled up in a ball beside the shed, hoodie pulled tight over his face, Danny lay shaking. His skinny body racked with sobs he tried muffling behind his hands.

Nate froze. *Oh, c'mon… What's he doing out here away from Philip?* He stepped back, but Danny jerked his head up, bloodshot eyes narrowing. Nate couldn't lie—the boy wasn't someone he trusted at all. *He's just a kid, right? No. No, he's not just a kid. George took that away from him a long time ago.*

"Whoa, easy," Nate said calmly. "I just heard you–"

"Leave me alone." Tears streamed down Danny's pale face and ran over the thin scar down his cheek. "I just wanna be alone."

"Is Philip OK?" Nate frowned.

"Like you care?"

"Why are you out here and not with your brother?" Nate said. *Not sure why I'm asking, since I can't help him feel better or give sage advice. But I can't leave the kid out here in the dark.* He knew how difficult it could be, curling up outside in the dirt and waiting for the dawn's light to wash over your shivering body. He knew how hard it was watching people get hurt and not being able to stop it.

Danny gulped hard, rubbing his eyes with one hand until his tears subsided and a cold expression crept over his pale face. "Phil's OK."

"Good." Someone else might've asked if Danny were OK, but it was obvious he wasn't. And Nate knew why. Danny and Ed had a stronger bond than blood brothers—maybe even more than Philip. But Ed Brooks was gone, and Daniel Dunnham had to live on with the fact he was never getting him back after he'd spent years yearning for another brother.

"Nate?" Danny finally whispered.

"Yeah?"

"Have you ever lost a brother?" A strong voice for a boy who's chin quivered.

"Yeah," Nate said quietly.

"Does it stop… hurting?"

A lie, "Yes, it does."

"Ed promised me if he died that I would be OK, but I…" Danny lowered his head, staring at some object in his hand. "He never lied to me, but I think that was a lie."

Nate shook his head firmly. "Nah, he wouldn't lie about that." Another lie. How easy it was to lie when it would soothe a person's heart.

Danny rubbed the thing in his hand, over and over. His whole body grew limp as he lifted his hand. A small, sharp arrowhead lay in his tight grip. "Eddie gave this to me. He'd tell me a lot about the Indians… Said he had Seminole in his background… He was all over the history and stuff."

Nate offered a smile. "That must be pretty old, huh?'

"Yeah… Very old…" Danny held it close against his chest again. For that split second, he didn't look so scary or tough or angry. The softness of his youthful face, despite the scars along his face and neck, jabbed at Nate's heart. The tears in Danny's dark eyes weren't falling, either, like the boy wouldn't allow himself such a weak portrayal of emotions. *But he's still a kid.* And he was alone, even if he did have Philip back, because he didn't know Philip as well as he had Ed. He was leaving behind everything, including Ty, for an unknown world. Who wouldn't be terrified?

"Danny?" Nate asked, keeping his distance but wishing the boy would look at him.

"Yeah?" Danny lifted his head. He was terrified and bold at the same time. How could he be that? It'd taken Nate years of practice before he'd been horrified and still did things with the fierceness of a lion. Yet, here sat a fifteen-year-old, who'd learned the lesson much faster than Nate.

"If you ever need me, you call." Nate gave him his number. "Use the radio, if you have to. I'll find your line through Philip."

Danny muttered the phone number a few times, then looked away, hugging himself. "You don't mean that."

"I said so, didn't I?" Nate shrugged. "Let's get inside. AJ makes breakfast at the crack of dawn, and you don't wanna miss his scrambled eggs and coffee."

Danny blinked, probably taken back by Nate's change of topic and easy-going tone. "O-OK…" He slowly got to his feet like his left leg plagued him.

Nate led him inside. AJ stood in the kitchen, brewing coffee, bringing out fresh eggs from his little flock that roamed the yard like winged sentries. He glanced over, smiling. "Mornin'."

"Morning," Nate sighed. "Mind if we join you?"

"I wanna go to Phil," Danny muttered, not following Nate any closer into the kitchen.

He doesn't trust AJ… guess I shouldn't push him. Doesn't matter if he does, anyway, since he'll be gone soon. "I'll bring you some breakfast shortly." Nate nodded.

Danny disappeared down the hall.

Nate helped AJ scramble eggs, yawning. He hadn't slept much in days. He dumped some eggs and bacon— the meat was courtesy of Ben, AJ's best friend and comrade, who went out of his way to raise farm meats— onto a plate. "I'm not too hungry this morning. I think I'll take a nap for a bit before Simon wakes up."

"You need to eat."

Nate scoffed. "C'mon, I'm not gonna die. Don't start acting like a grandmother."

AJ threw a dish towel after him but Nate avoided it, hurrying to Philip's room. Danny sat on the floor and Philip lay still under the bed covers, both pale as death.

Nate carefully set the plate of food beside Danny. "Here, bud."

Danny flinched. "Thanks."

"I'll be in the living room if you need me." Nate left, disliking the heavy air in that room and how the silence tore at his gut. He collapsed on the couch, tossing a blanket over himself. Jack was with Ty and Spencer must've wandered off. Simon and Rene' slept while Mr. Fisher watched over them.

Just for a bit, Nate could sleep without fear. *So why can't I calm down?*

TWENTY-SIX

AUGUST 3RD, 2027

GIDEON STOOD ALONE IN THE small torture room, his solemn resolution keeping his breathing slow and steady. He didn't look at the table nearby covered in various tools—he'd already used most of them himself on others. He'd worked his fingers to the bone for this day. The day his covenant was final with George Johnston. The day the man marked him like a rancher branding his cattle.

A human would be ashamed at the reality of the situation. A human would be shaking and vomiting at the upcoming agony they'd face. A human would weep over the things they'd done to earn George's trust.

Gideon was not human. He did not weep, feel shame, or shake in fear. He was a monster of his own design, and this mark would prove he'd done everything it took to make his father proud. He might not be as barbaric as the hybrid monsters the government whipped up in secret, but he was close enough for George to call him his best.

Focus on the job. No time to think of what you are or what your father tried to make you to be. To handle pain, you must go deeper than that, Gideon.

The door opened without a sound. "Ah, you're punctual, as usual." George stepped in, wearing a dark suit and snazzy tie, though his hair was slightly disheveled. "Alex won't interrupt, I presume?"

"No, sir." Gideon met his gaze. Alex had no idea what was happening—Gideon sent him to AJ's to help Ty when Jack called saying he wasn't resting any longer. Alex had sleeping pills that would do the trick. Gideon had lied to his brother when he'd said he'd be gathering more supplies for AJ's makeshift hospital. Instead, he'd gone straight to George's warehouse, only three hours away.

"We're both busy men, let's begin." George handed Gideon a needle from the table, one full of a poison he rarely saw—it was a precious strand available only to George himself. George playfully titled it Dead Man's Bliss, but Gideon didn't know the scientific title. He knew the strand was rarely produced by the government, but George had men in China who made small batches. Dead Man's Bliss was a long-lasting substance that, when injected into a man's bloodstream, would attack the neurological system, causing hallucinations, severe pain to the nervous system, and other side effects Gideon didn't think about. *Death's a sure possibility.*

Gideon hadn't seen a man take it. No amount of

research could prepare him for the pain. He injected it into his own neck without a sound. He pulled his shirt off and sat on the cold metal table.

"What happened to Daniel was your fault," George said softly. He didn't comment on the poison or the torture that loomed ahead. "Did you receive the footage of Ed?"

"Yessir," Gideon answered, voice void of any emotion.

"I hated to end such a valuable member, but while you are in charge of Daniel's safety, Ed was with him during the kidnapping. I could not allow such weakness and poor guardianship to pass unpunished. I have men complaining that I'm growing soft." George chuckled. "I don't listen to gossip, but it never hurts to kill a man. Let the whiners know who is boss. Philip is becoming just as good as Ed was at sniping, anyway."

Gideon didn't let himself think of Ed or Philip. Already, the poison crept into his nerves, sending sharp tingles through his fingertips, jabbing into his shoulders like thousands of needles piercing his skin.

George shoved the table aside, the metal tools jostling. "No one disinfected these," he muttered crossly. "Looks like I'll have to use Bebe." George unbuckled the long, one-of-a-kind knife that he carried like a trophy from his waist where it hid under his coat. Gideon remembered the screams it'd caused the last time he'd witnessed George's rageful use of it.

Still, Gideon was not afraid. Not even with the poison darting into his head and sending sporadic, iron-like jolts of pain through his skull. *So this is what it feels like.*

"I know it is pointless now, since the boy is dead, but can you explain your failure? We wouldn't want it happening again." George smiled.

"The kidnapping happened at night and the lights at their shack broke, sir. They did not see the kidnappers in time due to poor conditions," Gideon explained calmly, grateful he could speak. "The boy slipped out when the brothers were sleeping— by the time the alarm sounded, he was gone."

"It was Edward's fault, but as the leader, you shoulder the burden, as well," George said softly. His hungry eyes studied Gideon for a long, thoughtful moment. "I trust you learned your lesson?"

"Yessir."

George gestured for Gideon to lie down. Once Gideon was flat on his stomach, George stepped closer. "There's something in you the others don't have. There's a coldness in you, Gideon. Something not human and you don't fear it. If you wonder why I give you this covenant, after every triumph and every failure, it is because of that secret."

Gideon's heart rate sped as his body fought the

poison. "I understand, sir."

"Tell me what this bond means." George held the knife over Gideon's back. Gideon couldn't see him well but George's presence made his stomach twist—like a hawk waiting to swoop down with his talons and rip into his prey's flesh.

"The branding is a covenant of our bond—my loyalty—in the form of bloodshed. You remain in control. I sin, but you will guide me home. I will be what your nation needs me to be." Gideon spoke those words with no emotion. He'd spent years preparing for this—when George accepted him entirely. As a teenager, he'd begun to study George's words and speeches, and got sick countless times whilst doing so. That had passed quickly. Now, the words he spoke tasted like dust when before, they'd had the power to make him weep.

Right now, under the demonic eyes of George and with a blade inches from his bare back, Gideon's heart was as empty as a city night sky. *Only because it has to be.*

George hummed softly. "I am glad you understand, Gideon. Perhaps losing Daniel taught you a lesson I never could."

Gideon didn't react, didn't let himself picture Danny's face in his mind, didn't let himself recall all the people he had lost along this ruined path. The poison traveled faster through his nervous system—it was these kind of poisons that made a man take his own life in a torture room. Fill a man with something that ate through his blood, he'd fight, but if you screwed with a man's nerves, he'd end himself.

A long breath filled Gideon's lungs and escaped through his mouth as he felt the blade touch the top of his back. George braced his free hand on Gideon's left shoulder. *Here it is. I'll make you proud, Dad. If a cold-eyed monster possibly can.*

"A wrong choice can pull you far from me, Gideon, but as your leader, your friend, I will guide you back. Do you trust me?" George asked calmly.

"Yessir."

"Explain why." The blade sank lower but did not cut far into Gideon's skin. George's voice dripped, soft as velvet, wicked like a snake.

"You brought me in when I needed shelter. You taught me your ways. You had my back when Markus betrayed me. You blessed my work." Gideon didn't flinch at the knife, but it grew harder to lay still with the poison searing through his body.

"That is right," George murmured. "And we will have this bond until your life ends?"

"Yessir."

Gideon held himself together for the duration of the mark. Clamped his eyes shut. Took a deep breath, another, another, another. Hot blood poured down his back and dripped onto the table, but he didn't whimper or scream. He didn't break and beg that George stop.

George kept going. "Scream, boy."

Gideon's hands jerked. The poison was wearing on him. *I have to do this. I have to. Face the pain, just like Dad said.*

The knife went deeper, picked up, then dug in again. How long did it take the beast to carve his initial into Gideon's back?

"You screamed when you first came to me, remember? You screamed and screamed because you were alone, afraid, and doomed. Who gave you a future?" George's voice barely reached Gideon's mind.

"You…" Gideon choked. He jerked, panting, gripping the sides of the table. *Face it.*

"You've been strong many years, Gideon. Now, you may scream to your heart's content."

Gideon gasped in agony. The poison shot throughout his body like a million needles tearing his nervous system into thousands of pieces and pinning them down against a table. His lungs constricted and he couldn't control his body. *Oh, God… Face it… Face it… don't scream. Do not scream. I can't do that.* His body begged for it. *Scream. Just scream!*

If you follow Me, I will heal your heart.

Gideon jerked again and groaned.

"Scream, Gideon. It will help you, son…"

If you follow Me, I will bind your

wounds.

What is that? Gideon gasped violently but bit back his ragged cry. What other voice kept whispering in his mind? *I'm losing it. No, no, no.* He opened his eyes. *Focus on something.* Sweat poured down his face and he saw a man in the doorway. A tall man, mostly naked, dark blood dripping from his pierced hands. He just stood there. Silent. Any other man would cower in shame but this man stood like a lion. Did he not care that he was naked and covered in scars and blood?

Gideon looked around, a scream tearing from his throat. Markus stood by, as well, shaggy haired and wearing his smug grin, laughing: "I told you that you needed me, brother. Look what you became when I left!"

Gideon cried out again. The room was full of people, full of faces, and they all came closer. Raised the knives in their hands. They laughed like a horde of demons— Alex, too, approached with a knife. "You deserve this," he whispered softly, right into Gideon's ear.

The only one who did not come near for blood was the broken man in the doorway, but Gideon couldn't see him through the room of people.

Gideon screamed. The blade withdrew from his body and he lay frozen on his stomach, shaking hard.

"It is over," George said softly. He ran his bloodied hand over Gideon's sweaty hair, voice sweet as honey.

"Vince will come to take care of you. You did well. I knew you would."

Gideon didn't try lifting his head, sweat pouring down his temples and blood running down his wounded back. *It's over. It's over. But it isn't. It never will be.*

His body was on fire. His vision was blackening. His hope drained from his body like a dying sparrow falling out of the sky. The room full of people pushed around him, their hands and knives stabbing him repeatedly, and he couldn't fight any of them, nor did he want to.

"Gideon, keep breathin', boy. I'm gonna give you some painkillers, but they won't help the poison. You gotta fight that yerself." A voice, Vince, somewhere close and so far away.

Follow me, I'll heal your heart and bind your wounds. Gideon kept screaming.

TWENTY-SEVEN

AUGUST 3RD, 2027

"**I'M NOT SO SURE IT'S** a good plan, Nate," Simon muttered, sitting down heavily on the back porch steps as the morning sun peeked from the horizon. He'd said those same words hundreds of times. Nate wasn't exactly the best schemer.

"What other choice have we had for *years*?" Nate crossed his arms, leaning against the porch railing. "Kaleb and Jordan have raised us to always go back to base and do what they need of us. Our little far-flung dream of having a shot at roughing it ourselves isn't happening, and it almost got Graham killed."

He's right. I'm level-headed but that doesn't mean my heart is. But right now, logic says to go back to what we know. Simon couldn't disregard the fact their attempt at a far-flung dream had been cut short. It'd almost gotten Rene' killed, too. "So, we go back?"

"We gain total trust from our dads and George." Nate nodded as if that was a totally easy thing to do.

"You've changed," Simon mumbled. "You never wanted this to end like that. I mean, my dad has our trust. But…"

"We were fools for trying anything different. It got Graham and Rene' both hurt. I'm not gonna let that happen again."

"You'd rather live forsaken? You'd rather live in a cage and be a broken man and work as a slave?" Simon looked up, indignation flashing in his chest. "Come *on*, Nate. There's gotta be more to that plan. Do we gain trust so we can help people and trick them out?"

Nate scowled. "We've tried to be the spies and liars, Simon. I want to be with everything in me, to best my father and leave this life behind, but we're good at it. Letting our hearts get in the way," he gestured to the house where Rene' slept, "was a mistake."

"You think being a cold monster is worth it?" Simon asked coolly.

"No, I don't think we should fight without something to fight for, but we gotta fight smarter." Nate sat down beside Simon. "Better than we have been. Maybe, if we get close to Kaleb and Jordan again, do well on their jobs, we can learn more. Have more resources. We've been rogue, but maybe it's worth living a lie if we can help more people," Nate whispered, staring down at his calloused hands.

Simon paused a long moment. He'd been thinking the same thing. "I think it might be best, too. We can help better if we're better at what we do." He closed his eyes. "But I can't leave Springtown hanging high and dry." *I can't leave Rene' behind.*

Nate studied him closely. "I know. They need supplies, but George knows what we did, Simon."

"You're sure?" Simon frowned.

"Yeah. Kaleb called me. George let him know what was going on. Not sure how he found out but he knew. Kaleb won't punish me if I come back." Nate admitted tightly.

"He's not gonna do anything?" Simon hesitated. It didn't make sense for George to not take this chance to set them straight.

"No."

"Well, if that's true, and even if it isn't... I guess we gotta go back. No sense in being prideful over staying away when we can learn to be better than them if we return." Simon gritted his teeth, rubbing a scar on his arm. They'd hardly been rogue for a year but he'd miss that way of life. *I have to protect Rene', and the only way to do that is survive and become stronger, smarter, better... And I can't help Springtown if George destroys them out of spite. At least Jordan will help to some degree. I can trust him.*

"Guess it's decided," Nate muttered. "I'm sure all

the sorry cusses sure will be happy to see us move back in."

Simon didn't return the banter. "We'll have to figure out a way to get Springtown supplies."

"I'd suggest Gideon and Alex, but after the kidnapping, I doubt they'd be trusted to do that, even though they're capable of such a big secret." Nate scowled darkly and rubbed his neck.

"Maybe Jack…?"

"I doubt it."

"We have to find someone. We can't keep doing it for a while. We'll be closely watched, and George won't allow another mistake." Simon ran a hand over his face, heart heavy. "I guess I'll talk it over with Mr. Fisher." *No use in being upset, Simon. Rene' will be OK, and she probably won't trust you after this, anyway. Focus on providing for the town.*

"They'll head out soon. Let's catch him and AJ together now." Nate sighed, getting to his feet and offering Simon a hand.

They went inside quietly, not wanting Rene', Philip, or Danny waking from where they slept in the rooms. Ty'd been awake since a few hours ago—he'd woken screaming and only Danny had been able to comfort him.

AJ and Mr. Fisher were making some breakfast, neither talkative and both reeking with exhaustion. Simon went over, taking the bowl of eggs and whisking them so Mr. Fisher didn't have to. "You guys heading out soon?" He knew the answer was, but what else did he say?

Mr. Fisher nodded. "I think Rene's strong enough to travel. She needs home, her mother…"

"We need to talk to you two," Nate spoke up. He and Simon carefully explained their plan—and the lack of idea for who would bring supplies. Neither men showed much reaction, since they'd probably been one step ahead of the boys.

"We don't have it sorted out yet, but we knew it would be unsafe for you both continuing the supply drops." AJ set his plate of fried eggs onto the wooden table. "Gideon and Alex might not be the best choice, even if I know they could pull it off."

Mr. Fisher's eyes narrowed but he nodded without a word.

"Well, I don't know anyone else capable." Nate didn't meet anyone's gaze, helping AJ finish the sausage. "It's a lot to pull off and most everyone couldn't be gone that long without getting suspected."

Mr. Fisher made a small plate of food, expression dark like a summer storm. "There's no one capable of the job and able to keep the secret. I don't know if we can afford beating around the bush."

"You guys can't go on without outside help," Simon said tightly. "We have to find someone, soon." Nate was right. Even if they knew men who'd get the supplies, how would they get them to Springtown without being caught?

"What if I had a group who could get it done?" Another voice came from the hall, and Jack stepped into the room, keeping his words quiet. "It might not be as flawless as the work you've been doing." The glance he gave Nate and Simon almost resembled respect. "But it'd count, right?"

"Who?" Mr. Fisher asked calmly.

"Some thugs who do good work, just didn't climb up George's ranks. They're kinda their own group. They could take this job, stay quiet about it, and not get you guys involved in the wars or battles." Jack braced himself against a table chair, jaw tightening. "I can't exactly give more info."

AJ flipped a pancake, huffing. "I dislike vague plans, Jack."

Nate glanced at Simon, almost fuming. If his cousin could come up with a solution and he couldn't, he'd be as mad as a honey badger. Simon didn't care, because a good solution was a good solution, and that's what they needed. *Now, if only Jack's solution can be a good one.*

"I understand you want explanations, but some things are best left unsaid, sir." Jack met Mr. Fisher's calculating gaze.

"Does the group work for you?" Mr. Fisher asked.

"Not exactly."

"You said they weren't directly under George." Mr. Fisher picked up the plate and a fork. The way he held the utensil almost made Simon flinch.

"No, sir, not exactly." Jack cleared his throat. "They're low enough to pull it off, and I think that's what matters most. They will not bring harm to the town, for sure, they'd never pull something stupid."

"They're a group of men, they're bound to pull something stupid," Mr. Fisher snapped. He had a town and a family counting on his protection—Simon didn't blame his anger. He just wished he could fix it all, like he'd promised he would.

"I understand, sir, but I don't think we have much choice. I want to help." The bags under Jack's eyes and sagging shoulders reminded Simon just how much the man needed, depended on, and missed West. Jack was terrified for his brother but was stuck here, fighting on, defending others. Simon couldn't imagine leaving Nate. Maybe it made him less of a man, but he didn't care.

AJ and Mr. Fisher exchanged a brief, somber glance before Mr. Fisher gave Jack a piercing glare, but Simon could see the sadness in his green eyes, too. Mr. Fisher was fighting as hard as possible, but he needed help. How could he pick which help he got? "All right. I will discuss it with the town, but if it is our only hope…" He trailed off, going into the hall with the food.

Simon stiffened, hurrying after him. "Mr. Fisher—"

Mr. Fisher stopped and turned, studying Simon with those eyes that made Simon cringe inside.

"I… I'm sorry, sir."

"You cannot help us without endangering us and yourself," Mr. Fisher said quietly. "I understand. This war makes men out of all of us." No anger lingered in his tone or eyes. Perhaps he knew how little vengeful or bitter anger helped a man.

"I'm sorry. I'll do everything I can, sir," Simon whispered, clenched fists shaking. "Please…" *Please, what? Don't push me away? Don't hate me? Who am I to ask this man for single thing? I should beg on my knees for his forgiveness, not his love.* But Mr. Fisher had already forgiven Simon and the fruit of that decision cut Simon's heart. *I want to make him proud, and I've already ruined that. I almost lost Rene'.*

Mr. Fisher paused, resting a firm hand on Simon's shoulder. "What is it, Simon?"

"Why aren't you angry? You explained but I still don't understand, sir. I tried so hard but I failed the whole town. The one chance I had to protect Rene'? I failed. I can't undo it. The only way to help now is to leave you guys behind like some kind of monster, sir, and I… I'm sorry." Simon's voice grew unsteady. His eyes burned with tears, but he'd shed enough tears while holding Rene' as she met death in the face, days ago.

"You are not a monster. If God is changing our paths for this time, we do the best we can, Simon. Hear me? What happened wasn't you, it was God. I don't understand it, I really don't, but I do know that Rene' helped that girl deliver an innocent baby. If this whole mess was for that and that only… That's enough." Tears rolled down Mr. Fisher's cheeks but his voice was as strong as a stone wall. "Don't doubt God." The words sounded as if they broke him.

What a command for a gangster's son! Didn't Mr. Fisher know what Simon was? What he'd done? "I'm trying, sir."

"And another thing..." Mr. Fisher controlled his emotions carefully. "Rene' won't let you go so easily. I expect you to at least call if you can't visit." He wiped his tears with his shoulder.

Simon stared. *Is he… is he joking?* "I… How do you know?" He didn't try hiding his disbelief.

"I'm her father," Mr. Fisher straightened and cut his eyes at Simon. "I know everything." He went into the bedroom, closing the door behind him.

I wanna see her, but I'd better keep my distance. For now. Simon licked his lips, going into the kitchen, grabbing some food.

Whack.

"Ow," Simon shoved Nate off, rubbing the new sore spot on the back of his head. "What—"

"Stop looking like a lovesick puppy," Nate whispered.

Simon set his plate down and hit Nate hard in the gut. "Shut up." Nate had no idea what he was talking about, and Simon wasn't in the mood to play around.

Nate guffawed. "Hey!"

"Both of you knock it off," AJ warned. They knew him well enough that they behaved themselves—when he was looking.

TWENTY-EIGHT

AUGUST 3RD, 2027

THE SUNLIGHT WARMED RENE'S PALE, cold cheeks like a kiss from God Himself. It'd been almost a week since she'd been outside, and the summer humidity clung tight but she couldn't help but rejoice in it. *I'm alive. I'm going home. I'm gonna be OK.* Sitting on the front porch, exhausted from the walk out of the house, she fingered a rose flower nearby in the soft dirt. In the past few days, she saw life through a distant lens, like watching a movie while dozing off. Other times, like right now, it felt real again, like she was a part of it.

Simon stepped from the front door and stooped beside her. "Ready?" He picked one of the rose flowers.

"Yeah. More than ready." *Lord, let Mom, Terri, Lee, and the babies be OK... and Beth... and everyone else...* She missed home so badly she couldn't see straight. Or maybe those were the painkillers messing with her mind.

She didn't know if it was the pain or the painkillers making reality worse, like seeing her father weeping beside her in the dark, his whispered prayers lingering in her mind. He was broken over what happened to her and furious at Brian. She wondered how her family would deal with Brian's decision. She had no strength left in her to even think of what'd happened. It hurt too much to pray about the war going on, too.

Simon placed the flower behind her right ear. "I'll carry you to the truck."

"I can walk," Rene' insisted. "Please? I'm sore."

"You need rest."

"I'll rest during the long roadtrip," she scoffed, taking his arm and leaning on him as he helped her stand. "Thanks…" Her vision and balance took a moment before steadying. *I'm weak and pathetic and—no, don't think that. Those are lies.* Swallowing the lump in her throat and battling the voices in her head, she smiled. "You haven't seen Aiden yet, have you?"

Simon took little steps, helping her along. "Nope."

"You'll love him," she murmured.

"I've never really been around kids, but if they're related to you, I'll love them."

Rene' smiled softly, squeezing his steady arm. *I'm safe with him. I know I am…* "You'd better."

"Oh?" Simon raised one eyebrow. "Is that a threat? Because I love a good threat. I'll make a bet that I'll love that baby more than even you do."

"Hmph!"

"I'll bet!" He stopped at her father's truck, opening the back door. He'd already prepared the backseat with blankets and a bag of food and water.

"Bet me that you'll visit again." The words left her mouth before she could overthink them. She knew he thought she hated him for what happened, but that was far from the truth. *I need him. How can I prove that now?*

He frowned deeply. "Rene'…"

"You said you would." She leaned against the truck and looked up at him dead in the eye.

"I did." He didn't look away. A smirk tugged his lips and he offered her a pinky.

"I don't do pinky promises."

"I know. I just wanted to have an excuse to hold your hand again." He grinned like a schoolboy.

"You're not a bright penny." Rene' hugged him close. *Warm and safe and solid. Lord, please, protect him when I can't be there. I can't lose him.*

"Oh, c'mon, you're both going to the same place!" Nate called roughly, hauling a duffel bag from the house and toward their van. "Let's get a move on!"

Mr. Fisher bid AJ farewell and got in the truck with Rene', cranking the engine. Simon and Nate got in their van and led the way, down the driveway and onto the narrow road, headed for Springtown.

"Baby girl?" Mr. Fisher reached into the backseat and squeezed Rene's hand gently. "Get some rest."

"I love you, Dad." Rene' had no strength to argue, relaxing in her cocoon of blankets and closing her eyes.

THE TRUCK JERKED TO A stop. Wincing from pain shooting down her legs and left arm that she was sleeping on, Rene' lifted her head up. "Dad?"

"Get down, now," he ordered sharply.

Heart crashing into her throat, Rene' obeyed and stayed close to the seat. A million questions raced through her mind—where were they and what was going on?

Mr. Fisher unholstered his pistol. "Stay here and if you can get away, go." He opened his door. Rene' gasped. "Dad, no—" He shut the door behind him.

Whole body shaking with anticipation, Rene' held her breath, but no gunshots followed her father's departure. *God, protect him. Whatever's going on, protect them!* She heard Simon's voice, loud but muffled through the truck.

"If you want mercy from George Johnston, get out of the way." She clamped her eyes shut briefly. *Lord, help them. Help us! Don't let us get killed.*

"We need supplies." An unfamiliar voice rebuked Simon sharply. "We won't hurt anyone if you hand it over, Bucks." "You're a fool," Simon said.

What is he doing? Rene' took a weak breath and tried to prop herself up—just one peek wouldn't hurt. But her vision blackened and she groaned, falling back.

"I have a daughter who has gotta get home—she's sick. She was almost killed, and I can't spare anything," Mr. Fisher said sharply. Or, Rene' thought that's what he said. It was hard to hear over her pounding heart and through the truck door.

A gunshot echoed through the little valley.

A scream tore from Rene's throat. Shaking, she reached out, grabbed the seat. "Dad!" She wasn't thinking straight but she couldn't help it—she had fought all this way for her family. She couldn't lose anyone now.

When she looked out, Mr. Fisher, Simon, and Nate stood strong and close together, a barricade in front of the truck.

A body lay dead in the dusty road. Rene's eyes slowly traveled up—the man with the gun still aimed at the body stared right at her. His mullet was tangled, his skin tanned, and his worn clothes showing how he lived and acted like a rogue. Despite his unruly appearance, there was a terrifying strength about him.

Rene' sobbed and looked away from the body. *It's not Dad, or Si, or Nate… It isn't them. They're OK. For how long? Oh, God, help us. Please.*

After a long moment of silence that lasted a lifetime,

Rene' looked over again. The mullet man was speaking with Mr. Fisher, both men's guns holstered—perhaps it'd been a mutual agreement for the mere sake of no one else dying—and the other thugs hanging around were now unarmed, too.

Rene' blinked back tears. Simon opened the door and quickly pulled her into a firm hug. "It's OK. It's all right."

She held him tight. "What's going on?"

"That's Travis. He used to run with Kaleb, but he kinda faded out. He has his own group now." Simon smoothed her
hair back, frowning. "Did you hurt yourself?"

"Wh-why are they talking?" Rene' mustered.

"Travis thinks he can help some, if Mr. Fisher needs him." Simon kept his voice down, grabbing a blanket and picking it off the floorboard. "Sit back. You'll hurt your legs."

"I'm fine. I've just never seen Dad go so ready to kill someone to talking quite so fast…" She gripped Simon's hand. "You OK?"

"I'm always OK." Simon smirked. "I knew Travis wouldn't kill us when he saw that we were trying to get you home safe." "What?" The blood rushed from her face.

"I'm kidding," Simon said quickly. "I just mean that he's stopped Nate and I before for supplies when they get

---

really tight or just wanna annoy us."

"Oh." She sucked in a breath, glancing outside. *I wanna go home, Lord. Dad does, too…*

"We'll be back on the road soon." Simon squeezed her hand gently. "Don't worry too much. Nate and I know this nation's roads better than we know ourselves."

"That's not comforting," Rene' mumbled.

Simon closed the door, going back with the others. After another five minutes, Travis led his men back into the woods without looking back, like a pack of wolves slinking off for blood. One large man walked with the corpse over his shoulders. Rene' wondered how many corpses the stranger had carried before.

Mr. Fisher quickly opened the truck door and hugged Rene'. "Let's go home. I'll explain on the way."

RENE' DIDN'T WAKE UP MUCH when she got home—everything moved in a blur. All she felt was her mother hugging her and not letting go and her father helping her to bed. Rene' clung onto her mother. Everyone else was there, too, but she hardly could focus on them.

Lee led them into her bedroom and pulled the bed covers back.

"I wanna see—" Rene' tried pulling back. *The babies, the animals… I gotta make sure everything's OK.*

"Everything is just fine, dear." Mrs. Fisher brushed

Rene's cheek. "You get into bed and rest this instant. We'll be here."

Tears ran down Rene's face but she obeyed. *They'll be here.*

And they were. Everyone came in, gave her a kiss and a hug, then left so she could get rest. Lee stayed with her when Mr. and Mrs. Fisher left the room.

"They'll get some food and be back." Lee sat on the edge of her bed. "Simon and Nate are waiting outside. I talked to them— they said we'll still have help. From a group with that Jack guy and maybe that weirdo who stopped y'all…" He trailed off.

"Hey, don't cry, sis."

"Sorry." Tears fell from her eyes and hit the pillow.

Lee wiped her wet cheeks and took her hand. "It'll be OK, Rene'. I promise. Don't think about what happened… If you need to talk, I'll listen, but just relax. You're home and we're all

OK…"

"I missed you." She hated being so weak in front of Lee, but she couldn't suck it up or block it out.

"We missed you like you wouldn't believe." Lee sighed, rubbing her hand. "You'd better try and get some sleep. I'll be here. And I'll make sure Simon and Nate stay until you wake up." "Are you mad at them?"

He looked away. "Of course I am. But Dad keeps assuring me they did all they could… But I wouldn't have let it happen. And honestly? I want to make Brian pay more than anyone else."

She wished he wasn't angry at Simon and Nate, but she couldn't make him believe anything else right now. She couldn't ease his rage against Brian or help him find peace in God, nor did she try. Not right now.

"It doesn't matter right now," he concluded gently. "The doctor will be here soon to check you over. Sleep until then. Don't worry about us." He leaned down, kissed her forehead, and said, "Love you, midget."

"Love you, beanpole."

TWENTY-NINE

AUGUST 4TH, 2027

WEST GRABBED HIS DUFFEL BAG from his apartment room, filling it with his few possessions that weren't guns, clips, or other weaponry. He hid his small pamphlet—the Gospel that Ed had snuck him years ago—in a coat pocket, folding it deep into the bag. He didn't have much else that he needed to bring with him to George's mansion. *Home. It used to be home. Not anymore, even if Mom never leaves the grounds.*

"Special business," George said when he ordered that West return home. "You'll need to be there and there's no need for you staying behind when you can join me."

Taking a deep breath, West glanced around the room. Empty. As bare as it'd been when he first moved in years ago. A soldier always packed necessities, and West lived on much less than an Army soldier.

He headed outside, tossing his bag in the trunk of his new car that George gifted him hours before. One of his minions had parked it outside, tossed him the keys without a word, and walked away. West knew it'd been from George, and he wasn't refusing the gift because that'd cause problems, and he didn't need more problems.

"West!" a voice shouted.

Tensing, West ignored Jack's car stopping on the nearby curb. *They know better than to come. They know I have to do this. I've warned them.*

"West, dammit, look at me!" Jack slammed the driver's door shut.

West opened his car door without looking over.

"West, please." A weaker voice. Tyler.

West turned around, heart crashing into shatters. Ty and Jack hurried over. Pale-faced, eyes bloodshot, shoulders sagging, Ty didn't say another word, throwing his arms around West.

West wrapped the young man into his arms, wishing he could take away his pain, his grief, his loss. But West couldn't bring Ed back. He could only ensure Ed hadn't died in vain. That meant giving himself to George so that the others would be free. *Or more free than if I keep doing what I'm doing, anyway.*

Face buried against West's chest, Ty shook with silent sobs. West set his jaw. *Who will protect him? Who will wake him up from his nightmares now with Ed and I gone? Who will sing and play music with him? Will he ever sing again?* "I've got you, Ty." "Please, stay," Ty whispered.

Jack stood with his arms crossed against his chest, face red with rage, his eyes wide and fearful. He kept silent for now but that wouldn't last long at all. Savage men didn't shut up for long.

"I can't, Ty. I've warned you guys all this time that this is how it ends. We knew that." If West had made his decision sooner instead of letting his brothers talk him into hope, Ed would still be alive. *So many would still be alive.*

West couldn't take it anymore. His spirit was shriveled up like a dying oak tree. Broken, snapped, pulled up by the roots and suffering under the elements. His mind and heart lay six feet under, his lungs couldn't reach air, and his eyes refused what the world offered him. No hope, no faith, no love that would last forever and through hell. Oh, how he longed for God to be real, but He wasn't.

West wouldn't end up like his precious brother Ed. He'd be stronger than George. He'd protect them all alone by any means necessary. Even if it meant bidding them goodbye. He would say his goodbyes, head held high, heart of stone, and promise his blood would be enough for their protection.

"No. We all agreed it *wouldn't* be how it ended!" Ty

choked, pulling back and grabbing West's arms tightly. He shook like someone was sending electric waves through his body. "You just *shut up* about playing God!"

"I have to, Ty. George won't stop unless I please him. We tried every other way." West rested a hand on Ty's lanky shoulder. "You can't change my mind. Please, don't make this harder."

"You aren't getting rid of us. You know that. Deep down, you aren't stupid," Jack snarled. "We're not leaving. We *promised*—"

"But you will keep your distance," West said calmly. "I'll do what I said I would if all else failed." *And all else failed. Ed and Ty's prayers did nothing. Mr. Fisher's faith is strong, but he doesn't have my life—he doesn't see the demons I face every day. If he did, he wouldn't believe in God, either. I'm giving them all a shot.* As hard as he tried to believe those words, his heart of steel wavered.

"West, you're not… not thinking straight." Ty held on for dear life. "You promised… you'd stay."

"I promised protection."

"Your protection isn't worth anything if you aren't with us! You're out *brother*." Ty's eyes flooded with tears, his gaunt face twisting in agony. "*Please*!"

"I'm George's son." West steadied him.

"I lost Eddie, don't make me lose you, too!" Ty's broken voice dropped low.

West's heart shattered but he pushed emotions

aside. He held Ty's arms firmly, speaking without hesitation. "You'll never lose me. Never. I love you. Hear me? West Johnston loves you." *The brutal, cruel, monstrous, filthy, wicked West loves the kindest Christian brother he's ever known. Love isn't enough without me leaving and protecting and giving myself up. Any man can let himself go. It's the family behind him that holds on too tightly.*

"We'll lose you if you walk away." Ty shook West weakly.

West shook his head. "He can't control everything. We'll take jobs together still, I'm sure. I'll just do things with him, too."

Jack stepped closer and grabbed West's shoulder tightly, fingers digging in painfully. "West, whether you've planned on this for years or not, it's crazy. Don't do it. Tell him you just need—"

"More time? It's been years, Jack. The sooner I get the test, the sooner I can control things for once," West snapped.

"And if you die? Like Hunter did?" Jack gripped tighter. For a moment, his eyes flashed with pure rage instead of fear. "*Nothing's* saying you pass it! You're not immune to that batch of poison he uses for the test, no one is, and God only know what kind of psychological torture George does!"

"I'll survive." *They know they can't stop me.*

Jack's grip shook. The fear returned in his burning

eyes, but he hissed, "I'll come for you."

"You will *not*."

"The moment you take the test, I'll come for you, West." No doubt, hesitation, or fear lay in Jack's bold voice. Just cold rage. The kind of rage a Savage man survived on.

"How will you even know when it happens?" West demanded.

"I'll know. I'm your brother and a Savage. I'll always know when you need me." He must've had something up his sleeve— maybe he planned on begging George for that date and location when it came. Jack wasn't above asking such a thing. His pride disappeared for his brothers.

West nodded slowly, pacifying him. "All right." He glanced at Ty's tear-streaked face. "We can get through this, Ty."

"Maybe you can." Ty stepped back, his shaking hands falling. "I'll see you, West." Ty didn't say another word, getting into Jack's car and staring into oblivion. His detachment scared the life out of West.

For Ty's sake, it wasn't goodbye, so West didn't go and hug him again and wish him the best. He faced Jack calmly. "Jack–"

"I understand, West. We've talked, you've warned, and we tried making another way… But it doesn't end like this. Hear me?" Jack met his gaze, eyes hard and demanding, thick voice rough.

"I hear you." West wouldn't fail this time. His brothers needed him.

Jack patted him hard against the back. "Keep in touch." He now acted like West was merely going on a one-man job for a weekend, not going home and signing his soul away.

"Don't miss me too bad, loverboy." West got into his car. As he drove away, he turned the CD he'd snatched from Jack's truck earlier. He blasted it loud and rolled the windows down, waving out one hand but never, ever looking back for Jack and Ty's reaction. *He'll be mad I took the rock music, but if I look now, I'll see his pain. His rage. His grief. I'll just imagine his annoyance. This isn't the end. It's a beginning.*

THIRTY

AUGUST 10TH, 2027

"IT'S BEEN A WEEK, SIMON. I've held Kaleb off as long as I can, but we need to leave. Soon." Nate watched Simon herd the Fishers' goats into the barn. Lee'd been more than happy letting them deal with the pests during their stay at the Fisher farm. Pouring sweat, hungry, and sore, Nate and Simon were a pathetic sight, and the sneaky creatures pressed their buttons.

Simon swore when a baby goat headbutted him in the rear.

"You made him angry!" Nate scowled.

"How? He's a goat!"

"You didn't give him his own pile of feed."

"So?" Simon shut the barn stable door, locking it as if locking a room full of banshees. Nate figured Lee watched them work in the shadows, laughing at their stupidity.

"You aren't a good farmer," Nate mumbled. Neither was he but it didn't matter to him. "C'mon. Dinner should be ready." He didn't bother hiding his adoration of Mrs. Fisher's cooking skills and wouldn't dare be late for dinner.

Simon brushed some dirt from his shirt. "OK…"

He glanced around. "Where'd the others go?"

"Lee went to Terri's—the kids needed help picking stuff from the garden." Nate sighed. "Mr. Fisher and Howie will get here soon. They can't be needed much longer, right?"

"Springtown seems pretty lost without them," Simon mused somberly. "They're getting pushed too hard. They need rest."

"Doesn't everyone?" Nate shut the barn doors up tight. The setting sun cast a light, golden glow over the farmyard. *Even if it isn't my kinda life… This town, this farm, none of it is like the gang. It's beautiful. None of it's like the barbaric wars going on. It's like how it all used to be…*

"Hey." Simon nudged his arm. "Did you hear me?"

"No. You're boring." Nate caught himself and plowed over the worn yard, ignoring the flowers, ignoring the grazing horses, ignoring how his heart yearned for a dinner surrounded by people—good people.

"I said that we'll head out tomorrow. Mr. Fisher said it'd be best. We're kinda stressing Springtown out, anyway." Simon kept his voice down.

"We don't bring supplies now—we're the enemies again," Nate said matter-of-factly.

"I don't think the people in this town are that heartless—"

"That's what they're thinking, heartless or not. It'll work out fine. We're not hanging around anymore and they'll get supplies. Bingo." Nate opened the front door, going inside, knowing Simon wouldn't keep arguing now.

The hot, welcoming smells of dinner—venison, vegetables, and bread—wafting from the kitchen hit Nate like a train. He and Simon washed up hurriedly. Simon chatted with Mrs. Fisher and Terri as they helped set the table.

He's only hurting himself. If we don't get attached, it will hurt less when we leave. But Nate didn't stop him. "I'll go get Lee and the kids," he said easily. *Anything so I don't have to hear Simon sound so... happy. It won't last. This isn't right.* Without waiting for a response, he left the farmhouse and jogged down the road.

The kids were trudging inside Terri and Howie's home with armloads of fresh produce. Lee, leaning against the porch beam and chatting with one of his friends, Mo, glanced over. "Hey, Nate. Dinner ready?"

"Yeah." Nate didn't look at Mo. The short, skinny Indian looked rather uncomfortable, and Nate decided since he'd never seen much of him, Mo probably didn't like him.

"Kids, let's go!" Lee called, adjusting his dirt-stained t-shirt. Mo smiled nervously and helped the girls come outside, leading them down the road. Lee walked beside Nate. "You guys leaving soon?"

"Tomorrow morning, probably." Nate understood the brother's anger and disdain against Simon and him now. They'd failed and Nate wasn't pretending they deserved anything else except loathing. The fact the family allowed them shelter and food for a week blew his mind.

Lee hesitated. "You guys better be careful."

"Thought you didn't want us visiting?" Nate kept his eyes on the road.

"I don't, but Rene's awfully worried you'll leave forever." "You wouldn't mind that," Nate mused dryly.

"I'd mind my sister's heart getting broken," Lee said. His expression made Nate fall quiet.

They all filed inside the Fishers' home, the kids loudly talking and greeting "Mommy" and "Granny." Lee washed up, going and bringing little Aiden into the kitchen. It took Nate only one day with the family before realizing how attached Lee was to his nieces and nephews. Lee constantly held cranky Aiden and smothered him in adoration.

When everyone sat down at the table, Mr. Fisher and Howie came inside, greeting their family. Simon helped Rene' into the kitchen, sitting her down, but letting Lee and Mo take their spots beside her. While the teenage boys didn't like Nate or Simon very much, they adored Rene'.

"How was the ride, dear?" Mrs. Fisher kissed her husband after he'd washed up and sat down at her side.

"Dusty," Howie answered for him. Terri patted his arm comfortingly. "The town's doing well. We'll last a bit longer yet before the next supply trip. So long as the teens stop causing trouble."

"Quinn and Jason still acting up?" Lee stiffened at the idea of the guys he worked with in town causing issues, but Nate didn't think it that big a deal.

Mr. Fisher nodded. "Afraid so. But I think we scared some fear of God into this time." Glancing about the table, taking his wife and Terri's hands, he bowed his head for grace. Once the prayer ended, everyone dug in and passed dipping dishes around.

It was strange, even after a week, how right it felt being surrounded by people with joy in their hearts. Nate kept his head down while he ate but couldn't help but ponder it. *Surrounded by food hard wrought. Surrounded by hope. Like the world isn't damned and they all have a chance of making a difference.*

He glanced around. Simon's shining smile as he kept

looking at Rene'. Lee and Mo joking around. Mr. and Mrs. Fisher speaking of farm plans. Howie making silly faces at baby Aiden, who cuddled against Lee's sweaty chest.

Nate set his jaw. *It will hurt less if I don't do this. Simon does this and that's why he wants to stay, why he loves them all, and I have to be stronger than that.*

SIMON LOVED WAKING UP WHEN the rooster screamed bloody murder from below the barn loft. It really got his blood pumping. Jerking awake and nearly smacking his head on the wooden wall, he groaned. "Nate. Wake up… Wake *up*." Arm flailing, he whacked Nate in the face, but it was Nate's own fault for sleeping so close beside Simon in the prickly hay. The blanket they used as a sheet didn't make the hay a 5-star hotel comfort stay.

Nate growled. "Get off me."

"We gotta get chores done." Simon liked the farm life—the heat, fresh air, animals, the amount of production he got done every day with the others. He liked it better than dealing with Springtown's people over the week. They hated him now. Animals didn't hate—not even annoying goats. *Well, Sugar doesn't like me, but she hasn't bitten me yet.*

Throwing his shirt on, Simon clambered down the loft. He'd do all the chores himself this morning. Mr. Fisher, Howie, and Lee deserved that much. He released

ANGELA R. WATTS

the goats into their pen, fed the snickering horses, and checked on the lazy cows. Everything seemed just fine, though he was no farmer, and he'd no clue how to milk a goat. Lee would have to milk the monsters later.

Nate fed the chickens, swearing like a sailor when a hen attacked him. He finished putting the sacred eggs in his scoop. "Get off!" he nearly shrieked.

Simon bit back laughter. He locked the chicken coop behind Nate. "You OK there, Mr. Savage?"

"I'd like to see any grown gangster go against a mad mama hen!" Nate snarled, smoothing his wrinkled shirt.

"I'll ignore the fact you scream like a girl."

"You'd better."

"C'mon, let's see if everyone's up." Simon smiled, heading down the beaten path toward the farmhouse.

Nate followed, sighing like the world weighed on his shoulders. "Si?"

"Hm?"

"We're leaving."

"Really? I didn't know," Simon said sarcastically.

"Why are you getting so attached to this family?" Nate insisted tightly.

"We're already attached, Nate. Don't think I'm making it harder on myself," Simon said calmly. He'd been attached when they'd done supply drops, but he'd never been this close. It wasn't possible for him to miss Rene' more than he was going to before the week's stay.

304

This week will make me remember why *I'm fighting. For once, I didn't break something I touched.*

"But you are." Nate shook his head.

"This week has only made me remember why I'm fighting. Paradise, the jobs, the world, it won't seem so bad when I'm fighting for this, man. It's not just a dream anymore. This is real." Simon gestured all around. "And I get to protect it all knowing they care, too."

"Not everyone in the town you fought and bled for cares."

Simon met Nate's gaze, stopping in his tracks. "*This* family does and that's enough."

Nate rolled his eyes. "Fine. Let's go."

"You'll see it one day, Nate. I know you will." *If you haven't already, you little turkey.*

"CALL AND TEXT, WHATEVER YOU have to do, and often. Please." Rene' hugged Simon with all her might, like he was Superman about to fly into some great battle. He gently returned her hug but made sure she didn't move and hurt herself. She insisted her wounds were healing up, but he couldn't be sure.

"I will." Simon smiled. "Keep me updated on everything." He meant everything but didn't go into his detailed list, consisting of the family, kids, animals, and of course, Springtown's situation.

"We'll keep in touch, sir." Nate got into the truck,

addressing Mr. Fisher. "Let us know if we're needed."

"I think we have all our plans and contacts together. You boys be safe." Mr. Fisher stood tall with Mrs. Fisher, Howie, and Terri in the front yard. Lee had the kids inside for playtime.

Simon met Rene's gaze, wishing her eyes didn't ache like that and her smile weren't so sad. He wished there was something he could do to make her happy and see her smile one last time before he left.

"Yessir," Nate said. "Thanks again for the week. We appreciate it."

It'd kept them from the gang, from Jack's anger, from Ty's pain. For a week, they'd successfully run away—and into a family, no less.

"Thank you all." Simon got into the car, giving Rene' a salute out the open window. "And I look forward to the stories of baby Aiden."

She grinned a real grin, her blue eyes shining, and Simon's heart lifted slightly.

As Nate drove them away, the family waved after them, and Simon waved too, but for once in his life, he believed it wasn't a farewell. *Maybe I've lost my mind, but God, I really think You're in control. I'm not afraid of what I've gotta do and that's a miracle.*

PARADISE HADN'T CHANGED AT ALL—busy, secure, and foreboding like a bad storming haunting the horizon.

Except that horizon was Nate's life, and Paradise was the storm he couldn't escape. More specifically, Paradise stood for everything his father expected of him, everything he hated, everything he had to be.

I'm ready. Readier than he'd ever been.

Parking outside the bar Kaleb often visited, he went inside, leaving the warm night behind him. He'd convinced Simon to stay at their new apartment with Graham. "I gotta face Kaleb myself, Simon, and Graham needs you," had sealed that deal.

The bar wasn't busy—most men busied themselves on jobs during the weekdays or had elsewhere they'd rather be—and it greeted Nate with a strong aroma of mixed alcohols and the stench of sweaty, tired men. Men sat around and played card games, gambling money or cigarettes. Others played pool in the corner. The United States might be at a brotherly war, but that didn't stop Kaleb Savage from having a classy bar.

Kaleb sat on a bar stool, leaning on the counter with a drink in his hand. His blond hair smoothed back but falling in his face from his long day, he didn't bother looking up. "Hello, Nathan."

"Kaleb," Nate said calmly, standing at his shoulder. "Things are in order, sir. No more procrastinating." *No more running.*

"How's the brat that caused you so much trouble?" Kaleb took a sip of his whiskey.

"Healing." Nate hated Rene' being disrespected. *Kaleb knew about Springtown and the Fishers—no going back and no fixing mistakes.*

I gotta face it.

"She was in Jed's hands, she isn't *healing* any time soon." Kaleb chuckled. "I hope the whole disaster won't affect you boys' abilities?"

"Of course not." Nate glanced around the bar one last time. No one could hear them, of course.

"Good. George will let the situation slide…" Kaleb looked up and practically pinned Nate against the table with his dark, piercing glare. "You understand how rare that is."

"His mercy will not be needed again, Kaleb," Nate said simply. His blood boiled—did Kaleb think him a child? He knew George sparing Springtown was a merciful miracle, but George wasn't without personal motives. Even so, Nate wouldn't make such a mistake or be at George's mercy ever again.

I'll just live under Kaleb's hand like a puppet. A soldier. A good little warrior. For my brothers, Springtown, and myself, I'll do it. One day, I'll break free, by my own doing, and I'll show Kaleb he was wrong about me. All this time, he's been dead wrong.

One day. But not tonight.

Tonight, he handed his soul over to his father in a grand lie. A con Kaleb must believe or all else failed. In one way, it was a lie—Nate would break free and prove

Kaleb wrong. He'd be better. He wanted to learn Kaleb's ways and he still, blast it all, wanted just one word of confirmation from his father.

He'd get it all now. He was smarter than he used to be, and he'd get everything he wanted while protecting the others. *Better than Kaleb ever did.*

After the silence lingered, Kaleb nodded. "I believe you. You've come a long way, Nathan. It's time to see what you've got." He lifted his glass. "Welcome home."

Nate pulled a small golden ring from his pocket, the one he'd stolen from his father years ago, what he held onto to remember that his mother hadn't wanted to leave—she'd had no choice. He kept it to remember Kaleb had loved him at one point, until it was Nate's fault Katie had left. *There's a chance Kaleb loves me.* He shoved it into Kaleb's hands without a word.

Kaleb's eyes flashed with anger. Or pain? Nate didn't catch it. Kaleb stuffed it into his shirt's chest pocket.

"When's our first job?"

"Now that you asked…" Kaleb ordered another drink. "Sit down and let's talk, father and son."

And so it began, the end of Nate's dream, but the start of another, that most likely ended with him conquering all. Or he ended up six feet underground. His spirit yearned for both, but his mind would only allow the first option.

He spent the next hour and a half scheming a job

with his father, just like old times, and he'd be a liar if he said he didn't enjoy every minute of it.

THIRTY-ONE

AUGUST 10TH, 2027

A DULL, SOFT PAIN SPREADING throughout his body woke Gideon from his nightmare and forced his eyes open. His familiar bed beneath him creaked softly at his slight movement. On his stomach, his neck aching, he managed a brief glance around in the dim room. He saw nothing but Alex on his knees, heard his choked, soft voice as he sang. Alex sang often—his voice better than Gideon's—but Gideon didn't remember this song.

"It is well…" Alex's voice shook. *"With my soul…"* Ironic words for a broken man. Gideon heard the tears in Alex's pained voice. He couldn't make sense of the lyrics, but he'd never understood Alex's love for church songs. He didn't understand praising a God who allowed the nation's demise, who allowed torture upon His followers, and death to little screaming children.

Alex spent years explaining God's love, but Gideon

studied the Bible more than most Christians he knew. He dug it apart, matched dates, remembered names— but the laws and merciful verses fell deaf on his ears.

But the voice in the room with George, that voice in my head, that man in the doorway, the holes in his hands… Familiar. He was familiar.

Alex kept singing, but as the song grew in power, his voice sank even lower, like he couldn't force himself much louder. His spirit was in the song but his body couldn't follow. He wept the words softly, head down, shoulders sagging against the bed.

I've gotta comfort him. Gideon got his tongue working, whispered, "Al?"

Alex jumped up. "Gid!" He stood up and grabbed a glass of water from the bedside table. "How do you feel?" "Can't feel anything," Gideon mumbled.

"Yeah… Vince kept you in a medically induced coma for… I think it's been about a week. You've done well, Gid. It's healing OK. Vince gave instructions for the painkillers and stuff, I have it written down… You haven't stayed awake for long, but that was our doing." Alex helped Gideon drink some water.

Gideon didn't react at the timeframe he'd been out cold. It made sense and he'd expected it. "Any updates on the others?"

"Rene' got home safe. Simon and Nate are at Paradise again. Philip and Danny are still hiding at AJ's, but he's healing fast, probably will find a place to go next with AJ's help. West didn't leave George." Alex set the glass down, expression grim. "Jack's sorting out your guys for the supply drops. He kinda took that over. Hopes you don't mind."

"They're not my group officially yet," Gideon responded simply.

"Basically, they are."

"Anything else?" Sleep tugged at Gideon's mind, but he couldn't pass out yet.

"Not for you," Alex said quietly. "Get some more rest."

Gideon closed his eyes. "That… that song…"

"I can shut up—"

"No… It's not bad."

Gideon passed out into a world of darkness. He dreamed of every person he'd ever cared for hanging from nooses in a large black room. He tried saving them, but the noose around his own neck jerked him immobile. He tried screaming for help but, looking up, saw a weeping man in the midst of the dead. The man turned, eyes burning like fire and tears wetting his face, holding out a hand for Gideon.

ALMOST TWO WEEKS LATER, GIDEON had healed enough to do simple things for himself. He woke that morning determined to do at least one thing for himself. He wasn't concerned over his wound which was healing perfectly.

"Just rest. You have to." Alex stopped him from getting out of bed promptly.

Gideon studied him, the worry lines in Alex's forehead, the bags under his eyes, and his pale complexion. "No, I don't," he said calmly. "You look no better than I do."

"I am your best friend," Alex began slowly as if gathering his wits about him. Like something had simmered in his mind for too long and he couldn't take the silence anymore. "If I wanted to manipulate you and con you into telling me the truth, I could. But I won't, Gid, because I trust you. I trust you to trust me. But you *don't.*"

Surprise flickered in Gideon's tired brain. "What are you talking about?" he asked tightly. "I trust you mor—"

"You haven't breathed a single word of what's happened." Alex didn't look away, tone firm and steady.

"Talking about what's happened helps no one." Gideon tried standing sorely but stopped when Alex started again.

"I've watched you for two weeks, but you won't even let yourself process anything, you just keep pushing on, like you're superhuman. You're bloody *not.* Maybe your body is healing fast and you can gain your strength back, but that's not how your mind is gonna react."

"I *am* fine. It isn't like I haven't been tortured before, Al." Gideon disliked speaking of things that he had no control over. Failures and torture had their place, but they were also best locked away where he couldn't ponder them.

"It's not something you grow immune to!" Alex sat down on the chair beside Gideon's bed. "No one does. Remember the Fodder job?" It was the nickname they'd given the job Alex had taken seven months ago, when he'd been tortured until Gideon had retrieved him single-handedly. "I talked to you. Remember? I didn't want to, but you kept worrying, so I did. You can't have that same mercy?" Fear was heavy on his face, his pain dark in his eyes, and his heart completely open.

Gideon took a shaky breath. *Strong. I have to be strong. I can't break.* "I'm not strong enough to feel it all like you do. I push it aside because that's all I can do. If I don't talk, it isn't because I don't trust you. It's because I can't. I can do terrible things, Al. And you've seen me do those things. But I can't show you the inside of my head, because if I did, I wouldn't be able to stop."

Alex grabbed his arm firmly. "I'm your brother. You'll never scare me off."

"I'm not worried about *scaring* you," Gideon said weakly. They'd seen the inside of each others messed up minds. They'd seen the other poisoned, near dead, and screaming bloody murder over PTSD flashbacks. "I'm

ANGELA R. WATTS

scared I'll break and not even *you* will be able to pull me back together."

"I can't, Gideon, I never could," Alex said gently. "But God can." His hand shook on Gideon's arm but his resolve almost transferred into Gideon's heart. Alex had undergone as much pain as Gideon had during his lifetime, but he didn't shut off or shut down. He fought the pain and pushed on, too, but he did so with God.

Gideon searched Alex's eyes. *If anyone knows what that man standing in the doorway meant, it'd be Alex. But I can't bring it up now. I can't get his hopes up. Not just yet.* "Alex?"

"Yeah?" Alex leaned back slightly, releasing Gideon's arm.

"Don't ever think I don't trust you," Gideon managed.

Alex shook his head. "You can talk to me. Always. If I can't help you, I'll just listen. You can't carry your demons alone. You don't let me do that, remember?" His accent grew thicker with emotion.

Gideon closed his eyes and leaned back. "Don't think that what happened scared me." Hopefully, that truth comforted Alex, because if it was one thing Gideon couldn't stand, it was the times Alex had been hurt while being terrified.

"Being afraid isn't a bad thing, Gid. Look at me. I don't screw up too much anymore, but I'm still scared when I go on jobs. It's just human nature. PTSD.

Whatever you wanna call it."

Gideon didn't open his eyes. *I wasn't afraid of the knife, the poison, or George. I was only afraid you'd find me, Alex. I was terrified you'd find me like that.* "Alex… I'm sorry. I'm so sorry I lied to you."

Alex rested a hand on Gideon's shoulder. "I'm not angry at you anymore… But if you ever do that again, I'm putting you in a box and burying you."

Gideon's eyes snapped open. "You forgive me?" he gaped at Alex's somber face.

"Of course, you bloody bogan."

THIRTY-TWO

AUGUST 24TH, 2027

SIMON AND NATE ACCOMPLISHED VARIOUS jobs during the first two weeks, some alone and some alongside Kaleb. Simon fit right back into the gang as the quiet one who watched everything. Nate, always the troublemaker, hadn't caused a fight yet. Simon was rather proud of his peaceful, calculated efforts that paid off. So far, so good, in all scopes of moving back to Paradise.

The only thing that could ruin their groove was either flunking a job or Randy Anderson. Flunking a job was pretty self-explanatory, but Randy was a problem. Not for Kaleb, the gang, or Simon. But he was Nate's nemesis.

Simon headed down the road on foot, enjoying the time alone, sorting his thoughts. Tomorrow morning, they'd have another job from Kaleb, but Kaleb wouldn't go this time. A big job. A big pay off. A big chance.

Simon prayed they pulled it off.

Prayer became a part of daily life. Simon couldn't help it, but every morning and every night, he allowed himself time with God. Rene' and her family prayed for his and Nate's safety, so it was only fitting he prayed for theirs, too. He prayed that Nate's heart would soften. The more he saw Nate struggle around Randy, the louder that prayer pounded in his heart.

"Hey, Simon!" Randy called from across the street, flashing his charming grin that reminded Simon of Spencer. In his usual squirrel-like ways, Randy darted over the asphalt, coming up behind Simon.

"Hi, Randy." Simon kept walking, stomach growling. If he didn't reach mess hall, he might die, and that was saying something, considering mess hall food sucked and he missed Mrs. Fisher's cooking.

"Where's Nate?" Randy shoved his hands into his pants pockets.

"He's coming," Simon said. *He'll hate me if I don't get rid of Randy, but how? Shaking an Anderson is impossible.*

"I know Nate doesn't wanna talk, but I gotta tell him something, so could you pass it on?" Randy glanced at him briefly. "Please?"

"I guess." Simon glanced back, but Nate and Graham were nowhere to be seen. They'd been stashing some supplies, both reassuring Simon could go ahead before he "died of starvation."

Randy sucked in a deep breath. "OK." His hands went over his head. "It's about Kaleb—"

"I don't think that's your business, Randy," Simon said casually.

"No, it's not, but, I mean… Just listen. Please." Randy shook his head. He was a smooth talker—his obvious discomfort left Simon confused. "It might not matter to Nate, but Kaleb cares.
He really does."

"About Nate, you mean?" Simon raised one eyebrow. "Yeah, about Nate."

"Randy—"

"I know what you're thinking, but hear me out." Randy stopped him in the middle of the path along the road, eyes flashing.

"Fine."

"I was a newbie here two years ago, remember?"

"Right."

"But I saw Kaleb after he hurt Nate. I wasn't supposed to, I'd come by because I got kicked out of my bunk, and I saw Kaleb," Randy whispered. "He cares, Simon."

"This really isn't your business. You should talk to Nate." Simon cocked his head, taken back by the fire in Randy's eyes. "I've seen him worry about Nate when he's gone."

"That might be true, but Nate isn't gonna care."

Nate wouldn't believe Randy's word, and he wouldn't believe Kaleb cared unless he saw it himself.

"Please, Simon." Randy stepped closer. His worn clothes reeked of sweat and dirt. "That kid hates me and I don't blame him, not at all, but I can't stand living with him hating himself. Kaleb's a sick man, but that's not Nate's fault."

Simon set his jaw, taking a step back. *Andersons know nothing about personal space.* "I know better than anyone, Randy. Nate'll come around."

"I-I gotta help." Randy looked away, clenching and unclenching his fists he rarely used for violence, unlike his older brother.

"I've got Nate's back, Randy." Simon tried burying his defensiveness but failed.

Randy studied him, determination slowly crawling over his face. "I've got both of yours," he muttered. "You guys aren't the only stubborn buggers around here, you know."

"Never thought we were. You're an Anderson, after all." Simon smirked. Leonard Anderson might not have been a powerful ganglord, but he'd striked fear into many and won over much power in small, local government. That'd been enough for Kaleb's alliance, and after Leonard's disappearance, Spencer and Randy chose George and Kaleb as their new leaders.

Randy's eyes narrowed. "I am." He bore his father's

name with silent pride.

"Hey!" Nate's taut voice called from down the path. "Are we gonna eat or what?"

Simon glanced over, sighing. Graham walked silently, head down, fingering the edge of his worn, gray sweater. Simon gave Randy a firm nod and stepped on. "See you, Randy." *I'll be seeing too much of you.*

"IS S-SHE NICE?" GRAHAM MUTTERED, curling up under his fortress of blankets. He slept in Simon's room, because the tiny house couldn't hold much, and because Simon was the only one who could comfort him after nightmares.

"Yeah, Rene's really nice." Simon took his shirt off and folded it, placing it on his tiny dresser. "You'd like her."

"What about the farm?" Graham kept his voice soft so he wouldn't stutter too bad.

"They've got horses, cows, goats, chickens… It's really nice. A bit hard to care for without feed and stuff, but they do OK." Simon turned the lamp off and crawled into bed.

"You guys helped with supplies?"

"Yeah, bud, we did."

"Maybe you can again."

"Maybe," Simon yawned.

"Maybe I'll meet them all…" Graham whispered.

"Yeah, maybe you will. Lee's about your age, a bit older, maybe." Simon considered how he could get Graham over for a visit. *Is it possible...?*

"I'd like that." That was the last thing Graham said before he fell asleep. Simon stared at the ceiling until he was sure Graham wasn't waking up, then pulled his secured phone, texting Rene'.

Rene's update said, *"Aiden's doing fine. Goats miss you almost as much as I do."*

Simon smiled, rolling over onto his side. *"How are you? You didn't answer that question."*

A long pause before a reply sent. *"Healing fine."*

"No, YOU."

"Happy I'm home. Trying to help."

"You should rest."

"I've rested enough."

Simon gulped. *"You're a stubborn woman, Rene'."*

"How are you?"

"Fine."

"We shouldn't be lying like this."

"Guess we shouldn't. I'm doing OK. Graham's gone a few days without another nightmare. Nate's staying out of trouble, so far."

"Lots of miracles going on, huh?"

"You could call them that." Simon closed his eyes. *Yeah. I can call them that. Lots of little miracles.*

"GOOD MORNING, BOYS. HERE'S THE job." Kaleb slid a file across his wooden desk that was strangely bare. If an enemy ever broke into his office, they'd have no sentimental material or important evidence helping they distinguish what made Kaleb Savage tick.

Nate leafed through the ID file, personal details, and various other information. "Isof works for the Brazilians, sir?" A hunger for challenge gnawed at his belly.

"Isof?" Simon snatched the file. Randy, keeping his distance from Nate, leaned over Simon's shoulder, eyes widening as he read the file.

"Obviously." Kaleb cut his eyes up at Nate. "He's a trusted source of income to George's society, but he slipped up recently—allowing a settlement of Brazilians past the New Mexico border. George called for their rebuttal and Isof didn't act on that message."

"We kill him?" Nate asked flatly.

"I would, but George prefers sending a message to Isof's handlers." Kaleb picked out a small metal container from a desk drawer. "One dose of this should do him in for a bit." He chuckled softly. He himself was immunized against most strands. Nate bit back a satisfied smirk. "Yessir."

"I chose you three for this because you're no longer children. You want a job, you take it, no questions or doubts asked. You know that." Kaleb leaned back, picking up a book from his desk.

"We just find him here?" Simon tapped the paper. "In Arizona? His house? Which is heavily guarded?"

Kaleb laughed. "Don't look so nervous, Simon. Your father's pulled off worse."

"We'll handle it," Nate said.

"You have eight days before he leaves Arizona for a meeting. Handle it fast." Kaleb continued reading.

They left the room hurriedly, leaving the little, quiet warehouse building behind them. The summer sun beat down on Nate's back mercilessly, sweat making his shirt cling at his back. He got into his car with Simon, Randy crawling in back, much against Nate's preference. He'd rather them drive and Randy follow on foot, but Simon had thrown a shoe at him when he'd suggested it that morning.

"I guess we don't have much choice." Simon handed Randy the file. "We'd better get back and plan it." Nate smiled. "This should be fun."

THIRTY-THREE

AUGUST 24TH, 2027

BETHANY TANFORD, RENE'S CHILDHOOD BEST friend, came to the Fisher farm that morning. Rene' hadn't seen much of her and hadn't wanted company after returning home from the kidnapping, but she'd craved her friend's presence recently. Bethany's kind spirit, reassuring words, and comforting hugs were medicine for Rene's heart that day.

Bethany didn't ask what happened. Didn't press for answers. She simply stayed by Rene's side throughout the day, brushed her hair and braided it, and kept her attention elsewhere.

"Drat!" Bethany groaned, withdrawing a rather sunken loaf of wheat bread from the propane oven. She wasn't used to propane stoves, since the fuel was a rarity from Simon and Nate, and it showed painfully in her cooking skills. "Sorry, girlie. I wasted y'all's flour."

Rene' glanced up from stitching a pair of Dax's jeans, sitting at the kitchen table. "It's fine. Terri's not a great cook, either."

Bethany laughed weakly and put the pan down, trying to salvage the browned bread. Elvis came and sat at her feet, cocking his furry, canine head, whining for a piece until she tossed him one. He gnawed on it happily.

As Bethany sliced the steaming bread with hands of steel, she met Rene's gaze, her hazel eyes worried. "You haven't said much… You can always talk to me, ya know."

"I know," Rene' said gently. "I trust you." No more words came out, though she desperately wanted to explain how she simply couldn't speak about what had happened. If she tried, she'd never stop crying.

Bethany stepped around the table, wrapped her arms around her best friend gently. "I'm sorry I haven't been around. I've been consumed at home since my grandmother died."

"Don't be sorry, it's tough for all of us." Rene' hugged her. "I'm glad you're here now, though."

"Mama Fisher told me about Simon…" Bethany drew back and sat down beside Rene', clasping a hand, small but strong from washing clothes, over Rene's. "He's special to you?"

Rene' never kept secrets from Bethany, never tried gathering her thoughts together before spilling her soul.

She was far too tired to filter her heart now. "Yeah…" She bit her lip before forcing out, "He could've left me. He didn't." *Unlike Brian.*

"He's your friend," Bethany said softly. "I don't think that wild card would ever leave you. No matter what anyone says."

Rene' shook her head. "I don't understand why he came, or why that man, Spencer, helped. None of them had to. They could've let me…" she trailed off, voice ragged, eyes downcast.

Bethany squeezed Rene's shoulders. "Flesh and blood doesn't equal love. Sometimes, the people we love most won't take a bullet for us, but that doesn't mean someone else won't." She brushed Rene's long hair from her face. "Rene', look at me." Rene' obeyed, eyes swelling with tears and her chin quivering like a child. "You have no idea what this did to Mom and Dad, Beth. It's my fault for leaving. If I hadn't left, then Brian leaving me for dead wouldn't have broken them…" she choked.

"Your parents are as strong as mine, and they'll get through this, too. It hurt them when Brian left, but they made it. What he did, he did to all of you, but that's family, not your fault." Bethany always knew just what to say.

Rene' wiped her eyes vigorously. She broke too often in front of her family. "I didn't wanna hurt anyone.

I just wanted to help."

"You did," Bethany smiled. "Onya's called you once already, right?"

"Yeah…" Rene' managed a nod. Onya had called briefly a few days before, telling Rene' how good Jordan's people were to her and her baby, Rene's namesake.

"Don't be afraid of anyone else walking away, Rene'. That's life. Your siblings, Brian and Kelsey, they left and their loss is on them, not you. People leave, but people stay, too, and we gotta hold onto that." Bethany's eyes narrowed as she mentioned those names but then she teared up. "We might've lost Brian, Kelsey, Charles, and Grandma, and countless others, but we've got each other." Charles was Bethany and Rene's old friend who'd passed away last year from a small defense against outsider thugs.

Rene' hugged her friend with all her might, crying but offering comfort, too. "I love you."

"I love you, too, bestie."

It was enough. Simple words were always enough for best friends.

EXHAUSTION ROLLED THROUGH HER BODY like harsh waves of water against a sandy shoreline. Rene' sat on the front porch and watched the sun disappear behind the yellows, reds, and violets that sloshed across the sky.

The horizon offered comfort—before she'd left Springtown and saw what the world had left. She didn't find peace from the horizon now, just a lingering fear and sickness. *Springtown's the only place left. And how can it last? Will the Confederates win, will the United States ever be united again? Mom and Dad are so worried, they talk about it all the time, and we pray constantly, but the war doesn't end.*

Please, God, forgive my trembling heart and broken spirit… Help me…

She'd spent the day dwelling on her family—savoring every voice, every hug, every kind action from her loved ones.

She dialed Simon's number. She needed his voice now. Just for a bit, even if he couldn't talk long.

"Hello? Are you OK?" Simon answered almost immediately. "I'm fine, sorry."

"Oh. Hey." Simon sighed. "You scared me. It's not even nighttime yet."

"Sorry."

"No reason to apologize. It's good to hear your voice," Simon said quickly.

"How's Nate and everything?"

"He's talking to me, at least, even though I stole his chocolate pudding today."

Rene' smiled and leaned her back against the porch railing. *He's OK.* "You sound kinda rough."

"I'm doing just dandy. I sounded rougher when I

had a goat baby ramming my body every day," he joked.

"They're called kids."

"That's an insult to human children."

Rene' laughed softly. "Si?" She rubbed her arm, lost in thought and worrying too much. "I'm praying for y'all, nonstop." It hurt praying for people she couldn't see, for situations she couldn't watch unfold. It hurt praying like a blind child having faith their steps wouldn't lead them astray.

Rene' didn't want Simon without hope. Without hope, he was crashing around at a tumultuous sea in a holed-up, rotting rowboat. Simon knew that—he'd asked her question after question about God, not because he was faking it, or because he was weak, but because he had a whole world to fight and couldn't do it alone. He wanted God's help for strength and wisdom to win his battles, not just an easy from his troubles.

Simon slowly spoke. "I know you are, Rene'. It's what gives me hope everyday, you know. This world isn't easy. It's broken and messy and full of wickedness… It's full of slaughtering and martyrdom and prisoners and destruction… There's so much darkness that I can't stop. The Union and Confeds can't stop it all, and they fight each other, instead, like the victorious team can patch the rest of the nation—but they can't. No one can save America, except God, and none of us believe He even exists anymore. Maybe that's why we've fallen this far." He took a deep breath. Rene's heart pounded—was he crying? No, that wasn't right, his voice was too strong and bold.

"For the first time in my life, I heard someone talk about God and I couldn't help but see the truth. And that was you. I never spent enough time around Ed and Ty, but all of you have something in common, you Christians. You guys can lose so much, watch a brother die, and you still have hope. Joy. Faith. Whatever it is, you have it, and you only fight harder. The strongest man I know, without your God, would end it all after what you guys face." Simon laughed bitterly but spoke like if he didn't get it all out, it'd rot in his mind forever and never be found again.

Rene' listened closely, wiping tears from her cheeks. *Lord, please, help him…* A broken plea but what else could she ask?

"All of that to say…" Simon paused again, gathering his bearings, no doubt. "I know you're praying, because I've started seeing things different. I've started praying, too. Things are just as bad as they were before, but I'm fighting even harder."

"I love you, Simon." She didn't know what to say, and she wanted something to say that'd comfort him, strengthen him, but perhaps that's what her prayers were for, and words couldn't match that. Telling him such a simple truth could almost equal a prayer. The simple truth was she loved him.

"I love you, Rene', more than you know." His voice grew pained. "It'll be OK, yeah? Whatever you're facing, I might not be there beside you, but I'm praying."

Closing her eyes and burying her forehead in one hand, shaking, Rene' whispered., "See ya later, Si." *I won't say goodbye. I can't.*

A FACE, WRINKLED AND TIGHT, *a smile curving his lips upright. Honey-like words spilled from his mouth and clawed at her heart.*

Two hands. Big and steel-like. Around her throat and clamping down harder. Harder. Harder. Air pulled from her lungs and she fought for another breath but couldn't make her lungs work, couldn't open her mouth.

Sweat poured down her temples and back, nightgown clinging to her body like a mummifying death trap. Rene' shoved off her bed covers. Her breath came in ragged, frantic gasps, and she couldn't shake the nightmare from her head. It burned into her soul like red hot iron against flesh—she didn't stand a chance of winning. *Help me. God, help me!*

Sobbing, she yanked her gown up. Her wounds weren't bleeding, patched up nice and neat for the night. *Just a nightmare. Not real…*

Elvis lifted his furry black head from his paws, whining. Rene' shakily rubbed his velvet ears but couldn't make a sound, because if she did, she would never stop screaming. She choked back the sobs and drowned out the voices in her mind.

Elvis crawled into her lap and licked the salty tears from her hot cheeks. Rene' didn't mind his doggy breath so much just then.

It was all my fault. Everything is ruined because of me. If I hadn't gone to help the girls, Springtown would still have supplies. Simon and Nate would be free. West wouldn't have given himself up. Edward would still be alive.

They're prisoners again because of me. Ed is dead because of me. Did I really do what You asked, Jesus? Oh, God, I was so sure and now… How could those things happen if I was obeying Your will?

Tears continued pouring down her face. Powerless against the wicked claws of fear tearing into her heart, she sank against her pillow.

Brian was right to leave me for dead. My brother was right. He knew that our town would find its demise one day. One video of me getting tortured meant nothing. I'm a fly he can brush off his badge-covered shoulder.

Spencer saved her, and unlike her father or Simon, he'd had absolutely no reason behind his noble actions. He could've watched silently as she was tortured. Instead, he risked it all, giving her the slightest bit of comfort and fooling Jedediah.

He should've left me behind like Brian did. They all should've. No one would be hurt if I hadn't been so stupid.

No, no, no. Remember what Mom said, what Beth said, what Simon said… I have a family, they love me, they don't hate me. I have to have faith that everything will be all right, even with Brian. We'll forgive him, even if he never comes home. Even if Dad never welcomes him back like before.

She fell asleep, Elvis heavy on her chest, and let the nightmares cover her like dense fog. In them, she could never find her way home.

THIRTY-FOUR

AUGUST 24TH, 2027

AVOIDING GEORGE AND CINDY JOHNSTON in a large mansion lay in West's blood. He'd trained himself since a young age to avoid them unless they called or needed him. Never had he gone for a bedtime story, a hug, a kind word, anything. Being alone wasn't so bad, and after spending time with his parents, West preferred it.

This time, however, he was a grown man and not a child.

He ate dinner with them but sat stiff and spoke to Cindy as if she were a stranger. He spoke slightly more with George but never relaxed.

Cindy didn't speak. She'd changed since the last time West saw her. Hair grayer, wrinkles around her empty eyes, and lips in a stoney line. *All the life's drained from her. I always knew it'd happen. She loved George from the beginning, she couldn't let go. Still can't. It's killing her.* He steeled himself and locked this reality away, far from his heart, so it wouldn't interfere with his mission.

George told West of the Confederates' gaining strength, their incoming ambushes that he'd been warned about from his spies, and how the Union would win this Second Civil War, also.

"A war is won in a day or it is not, but long-lasting battles are too entertaining and profitable for despising." George finished his supper with a smile. "The Union has too much government funding to fail, just like the 1800s. A pity, really, the radical rebels couldn't get that through their stubborn skulls the first time around."

West chuckled. "That's the Confeds for you."

"Their pride matters more than their dying children," George muttered disdainfully. "If they surrendered to President Kade, they'd be offered survival."

"They'll learn the hard way." West knew that wasn't true. If the Confeds surrendered this time around, they would be slaughtered, shot down like pigs, and their homes ransacked. This generation held no mercy.

George smiled at West, eyes growing hungry. "Indeed they will. You'll do them all good."

WEST SAT ON HIS BED without a single emotion running through his heart. The bedroom he'd grown up in now stood stark, holding only the bare necessities a man would need—none of the possessions it'd contained when he was a little boy. He hardly remembered how the room used to be. He'd never had many toys or comforting items.

He'd already showered, dressed, and gone over the upcoming plans and meetings with George. Nothing left now but sleep. He shuddered, forcing himself down onto the bed, pulling his phone off the bedside table. *I promised…*

Taking a breath, he texted a coded message to Jack's cell. Even if George found the message, he couldn't crack it. Jack would read it simply: "Safe. Msg Tues."

Tuesday would be the day after he left the state, accompanying George to a meeting of elect government officials and leaders.

I can't tell Jack what I'm actually doing. He'll worry either way, but it's best I stay silent…

He closed his eyes after shoving his phone onto the table. *I'll do what I must. I'll be a monster. I'll survive. I'll conquer. I'm a Johnston, after all.*

THIRTY-FIVE

AUGUST 25TH, 2027

"HE HAS FIVE GUARDS ON site." Randy tapped the map rolled out across the kitchen table. "We have a freakin' Arizonian home, surrounded by sand, with no cover, and we'll be facing five trained butchos. And you just wanna shoot a dart as he heads inside for his evening tea?"

"No one said that." Nate smirked cockily.

"All right… Explain this like I'm five and need colored crayons, because I'm not following." Randy crossed his arms sulkily.

Nate liked knowing something Randy didn't. Randy's lack of courage only proved how he didn't deserve Kaleb's love or protection—but Nate would prove that to Kaleb.

"He means that we'll cause a brief distraction, and since Isof has such good security, he won't expect anything to get him… He's rich, fat, and spoiled. He'll only run for his life if someone pushes him." Simon cast Nate an annoyed glare.

"He won't think danger will reach him?" Randy blinked.

"Nah, not if we keep the distraction small enough. Two or three guys check it out, we take out the remainders, poison Isof, and get out." Nate drank the milk in his bowl and licked his lips. *I can almost feel the dart gun in my hand now. Better get rid of my itchy fingers before the job.* He could spend a few hours at the shooting range down the street. That'd calm his nerves.

"How do we get out? It's in the desert!" Randy scowled. *"We can't get close without being caught!"*

Simon chuckled. "We don't target him when he's at home, man."

Randy paused at Simon's irritable expression and cold laugh. "But Kaleb said—"

"Kaleb said do it before he got outta state. He gave a location so we knew where to begin…" Nate grinned. "We're taking these guys out on the road."

"We do the distraction up the road?" Randy slowly nodded.

"Yep. We find a place to hide along the road and take our shot. Then we ride off into the sunset on our iron horses." Nate leaned back in his seat, satisfaction bubbling in his chest. "We head out soon, and we'll strike the morning he leaves."

THE RAGING ARIZONA SUN FESTERED in the crystal blue sky like it mocked the world below. Despite pouring sweat and hating the desert sand, ragged terrain that jostled the vehicle as Nate drove, Nate was steadfast.

Randy, Simon, and he had spent the past nine days working on this job. Hour after hour, scouting the terrain and road from Isof's current quiet hideout to the fork in the road where they could scurry back east without a moment's break.

Everything ready, everything planned out, they drove and parked at their hiding spot. It was a space big enough for their vehicle behind a cleft rock that hid the truck. To avoid a glare on the metal, they'd covered the car with dull paint and brown netting. The asphalt road being only about twenty yards from the cleft in the rock, Nate had a clear shot of Isof's vehicle from where he lay on the top of the rock, just hidden from view of the road.

The distraction lay up the road, hidden on either side of the asphalt in neat little bomb riggings. Just enough to upturn the first security escort. The second escort would try covering Isof's vehicle after the initial explosion, but Randy, like a modern day Robin Hood, would send a rather hefty explosion arrow into the SUV's rear end. He only had one of the Army grade missiles, which he called arrows, because he was an idiot, and he refused anyone else shooting it off. Nate hoped he had good aim. If not, they were screwed.

"Ready?" Randy spoke over the radio.

"Ready," Simon and Nate chorused. Nate put his radio away for the last time. Lying in wait was his least favorite part. He kept his keen eyes on the road.

Less than fifteen minutes of waiting in the ready, three SUVs plowed from the asphalt road, speeding like they had to beat the time of a helicopter. Due to the rather large holes in the road where Nate hid, they'd slow down enough, and the bombs would go off for him and Randy to get clear shots.

Nate knew he'd get a clear shot because Randy had, God only knew how, hacked into the SUV's electrical system. Randy had hacked into Isof's electric cars, making the windows go haywire so they wouldn't close.

As the vehicles came closer, Nate smiled once he saw the windows were down—they hadn't had time to fix them. *If there is a God, He has a strange sense of humor.* Nate disliked little risks, such as counting on a broken window for a job to stay smooth, but they sure sent thrills through his veins.

The SUVs sped closer. Closer. Closer.

Fifteen seconds.

The sun beat down against the black car hoods. Nate watched through his goggles.

Ten seconds.

Everyone was ready. In the seconds leading up to such surges of crucial actions and bloodshed, a man's true spirit came out with fangs bared and claws slashing. An animal roaring awake for battle, whether the battle be cold and calculating or violent and bloody.

Nate saw Isof sitting in the backseat of his SUV, fanning himself against the terrible heat, his fat face red like an apple. Nate saw this in a flash of time. Aimed his dart gun down at the open window.

Now.

The first SUV hit the bombs that detonated in a flash of fire and smoke, heaving the car onto its side. It rolled off the road like a crunching tin can.

Nate fired at Isof once before the vehicle Isof was in swerved, tires screeching in a vain effort to avoid the danger zone. The third SUV went up in smoke like a dud of a 4th of July exhibit—Randy obviously hit his mark.

Done.

Nate scrambled backward on his belly, clambering off the rocks with his dart gun swung around his shoulders. Simon sat in the car, cranking the key. "Go go go!"

Randy ran like a cheetah, and Nate hadn't even seen him come from his hiding spot on the other side of the rock, jumping into the backseat. "Move!"

Simon shoved the Landrover into drive and hauled

off into the desert like a camel running for water. Or, Nate thought so, jostling around in the passenger seat like a rag doll. He kept his eyes on the asphalt road, but no one followed. Dazed men crawled from the wreckage, but no one tried shooting after their attackers.

"Home free!" Randy shouted, laughing. "We did it!" He set his large piece of weaponry, heavier and more mechanical than a crossbow but similar in design, in the floorboard.

Simon didn't slow down until they finally crossed the blasted, hellish desert and sped down the asphalt road. He didn't laugh or rejoice over the job well done. Just focused on getting them out of there.

Nate smiled. "Yeah, we did." *The escorts neutralized, the target poisoned, and no one on the team injured?* They'd gotten George's message across, loud and clear, and Kaleb could be proud of that.

THIRTY-SIX

AUGUST 30TH, 2027

"HOW DID THE FIRST SUPPLY drop go?" Simon asked quietly, keeping his voice down so Nate couldn't overhear from the kitchen. He hadn't called Rene' in two days and ached for her voice.

"No one expected it this fast." Rene' sighed. "It went fine. Some guy named Joel and another apparently named Socks brought it to the border. They let us drive it in, unload, then bring the truck back. The town seems accepting."

"You don't sound thrilled." Simon tossed his bed covers back. Pale moonlight poured through his small bedroom window.

"I'd rather talk about you. How'd the job go?" Rene' asked tiredly. "Thanks for messaging me as soon as you could earlier." "I'm beat. Kaleb was thrilled about how well we pulled it off.

We might've done too well…"

"Why?"

"Because Kaleb now wants us to do the same kinda lesson with some old family friends," Simon muttered. Dickerson and Reynolds had watched Nate and Simon grow up, but after causing slight strife among Kaleb's followers, Kaleb needed them silenced. They were too old to keep pushing others around and playing heroes or rulers.

"What does that mean?" Rene's worry rang clear in her weak voice.

"Well, it means the job's not complicated, we just hate teaching old guys a lesson." Simon's gut nagged and nagged— something wasn't right about doing this job. But what? A simple ambush, poison the vets, hit the woods, nothing more than standard procedure. Nothing more than a thorn in the old men's side that'd slow them down, make them think twice about questioning Kaleb. *Too easy. Why would Kaleb put us on this job when it's so easy? It's gotta be hard, and I'm just missing how…*

"You said old family friends? What's that mean?"

"It means two old men are causing too much trouble in Kaleb's gang, and he doesn't want them trying to take his place anymore. He'll have us give them a bad bout of medicine and hope that straightens it out."

"Doesn't seem like it would."

"It doesn't, but Kaleb knows their weaknesses.

They'll obey the strongest leader." Simon hid the disdain from his voice.

"Poisoning them doesn't make Kaleb the strongest leader…" Rene' hesitated. "I'm confused."

"It isn't the grandest scheme Kaleb's gotten, believe me." Simon laughed bitterly. "It's just a quick fix, scare 'em back into submission. They're too old to fight much more, and they've always been cowards." *Not like AJ or Ben or the vets—not tough as nails or brave. They'll back down after poison because they like living in luxury while the world burns, and Kaleb's giving them that life.*

"Sounds…" She hesitated.

"Deranged?"

"I was gonna say scary."

"Yeah, scary fits." Simon climbed into bed, body aching from utter exhaustion after labor and extensive time in the desert heat.

"I'll be praying it goes well," she said gently. "You'd better get some rest now."

"I'll call you tomorrow."

"You'd better, bucko."

Simon smiled. "Goodnight." He might be a state away, but he couldn't help but feel close to her. He wasn't lonely or dreading the dawn, he was close to her in spirit, and somehow, that helped his mind calm down. It helped his spirit hang on despite the destructive journey that lay ahead.

"A WEEK ISN'T MUCH TIME," Randy muttered, leaning back against the chair, closing his eyes. "How do we scope these two out enough for the ambush to go smoothly in such short notice?"

"Got a better idea, weirdo?" Nate scribbled down more notes in his notebook.

"I wish." Randy glanced at Simon. "We scope it out and just ambush them? They're pros. They'll shoot us dead before we get the chance!"

Simon picked up the file, opening it. "They have four Dobermans. They let them out at seven o'clock sharp every night, before bed."

"That's just one man, though. We're supposed to dart both…" Randy's eyes widened.

"We take out one, and when the other comes out swinging,

we dart him out cold, too." Simon shrugged.

"Where will we hide so they can't drop *us*?" Randy demanded. Obviously, he didn't enjoy jobs with Simon and Nate.

Nate laughed. "They live in the middle of the West Virginian wilderness. Pick a tree and run."

"That's—"

"Crazy, but we can manage it," Simon interjected easily. "It will be no riskier than other jobs we've all done. It just seems intimidating because they're old guys."

Randy huffed, but he'd learned by now that arguing was pointless. He poured himself a cup of coffee and sat down. "Let's plan."

Nate handed Simon and Randy his notebook where he'd laid out his scheme.

This job was the chance he'd dreamed about since he'd been six years old. He remembered the exact day his hatred for Dickerson and Reynolds kindled inside him, too.

It'd been the middle of August, after a long day of Hunter teaching little Nate how to properly shoot a bow and arrow. Nate hadn't been big, so the bow was flimsy and the target a soft bag, but Nate'd felt on top of the world. His uncle was a great teacher and Nate hungered for more knowledge on how to fight—how to make Kaleb happy.

He hit bullseye after bullseye when Hunter finally stopped him. "Let's get some water, bud. You've done well, but this heat is getting unbearable." "Did I kill all the bad guys?" Nate asked solemnly.

Hunter smirked, ruffling Nate's blond, sweaty hair. "Yeah, you killed 'em real good."

Satisfied, Nate bounded onto the porch, grabbing a bottle of water off the steps and drinking it. As he relaxed, Dickerson and Reynolds came out the back door of the mobile home. The stench of beer hit Nate's nose and he frowned, standing. Uncle Hunter won't let them hurt me again.

"Hey, hey, we just wanted to congratulate you," Dickerson *slurred, grabbing Nate's shoulder. His hands were so big.* Like Dad's.

Nate scowled but didn't dare jerk free, even though he knew how, because that'd make Dickerson mad.

"Killing a puppy is quite a big thing for a little boy to do." *Reynolds stepped closer, grinning. What was so funny? Why was his laughter so cold? Nate's stomach flipped and he tried to step away. He always grew sick when he thought of tiny Daisy—the stray mutt he'd found under the porch. He'd tried to save her, but she'd been too sick. Nate had asked his father what to do, and Kaleb had told him to put the dog out of its misery, so Nate had killed the dog in the backyard, all by himself. He couldn't stand his uncle finding out—he'd be ashamed that Nate did such a thing.*

"Back off, Reynolds," Hunter cut in sharply. He stepped, pushing both men back. *"You're both drunk. Go back inside with Kaleb."*

"You're not our boss, young man." Dickerson smiled. *"We're just talking to the boy about his accomplishment. It takes a very cold-hearted boy to take an innocent life."*

Nate couldn't take it anymore. Shoulders jerking with sobs, he ran. Out of the yard, down the dirt path, heading for the treehouse his uncle built in the tiny patch of forest a quarter mile away. His sneakers pounded on the dry dirt. He didn't stop or look back and his tears blurred his vision.

Cold hearted. Killer. Uncle Hunter will hate me.

Hunter found him minutes later up in the fort and pulled Nate into his strong arms. He didn't hit him for crying or shaking, just promised that the puppy forgave him for what he did, and he'd done all he could.

Despite Hunter's attempt to strengthen Nate, Dickerson's words had remained etched in his psyche. But now? Dickerson would pay.

Simon and Randy finally spoke after taking in the detailed description. "Well, this could work," Simon said. "There's just one thing, Nate. I think we should talk a second outside." He got up, tossing the notebook onto the table.

Shaking his memories off like a bad dream, Nate followed Simon outside of the apartment. "I know what you're gonna say, Si."

"You've lost this mission the moment you let it become personal." Simon's eyes narrowed dangerously, tone tight, but his quietness yelled volumes.

"Don't pretend revenge is a sin." Nate smirked coldly. Simon never was one for vengeance, but he'd never condemned Nate for yearning for it. Simon might be choosing the Christian path, but Nate wasn't. He wanted revenge and wasn't waiting around for God to fulfill it.

"This plan is our only chance, but don't think I'm stupid, Nate." Simon clenched his fists, face growing red.

"I didn't think you were. You don't want me making this personal?" Nate laughed sarcastically, cocking his head up at

Simon. "What about you making Springtown so personal, huh?" "That was different and you know it," Simon hissed.

"Was it because of Rene'?"

"No, not because of her, because they needed us. A whole freaking town needed us, Nate! Yeah, it got personal, but it didn't end like *this* will." Simon rammed his hand in Nate's chest. "This is gonna end with someone hurt. I said we needed to take a risk to win, I didn't say we needed hatred to cloud our judgment."

Nate shoved him off. "Don't change the subject." He knew Simon was right, but it wouldn't stop him.

"You gotta stop, Nate." Simon didn't push him again, but his voice grew pained, expression dark. "You have to stop *now*."

"I'm doing exactly what we said we'd do. I'm making Kaleb happy." Nate crossed his arms, rage rising higher and higher. What did Simon think he was doing? Nate wasn't being foolish.

"No, you're not. We agreed to be the good little soldiers and do our jobs and protect," Simon whispered, but his fists shook from all the things he didn't say. "We never agreed we'd let it all consume us again."

"I'm not letting anything consume me. I'm *working*," Nate shot back.

"This job isn't just a job and you know it."

"Simon, just focus on the job." *I've made him more than angry. I've hurt him. I'm keeping the truth from him and lying about what I want. I want those men in pain. I want to show I'm better. I want Dad to be proud. But I don't want my brother ashamed of me.*

Simon stepped back. "You seriously aren't gonna talk? I've been your brother since we were toddlers, and you wanna act like you gotta protect me from yourself now? You hate that trait in West, and you're doing the same thing!"

"Drop it," Nate snapped. *Don't say anything or do anything you'll regret.* If another regret stacked on his conscience, he'd be a crippled man.

Simon studied him one last moment and stormed off into the apartment, slamming the door behind him. Nate took a deep breath, looked around—no one was around for that little show—and went inside.

A COOL BREEZE DANCED THROUGH the heavy trees that reached for the sky like giant sentries standing guard over the lush forest floor. Nate couldn't identify many of the trees, but most were large enough for solid cover in the case of gunfire, and that's all that mattered. Creeping through the forest, silent as a mouse, he wished the gun in his hands carried bullets instead of poison darts.

Elsewhere in the woods, Simon and Randy traveled towards the bachelors' cabin, but Nate, of course, didn't see them or hear them. *Randy's not a ninja. Or a quiet person in general. I'm surprised he's not screaming bloody murder because of some spider finding his face by now.* In the dark, Nate stayed low and made each step count. About a hundred yards now. The light from the cabin couldn't be seen through the trees yet, but the notes Kaleb gave them assured the lights stayed on until the dogs went out.

Simon and Randy had dog duty—one quick dart to each dog before they got off the front porch and tore the trespassers into shreds.

Kneeling comfortably behind a large oak tree and a bush— *please don't let that be poison ivy*—Nate set his eyes on the cabin's porch. He was just far away enough to blend in the shadows and close enough for a good sighting. He propped the dart gun up through the bushes, making sure he could see clearly and no limbs or branches got in his way. "All set," he whispered into his ear comm.

"Ditto, roger that," Simon and Randy responded quickly.

They all remained quiet and in position. Ten minutes ticked by. An owl hooted deep in the forest and a squirrel's pattering feet in a tree above filled Nate's ears.

The cabin door opened, Reynold's drunken laugh—

Nate could recognize it anywhere—bursting into the night like a drum. "Shut your trap, old man, I won fair and—"

The dogs scrambled past his legs but didn't get far. They dropped, two by two, thudding onto the porch like dominoes. Reynolds' eyes widened but he never made a peep.

Nate fired the dart just in time. Reynolds fell on the pile of dogs. Nate bit back a smirk. *One more shot. Come on out, Dickerson.*

"Not a bad plan, sonny. But you forgot back up." A gravelly voice came from right behind Nate in the darkness.

Nate jumped upright, gun ready, but his efforts were in vain—Dickerson's pistol stared him in the face. Nate wasn't close enough to get the gun out of his hand. Maybe it was the lack of moonlight, but Dickerson's ruthless smile and cocked head reminded Nate of a demon.

"You did well, boy, and you'll do great things. I always knew you would. This isn't your fault. It's your father's." Bang!

Nate's finger tightened on his own trigger, but he was too late. He hit the hard forest floor. The scream tearing from his lungs was the last thing he was aware of, like an echo, and then nothing.

THIRTY-SEVEN

SEPTEMBER 7TH, 2027

ONE GUNSHOT. ONLY ONE. IT echoed in the forest and then the whole world fell silent like the trees didn't dare whisper in the wind.

"What the hell was that?" Randy's sharp voice rang in Simon's ear.

A gunshot meant another man was with Nate. Dickerson never came out of the cabin.

Simon burst through the woods, barely touching the ground, branches hitting his face and arms. *God, no, have mercy.* Simon stumbled into the tiny patch of clearing. He made out the figure of a man running into the woods and knew it must be Dickerson, but he didn't have time to hunt the brute down right now.

"Nate!" Simon dropped down, pulling Nate's limp body into his arms. He pushed the headlamp on so he could see in the dark. A bullet wound oozed dark blood from Nate's chest. Panic snatched Simon's heart and his stomach twisted violently, but he had to think fast.

"Oh, God, Nate… Nate!" He pulled his backpack off with one arm, digging the sponge injectors from the side pocket. "Stay awake, Nate. I've gotcha."

Nate didn't make a sound, struggling hard for breath. The last time his eyes had held such terror…

Randy swore loudly, panting, crashing beside them. He grabbed Nate, holding him steady while Simon injected the gunshot wound with the sponges. "Nate, I'm sorry!"

Nate screamed in pain, biting down on the piece of leather Randy gave him out of his pocket.

"We gotta get outta here," Simon gasped. "Help me carry him!" He couldn't keep his heart steady, though his hands and mind never faltered.

Randy and Simon hefted Nate between themselves, hauling him into the woods. The light from Simon's headbeam pierced the pitch blackness that surrounded them like a blanket of death. Nate groaned.

"Don't look," Simon ordered. "Don't look, Nate, just breathe."

"Simon, it looks bad, but it… I don't think it actually hit anything…" Randy's voice shook.

"Just help me get him to the car!"

Randy gripped Nate, carrying more than his thin frame appeared capable of handling, long strides fast like

Simon's. When they finally reached their hidden car, they tucked Nate into the backseat and Randy got in, cranking it.

Simon held Nate, snatching his comm out, dialing Kaleb's number. His bloody fingers streaked the phone screen. "Kaleb? Nate's shot bad," Simon blurted. "We can't reach Paradise—we need Vince!" A thousand things jumbled through his mind, but staying calm was his job.

"The closest hideout is an hour away. I'll send the coordinates to Randy's phone. Where is Nathan hit?" Kaleb asked calmly, not a smidge of fear or worry in his voice.

Simon struggled for words. He could barely look at Nate's bloody chest, but he described the wound the best he could.

"Dickerson wasn't shooting to kill or he'd be bled out by now. The bullet avoided organs—the blood loss is the problem.
Did you stop it?"

"What do you think?" Simon snarled.

"Is he conscious?" Kaleb ignored Simon's rage and fear.

"Yeah, sorta." Simon brushed hair from Nate's forehead, whispering, "Stay with me, bud. Keep breathing."

"Give him morphine."

Simon grabbed a dose from his bag and quickly jabbed it into Nate. "I did it."

"Try to keep him awake until Vince gets there."

"When—"

"It'll take him about an hour after you get there, he's not far tonight."

"It was a trap, Kaleb! Dickerson was waiting for us, it was all a trap, and Nate's hurt because of it!" *He's probably dying! Why can't Kaleb show the slightest bit of fear for his own son?*

"What do you want me to do, Simon? Nate's strong, he'll hold on. Do as I say and use your head—you've done it before." Kaleb hung up abruptly.

"He sent me the address," Randy piped up. He drove steadily on the narrow road but sped up some after getting his GPS coordinates together with one hand.

Simon dialed Jack as fast as he could, telling Nate, "Hang on. Just breathe. The morphine'll help, just breathe. Hold onto me." He took Nate's hand with his free hand. Nate just lay there, tears running down his face, never making a sound.

Simon told Jack where they were headed. Unlike Kaleb, Jack's fear conquered his voice. "I'll be there as soon as I can. Keep me updated, please."

Simon put his phone away shakily. "Nate, you gotta pull through this…" He held the side of Nate's face.

"Hear me?" Nate gave a ragged gasp but didn't speak.

"I've got you," Simon choked. "It's gonna be fine."
God, let it be OK. I can't lose him. He can't keep doing this. He's not invincible.

An hour driving into the night never lasted so long. Between keeping up with Nate's vitals, comforting him the best he could, forming a plan of action with Randy, and praying, Simon felt like he'd left his heart behind in the forest. His mind and his body worked on autopilot. Somewhere, in a corner of his mind, Simon added Dickerson's name beside Jed's to the list of people he would destroy with his bare hands.

THIRTY-EIGHT

SEPTEMBER 8TH, 2027

"THERE ARE THIRTY OF GEORGE'S men making a beeline to Springtown right now…" Alex laid both hands on Gideon's shoulders firmly.

"Don't you dare get outta bed, let me finish!"

Gideon scowled. "Finish!"

"George warned me yesterday that the little brigade would form—"

"You didn't tell me?" Gideon managed, shoving the grogginess away from his mind, cursing the painkillers' effects.

"What was the use? They aren't going to blow the place up–"

"What else are they doing?" Gideon tried shoving Alex off but snarled in pain, collapsing again.

"Bloody hell, would you sit down and let me finish?" Gideon didn't move an inch.

"George said they got orders from one of his allies to scare Springtown a bit—no severe damage, no kills, just scare them. They said something about the mayor working with some Union guys, some gangsters, ya know? The town didn't know." Alex frowned deeply, releasing Gideon. "Crikey, was that so hard?"

"George would kill innocents if he wanted to scare the town into submission," Gideon groaned. "That town is my responsibility. I have to protect them." He pushed himself up onto his elbows. "Help me outta bed so I can warn them."

"Gid, you're hurt." Alex shook his head like dealing with a toddler.

"Whatever George is up to, it'll get people killed. Help me out of bed!" Gideon's mind raced. He had to get to Springtown. He had to stop the squads from reaching it, and he had to figure out who spurred the movement, since George didn't bother with small scale acts of fear mongering.

Alex helped Gideon get dressed and grabbed a duffel bag from the hall closet. Gideon didn't refuse his help to reach the car outside and got in wearily, not putting his back against the seat but hardly caring he'd be in pain for the whole trip.

Gideon pulled his phone and called George. "Hello, sir. Have a moment?" He knew he would—George had no meetings today.

"Of course." George's voice was smooth as oil.

"What do you expect from Springtown after the attack, sir?" "It's hardly an attack."

"It is unlike you to scare them and not slaughter them," Gideon said easily.

Alex got into the car, cranking it and pulling onto the road, casting Gideon a brief, disgruntled expression.

"No, it's not. I have no use for the town, Gideon. It is not my mission."

"Whose mission is it?"

George chuckled. "If you want the town to be spared from scrapes and bruises, you'll just have to do it yourself. I can't give the identity of this ally."

"Understood, sir."

"I can tell you that I won't stop you from doing what you see fit."

"Thank you, George. Goodbye." Gideon hung up. "The less ready that town is, the less mercy the men are ordered to have." "What makes you say that?" Alex frowned.

"That's what my gut is telling me. This isn't a slaughter or a mongering tactic—not entirely. It's a test. The fittest survive. We gotta make sure they're fit."

"I guess that makes sense. We don't know who ordered this?"

"No." Gideon dialed Jack, ignoring the dull throb throughout his body. He couldn't take any more drugs to ward off pain without losing his mind's ability to work. He'd just live in pain until the job was done. "I'll get the contact information to Springtown's leaders. We have a chance to prepare them for whatever's coming." *Like it or not, it's my job. I can't fail it. George doesn't seem to want me to, either. Strange.*

THIRTY-NINE

SEPTEMBER 8TH, 2027

THE HOUSE KALEB TOLD THEM about lay tucked away precariously on the side of a cliff up a long, narrow slope of road, the rest of the surrounding rugged land barren. Simon hid surprise when they arrived with Kaleb standing on the porch.

Randy jumped out with Simon.

"Get Nate inside now," Kaleb ordered. "There's a cot waiting and supplies to patch him up until Vince arrives."

"How'd you get here before us?" Randy mumbled, helping Simon pull Nate from the car.

"Move!" Drill sergeant tone sharp as death, Kaleb led them inside. Simon and Randy rested Nate's unconscious body on a cot near a small hearth, the living room meticulous and stark. A large light illuminated the whole one-room cabin. "Get me the gauze from that bag over there, Simon."

Simon hastily dug into the black duffel bag near the cot, heart hammering hard like a drum.

Randy locked the front door, hurrying over. "What can I do?"

Kaleb didn't look up from tending Nate's gunshot wound, his large, worn hands working with deceitful grace and gingerness. "Nate's responded well to the painkillers, and the bleeding was gotten under control. You both did fine," Kaleb said coolly.

After an eternity, Kaleb stood up, blood-covered hands falling at his sides. His SOG pants hung heavy, full of supplies and knives and other things Simon couldn't make out from his brief glance over. *He was on a job...* He wondered why Kaleb had such a furious glint in his eyes if Nate was going to make it, then remembered that Dickerson and Reynolds betrayed him. *He'll be out for blood.*

"He'll make it," Kaleb whispered. His hands didn't shake but his voice almost broke. He went into the kitchen and washed up without another word, as if showing how afraid he'd been was a weakness he couldn't afford.

THREE HOURS LATER, NATE LAY stabilized on his cot, sleeping without a sound. Vince thoroughly fixed his wound and watched over him, but it was clear he'd make it, even if healing would be a slow process.

"It was a chest wound. How's he not dead?" Vince shook his head, sipping his steaming coffee. He and Randy sat at the tiny wooden kitchen table, drinking coffee. Simon sat on the floor beside Nate, constantly making sure he was still breathing.

"Dickerson knows where a man can be shot and survive, but he played a risk. Avoiding vital organs, yes, but blood loss…" Randy spoke bitterly.

"The bullet wasn't a bullet, Vince." Kaleb spoke up, voice cold, hollow.

"What?"

"It didn't kill him because it wasn't a real bullet." Kaleb knelt beside the duffel bag near Nate and unzipped a pouch. "There's a new experiment from the Union's warfare department—a piece of weaponry that explodes seconds before impact, causing a similar wound as a bullet with shrapnel. It's painful and can cause death, but it wasn't designed for fatalities."

"Then what was it for?" Randy demanded.

"Training for Union men, under normal circumstances, like hardcore paintball gun but for soldiers. Dickerson has access to it. He couldn't kill Nathan without repercussions, but a warning like this isn't breaking George's rules." Kaleb pulled a small bullet-looking piece of metal from the pouch, holding it up.

Simon stared at the fake bullet, then gripped Nate's

hand tightly. "Will we kill them?"

Kaleb poured himself a steaming cup of black coffee from the old pot without looking up. A cold smile came to his face. "Leave that to me, boy."

FORTY

SEPTEMBER 9TH, 2027

TWELVE HOURS AFTER GIDEON'S INITIAL warning to the townsfolk and officers at the courthouse, Springtown formed the strongest line of defense at the border they'd ever built. Vehicles lay upturned as a barricade across the entry roads. Guns, ammo, and various other weaponry were brought to the courthouse and prepared for every able-bodied man. The best shooters were assigned their positions near the border where they could shoot attackers in hiding.

Rene' rode into town—she'd babysat her nieces and nephews, along with countless other children, with her mother and Terri for the whole duration of time—with her father. Physically, she needed the break, but emotionally, her mind whirled like a bucket of sand tumbling around in a blender. Her prayers, however, remained steadfast.

"It'll be all right," Lee piped up from the backseat of the truck. Grimy and shirt damp with sweat, he sure didn't resemble his statement.

"Yeah." She smiled. "God'll take care of us." She prayed for a miracle—God would protect Springtown and not let a soul get hurt. It was a vain hope during a war. Loved ones died in war, but Rene' couldn't accept that. *It's more likely we'll die or be persecuted, like You promised we would be for Your Name's sake, Lord… I don't think I'm strong enough for this.*

Outside the courthouse, dawn's gleam glowing like a promise to them all, men readied AR-15s and bows.

Gideon had promised his back up would come, and the town was counting on it, but they would go down swinging regardless of whether they fought alone or with hopes of seasoned fighters. *That's how Confederates fight.*

Rene' licked her lips, reaching tiredly and squeezing her father's shoulder. "I love you guys." She couldn't say it enough but only mustered those words once, lump forming like a rock in her throat.

Springtown could lose everything by George's little militia. Gideon, Alex, and their group might be coming as hidden defense, but this was a battle Springtown faced together as a body of people. They weren't soldiers, but they were fighters, and it would be enough. They had no choice but to win against the odds—which stacked high against them. *It's George Johnston's men with weaponry and power, but we have God.*

"Gideon just arrived!" Officer Art shouted from the courthouse doors. "Sean and Mikey are letting them in on the lines for last minute preparations!"

Mr. Fisher took Rene's hand gently as he rolled his window down with his other hand. "Simon will be here soon. I radioed them right after Gideon alerted us."

Lee got out of the truck, heading over to where his friends prepared guns on the back of a flatbed truck.

They're just teenage boys. Not soldiers. They barely saw the world before it shot itself to hell. And people wanted these wars, they wanted action instead of talk. Well, they have it now, and my brothers are the one taking action. My family is suffering from the wars those civilians wanted, and what good has it done us? She hastily wiped her eyes so her father didn't see her tears.

They drove to the border, though Mr. Fisher insisted Rene' didn't have to, but she wanted to. *Gideon might've kidnapped me, but I gotta get myself understanding he was protecting me in the only way he could—and it hurt, but he's here to protect the town, and I will not be afraid.*

She held her father's hand anyway when they left the truck parked along the other vehicles and approached the front line. Alex was passing out boxes—she couldn't tell if they were just ammo, or guns, or bombs, or strange other tech—and telling the surrounding townsmen exactly how the weaponry things worked.

Gideon was nearby but kept one hand on the side of the car, talking to a few other men, including a bloodshot-eyed Sean who waved Mr. Fisher over. Rene' released her father's hand quickly, not going over, but forcing herself near Alex, instead. She couldn't get a good look at the boxes no matter how hard she tried. She didn't look back at her father or Gideon.

Alex grabbed a box from the truck, stiffening when he saw her. He smiled. "Hey. Are you OK?"

Rene' forced a smile, but it didn't match his in strength. "Yeah."

"Beauty!" He grinned like that was the best news he'd heard all week. Rene' assumed "beauty" was just another word for "great."

"Wanna see?" He asked, showing the little wooden crate.

"If we have these supplies, won't George's guys recognize it…? You guys will be in trouble."

Alex's smile faded. "We're actually supposed to be here."

"But, George… He…" Rene' stumbled. *That doesn't make any sense for George, the massacre, the power thirsty god…*

"He couldn't tell us *who* ordered this attack," Alex said, handing the crate to a teenage boy, still talking to Rene' like she was an old friend. "But he doesn't mind us caring for you guys now, this once. Not sure why and I wish I did." "Is it a trap?" Rene' asked weakly.

"Nah." He paused. "You should sit down."

"Rene'!" A familiar voice came from behind her and she tensed.

"C'mon." Xander grabbed her arm, pulling back from Alex. She tripped slightly but followed her friend over to the vehicles again, the cool September breeze ruffling her hair despite the warm sun above.

"I was talking." She scowled.

"You were gonna pass out. Sit down here." Xander shoved a shotgun out of the way so Rene' could sit on an ATV. Her knees buckled but she faked strength, thanking him quietly.

"What were you talking to *him* about?"

"I don't understand everything."

"Mr. Fisher didn't explain it all?"

"I think he left stuff out," she admitted.

Xander crossed his arms. "I'll explain. George didn't actually start this, some other ally did, God only knows who, probably some Union—" he stopped short from swearing, then continued. "The group of guys are just some of George's workers, I guess. They'll be here in about six hours, give or take. Gideon and Alex have permission from George to protect us. They don't think it's a trick, but they're not taking the risk of not being here." A pause. "Following me?

"I think so." Rene' wished her head weren't so fuzzy. "I don't understand why George wants them to help but didn't allow Simon and Nate to help us."

Xander shrugged. "Now *he's* in control over the situation? Who knows. All that matters is we have a shot right now. The Union might have a ton of gangs working for them, but if some start helping us, we could really have a chance at taking the nation back, Rene'."

"Guess so…" She rubbed her face.

"You're worried. You shouldn't be. You're still hurt, you know, you should go home and get some rest before you hurt yourself more. You girls have a lot to do, handling all the kids while we handle this." He spoke as if nothing could possibly go wrong. "It'll be fine."

Rene' didn't know if he had faith or if he just thought saying something made it easier to digest. Either way, it helped her feel better. "Guess I'd better let you get back to work."

"We just have some last minute weapon additions. We're all set, really, and should be fine. Everyone's got an idea of our plan."

"Which is?"

"Gideon will try talking the jerks down first. If it comes to a fight, we use everything we have." Xander didn't bat an eyelash at his words.

Rene' hid a shudder. "Ah. You make it sound…"

"Simple? It is."

Rene' prayed it wouldn't be a struggle for the town to do what was right. *God help us. I won't be out here fighting, but I wish I could be. I've got other things to care for that I'm capable of doing, but the guys I love will be in the battlezone, and I can't be with them. All I can do is pray over them.*

FORTY-ONE

SEPTEMBER 9TH, 2027

NATE SLEPT LIKE A ROCK in the backseat of Simon's car, but Simon drove as carefully as possible, knowing they had a fair trip ahead of them before reaching Springtown, and he wasn't sure if Nate would handle it well. Vince said as long as they kept slow and Nate rested once they arrived, he'd be no worse than staying at Kaleb's cabin. Nate'd been dead set on getting out of there.

Simon reached Springtown's border just in time. Officer Art escorted him through the border—men moved a vehicle and he drove straight to the farm. Nothing had changed there since he'd left—the horses grazed like all was right in the world, the chickens darted away from his car, and Elvis barked wildly.

He got out, opening the backseat door. "Nate—"

"I'm awake…" Nate mumbled, eyes glazed over, weaker than he'd ever admit.

"Simon! Nate!" Rene' exclaimed, leaning on the porch railing, eyes wide with relief, then worry when she saw Simon lift Nate out of the car.

"He's fine. I'll just take him to Lee's room like Mr. Fisher ordered." Simon carried him inside the Fisher home. He situated Nate into the waiting bed, grunting. "You gotta lay off the pizza."

Too groggy to insult him back, Nate curled up in the covers slightly, falling fast asleep.

"Is he OK? Are you OK?" Rene' asked softly. "You said he got hurt and was doing OK, but he doesn't look so OK—"

Simon turned and wrapped his arms around Rene' tightly. *She's safe.* "He's still drugged up from painkillers, but the wound is healing just fine. He'll be back to his highly annoying self in no time."

"And you?" She lifted her head, eyes searching his closely. She could ready every secret behind his eyes, which was why he never looked close for too long. He couldn't risk her finding every secret, every truth, because it would hurt her. Her heart was too big for his burdens. He wanted to protect her, not break her, and right now, he had a second chance to do just that.

"I'm going to help, so I'd better head over." He squeezed her shoulders.

"Everyone else is, except kids and moms and…" She trailed off, slowly grabbed his hand. "Simon?"

Heart lodged in his throat, he mustered, "Yeah?"

"You made me a promise. And I'm not one for promises, but this one…" She never tore her eyes from his, jaw so tight her chin quivered.

"I'll be coming back." Simon smiled, voice firm. "Don't think you'll get rid of any of us this easy. You got a group of Springtown men and gangsters against some underpaid thugs. Don't say you don't have faith in us." He cracked a grin but only found relief when Rene' smirked at him.

"I have faith in *God*, and I know He'll take care of you, even if you're pea-brained." She patted his arm. "Be careful, Si."

"Yes, ma'am." He headed outside, looking back with a smile, and drove down the dirt road.

When he reached the border again, the men were preparing for war. No matter how many times Simon fought, he never grew accustomed to the air of apprehension bearing down across the group of fighters like smoke.

Gideon remained near his truck, explaining one last time to the men how things would most likely go, and how they must be ready on offense and defense. Once the planning and scheming finished, it was Mr. Fisher who stood before the crowds of townsmen, all bearing arms and sober expressions weighing heavy, and he rallied them for war.

Of all the leaders Simon followed, of all the war cries from his father, Kaleb, and even George, none of them compared to Mr. Fisher's words. They were not merely moving the men for blood and power. Every word hit Simon like a knife plunging into his heart.

"We're facing men who will toy with us, make us run or submit—but we will not be moved. We will not faint. We will not lose. God is with us and we will fear no man, no bullet, no death. There is not a single thing that can separate us from our Creator, and we'll fight until the death for our families, our land, and our honor." Mr. Fisher lifted his black rifle toward the sky and countless followed, including his teenage son at his side. "Let's pray."

It wasn't until a pastor wearing a bow and arrow finished his brief prayer that Simon felt hot tears running down his face. Shaking himself out of whatever spiritual battle raged within his chest, Simon went over and offered his help wherever he was needed.

"With me," Lee spoke up. His eyes dark and betraying nothing, he repeated, "You stay with me."

FORTY-TWO

SEPTEMBER 9TH, 2027

GIDEON WANTED SLEEP. PAIN AND exhaustion pulled on him, but reminding himself the large J carved into his back really wasn't the worst form of pain he could be bearing, he pushed onward. Alex gave him some painkillers about an hour before the company arrived. Gideon's own group consisted of eighty men willing to take orders and fight for a town they'd never see again. They'd all arrived in record time, going to work immediately. Enemy company consisted of forty armed men eager for a fight so they could head back to their fort for cash. Gideon didn't know who their buyer was, but he must've named quite the price for this little endeavor.

Gideon hoped he could stop the destruction before it began, but in the Second Civil War, what kind of childish dream was that? The kind of dream none of the others expected, either, which explained why the surrounding woods swarmed with hidden men ready for death and teenagers terrified over pulling the trigger in defense of their home.

The militia of vehicles parked along the road. A tall man with a buzzcut stepped out of the lead truck. He approached slowly but didn't show any nervousness at the men crouching behind the overturned cars, their guns targeted at him and his men.

"Shane, I knew you took this job." Gideon stood near an upturned vehicle without going out in the open. *Whoever wanted this town under attack is strategically ruthless. If this is a test for me, then it just became quite real.*

Shane was a rogue Confederate traitor and went into hiding with George about a year ago, working his way up as a ruthless killer. Gideon had told Springtown that before this disaster, Shane had bought Mayor Knight out. In response, the town locked Mayor Knight up immediately. He'd risked the town more than once, and they'd been clueless before. Not this time.

Shane flashed a charming smile. "I was warned you'd be here playing hero. George doesn't find this town a threat and neither should you. This is merely a small act of business."

"You're the last man that needs this town's demise under your belt, Shane." Gideon studied him close. He wore fancy clothes and a pistol on his side, and his lack of care in his own protection told Gideon he underestimated the town's strength.

"You're right, this isn't a trophy game. Just fun." Shane smiled, eyeing Mr. Fisher. "Where's the mayor? Too scared to come meet his buyer?"

Gideon frowned. "You think he'll come out in the open before you open fire at this town?"

"You told them already, didn't you, Hochberg?" Shane eyed Mr. Fisher as he clapped his hands together eagerly. "I came offering a treaty!" He shouted so all could hear.

Gideon had warned Springtown of the treaty Shane might offer already.

"I will offer protection and supplies for the whole town. No limits. No rules. In return, all able-bodied men will work for my group," Shane called out, a smirk tugging on his lips. He didn't specify his group allied with the Union, the opposite side this town was on. "You won't get a better deal! Anyone else will slaughter a God-fearing town right off the map—you've seen it done."

Mr. Fisher responded without a moment's hesitation. "We refuse your offer. Leave, before anyone must die."

"This is not a game, Mr. Fisher. This is life or death. I am the only way to save your children." Shane's smile disappeared. He gestured to the barricade, raising his voice. "I am the only way any of your families will survive and you know it."

"They made their decision," Gideon spoke calmly. "I strongly suggest you leave."

Shane's countenance fell from welcoming to threatening, expression darkening as he stepped back. "Very well. They chose."

The first gunshots loosed from Shane's group, ricocheting off the cars and pounding away like hail. Shane fell with a bullet to the head—Gideon had warned the town that chest shots would do nothing against the bulletproof body armor he constantly wore.

Gideon ducked down behind a car, back searing in pain, grabbed the rifle waiting for him.

In a war zone, time ceased to exist, both stopping entirely and spinning so fast a man couldn't keep up. Gideon kept up with the enemies—he fired precisely at every head that lifted too far from their crouched positions. But it wasn't the bullets that broke Shane's group. It was the grenades.

Mr. Fisher's hidden group pulled the pins of the recently evolved government-grade grenades and chucked them down the road.

Gideon kept firing until one of his own men dropped beside him. A second, just a teenager, cried out as a bullet hit him. Blood splurted across Gideon's face, and he hunched down, reaching for the boy. He tried stopping the bleeding until he saw the bullet had torn the boy's jugular. Instant death. Gideon lay the body down, taking his gun up and going back to shooting at the men diving for the cover of the woods. He was just cover fire, but he wasn't losing the common ground they had.

Grenades went off, shrapnel flying from the vehicles that spun off the road from impact. The men who ran for the woods were shot down by bullets or the occasional arrow. It wasn't the most methodical war Gideon ever formed, but Springtown wasn't losing, either.

Yells rang out under the falling sun, men falling like sparrows from the sky on both sides of the barricade. Screaming men ran from Shane's vehicles, bodies aflame, but they were shot before they burned alive.

FORTY-THREE

SEPTEMBER 9TH, 2027

A SOLDIER WAS TRAINED TO follow orders, shoot when spoken to, and move on when his brother was hacked to pieces beside him. For a soldier, heated battles were their job, and having a mission trumped any horrors they saw. But Springtown wasn't a town of soldiers, Navy men, or police officers. The three hundred men were husbands, fathers, builders, farmers, businessmen, everyday workers who defended themselves knowing they'd die without a medal or a ribbon.

Simon couldn't watch it unfold. Couldn't watch a town stand at its border and fight off trained killers like hundreds of flies swarming at sharp-toothed wolves.

So he focused on his duty and ignored the screams, the gunfire, the pleas for mercy from the youngest town fighters before they were slaughtered.

He sat crouched near a large cedar tree, firing

mercilessly toward the enemy's formation, but five men were entering the thick forest like cougars. He knew they were trained for this part of war—infiltration and surviving in elements that the opposite side knew more about.

"Lee, take them out!" Simon gestured at the woods before them. Lee, at his left side with Mo, nodded and set his AR-15's crosshairs on the first infiltrator that lifted his head above the bushes.

Lee fired, too, but he stiffened when a young man ran from his position in the woods. Screaming, half of his left arm gone and leaving a gushing wound. "Too late!" Of all he cried, Simon could only understand those two words.

The infiltrators grew dirty with close combat. If they didn't shoot them out before they got close, the four men would use knives. Simon couldn't let that happen.

Simon kept low and waited for his chance, but he waited too long. The four men disappeared as some of the Springtown men opened fire on them.

A grenade flew toward the Springtown men's group. Simon shoved Lee roughly. "Back!" The bomb snapped a tree in half but Simon couldn't tell if it'd hurt anyone.

As Lee scrambled up, he suddenly dropped low into the moss again. "Mo!" Mo's left leg oozed blood that covered the ground but he wasn't making a sound, just grasped Lee's shoulder and tried standing.

Another grenade exploded to their right but none of the shrapnel reached them, though screams followed from men too close to the destruction. Simon covered Lee's back, shooting another infiltrator down who was hacking into a middle-aged man with a knife.

"We need more men!" Simon shouted. "Stand! Don't retreat!" If the civilians began backing up or breaking apart, they'd lose their ground.

Lee tossed Mo onto his shoulders. He ran deeper into the woods, staggering and keeping low. Simon watched him only a moment to make sure he reached the dense trees before turning around. The infiltrators hadn't come any closer, like cats waiting for the untrained men to snap and come closer so they could pounce.

"Don't leave your positions!" a man shouted. Simon prayed the people would listen or they'd be lost.

The infiltrators must be killed, and they could not be hit by bullets where they were now. They would be forced out like rats. Simon pulled a grenade from his pocket, crept closer, gunfire ringing in his ears. He only had this grenade, and the three enemies wouldn't be hiding together in one spot, but it was his job to protect the town. If that meant facing three trained assassins with his bare hands and a knife, so be it. He'd kill all of them before his last breath.

He spotted the first man in a small thicket like a viper

blending in with his surroundings. Simon ducked for cover just in time—the man fired at his head but narrowly missed. Someone from Simon's side killed that vermin.

A shrill cry echoed from the woods ahead of Simon. Had someone left their position and gone over the forest border? Low and steady, Simon moved closer through the woods. In a tiny, blood-stained clearing, a young teen was on his knees before one of the enemies. *A farmer's son.* He begged for mercy, kicking hard and struggling against the large man's gun against his head.

Simon aimed for the man's head and fired, but he'd been too late. Two gunshots rang in the air and only one came from Simon's gun. The teen fell dead to the ground, the enemy crumpling beside his victim's body. Out of the woods from Simon's front, where no men were positioned, he heard a swear. Simon lifted his gun to fire.

"I'm with Hochberg!" A dark-haired young man with tattoos along his bare arms and neck came from the trees, briefly eyeing the teen's body before smirking at Simon. "A pity. He was a beautiful kid."

Simon frowned, hearing another scream from his left. He ran for it, gun ready, the other black-haired man following.

"How many have passed the border?" Simon asked under his breath as they moved.

"I finished the rest of the five soldier boys from behind," the man said. "You're welcome."

They ran through the woods and over a few civilian's corpses sprawled across the forest floor. A man in black ran toward Springtown, leaving his wreckage behind, but Simon fired and the man fell dead.

"Let's get back to our positions now," Simon snapped at the tattooed man, keeping low and moving fast through the trees and thickets. He'd promised to watch Lee's back, and wherever the teen had gone, Simon needed to find him again, now that the infiltrators were gone. The tattooed man followed him closely until they reached the border. Civilians ceased fire for a matter of seconds until another enemy neared.

They reached their side safely, but Simon didn't stop moving forward, jumping over the dead, avoiding the crossfire, staying close to the ground when he could. Lee was tending Mo in a small ravine, trying to bandage his friend's leg. Xander was in the hole, too, giving cover fire when he found an enemy.

"Just me, I can help!" Simon almost fell into the hole but caught himself, easing beside Mo's shaking form. Lee bandaged Mo's leg but vomited immediately after the deed was done.

"We don't have morphine," Xander snarled at Simon. "Help him!"

Simon gave Mo a dose of painkillers. "Here, bud…"

They're three damn kids, not soldiers. But this was no time for fleeting thoughts. Lee kept throwing up violently until blood dripped from his mouth.

"Xander, switch with me." Simon crawled up the side of the hole with his gun to watch their backs. The gunfire had already grown slightly more quiet. It sounded like most of the damage was on the road by now. *God, let us win.*

Xander calmed Lee down, speaking firmly, making him focus on himself and Mo. "Don't think, don't think, just focus."

They might be able to focus on the battle at hand for now, but what they'd seen would haunt them. Forever. They wouldn't forget anything, no matter how hard they tried, no matter how much they needed to. The horrors of war never left a man's mind. War didn't differentiate between men and teenagers.

Simon caught one enemy clad in black creeping through the civilians. He shot him in the head and let the satisfaction burn in his belly.

FORTY-FOUR

SEPTEMBER 9TH, 2027

OVER THREE HUNDRED CIVILIANS STOOD against the forty trained assassins. Forty minutes and the raging battle fell to a soft whimper, vehicles burning on the road, men sprawled like dead insects littering the ground. It was finished.

Men from Springtown rushed out to see if any survivors lay among the forty, others carrying their brothers to safety where the doctors and nurses waited in safety.

"Your wound is bleeding, mate." Al's voice came from close by, but Gideon's ringing ears adjusted to his voice slowly. He turned his head, covered in the teenager's blood, silent.

Alex paled. "Gid…"

"We won." Gideon put his gun down on the dirt. His eyes traveled across the field—he spotted Mr. Fisher helping wounded with Lee at his side. Simon carried a skinny man to a medic.

"Let me patch your back before you bleed out." Alex opened a black medical bag he'd grabbed from another man, removing Gideon's shirt and working fast.

Gideon closed his eyes. He couldn't look at the bodies of his own men—he'd be overseeing their burials soon enough. The stench of death and smoke and gunpowder flooded his senses like a hurricane.

"We'll bury them here," Alex whispered softly.

"They'd like that." Gideon opened his eyes and watched the civilians pick up the pieces of what the battle left them.

A man shouted in agony, dropping to his knees beside the body of a young man—his son, no doubt, and no one tried consoling him. How could you console a father who fought beside his son and survived instead?

Gideon watched the town work together, weep together, and while the town had won, not a soul rejoiced aloud.

Is this You, God? Is this victory by Your hand?

Simon covered the body of an older man who'd fought for his family until his last breath.

I have nothing to offer You except endless blood on my head and a cold heart and a ruthless spirit, Lord. You can't possibly want me. Look around—I led this.

Follow me.

Gideon slowly got up once Alex finished patching his wound. Turning away from the destruction, he called for a few men, ordering them to help clean up and leave the dead for now. He stiffly made his way over to Mr. Fisher and the wounded.

If following You means having the strength this little nobody town possesses... You have my attention, God. So, let's find out who ordered this attack and why, because I don't think it was simply business between Shane and Mayor Knight. This was a test for me.

"DAD! LEE!" THE FISHER FAMILY cried out, racing off the front porch and clinging for Mr. Fisher and Lee. Once Rene' and the others were certain their loved ones were unharmed, they practically dragged Mr. Fisher, Lee, and Simon away from the car. The beam from the lantern sitting on the railing flickered steadily in the darkness, like a promise, as they trudged inside the farmhouse. Rene' had no words for that moment.

A family welcoming loved ones home after war. Such scenes are better left unspoken.

Lee passed out on the couch without a word and without cleaning the blood from his weary body. Mr. Fisher took his wife, Howie, and Terri into the kitchen. Rene' didn't know what they spoke of. Once Dax quickly took all the children into Rene's bedroom, Rene' collapsed beside the couch and wept, body shaking with every sob, clutching Lee's hand.

Simon knelt beside her, putting his strong arm about her shoulders. "His friends are alive."

Thank God. Rene' bit back sobs weakly.

"Don't cry…" He engulfed her in a hug, smelling like sweat, dirt, blood, and gunpowder. "It's all right… We won… We won… God took care of us."

Rene' wept into Simon's shoulder, curling up beside him and clutching the bloodied hand of her little, precious brother. *We won, but at what price? I asked for a miracle and I got one. Still, I grieve.*

Rejoice in the Lord. How?

"It didn't go near as bad as it could've, Rene', it… it's all right…" Simon whispered in the darkness.

Rene's tears slowly dried. *You were faithful, Lord… I'll rejoice.* Throat tight, eyes clamped shut and cheek against Simon's chest, she began humming, softly at first, until the words came. *"Our God is an awesome God…"*

In the dark living room, Rene' sang under her breath, praising the God who'd spared their town and offered them hope. She had no doubts left in her heart that He loved them. And though they might do terrible things, and weep, and bleed, and die, His love endured. He'd be beside them through every single thing.

And He was enough.

FORTY-FIVE

SEPTEMBER 10TH, 2027

GEORGE JOHNSTON STOOD IN HIS large kitchen with a glass of vodka and laughed his booming laugh that echoed throughout the high ceilings. "I told you Gideon would pull it off, Guns!"

Guns sipped his beer, smiling. "I didn't expect Shane would take the bait so easily. I'm glad he's gone now. I didn't feel like having his blood on my hands. Now it's on some little hillbilly's."

"Gideon told me it was a clean battle," George continued proudly. "A real Custer look-alike. Springtown had few fatalities."

"I shouldn't be surprised by the town's stigma and skills, but I'm surprised they allowed the gangsters to enter in and help their cause." Guns shook his head, downing the rest of his drink and leaning back against the bar stool.

"It went well, all things considered, and what a fun game!" George grinned. "A pity, losing a few valuable players, but most of them were doomed regardless."

"I sent a majority of cocky arrogants who started begging for death, like Shane," Guns said coolly.

"I don't doubt you, brother."

"I'm proud of Gideon." Guns sighed. "He shows great potential and proves himself repeatedly." A smirk tugged at his lips. "Just like your boy, hm?"

George laughed again. "West pleases me. His eloquence among the leaders and officials is uncanny. He can bust a head open with his bare hands just as easy as he can persuade one with mere words."

Guns laughed heartily, lifting another beer bottle. "To the next generation. May they continue our empire for millennia to come."

"I can drink to that." George clinked his glass. "Before we discuss the next official meeting and the batch of Union soldiers, Hunter will be here in…" He glanced up.

Hunter Savage, clad in black with a mask over his face, stood in the kitchen doorway like a doomsaying grim reaper.

"Ah." George smiled and sat back. "What was it you needed, friend? A keg of beer?" he joked loftily.

"You hired Dickerson and Reynolds to target Nate, or am I supposed to believe they rebelled of their own accord?" Hunter didn't come closer, nor did he remove his mask.

George raised his eyebrows at the audacious assumption. "You think I hired them to kill Nathan?"

"Don't play with me. Don't ever think you're capable of that."

"I hired them so Kaleb would end their lives once and for all and so Nate got some submissive fear. You didn't interfere, so you must not have thought the harm done was fatal." George never tired of his games, and there were so many games, all intricately woven into one giant web. He'd spent months being a serious ganglord, and he wanted just a bit of fun.

"You could've hired Kaleb to do that flat out, and there are more ways to scare Nathan than almost kill him—this is about me. So, what's it going to be? You needed an excuse to kill me?" Hunter pulled his mask off, a cold smirk on his lips and hunger burning in his green eyes. His scarred face sent chills up George's spine. "You forget, I like games, too, George."

"I know you like games. I know you considered the consequences of your actions beforehand so you refused to save him, and I know you considered my motives, as well." George leaned back with a sigh. "We're both playing a game when it's quite simple what the answer is."

"You wanted me to save Nate," Hunter said evenly.

"You wanted me to breach contract, but you breached it first. What for? You won't kill me."

"It's been five years. A man can only be a ghost for so long without yearning for life, and where your heart is, your mind is also." George set his drink down, voice cross. "I can't have you working jobs while you want your family. I've gone this long keeping my word, and you haven't lost your softness."

"You expected me to lose my interest in protecting my family? Like Williams?" Hunter chuckled. Williams had been a mediocre spy who, after three years of dirty work, shot himself instead of continuing his protection of his wife and child.

George tapped the files on the table. "I hired Dickerson because I needed them removed, and I needed you to remember why you fight. From now on, on your own terms, you may return to your family." A smile curved his lips and a satisfaction burned in his chest. Hunter served him well, steadfast and fierce as a wolf, and now it was time for the man to renew his spirit. It was fun, giving a man his life back.

If Kaleb and Jack forgive him, that is. If not, he will fight out of bitter brokenness. If they forgive, he will allow his bond to grow, thus strengthening his sense of dedication to my cause. Five years has been enough time, and with Nate the last of the legacy, now is his chance to build both young men into soldiers I can use.

A long silence followed. Hunter stared at him, his

expression unreadable, but his eyes slowly grew hard like coal. "I understand."

Guns put his empty beer bottle away, chuckling softly. "Happy early birthday, my friend," he told Hunter sarcastically.

George smiled but didn't share Guns' sardonic sentiment. He lifted his glass at Hunter. "If that is all?" The man had just had his whole world dumped back into his lap—he'd need time to think, consider, and plan what he'd do. George knew him better than he knew himself. Hunter wouldn't run home. He'd keep his distance because deep down, he feared what his brother, son, and nephew thought of him now that the truth rang out.

Hunter nodded, stepping back. "Good evening, George."

"Don't want to stay for a drink?" Guns lifted his glass. "Just because the rebels won over D.C. doesn't mean us egotistic prodigies can't enjoy a cold drink like gentlemen." He winked, often taunting Hunter's Southern roots. Hunter worked for the Union as a gangster, spy, killer, but his Texan roots remained the same, not that George cared much as long as his jobs were done well.

"No, thank you," Hunter said. "I have business to tend to."

George watched him disappear, smirking at Guns.

"No matter how cold-hearted a monster is, he will always defend his own before all else. That is why Hunter is a valuable member." Not a puppet, because Hunter was far from mindless, but a member that George could count on to do the unthinkable—all in the name of holy righteousness.

It was such men as Hunter than equipped George to dissolve the United States from the inside, watching it crumble like the Trade Centers back in 2001. Just like then, the nation was powerless to stop the destruction. "This war will end in a Union victory... If I expect Hunter to assist in reconstruction, I will give him his family now."

"You're a merciful leader," Guns mused dryly.

"This empire we are building will not think so. It is an ironic joke, working to unite the nations, and be viewed as a monster, is it not?"

"Beauty is in the eye of the beholder, as is wickedness." Guns eyed George, smile fading like a claw pulled it into the abyss. "Now, tell me how the session with Gideon went. Did you video it?"

George pulled the chip from his pocket and set it on the table. "You'll enjoy this."

FORTY-SIX

SEPTEMBER 11TH, 2027

"THE CONFEDS TOOK D.C.!" THOSE four words rang throughout Springtown like a resounding hallelujah. The news came from Simon that bright, crisp morning—he'd burst out of the barn, barely dressed, shouting the news. Gideon had called him minutes before with news the Union had lost the bloody battle and the army of Confederates gained solid ground in the US capital.

Men gathered at the courthouse. Sean got a radio hooked up, contacting Alex, who didn't have much more information than what Gideon had already told Simon.

"It happened this morning. The South has solid ground and nothing can push them back now... The Union fled this morning and won't waste any time preparing the next step, but it's a win, and that's that," Mr. Fisher told his family after returning from the courthouse, an hour later, exhausted but joy shining in his weary eyes. "You wouldn't believe it... Everyone was rejoicing and weeping..."

Mrs. Fisher pulled him into her arms and he said no more. Nothing more needed to be said. The United States had hope, with God, and this victory paved a new path for all of them, like a new dawn lifted its head over the nation and offered restoration through the dry, dusty plains and crumbled buildings. If they took their chance, if they greeted the dawn with both hands out, they could win. If they fought and prayed on their knees, the nation might not be doomed.

LORD, PLEASE, GIVE YOUR PEOPLE *strength*. Rene' helped her mother and Terri cook a meal for the celebratory feast in town square that the men and women of Springtown prepared for. She finished chopping up carrots, then cared for the children, watching Aiden suck his thumb. Dax had gone into town with Mr. Fisher, Howie, Lee, and Simon, so the other children played by themselves in the living room. They sensed the excitement and eagerly waited for the feast.

"Why are we celebrating?" Paisley asked softly for the hundredth time.

"Because the town wants to thank God for helping the Confederates win over D.C." Rene' smiled. "Since we have so many supplies from Simon and the others, we can."

"Will the men who helped Springtown be there, too?" Jaycee asked solemnly. She took great care in making sure Springtown's new alliances were helped, too.

"Yes," Rene' said. "Simon and Randy are helping set up booths and tables in town square right now."

"I like the scary men." Jaycee looked down at her worn sketchbook, her youthful eyes determined. "They helped us, and they deserve to be happy tonight, too."

Rene' brushed Jaycee's brown curls back. "They will, sweetie. We all will."

"Nate, too?" Lily asked in a childish slur.

"Nate, too." Rene' chuckled. Lily found great amusement in watching Nate sleep in Lee's room and it was difficult keeping her away from him. If Nate woke and noticed, he didn't say anything or scare the girl off.

For one night, they'd rejoice and be glad, as God bid them to. They'd remember the many fallen, and they'd have faith in the future that God held in His hands. Tonight, they'd do so as a united town. And next week, they would send Mayor Knight out of town as his punishment for betraying them for three years.

"THIS TOWN LOOKS BEAUTIFUL. Y'ALL did great pulling this together so fast." Rene' handed Simon a plate full of hot food she'd dipped from the tables of meals the women of Springtown had prepared within their joyful homes. A cool breeze ruffled her hair, and she took in her surroundings one last time: the tables and booths covered with food for all, the lines of people waiting to get their plates, and the children darting through the streets playing ball and tag. Various groups sang songs of rejoicing, while other people sat alone and wept, no doubt wishing the men they'd lost two weeks before could witness this triumph.

The United States was broken, but the South's victory burned bright for all who dared hope the world might change. Springtown had faith, after all they'd done so far, that together, they could thrive. Together, with God, they'd be a town undivided, forever.

Simon stepped closer and touched Rene's shoulder. "I honestly keep expecting to wake up from a dream." He glanced around in total awe, a smile tugging on his lips. "It's insane. All these people work together, mourn together, and rejoice together. I've never seen anything like it. I told Graham this morning I wish he could see it. Maybe one day, he will."

"Simon?" Rene' dipped another plate for her father, who sat with Mrs. Fisher and Nate, talking with Sean and some others.

The kids ran around, Dax chasing them.

"Hm?" Simon smiled.

"This wouldn't be possible without you." She

gestured at the food. "So, go sit down and enjoy it."

A soft sigh escaped him. "I'm not so sure this town wants me to enjoy it."

"They'll trust again," Rene' said firmly, taking the plate to Mr. Fisher and hugging her father, turning back with Simon. She grinned wide. "After all, who can refuse your charming smile?" It took all her willpower not to laugh at how red his cheeks grew.

"Nate and I will not stop protecting this town." Simon stepped closer to the booth, grabbing a water.

"Any word from Kaleb?" Rene' asked softly, stomach in knots.

"No. When we go back, it's going to be a disaster," Simon whispered. "But, let's not think about it now, yeah?" His worried expression faded into a hopeful smile.

Rene' followed and sat beside him at the table with her family. She listened intently to her friends and family, watched the celebration for hours. Children played into the dark while the adults rested in God's peace. For the night, they were free. For the night, they had a future, and their children had hope and full bellies.

As the sky lit up with stars, the town sang "Amazing Grace" as one, their voices all rising to the darkened sky like only God listened.

Rene' sat weeping and knew her mother and sister did as well, and while Mr. Fisher and Howie comforted their wives, Simon put his arm around Rene', too. He didn't sing the anthem, but he closed his eyes.

Rene' wondered what God saw when He saw a little town singing about being saved wretches, with many weeping on their knees and more yet with arms outstretched, reaching for the dawn that would arrive once the night fell away. And she decided what He saw was good.

FORTY-SEVEN

SEPTEMBER 12TH, 2027

"A MAN OF POWER WITHOUT *a home is a waste of breath," George said softly, putting his hand over his wife's as she sat beside him at the dinner table. "I own property all around the world, I have the government wrapped around my little finger, and I make men beg for mercy. But when the highs of war are over, a man can only continue on for so long." He lifted Cindy's hand and kissed it.*

West fought not to vomit. Ever since he was a boy, his father's affection often made his stomach twist into knots.

"It is important a master never lose what makes him a god, and that includes the skill of being gentle, just as you are cruel." George thought a moment before taking a sip of wine. He let his words settle in the air like fog. "To be a dictator with no kind hand is begging for defeat. But have people who depend and worship you, you must give them a reason to do so."

Cindy kissed his hand wordlessly. George chuckled. "It is a pity you will not find a woman as beautiful as your dear mother, my son."

*"I have no time for such a thing, father." West met his father's
adoring eyes.*

*"Not yet." George chuckled. "But you will when I find you
the right companion for your legion."*

West hoped he died before that ever happened.

West pushed the memory from last night away
angrily. He sat on the edge of his bed, chest as empty as
the bottle of beer in his left hand, staring at the worn old
photo in his right hand. He'd torn the edge of the photo
off to remove George, but eleven-year-old him and his
youthful, smiling mother remained.

It'd been about a month now, but he still couldn't
stand what his mother had become for him. She'd
become George's personal pet for the sake of her only
son, so he wouldn't be alone with George for the rest of
his life, but she wasn't much of a buffer in West's weary
opinion. Still, she was his mother, and he loved her but
couldn't save her from George.

He could save his brothers, and that's what he'd do
until his last breath.

*Sitting around aching for the love of a father, like Mr. Fisher,
won't strengthen me. Yearning for the faith Ed had before he was
killed won't make me bolder. None of that will help me do my job.*

His phone rang and he answered it, shoulders
straightening instinctively. "Jack?"

"West. Did you hear the news about D.C.?"

"Yes. Where are you?"

"The Union will get dirty. George—"

"—will use me where he needs me." West stopped him calmly. "I came for this purpose, Jack. I've tried for years to make you accept this. I have to do what I have to do. You can't stop the way the world spins."

"I can for my brother."

West closed his eyes tightly. "Jack, I know you'll try to rally Gideon and Philip and the others, but don't come after me. I am not in any more danger than before with you guys."

"Yes, you are, because you're *alone*." Jack wouldn't back down against West. Brothers never backed down. Even when they should, even when things would be easier, even when the fight was hopeless, a brother never stood down.

"I'm not alone. I've got God." West kept his voice quiet but strong, for Jack's sake, not his own, because if Jack heard a smidge of doubt in his brother's voice, he'd tear down the gates of hell to reach him. And West needed Jack where he was, with their comrades and friends.

"God?" Jack breathed.

"Yes."

"You believe?"

"I do," West said quietly. "I do, Jack. And I need you where you are. I need you to let me do this." He didn't fully believe like he said he did, but a small lie wouldn't harm Jack. Lies offered hope, too.

"Not alone," Jack said sharply. "God is with us, but He'd be the first one to tell me to stick with you. No matter what demon tries stopping me, West, I'll reach you. You're so determined to die for us—but we're all willing to die for you, too. Don't you dare forget that."

"I won't." West clenched his fist against his bed covers, struggling for breath.

A muffled scream came over Jack's phone line. West had heard that cry time and time again. "West, I—"

"Go to Ty."

"You remember what I said, West. We're coming for you." The line fell dead, like West's heart, and West put his phone on the bedside table.

He studied the photo in his fist. All his life, George raised him as his son, heir, and legacy. All his life, he'd fought it. He'd fought like a lion ready to die with endless zeal, but it wouldn't end like he'd dreamed. It would end as George wished. *I'll give George what he wants, do his jobs, be his picture-perfect heir, lead the Union… Once I pass his indescribable test, I'll be unstoppable. I won't die during the test like Hunter did, I'll make Hunter proud. I won't let Jack die, I'll protect him. I won't let a single man die in vain, and I will give the living a future.*

I'll kill George Johnston, even if it kills me. Show me You are real. Show me You're a God of justice.

God might have no love for him, but if the Confederates continued to win, the United sects might remain a nation under God, if West Johnston sabotaged his father, once and for all.

EPILOGUE

SEPTEMBER 12TH, 2027

BRIAN JONES LIVED FOR THE fight. He found more satisfaction in leading operations for the Union Army, surrounded by men and women willing to give their lives for their cause, than he did at home. His wife and children remained safe because of his own sacrifices. It had not been so long ago when the whole nation depended on him, also. The United Nations rested assured that the Second Civil War would close soon, because it was growing messier than anyone liked.

The South's conquering of D.C. was merely a fluke. With the planning we have, we'll demolish them in a few months' time. We'll strike hard and smart during winter, take out the leaders, make the Confeds too scared to strike a Union city again.

Brian leaned back in his chair, staring at the holographic maps before him. As a Union leader, he craved the war, the battles, the strategic planning that made every piece fall into place. The world was a puzzle for those willing to bleed for answers.

Such a role was not for everyone. His family had succumbed to the weaker side. He still recalled his step-father's words before the war broke out. "You can always come home."

Home was not Springtown. Home was with the Union. His family was not the Fishers, it was his wife, children, and his comrades.

He glanced at his private contact device. Alone, in the silence of his home office, he thought of his sister. It had been months since her kidnapping and torture. Hochberg had only told him she'd survived, and Brian hadn't asked for more details than that, though he wondered how she was now. He wondered if his family would ever come around. He knew they hated the war, but before 2024's election, they'd stood fast with the belief they must fight for their rights.

How they must regret such a radical idea now. Brian rubbed his aching head. *Or they don't. They must hate me. They must hate their son for leaving and fighting for the wicked government. They're too foolish to realize that I love them, that I fight for the side that will win and shed mercy on the weak, if they'd just accept it. They'd rather die than accept mercy.*

He was a soldier; he followed a creed; he made sacrifices. Had he been wrong in sacrificing his innocent sister? *Of course not. You don't have time to doubt such silly things. She is one innocent. If you'd left base to save her like some rogue, hundreds of soldiers would have been without you, and more innocents would've been harmed. You have a job, Brian. Don't look back.*

Brian stood and left his office. He'd fly to North California tomorrow. He needed sleep before his trip. He wouldn't get much of it when they struck Pennsylvania's Confed camp next month. *Fighting against a man's own flesh and blood is a cruel joke.*

TO BE CONTINUED...

ACKNOWLEDGEMENTS

I thank Yahweh for not only giving me The Infidel Books but giving me the courage to share them with the world. It has not been an easy road from the beginning. I've stumbled, doubted, and grown timid since God gave me the idea to the date of publication, but Yahweh guided me onward. It is because of His Love that this novel is in your hands. May it do you good.

I thank my family for their constant support and prayer. Thanks for listening to me brainstorm, helping me fix plot issues, and reminding me to take breaks. Without you, this book wouldn't be what it is. (P.S. I'm German.)

I thank Sydney, for being the bestest bestie and partner in crime ever. I finally got around to basing a character off you, girlie. I hope she does you justice.

I thank my friends, offline and online, for your encouragement and generosity. You guys mean the world to me.

I thank: my street team for their constant encouragement and teamwork. My beta readers: Addy, Aria, Esther, Faith, Hannah, Janice, Kailey, Kaitlyn, Kassie, Merie, Michaela, Olivia, Sarah, Shine. I also thank my editor, Abigayle Claire. My cover designer, Mandi Lynn. My formatter, Brian McBride. Huge hugs for all of you!

And lastly, thank YOU for reading this novel. I sincerely hope you join the ride in book two. Can't wait until then? Find me on social media and follow me for more news. God bless you all.

THE INFIDEL BOOKS #2 IS COMING SOON

SO SLEEP WITH ONE EYE OPEN.

ABOUT THE AUTHOR

Angela R. Watts is a homeschooled highschooler, and has penned stories since she was little. She lives at Step By Step Sanctuary with her family and strives to glorify the Lord in all she does.

www.thepeculiarmessenger.wordpress.com
www.facebook.com/AngelaRWattsauthor
Amazon – Angela R. Watts
Goodreads – Angela R. Watts
Twitter – @PeculiarAngela

Made in the
USA
Columbia, SC